KU-007-830

THE
REMBRANDT
SECRET

Alex Connor

Quercus

For my father

First published in Great Britain in 2011 by

Quercus
21 Bloomsbury Square
London
WC1A 2NS

Copyright © 2011 by Alex Connor

The moral right of Alex Connor to be
identified as the author of this work has been
asserted in accordance with the Copyright,
Designs and Patents Act, 1988.

All rights reserved. No part of this publication
may be reproduced or transmitted in any form
or by any means, electronic or mechanical,
including photocopy, recording, or any
information storage and retrieval system,
without permission in writing from the publisher.

A CIP catalogue record for this book is available
from the British Library.

ISBN 978 1 84916 346 0

This book is a work of fiction. Names, characters,
businesses, organizations, places and events are
either the product of the author's imagination
or are used fictitiously. Any resemblance to
actual persons, living or dead, events or
locales is entirely coincidental.

10 9 8 7 6 5 4 3 2 1

Typeset by Ellipsis Books Limited, Glasgow

Printed and bound in Great Britain by Clays Ltd, St Ives Plc.

A man who seeks revenge should first dig two graves.

Confucius

BOOK ONE

PROLOGUE

House of Corrections,
Gouda, 1651

This is the story of me.

I am writing it because one day someone will read it and know the truth. I write it believing that my history will get out of this place, because I never will. They have locked me in here, slammed the door on me. And when I panicked, water was thrown on me. It dried cold, the white cap which covered my hair stiff with starch, and spittle from one of the guards. After he had tried to feel under my skirt. After they searched me, looking in my mouth and ears, and in my private parts, forcing fingers into orifices, making an animal out of me.

They take your life away from you when they lock the door. When they say Geertje Dircx, housekeeper to Rembrandt van Rijn, has been committed to an asylum. She is a nuisance, she abused her employer verbally, accused him of breach of promise, sold the ring he gave her: the ring which once belonged to his late wife. She is immoral, she is ungrateful, she is mad with bitterness and

3

anger, telling lies, spreading gossip about how her master had promised he would marry her.

But she is silent now.

Only these pieces of paper hear my history ... I lay with him when I had been at the house for some few weeks. He was grieving for his dead wife and I was eager to be promoted from kitchen to bed chamber, lying next to him and dreaming that the child I had been hired to take care of might – one day – become my stepson. Sssh ... I hide these papers when I hear a noise. A footfall on the corridor outside means guards and people who peer in on me, watching me even when I relieve myself. Watching me, because I am labelled now. Locked up in the House of Corrections as a woman of licentious habits. A danger to myself, they said, when they took his part – which I should have known they would. Powerful and respected, how simple was it for him to have one mistress put aside for the newcomer. A girl younger than myself, with plump, country flesh that he will explore and probe. And then he will paint her. As he painted me.

She will look after him and his son, and sweep the floor, with its monochrome tiles, when the sunlight comes through the stained glass of the windows and makes fireflies on the panelling. She will smell the linseed oil and rabbit glue, and know the sound of the pestle grinding the colours with the oils and turpentine which burn the back of her throat. I know she will creep upstairs and watch his pupils work, and watch him too. She will rummage amongst the heaps of costumes and props he collects for his paintings and hang back in the shadows when patrons come to the studio. She will find herself glancing at her reflection in the mirror a little

4

longer than she used to, counting her attractions, because she wants the image to please him. She will do all this because I did. And I watched him watch me, and watched his expression turn from affection to love. I watched it – let no one say otherwise.

Sssh . . . I am pausing now, hiding the paper under the skirt of my dress as someone's eyes scrutinise me through the peevish little hatch in the door. I perform a crude gesture and the guard walks away, making a sucking sound with his lips. They think I'm promiscuous. I was once, with a few men, in the tavern where I worked, after I was widowed. I was, once. But they gave false evidence against me later. Not just my neighbours, but my own brother . . . What was he paid to lie? What amount was enough to have his sister committed? Does he lie awake in Amsterdam and look out of his free window at his free moon and wonder what sliver of captive sky his sister catches through the bars . . .?

I could have ruined van Rijn then, but I stayed silent. Could have exposed a secret which would have hobbled him and got all Holland grinding him under the heel of their righteous Dutch boot. But I stayed silent. Only asked for what he promised, what he later denied me . . . It's getting dark now, I can hardly see to write anymore. But tomorrow I'll continue. My history will be told and I will destroy you, van Rijn. From the asylum where you put me, out of your bed and your life, from here, on scraps of hidden paper, I will chart your ruin.

I shall write these letters to myself. I shall keep my sanity by this record. And one day, when they are read, the world will know you. They will know me, and you – and Rembrandt's monkey.

1

Amsterdam

His body was bent over, his head submerged in the confines of the basin, his knees buckled, trousers pulled down. Blood seeped from between his buttocks, intensive bruising around the top of his fleshy thighs. On the floor beside his puffy right knee lay the toilet brush, its handle bloodied. A series of small nicks covered his lower back and the skin of his scrotum was mottled with burn marks. Although his head was submerged, the back of his neck showed the imprint of fingers; his wrists bound together with the same gilt wire often used to hang paintings.

It had taken him a long time to die. As he fought, he had struggled, his wrists jerking against the wire as it cut deep into his flesh, down to the wrist bone in places. Repeatedly his head had been dipped into the filled basin, then pulled out, then submerged again. When the water finally began to enter his lungs, his body had reacted, foam spittle gathering at the corners of his mouth. Much later it would rise from the corpse to make a white death

6

froth. Against the push of water, his eyes had widened, the pupils turning from clear orbs to opal discs as he stared blindly at the bottom of the basin.

The killer had made sure that the death of Stefan van der Helde would horrify not only the people who found him, but also his business associates and his cohorts. In sodomising him they had exposed Van der Helde's hidden homosexuality, humiliating him and bringing down one of the top players in the art world. But there was more to it than that: a reason why no one would ever forget the death of Stefan van der Helde. When his body underwent post-mortem examination the pathologist found stones in his stomach. Apparently, over a period of hours, he had been forced to swallow pebbles, one after the other, each one larger than the last, until they threatened to choke him. Even when his oesophagus reacted and went into spasm, he was forced to keep swallowing, his gullet bruised and torn in places by the stones.

They found twenty pebbles in Stefan van der Helde's stomach. They found the water that drowned him – and the twenty stones. The pathologist didn't know what it meant. Neither did the police. No one knew the meaning of the stones. By the time they did, the world would have plunged into recession; the auction houses losing fortunes on collapsing sales; and dealers forced into ruin as bad debts were called in and old favours demanded repayment. As the year ground into an unsteady and claustrophobic spring, the global art world was in a depression no one had foreseen or prepared for.

And from behind elegant façades and glossy reputations crept the venal underbelly of the art world. In a matter of months the financial collapse of the market was underscored by a moral malignancy that left no one unscathed. And four people dead.

It was, some said, a culling.

2

London.
The present day.

Tucked tight in the central kernel of the capital, in amongst the crochet of streets off the thoroughfare of Piccadilly, lies Albemarle Street. Every building is dissimilar. In shop fronts gilded with fashion logos, porters in funereal suits open doors for tourists and the wives of Russian oligarchs alike. Other shops have been there for over a hundred years; a dusty sprinkling of snobbery courts the passer-by with windows cradling bespoke shoes or hand-rolled cigars. And dotted among the By Royal Appointment signs and robin's-egg blue Tiffany boxes nestles the Zeigler Gallery.

It had first opened in 1845, but attracted no notice. After that, it had changed hands several times, closing during the Second World War. Left abandoned, its walls denuded of paintings, the building had sat out the fighting alone, the flat above remaining empty. The rates had been too high, the landlord too greedy. At the height of the war there had been a suspicious fire in the gallery. Some said it had been caused by a tramp, sneaking in and falling asleep with a lighted cigarette in his hand. But neither the tramp nor his cigarette – not even a stub – had ever been found. Yet soon afterwards there *had* been a real fatality: a soldier killed whilst on leave, his body left in the back of the gallery, hidden among the empty packing crates. The soldier – who had worn no dog tag and carried no identification – had never been named and the murder was never solved. But the death of the unknown soldier had cast a pall over the building and the gallery had acquired a ghost. Or so rumour had gone.

Then, in 1947, the gallery had been reopened by a Polish man called Korsawaki. He had come from Warsaw – where he had had been forced to leave behind a fortune and a family – to try to make his name in London. In his home city he had been a dealer of some note, but in the austere years directly after the war he made little headway in London. Forced into selling cheap prints, he was soon grubbing around for any means to pay the rent and, by the time 1949 came around, Korsawaki had left. A couple of other dealers followed, with little success, and the gallery gained a reputation for being jinxed. Left deserted as its neighbours flourished, it had one brief spell in the sunshine as a café. But soon the clink of dishes and the pulse of conversation ended, and the doors were closed and bolted once again.

And so they stayed, until one bitingly cold morning in 1963 when a young man had paused on Albemarle Street and seen the FOR SALE sign in the window. Curious, Owen Zeigler had leaned forward, peering in, but all he had been able to make out was a deserted interior with a staircase on one side and a skylight at the end of the room. He tried the door handle, but it was locked. Then he had stepped back – almost into the path of an oncoming car – to stare upwards at the flat above. The windows had given nothing away, but Owen had felt drawn to the place for some reason that escaped him. Intrigued, he tried the door again without success, and then noted the name and address of the estate agent.

That afternoon he had visited Messrs Lyton and Goldthorne, asking for details on the gallery. They – spotting a potential customer for a property which had proved virtually impossible to shift – encouraged his interest. In fact, Mr Lyton had taken Owen to the gallery within the hour, pushing open the door and waving his prospective customer in. A little probing told Mr Lyton that Owen had family backing and that his father was a dealer in the East End.

What Owen *didn't* tell the agent was that Neville Zeigler dealt not in fine art, but in a variety of 'collectables'; a Jew who had come to London before the war; a Jew who had learnt the business the hard way; a Jew clever enough to develop an eye for the marketable and, later, the valuable. And over the years Neville had instilled in his only child a terrifying ambition. He would take Owen to Bond Street and Cork Street and show him the galleries and tell his son – no, *insist* – that one day there would be a Zeigler Gallery within this cluster of culture and money. With a ferocity which might have daunted a lesser child, Owen learned to develop his natural appreciation into a skill. Neville's long hours of labour in the East End afforded Owen a university place – and the son repaid the father well.

When Owen Zeigler finally entered the bull ring of the art world, he was clever, adept and confident. He could pass as an upper class scholar, a natural inheritor of a cultural career. With his innate ability and his further education, his progress was seamless. But what people didn't know was the other side to Owen Zeigler, the side inherited from his Jewish father, along with Neville's shrewd, invaluable business acumen.

Encouraged by the widowed Neville, who knew the fortunes to be made in the art world, Owen was told to keep quiet about his background and 'get climbing'.

'You've a foot in both camps,' Neville told him. 'You know about culture, and you're street-savvy too. Use it. And remember – there's plenty of room at the top.'

Of course Mr Lyton didn't know any of this, but was impressed when Owen returned a day later having uncovered the gallery's erratic history – which he used as a bargaining tool. In short, by the time two weeks were up, Owen Zeigler had become the new gallery owner. And by the time three weeks were up, the interior had been painted, the flat above was furnished, and there was a new sign outside: after an uncomplicated delivery, the Zeigler Gallery had been born.

In that same bitter winter, Owen held an opening to which his neighbours came to gawp and to criticise, a few to predict disaster. But the dealers from Dover Street and Bond Street realised within minutes of walking through the door that they had a serious new rival. The market at that time was swamped with French art, and the Impressionists, the gauzy country scenes, were becoming commonplace – almost boring – by their very repetition. So Owen had chosen another speciality – Dutch art. Not the thundering names of Rembrandt or Vermeer, in which he could not afford to trade, but the smaller followers, and the still-life painters.

There had been only twenty paintings exhibited on that cold winter day in 1963, but by the end of the month eighteen had been sold. Owen Zeigler's career had been launched. Not perhaps as a grand, ocean-gobbling liner, but as a swift, clever little lighter that could ride the waves of the art market and survive . . .

And all this, Owen Zeigler's son, Marshall, remembered, looking at his father in disbelief.

'Where did all the money *go*?' Marshall asked

Owen put his head in his hands. Now in his seventies, he looked no more than sixty-five. Years of careful grooming, and long walks in London parks, had kept him lean, and his hair, although grey, was thick and well cut. In front of him was the desk he had used since the first

13

day he had begun business at the gallery. A desk on which many a cheque had been written, and across which had passed many a handshake. Above it hung a Dutch painting by Jan Steen. Valuable, as were all the pictures in the gallery, the insurance rising regularly over the years to accommodate and protect Owen's success. The burglar alarms, red lights flickering outside like out-of-season Christmas bunting, all connected to nearby police stations.

Still staring at his father, Marshall thought back to his childhood. His first ten years had been spent in the flat above the gallery, but as his father had prospered the family had been moved out of London to a country house, Thurstons. During the week, Owen had lived in the flat, spending his weekends in the Georgian stereotype of up-market success. But when Marshall's mother had died, Owen had returned frequently to Albemarle Street, leaving his son in the care of a nanny, and later the rigid arms of public school.

'Where did the money go?' Marshall repeated.

His father made a movement, almost a shrug, but the action dropped off, half-made. 'I have to do something . . . I have to.'

For the first time Marshall noticed that his father's hair was thinning slightly at the crown. Even his expert barber hadn't managed to disguise it, he thought, knowing that it would embarrass his father if he knew. Then he noticed the raised veins in his hands, the liver spots puddling the tanned skin. His father was getting old, Marshall realised, unaccountably moved. All Owen's little vanities were becoming noticeable, obvious . . . Marshall glanced away, thinking of the telephone call which had brought him back to London, his father asking him to return from his work in Holland.

'I need to talk to you,' Owen had said, his voice shivering on the edge of panic. 'If you could just come home.'

He had done so at once, because his father had never been possessive or demanding. Marshall might have longed for more closeness as a child, might have grieved alone for the loss of his mother, but in his teens he realised that his father's affection had never been withheld. Just neutralised. Having lost his wife so unexpectedly in a plane crash, Owen had spent the next decade in waiting, almost as though some other plane – real or ephemeral – might bring her back. As though, if he refused to accept her passing, she would one day arrive at some spiritual terminal. Where he would be waiting by the gate to bring her home.

But she never did come back, and Marshall watched as his father finally faced the truth, ten years after her death. He watched the grief, sitting with his father in the country house, staring into country fires or country views. He listened to old memories that had never been his, memories from before his birth, and realised that inside some men there is one space for one woman. And if that woman is lost, the space is never filled again. With a father so bereft, Marshall absorbed his own grief alone, and by the time Owen invited him to talk about his mother's death, she had been parted with. As beautiful, but out of time, as his grandfather's old French paintings.

His thoughts coming back to the present, Marshall prompted, 'You said the money had gone.'

'All gone,' Owen said, nodding.

'How?'

'Debts.'

'*Debts?*' Marshall was shaken. His father had never intimated that money was tight. 'You never said you were struggling. The last show was a success—'

Still seated, Owen turned his face upwards to his son, fixing his gaze. 'I've been cheated.'

I've been cheated ... The words seemed to swell in the gallery, skim along the picture rails, slide across the red silk on the walls, and then slither up the staircase into the dark beyond. A creeping sense of unease swept over Marshall, the same feeling he had had as a boy sleeping in the flat above, remembering the old story of the building. And listening for the ghost of the unknown soldier. The young man who came out at night, who walked around the gallery below, then crept up the stairs in the darkness.

'Who cheated you?'

'I should never have believed him.'

'Who? Who are you talking about?'

'Manners.'

Manners. The name fell like a corn thresher, slicing the air between the two men. Tobar Manners, one of his father's oldest friends and a fellow dealer. Tobar Manners, with his small pink hands and dandelion hair. Tobar Manners, quick, clever, mercurial, always so charming to his father, but another man to Marshall. Indeed, it was Manners who had told Marshall about the murdered soldier, taking delight in frightening a child with stories of a ghost and then laughing, insisting he was only teasing, but knowing that he had planted a poisonous thought. Many disturbed nights of his childhood Marshall put down to Tobar Manners. Many times, waking at a sudden noise, he blamed his unease on his father's changeling friend.

'What did he do?'

Owen shook his head.

'Dad, what did he do?'

'I've been in debt for some time,' Owen said slowly, the words crisp, as though he could keep back his panic by the control of his delivery. 'Business has been bad. The collectors aren't investing, and the auctions have been hit too. A couple of galleries have even closed down.' He paused, grabbed at a breath. 'In the last few years, I overbought. I came across some good paintings and thought I'd have no problem selling them. But then there was the credit crunch. Not many people buy at these times . . .'

'But the big collectors?'

'Are holding back.'

'All of them?'

'No, but not enough are investing to stop me going under.'

'Christ!' Marshall sat down next to his father. 'What about the house?'

'Remortaged.'

'The paintings,' Marshall said, feeling some panic himself, 'sell what you've got. You might make a loss, but you'd raise some money.'

'Not enough,' Owen replied quietly, his hands clenched together. 'I didn't want to tell you how bad it was. I thought I could get out of it, I thought if . . . I sold the Rembrandt . . .'

Slowly, Marshall lifted his head, staring at his father. The painting had been in the family since 1964, when Owen had bought it in Germany. At first he had believed it to be painted by Ferdinand Bol, a pupil of Rembrandt's, but after numerous tests and some intensive research, it had proved to be genuine. It had been the first spectacular triumph of his father's career. A seal on his talent as a dealer. Marshall could remember hearing the story repeated by his father, and by Owen's mentor, Samuel Hemmings. *Watch your back now*, Samuel had warned him, *now you have enemies.*

'Did you sell the Rembrandt?'

'I took it to Tobar Manners . . .'

'And?'

'He said it wasn't genuine. That it was by Ferdinand Bol, as we had originally thought—'

'But it *was* genuine!'

'It's all in the attribution, Marshall,' his father said shortly. 'There's no cut and dried proof—'

'Samuel Hemmings backed your opinion,' Marshall interrupted. 'Surely his name carries enough weight?'

'Samuel is a controversial historian, you know that. What he says is accepted by some people and vigorously denied by others.'

'Usually when there's money involved.'

At once, Owen flared up, his unruffled urbanity overshadowed by hostility.

'I know what you think of the business, Marshall! There's nothing you can say about it I haven't heard before. You made your choice to have nothing to do with the gallery or the art world. Fine, that was your choice, but it's my life, and despise it all you will, it's my passion.'

The argument was worn thin between them. Owen might be committed to art dealing, but Marshall wasn't blinded to the realities of the trade. And trade it was. A hard, tight little trade where a pocket of honest men traded with a legion of those without scruples. Dealers who had inherited galleries, working cheek by jowl with titans who had bought their way in. Deals brokered between old-school traders and the hustlers who drafted in dummy bidders to up the price on a gallery's painting at auction. Not that all of the auction houses were blameless; the process of *burning* was well known. If a painting didn't reach its reserve, it was supposedly sold, but instead it was *burned*, put away for years until the market had either forgotten about it, or presumed it had been put back on sale again by a private buyer. That way no famous name was seen to lose its kudos and market value. Because market value was imperative. For every Cézanne that scorched through its reserve and set a new benchmark, a dozen other Cézannes in museums and private collections rose in value. Over the Sixties, Seventies and Eighties the art market had inflated the value of Van Gogh to such an extent that one purchaser had to put his painting in store for twelve years for insurance reasons. Art was being priced out of the galleries and off the walls into the steel tombs of bank vaults.

Sighing, Marshall realised that this was no time to resurrect the old argument and moderated his tone. 'So Manners said it wasn't a Rembrandt?'

Owen nodded. 'He said it was by one of Rembrandt's pupils. Besides, there was no signature on the painting—'

'There's no signature on many of Rembrandt's paintings!' Marshall snapped. 'That never stopped them being attributed to him. And God knows there are enough paintings *with* his signature that people doubt are genuine.'

'Tobar was sure mine wasn't genuine. When I asked him to buy it, he was told that it was by Ferdinand Bol. He had it looked at twice, thoroughly investigated.'

'By whom?'

'By specialists!' Owen barked, hurrying on. 'Tobar was so sorry. He said that he would give me as much as he could, but nothing like I would have got for a genuine Rembrandt . . . Jesus, I *trusted him*. I've known Tobar for years, I had no reason *not* to trust him.'

Unbidden, images curled in front of Marshall. Images

of Christmases, of private views, of visits to the gallery – and in every image was Tobar Manners. Always there. Sometimes alone, sometimes in a group. Manners and Samuel Hemmings, and other friends of his father's, talking, laughing, swapping stories about dealers or customers. Gossip flirting from one glass to another; snippets of information traded over caviar and canapés; cankers of venom floating into greedy ears.

'What did he do?' Marshall asked finally.

'He bought the painting off me.'

'And?'

'I just heard,' Owen said blindly, 'I just heard about it. The sale in New York. Someone showed me the catalogue, and there is – was – my painting. The same one Tobar had bought from me as a Ferdinand Bol. Only it wasn't. It was in the catalogue as a Rembrandt. *It had been sold as a Rembrandt.*' His words were staccato, gunning his story out. 'Tobar Manners gave me a fraction of its value! He cheated me!'

Shaken, Marshall stared at his father. 'Have you talked to him? Confronted him—'

'He said it wasn't his fault!' Owen replied, his voice raised, anger making bright spots of colour on his cheeks. 'He said he had sold it on to someone as a Ferdinand Bol, and they had cheated *him!*'

'You don't believe him, do you?'

'Of *course* I don't believe him!' Owen hurled back, getting to his feet and walking over to the window.

To his amazement, Marshall could see that his father

was shaking, his elegant body trembling, his hands clenching and unclenching obsessively.

'It made a fortune at the auction,' Owen went on. 'Broke all records for an early Rembrandt. *My painting made a fortune.* A fortune I could have saved the business with. A fortune that was *mine*! Jesus Christ,' he said desperately, 'I'm finished.'

Sensing his father's despair, Marshall tried to calm him. 'Look, you can sell your stock – everything you've got. There are thousands of pounds hanging on these walls, you can raise money that way.'

'Not enough.'

'It must be!' his son replied, feeling a sinking dread. 'Call your collectors, auction what you've got. Ring your contacts. There must be some way to get money—'

'It won't be *enough*!' Owen snapped, control gone. 'I have debts you don't know about. Debts to many people, some of whom are pressuring me now. I can't afford the upkeep on this gallery. I kept thinking that things would improve, and then times got tough for everyone. People still bought, but much less over these last months. I can't shift the stock, Marshall, I can't raise money. There was only the Rembrandt left. It was always in the background, like a safety net. I knew that would raise enough to pay off the debts and get me straight again. But Manners . . .'

He stopped talking, his anger drying up, and an eerie calm came over him before he spoke again. 'He won't admit it, but he *did* cheat me. He lied to me, knowing I was in trouble, he lied to me . . . How many times did that man come to my home? How many times over the years did I help him out? Lend him money to tide him over when he was struggling?'

Owen was no longer talking to his son, just staring at the desk in front of him. 'I'd only been here for a few weeks when Tobar Manners introduced himself. Your mother never really took to him, but I always thought that that was because he could be spiteful about people, and she never liked gossips. And when your mother died, Tobar was very kind . . .'

He was a leech, Marshall wanted to say. My mother saw it, and so did I, even as a child. And he wasn't smart, nothing like as talented as you. So how did he manage to dupe you? You could run rings around him once. You laughed at him with Samuel Hemmings. Not unkindly, more indulgent. But you let him in, too often and too close. God, why were you so stupid with the most treacherous of men?

'I've got a bit of money put away. You can have that.'

'No, I can't take anything from you,' Owen replied, then smiled sweetly, as though the offer momentarily obliterated the seriousness of his situation.

'What will you do?'

'Manage, somehow.' He was trying to fight panic, to press a lid on the scalding tide of his own despair. 'I'll talk to the accountant and the bank again.'

'Will they help?'

'I don't know. Maybe . . .' he replied, back in control again. The father, not the panicking man. 'Don't worry about me. I was just so shocked by what's happened. I shouldn't really have troubled you, got you worried. I'll find a way round this.'

Unconvinced, Marshall looked around the gallery. 'You need a change. You should get out of here for a while, Dad. It'll help you think. I could come and stay with you at Thurstons for a bit. I don't need to get back to Amsterdam straight away.'

'It might . . .'

'It would do you good.' Marshall pressed him. 'We can talk if you want, or you can just relax.'

Owen nodded but averted his gaze. He was embarrassed to be seen as a failure by his son. Embarrassed and ashamed that he had panicked, crying like a child. After all, what could Marshall do? He hadn't the money to rescue him, and couldn't have guessed at the full plunging extent of the debts . . . He had never been a gambler, Owen thought, he should have known. Should never had fallen into the trap of over-buying, then relying on a friend to get him out of trouble – even a friend he had helped, a person who owed him a debt of honour. The shock of his imminent ruin fizzed inside Owen's head, along with the queasy realisation of his own stupidity. He knew that the painting was genuine. He had looked at it for years, treasured it, admired it, petted it like a favourite child. It had never been a follower's work. It had been painted by the Master's hand. And he had sold it short. Confused and panicked, he had listened to a cheat and been treated as a fool.

*

'You need to get away from here,' Marshall said, breaking into his father's reverie.

'It's jinxed.'

'What?'

'The gallery,' Owen said softly. 'When I bought it, I knew about the rumours. Nothing succeeded here for long. People came and went. Perhaps there *is* a ghost . . .'

'Bull shit.'

To Marshall's surprise, his father laughed. 'I wish I was like you, Marshall. I really do.'

'I always wished I was more like you,' his son said honestly, touching his father on the shoulder. 'We could go to Thurstons tonight—'

'I can't,' Owen cut in hurriedly. 'I can't just run away.'

'But if you got away you'd clear your head.'

Owen sighed. 'There are things to do. I have to see to a few things here before I can leave.'

'All right,' Marshall agreed finally. 'Then let me stay here and help.'

'No,' Owen replied, straining to smile. 'I should never have got you involved. It's not your worry, I just panicked that's all. You're right, Marshall, there *is* a lot of stock; perhaps I can raise enough to pay back some people.'

'What about asking the bank for a temporary loan? Just to tide you over?'

Mirthlessly, Owen laughed. 'They didn't seem to think I was a good bet.'

'Then let me go and talk to *my* bank.'

'No,' Owen said, almost harshly. 'Leave it be, Marshall.

Just talking to you has helped. I'll go through the stock tomorrow and draw up some figures. There are some people I can talk to ...' He trailed off, looking around him. 'The Rembrandt would have sorted all this out, paid back all my debts. It sold for a *fortune*, did I tell you that?'

Surprised, Marshall nodded. 'Yes, Dad, you told me.'

'Manners cheated me.'

'So why don't we confront him together?'

His face set, Owen shrugged his shoulders. An odd gesture, resigned and feckless at the same time. 'What's done is done. I know this business, I made enough money out of it myself—'

'Not by cheating people.'

'No,' Owen agreed. 'And not by cheating friends.' He paused, then straightened up, smoothed his hair, his urbane charm restored. 'It might not be hopeless.'

'Are you sure that there's nothing I can do?'

'Nothing,' Owen said calmly. 'You go to Thurstons and I'll come at the weekend.'

Marshall nodded. 'I've some business to see to first, but I'll come back and we'll go together. OK?'

'OK, OK.'

Relieved, Marshall touched his father's arm. 'When you get away from here you'll feel different, I promise. It will all be different by the weekend.'

3

Teddy Jack was drinking tea made with two teabags, and four spoonfuls of sugar. Made by the fleshy woman at the Tea House on the corner, opposite St Barnabas's Church. She made it better than anyone else, and winked when she passed it to him. Gratefully Teddy patted her bottom, the soft flesh under her polyester skirt yielding to his hand. Taking another gulp, he wiped his mouth and beard with the back of his hand, then watched the workers coming and going from the main entrance of Smithfield Market.

Teddy could remember the place twenty years earlier, when he had just come out of Strangeways, having served two years for assault. His mother had said at the time, *if you want to amount to nothing, carry on the way you're going.* There and then he'd decided that he wanted to amount to something – something more than cheap food, a worn bed in a council flat on the ninth floor, with a view of the gas-works. Divorcing a wife who had borne another man's child while he was in prison, Teddy had left the North for London.

He came down, regaled with all the usual tales of the capital's streets either being crammed with gold or sleaze, depending on who he spoke to. But he had found neither. Perhaps his impressive physical size had warned many off; or perhaps it was his manner, which had been affable and threatening at the same time. Either way, Teddy Jack had started his new life washing up in a big London hotel. By the end of the month he had taken a smelly flat in Beak Street, Soho, sandwiched between the rooms of two working girls and above an all-night chemist with a relentless stream of addicts – the most desperate getting their stuff and immediately shooting up in the doorway of Teddy's flat. When he'd caught them, they hadn't done it again.

Teddy had then cleaned out the flat and got rid of the smell, fitted a new window where a mouldy board had been, and soon the working girls took to Teddy. After another month he had been 'married' to five different girls, his husband status warning off pimps and keeping the punters in line. In return Teddy had been rewarded with blow jobs or quickies, and for a time he had even fancied himself in love with a diminutive Asian girl – until she had stayed with him one night and emptied his wallet. After that, none of the working girls had ever slept over at Teddy's again. They had visited, talked to him in the Formica bleakness of the galley kitchen, or asked to use his bath, but they had only been friends, not lovers. Teddy was always a quick learner.

So quick that he had soon graduated from washer-upper

to doorman at a respected Park Lane hotel, his saffron coloured beard neatly groomed, his hair trimmed and contained under the green uniform cap. Dressed in the dark military style coat and trousers, Teddy had been a striking Norseman at the doors. A Viking in the middle of London, his bass voice adding to his overall aura of power. Soon he became a well known and trusted figure. Married guests arriving with their lovers had never had to worry about Teddy letting anything slip to their spouses. There was no embarrassing mix up in names, just the usual contained good humour which had seen Teddy's tips increase as fast as his colleagues' jealousy. Realising that a Northern outsider had become the unexpected favourite, the rumour mill swung into action, gossip reaching the management's ears that Teddy Jack had been bringing prostitutes for the guests. Hardly a revelation – it was something which went on in most hotels – but when the management heard of the bloated commission Teddy was supposedly getting, he was fired.

He never been given the reason, just turfed out, saying they were cutting back on staff.

Last in, first out, sorry, mate.

So Teddy Jack had given back the uniform and moved on, without a reference, and found work as a porter for one of the smaller art galleries in Dover Street. His physical strength had made easy work of the packing and unpacking of the paintings and sculptures, but he had always been under supervision. Teddy had never let on about his criminal record, but he had been sufficiently sketchy about his past to be viewed with caution. When he had once volunteered to deliver a customer's painting to Hampstead, the embarrassing pause which followed said, without words, that his employer had no intention of letting a Turner sketch leave the gallery – unaccompanied – with Teddy Jack.

In response to the obvious insult, Teddy had resigned. But he held onto the brown porter's coat which he reckoned as payment for the slight. Enraged, he had left Dover Street and walked quickly towards Piccadilly, accidentally brushing into a man and knocking him into the road on Albemarle Street.

Grabbing hold of the stranger he had unbalanced, Teddy had apologised.

'You all right, mate?'

The urbane man had shrugged. 'No harm done. But you're a big man, you take up a lot of pavement.' Owen Zeigler had smiled, then gestured to the porter's coat Teddy was wearing. 'Are you working around here?'

'I was.'

'What happened?'

'My employer didn't trust me.'

Interested, Owen studied the big man. He needed more help in the gallery and had been about to advertise the job when this man had literally crossed his path.

'Did your employer have reason not to trust you?'

And then Teddy Jack had done something he never usually did. He found himself confiding, opening up. Whether

30

it had been because he was pissed off, or just didn't care, he dropped the caution of a lifetime and answered fully.

'You be the judge of whether or not he could trust me. I'm twenty-nine. Never amounted to much, did two years in the Strangeways for assault. The man was my own age and he'd insulted my wife, so I did time for it, and when I got out my wife had had another man's kid. I'd fought for her honour a lot harder than she ever had.' Teddy took in a deliberate, measured breath. 'I've been down in London nearly six months. Worked as a washer-up and a hotel doorman, and I just resigned from a bastard's gallery round the corner. I live in Beak Street, rough as a bear's arse, rent due every Friday. I don't do drugs, don't thieve, and I only drink at the weekends.'

'Still got the temper?'

'Not so you'd fucking notice,' Teddy had replied, his unflinching eyes fixed on the elegant man in front of him.

As they stood on the London street, under a disinterested spring sun, they had made a mismatched couple. The red-bearded Viking facing the polished art dealer. And yet they had immediately liked each other, some mutual understanding passing between them.

'I need a porter at my gallery, the Zeigler Gallery,' Owen had said. 'But not just a porter, someone who can be flexible—'

'Like rubber.'

'I have two other excellent porters, but I'd want you to do more of the heavy work. Have you got a driver's licence?'

31

Teddy nodded. 'Car and LGV.'

'I don't suppose you've got any references?'

'Only from Strangeways,' Teddy had replied, finally smiling. 'Look, I want to make a life down here. I've put the past to rest. The old Teddy Jack doesn't exist anymore. I didn't want to keep company with him no longer.'

'I'll put you on a month's trial. If you're reliable and a good worker, the job will be permanent. But it might change, over time,' Owen had said, frowning. 'You know, circumstances, events. Things change. Needs change.'

Without hesitating, Teddy had put out his hand. 'I'm Edward Jack. Teddy Jack.'

Owen had taken the proffered hand and shaken it, smiling with genuine charm. 'And my name's Zeigler, Owen Zeigler.'

At once Teddy's eyes had flickered.

'What is it?'

'I know about you,' Teddy had replied, distantly amused. 'Heard quite a lot about you and your gallery, in fact—'

'*Really?*'

'—because the bastard I've just walked out on is Tobar Manners.'

The month's trial had been up before anyone had realised, and it was never referred to because within four weeks Teddy had created a niche for himself and wasn't going anywhere. Having learnt from past experience, he had made sure that this time he wouldn't become the favourite and alienate his co-workers. So he had treated the older porters, ex-Guardsmen Lester Fox and Gordon Hendrix, with respect and kept out of their way. In fact, Teddy had kept out of *everyone's* way and concentrated on the Zeigler Gallery instead. He had repainted walls, mended the staircase and taken on some of the basic plumbing.

'What now?' Owen had asked one night, coming into the basement to watch Teddy mending a broken packing crate.

'Needs fixing.'

And fixed it had been. Whatever it was, if it needed fixing, Teddy had fixed it.

That spring had passed fast, left without anyone noticing, until the smoky hot summer flush of 1994 had swung her broad hips round the London streets . . . Teddy thought back, remembering how the smog had cluttered the interlinking alleyways and shops off Bond Street, snaking around the dowager terrace of the Museum of Mankind and dozing at the entrance of Burlington Arcade. As the hot red London buses had veined their circulation through the city, Albemarle Street had marinated itself in a series of triumphant art sales. And as a Matisse trumped up the already inflated prices, the stalwarts of Dutch art had made their re-entry.

In that eerie quicksand of a summer Owen Zeigler had taken Teddy Jack to one side and, as though it was a matter of little importance, asked him to watch someone. Just watch them, take notes and report back, nothing much. Then later Owen asked him to follow them, then bug their phone ... It was the first of many times Owen asked Teddy Jack to break the law.

Uncharacteristically unnerved by the memories, Teddy Jack looked round and sipped at his tea. He thought briefly of leaving London and then changed his mind, thinking instead of what he knew. Of what Owen Zeigler had told him. Of the confidences he had carried for years.

... I'm looking for someone I can rely on, even lean on perhaps.

They had liked each other, both knowing more about the men they really were, behind the images the world believed. Flattered and needed, Teddy had been the ideal support, the perfect ally, the furtive spy.

And perhaps the only man alive who knew *all* about Owen Zeigler.

4

Knocking over a folio of prints as he turned, Samuel Hemmings cursed under his breath. With an effort, he bent over in his wheelchair to pick up the sheaf of papers, slapping them back down on his desk, a mug of coffee slopping liquid over the rim as he did so. Unperturbed, Samuel wrapped his dressing gown tightly around him, the droplets of coffee dribbling down his front as he sipped at it. Outside, the winter garden shook its spindly fist at him. Leaves were banked on top of the net over the pond, whilst a stone cherub stood gloomy watch next to a U-shaped space under the far fence where the foxes had visited for decades.

Thoughtful, Samuel cleaned his reading glasses absent-mindedly and stared into the sobering morning. He was, he thought irritably, tired. But then again, he was eighty-six and had an excuse for still being in his dressing gown at eleven o'clock. In the passage outside, he could hear the vacuum cleaner start up on the other side of his study door. Mrs McKendrick, his housekeeper, had been with him for over twenty years, but no matter how many times he told her, she would try and get into the study. *It needs tidying*, she would say, but Samuel liked the sheen of dust on the high bookshelves. Why remove it when he seldom needed those volumes? The books he *did* refer to were close at hand, used so often no dust had time to settle. As for the dust in his old sofa and easy chair, he liked that too. Found it comforting to settle himself amidst the flotsam of years.

The only thing Samuel missed was a dog. Since he had lived in the Sussex countryside – in the house which had sagged under neglect, and grown so out of fashion it had become fashionable again – there had always been a dog. Someone living, getting older with its master. Sleeping by the fire, steaming when they came in from a walk, or farting into old age, an animal had been as much a part of the house as the door knocker and entry sign – Samuel Hemmings, Art Historian.

Even though he had collected a batch of awards and letters after his name, Samuel liked to keep his identity simple. He could afford to, as can all illustrious people, knowing their reputations speak for them. Wincing as the vacuum started up again, Samuel turned to the papers on his desk. He was amused by the latest auction where a Mark Rothko was expected to reach a record price, and wondered what the picture would fetch in a hundred years. Would Rothko's reputation increase? Or sink as so many had done before . . .

Having had no truck with the art world, Samuel had

written numerous anarchic pieces on the absurdities of modern art and the gangster tactics of some dealers. Always outspoken, he had become even more so as he grew older. Courageous at seventy, he had become reckless as he turned eighty, and was hoping for martyrdom at ninety.

His thoughts were interrupted by the door opening behind him. Irritated, Samuel turned in his wheelchair, but his sparse eyebrows rose in pleasure when he saw who his visitor was.

'Hello,' Marshall said, moving over to the old man and taking a sheaf of papers off a nearby chair before sitting down. 'I was passing by and—'

'Liar. You've never *passed by* here in twenty years,' Samuel retorted, looking intently at his visitor.

He was reminded – not for the first time – that Marshall Zeigler bore little resemblance to his father. Where Owen was patrician, Marshall was more heavily built, his thick hair as darkly brown as his eyes. On the street, a passer-by might have taken Owen for a diplomat, while his son looked like someone in the media. Even their voices were dissimilar, Owen's elegant speech a world apart from Marshall's deeper, cosmopolitan tone.

'So,' Samuel asked, 'what really brought you here?'

'My father.'

Samuel's eyes fixed on Marshall. His sight was failing, his left eye milky with a cataract, but his right eye was brilliant, blue as a delphinium and missed nothing. 'Is he all right?'

'Not really. I saw him last night. He's in debt, badly in debt.'

'Your *father*?'

'Yes. I'd have thought he was the last person to get into trouble like that . . .'

Hearing the vacuum cleaner start up outside the door, he paused while Mrs McKendrick banged it against the panelling, and waited until she'd worked her way along the hall.

'It's serious too. He sold the Rembrandt—'

'*What!* When was this?' Samuel asked urgently, scooting his wheelchair over to his desk and clicking on the computer. Peering at the screen, he began to type, Marshall watching him. Samuel Hemmings might be well into his eighties, but he was computer fluent.

'I've had bronchitis the last two weeks, flat out in bed. Missed a bloody lot,' he muttered, sighing as a page came up on screen, with the details of the New York sale. 'Jesus, it fetched a fortune!'

'Which my father didn't get.'

Slowly Samuel turned in his chair, the front of his dressing gown falling open to reveal a V-necked jumper pulled over his striped pyjamas. 'What are you talking about?'

'Tobar Manners cheated him. My father was in trouble, so he went to Manners because he was a friend. Manners knew my father was desperate for money, but he said that the Rembrandt was by Ferdinand Bol.'

Samuel's fingers clacked on the keyboard, then he

scooted his chair across the room again and pulled down a thick volume of photographs. Back at the desk, he flicked through dozens of pages, then withdrew an image of the Rembrandt. Screwing up his eyes, he then read what he had written on the page next to it.

Supposed to be Ferdinand Bol. But no doubt Rembrandt. Provenance suspect, but colouring and brushwork obviously the Master.
Owen has done it this time. He's a dealer now. (1961)

Then he looked at the painting again, peering at it with a magnifying glass. Outside in the hall, Mrs McKendrick was still denting the skirting board with the Hoover, and in the garden, beyond the window, a thrush was taking a dip in a lichen-encrusted bird bath. Patiently, Marshall waited for Samuel to speak.

At first he had been surprised by the old man's appearance; he seemed scruffier than usual and had lost weight, but within seconds he had proved that his mind was as astute as ever. Looking round as Samuel continued to read, Marshall noticed the elaborate carving along the picture rail, in places grey with dust, in others the wood bleached by sun. He had stared at the same carvings when he was a child, the day his father had brought him to meet the famous Samuel Hemmings. The historian had been much younger then, not weak in the legs, but scuttling like a child's top around the haphazard terrain of his study. In amongst the books and papers he had secreted bottles of

cheap sweets, their incongruous primary colours at odds
with the muted surroundings. Talking quickly and with
animation, Samuel had only paused to take a handful of
sweets, swallowing a couple and throwing the others in
Marshall's direction, Owen winking at his son as he did
so.

To another child, Samuel's eccentricity might have been
unnerving, but Marshall was entranced. He loved the
crackle of energy, the stimulus of Samuel's interest. His
enthusiasm and honesty were a pleasant change from
many of his father's dealer acquaintances. And as time
passed – and Marshall learned that Samuel Hemmings
was a one-man iconoclast of the art world – his admiration grew. Those dealers who had been at the rapier end
of Samuel's tongue or pen might detest him, but his knowledge of art history – particularly the Dutch Masters – was
formidable. Indeed that was how Samuel and Owen had
first met.

Soon after Owen opened the Zeigler Gallery, the rangy,
bowed figure of Samuel Hemmings had visited. In his old-
fashioned suit and battered patent evening shoes, he had
looked almost comical, but his intelligence was phenomenal, and he was unusually generous with his knowledge. So when Owen, a relatively green dealer, asked
Samuel to look at his paintings, he had been expecting a
swift summation but, instead, received comprehensive and
impressive opinions. Instead of being offended by the brutality of some of Samuel's remarks, Owen had chosen to
learn from the older man, and a friendship was born.

But now, Samuel scooted his chair back to Marshall, scraping its wheel against a table leg as he did so. 'It's genuine. I said so at the time, and I was right. How could Tobar Manners say otherwise?'

'He told my father that he'd got it valued himself.'

'By who?'

'I don't know. I doubt my father knows either . . .'

Samuel raised a meagre eyebrow, but he said nothing.

'Manners said *he* was cheated,' Marshall went on. 'He said that *he* was paid for a work by Ferdinand Bol, not Rembrandt—'

'Which meant he could give your father a lot less from the sale.'

'Yes – and my father was relying on the Rembrandt to get him out of trouble.'

'Why didn't he come to me?' Samuel asked, turning back to Marshall.

'I think he was ashamed.'

'Ashamed of what?'

'Being a failure,' Marshall said, his voice muted. 'My father never said anything about being in debt. Not a word. I thought everything was going well, as always, but suddenly he said that we needed to talk, and then confessed that he was ruined. He said he'd been over-buying, that auction sales aren't as good as they were, and collectors don't have the same money to invest. My father's got too many paintings and not enough customers.'

'So what happened to his profits?'

Marshall shrugged. 'Gone.'

'*Gone?*' Samuel turned back to the desk and grabbed the ledger. 'It doesn't sound like your father. None of this. He was never reckless.'

'I know, but he's in a mess now. He says he's going to lose the gallery.'

'I don't believe that!' Samuel replied. 'That place is his life. He would never have gambled with it.'

'He thought he could get himself out of debt without anyone knowing a thing about it if he sold the Rembrandt.'

Shaking his head, Samuel stared into the fire. A minute or two later, Mrs McKendrick came in with two cups of tea. In silence, she laid them down on the Long John in front of the hearth, then passed one cup to Samuel. Taking it, he sipped the tea absently, all the while thinking.

It was several minutes before he spoke again. 'I can let your father have ten thousand pounds.'

'Oh God, no,' Marshall said, startled. 'I wasn't coming to you for money. I just wanted you to talk to Dad. He couldn't and wouldn't take money, but he's very low, Samuel, and he listens to you.'

'Not lately, or he wouldn't be in this mess.'

Marshall nodded. 'I'm worried about him. And I'd be less worried if you were in touch with him. I'm staying at the country house and he's joining me at the weekend, but if you could ring him in the meantime . . . Just talk to him, calm him down. I can't do it. I'm his son, he won't listen to me.'

'What about Tobar Manners?'

'What can I tell you?' Marshall said bitterly. 'He says

42

that he sold my father's painting on, and that the purchaser said it was by Bol and therefore paid Manners for one of Rembrandt's pupils. Manners is insisting that *he* was the one who was cheated.'

'Liar. Always was and always will be,' Samuel said coldly. 'I can't imagine why your father believed anything he said.'

'They were friends.'

'There are no friends in business,' Samuel retorted sharply. 'Your father panicked, that's what happened. He wasn't thinking clearly.'

'So talk to him. Please,' Marshall urged. 'He needs to talk to someone he respects.'

Nodding, Samuel sipped at his tea, staring at the fire. The logs shifted and dropped, sparks flirting up the drowsy chimney in front of them.

'Did your father ever tell you about his theory?'

'Which theory?' Marshall asked, finishing his tea and settling back into the armchair. The house was welcoming and outside the day was cold and uninviting. He felt suddenly like a boy again, listening to one of Samuel's stories and waiting for the sudden flurry of sweets to come his way.

'His theory about Rembrandt's monkey.'

'Rembrandt's monkey? No.'

'Perhaps he knew you wouldn't be interested,' Samuel said simply, glancing at Marshall and knowing that he had scored a direct hit. 'You never *were* interested in the gallery, were you?'

'No.'

'It was a shame for your father, but then again, we can't force our children into our shoes. It only gives them bad feet. Can even cripple them, or so I hear,' Samuel continued. 'Your father's very proud of your work. You do know that, don't you? He wonders how you managed to have such a talent for languages and translation.'

'I've got a good memory and besides, my mother spoke three languages,' Marshall said quietly. 'I suppose I inherited it from her.'

'But it takes more than just a skill to translate literature in another language. It takes passion and creativity.'

'Which I could have put into the gallery and the art world?' Marshall countered, reading the old man's thoughts. 'You're being unusually obscure, Samuel, why don't you just come out with what you're thinking?'

Samuel smiled, obviously amused, then reverted to his previous topic.

'Your father has a theory about Rembrandt. He did some research and checked his facts and dates, and then he came to see me to talk about it. Oh, this is a while ago, not long after he bought the gallery and we became friends. You were all living in Albemarle Street then, in the flat. All very cramped for a family of three.'

'Especially with that bloody ghost.'

Samuel laughed again. 'No one ever found out who killed the poor soldier, did they? But then again, there are ghosts and ghosts. Some who stay around the place where they were killed, some who stay around places they loved. Some ghosts can't leave, because of their tie to the earth. And then there are the living ghosts . . .' He paused, folding his hands across his narrow stomach. 'People who are in the background. Always hovering, always out of reach.'

'I don't understand,' Marshall said carefully, watching his father's mentor.

'Rembrandt was not at all as we think of him now. He wasn't well thought of in the eighteenth and nineteenth centuries, his work was found to be too dark and dismal. Other painters could run rings around him. Rubens, for example, could paint a rhinoceros without blinking, and a whole pageant of people in broad sunlight. No cheating shadows, no Brown Windsor soup backgrounds. And yet, over the years, we fell in love with Rembrandt van Rijn. We took his darkness as our own. Perhaps in the twentieth century there was too much Sigmund Freud and Carl Jung; people who made us look inside our heads and psyches, who talked about our dark sides, and made us believe that the soul was as accessible as a National Trust castle. We were taught to embrace our shadows. And shadows live without sun . . . Caravaggio was the first who made a career out of lighting, but his brute strength and violence were too much for him to have many apologists, and so we came to Rembrandt . . .'

Despite himself, Marshall's attention was caught. It was cold outside and he had no wish to leave. In the soft, dry nest of the old house, he found comfort in Samuel's voice, the story drawing him in.

'But we forget the facts. We forget that Rembrandt was

a miller's son, as brash, ambitious and boorish a man as possible. He came to Amsterdam thinking that he knew it all and was soon successful. But success swelled his head. You can see it in the self portraits. Rembrandt dressed up like a cavalier or some turbaned Eastern potentate, but whatever he wore, the same potato face looks out at us. Clothes could not make this man anything other than a boor.' Samuel paused, smiling wickedly. 'All this has nothing to do with his ability as a painter. He was supremely gifted, but where we've gone wrong for so long is in how we have chosen to *think* of Rembrandt. Your father found the *true* Rembrandt.'

Leaning forward, Marshall stared at the old man. 'What d'you mean? The true Rembrandt?'

'After Rembrandt's wife died he hired a housekeeper, a youngish, childless widow called Geertje Dircx. Before long they were lovers and he gave her one of his late wife's rings. But then another maid came into the house and Rembrandt switched his affections.'

'And?'

'Geertje was forced out, but she took Rembrandt to court for breach of promise. She said that he had promised to marry her – something which was taken very seriously in Holland at the time – and said that the ring proved his intention. Rembrandt denied it. He claimed that in the terms of his late wife's will, he would be virtually ruined if he married again and so – because of that – he would never marry anyone. He offered to buy Geertje off, tried to wriggle of out his responsibilities, but when

46

Geertje wouldn't agree to his terms in court, Rembrandt retaliated in one of the cruellest ways ever recorded. He had her committed to an asylum.'

Surprised, Marshall frowned. 'People don't talk about this.'

'Of course not. How would it fit with the image of Rembrandt the humanitarian? If we had known that he got Geertje's neighbours, and her own brother and nephew to testify against her, how would we have judged Rembrandt then?'

'As a bastard,' Marshall replied simply. 'So what was my father's theory?'

'That Rembrandt had a son by Geertje.'

'You're not serious?' Marshall exclaimed, astonished.

'There's some evidence that Geertje could have met Rembrandt before either were married, and that they had a brief affair when they were very young. We know that Rembrandt knew Geertje's brother, and that the families were acquainted. But after the affair Rembrandt went on to marry Saskia and Geertje married a ship's carpenter.'

'Is that it?'

Samuel gave Marshall a slow look.

'Bear with me. Your father believed that Geertje gave birth to a son – Rembrandt's child – in 1622, when she was only fifteen and Rembrandt fourteen.'

'That's a bit young, isn't it?'

'Only the other day there was a boy in the paper who fathered a child at twelve,' Samuel replied. 'Anyway, because Rembrandt and Geertje were kids and the whole matter was an embarrassing mistake, the birth was kept a secret and the child was adopted by a couple in Beemster. The adoptive father was in the town council and his wife was the local midwife, Barbertje. This is a very important fact—'

'Why?'

'Because a midwife could easily bring an unwanted child into her own family. Who could be better placed?'

'But why would she?'

'Your father has a theory about that too,' Samuel replied, pleased to see Marshall's growing interest. 'Apparently, Pieter Fabritius, the adoptive father who worked for the town council, had regular increases in salary. After a decade or so, the couple were earning a substantial sum annually. Owen believes that the Fabritius couple were paid to keep quiet.'

'And this adopted child—'

'Carel Fabritius.'

'—was the illegitimate son of Rembrandt and Geertje Dircx?'

'Yes.'

Blowing out his cheeks, Marshall leaned back in his seat. Outside the wind was getting spiteful, the day dowdy with rain.

'But how would Rembrandt get them to agree to taking on the child?'

'Rembrandt didn't. You forget that Rembrandt was only a boy himself at this time. His parents were desperate to cover up the scandal and, although not rich, they paid to have the illegitimate child adopted. Remember, it would be worth it to them. They knew their son was prodigiously talented, that a great future awaited him, and they weren't prepared to let that opportunity slip. It was probably sorted out between the two sets of parents, and then forgotten.'

'But if that's true, what happened to Geertje?'

'She went on with her life, worked in a tavern, and then married a ship's carpenter.'

'And never said a word to anyone?'

Samuel paused, throwing a log on the fire. Within a few moments the smell of applewood uncurled from the flames.

'But what if she did tell someone? Her husband, for example? Couples talk and exchange confidences all the time. Perhaps she confided in Abraham Claesz when it turned out that they couldn't have children. Perhaps they argued and he told her that it was her fault that she was barren. Wouldn't she have retaliated? What pleasure would it have given her to brag about the now famous father of her illegitimate child? Or what if – when she was firmly ensconced in his home and life – *she told Rembrandt himself*?'

Intrigued, Marshall reached out to warm his hands.

'Where was Carel Fabritius by this time?'

'Being raised in Beemster. By judicious planning, Pieter Fabritius was an amateur painter, so Carel's talent wouldn't have seemed out of place. And when he reached his teens his father, seeing a perfect opportunity for advancement, entered Carel into Rembrandt's studio as a pupil. All very neat.'

'When was that?'

'Early 1640s. Geertje entered Rembrandt house in 1643.'

Curious, Marshall considered the facts. 'Did she know who Carel was?'

'Your father believes that she did,' Samuel replied. 'Your father thinks that Geertje knew only too well that Carel Fabritius was her son. And that when Rembrandt's wife died, it was the perfect opportunity for her to re-enter the painter's life.'

'But if Rembrandt knew about Carel—'

'Ah, but your father doesn't think he did know that Carel was his illegitimate child. Not at first, anyway. He'd probably never even seen his illegitimate son. He would have thought the whole matter was over and done with long ago. Rembrandt was on a high – famous, ambitious and arrogant. He might be very pleased to see Geertje again, and fall back into their old love affair whilst she nursed his young son, but did Rembrandt know that his pupil was the bastard he had with his girl lover? Unlikely. He'd hardly have risked such a scandal by taking Geertje in, would he? To have his own bastard as a pupil? While he slept with the mother? No, I don't think so.'

'But if Geertje knew,' Marshall said carefully, 'God, what a hold she'd have over Rembrandt . . . Of course, there's one other *big* question.'

'Which is?'

'Did Carel Fabritius know who his real parents were?'

Sighing, Samuel sank back into his seat, his spindly

legs stretched out on the Long John in front of the fire, his old slippers curling upwards at the toes.

'Has your father never told you about *any* of this?'

'No, never.'

'Perhaps you should ask him.'

'*You* tell me,' Marshall urged him. 'You can't stop now, it's too good a story. Did Carel Fabritius know he was Rembrandt's son?'

'Your father doesn't think so. He thinks that Carel found out later.'

Marshall frowned. 'So what's Rembrandt's monkey?'

'Not what, *who*. Apparently there were some letters, written by Geertje Dircx, which corroborated the whole story,' Samuel replied, smiling enigmatically. 'Your grandfather left them to your father.'

Stunned, Marshall leaned towards the old man.

'So why hasn't he gone public? Why hasn't he sold them? They'd make a fortune—'

'And create a scandal. Undermine the whole art market, especially in a recession,' Samuel said quietly. 'Your father loves everything about the art world, and he's not the kind of man to set out to destroy the reputation of one of the greatest painters who ever lived.'

Marshall's eyes narrowed. 'You haven't finished the story. You still haven't told me who Rembrandt's monkey is.'

'It's not my place to tell you.'

'So you just told me enough to whet my appetite?'

Samuel nodded, his eyes cunning. 'Ask Owen for the rest. Let him have the triumph of telling you, it might help you both. You said you were staying with your father at the weekend? Well, ask him then. It would take his mind off his worries and he'd love to think you were interested in his pet theory.'

Smiling, Marshall studied the old man in front of him. 'Have you seen these letters?'

'What do *you* think?'

'Well, have you or not?'

'Let's put it this way,' Samuel said earnestly. 'I don't have your father's noble nature. I'd love to set the cat among the pigeons.'

'Just as I would,' Marshall said, 'which makes me wonder why you told me about them. You know how much I dislike the business, and now this trouble with Manners has made me despise it more than I ever did.' He remembered Owen's panic. 'If my father loses the gallery . . .'

'Is it really that bad?'

'He says so. If he lost the gallery, he'd be ruined. I don't just mean financially, his whole world would collapse. Albemarle Street and the streets around it, the galleries, the dealers, the auction houses – they're his life's blood. Dealing is his passion. I think my father could even take the loss of his reputation – but not the loss of his gallery.'

'Your father has many friends, myself included. Honestly, Marshall, I'm sure when he calms down he'll realise he can save the business. He might have to sell the stock and pull in a few favours, but he can do it. And remember, there's ten thousand pounds with your father's name on it.' The old man sighed. 'If you ask me, what Owen needs now is a break. Do what you said you were going to do. Stay with him at the weekend, let him talk. And ask him about the Rembrandt letters. Those deadly, secret letters.'

Getting to his feet, Marshall looked down at the historian. 'And Rembrandt's monkey?'

'Oh, yes, ask him about the monkey too.' Samuel laughed. 'Make him tell you what Rembrandt was *really* like.'

5

The rain was coming down in platinum sheets by the time Marshall reached the outskirts of London. Peering into the darkening suburbs, he swerved to avoid a motorcycle and then skidded to a halt at the side of the road. Unnerved, he stopped the engine, the windscreen wipers keeping up their mechanised droning. Reaching for his mobile, he called his father, but there was no answer at the gallery. Surprised, Marshall tried the country house, but again, no reply.

Then he realised that if Owen was in the cellars of the Zeigler Gallery he wouldn't hear the phone ringing in the gallery above. And it was more than likely he was downstairs, going through the stock, taking an inventory, trying to make some order out of the chaos . . . For a moment Marshall was tempted to drive to Tobar Manners' house in Barnes. After all, he knew the place well: an old house studded with paintings, Manners an effusive host, his regal Italian wife often away. She was, some wit once said, the Good Manners. Certainly she seemed to have little involvement with her husband's work or colleagues, only present for the Christmas party they threw every year. Marshall could picture her without trying – taller than her husband, broad shouldered, with a long Venetian nose and black hair – formidable, and yet inherently kind. And with an impressive lineage.

Many people wondered why she had married the small, homosexual Tobar Manners, with his aggressive feral ways in business and his pungent social charm. But the marriage had lasted, the Venetian grande dame as reserved as the Sphinx. Not that she missed anything. Rosella might not remark upon it, but nothing her husband did went unnoticed. Once, many years earlier, she had seen Tobar teasing Marshall and had caught the boy's eye, glancing at her husband and lifting her brows as if to say, *what a fool. And we both know it.*

Incensed, Marshall thought of Tobar Manners and his hands tightened on the steering wheel. Why shouldn't he go and have it out with him? Confront him, accuse him of cheating his father? Why not . . .? Marshall knew only too well. Manners would have his story crafted to perfection. He would insist that *he* had been cheated, and no doubt have some tame accomplice on hand to back up his version of events. He would shake his head and act flustered – embarrassed by what had happened – assuring Marshall that he would never, *never* have done anything to injure Owen. His hand would shake very slightly as he poured them a sherry, and he would avoid eye contact, his white lashes feathering the sly eyes.

Turning the engine back on, Marshall knew that any visit to Tobar Manners would be pointless. He had got away with it. For now. But if Marshall had anything to do with it, one day he would get his own back on his childhood tormentor and his father's Janus friend.

Nicolai Kapinski stared out of the window of the flat above the Zeigler Gallery, his thick glasses pushed onto the top of his balding head. Around him were the account books and every other piece of information he had been able to glean about Owen Zeigler's financial situation. Not the facts he had been given before, but the whole and unabridged version of a man's imminent ruin. Jesus, he thought for the hundredth time, why hadn't Owen Zeigler told him how bad the situation had become? Why had he lied, given Nicolai false accounts?

Pushing the ledgers away, Nicolai Kapinski continued staring out of the window, his pallid Polish gaze fixing on a barley sugar chimney stack in the distance. He had thought himself a friend as well as an accountant. How many times during the previous twenty years had he and Owen worried about money? Discussed plans? Triumphed when the gallery had had a particularly successful year – and there had been a number of those. But from what Nicolai could see now, the previous twenty-four months had seen a dramatic downturn, which had turned into a slide, then into a financial free fall.

He turned as he heard footsteps behind him. 'Why didn't you tell me?'

Owen shrugged and sat down. 'It was not a matter of trust, you know I've always trusted you. But I took some risks you wouldn't have approved of . . .'

'Is this all of it?'

Owen blinked slowly, regarding the narrow shouldered, slight man sitting at the incongruously large desk. Nicolai had come to Owen via a friend; was recommended as an astute accountant, originally from Warsaw. There was only one problem. With Nicolai's business acumen went a long-held manic depression. Medication controlled the condition eighty-five per cent of the time, but there were intermittent staggers of instability, and every time Nicolai slipped into mania he reverted to the same theme – the disappearance of his brother.

Luther had gone missing when they were children. Rumours had abounded of kidnapping gangs, gypsies, even a local man, who was questioned by the Polish police and then released. Driven out of the town, the man had fled but the mystery had remained. In time Nicolai's parents grew more accustomed to the loss. His mother retained her sanity by convincing herself that her son was dead and, being religious, accepted his fate. But Nicolai knew that his brother wasn't dead. All he had wanted to do was to find him.

In time circumstances forced him to leave Poland, and as his life progressed in London Nicolai married and had a son. His mental condition controlled, he became an agreeable little man, smiling and nodding his greetings to everyone as he arrived and wound his way from the ground floor of the gallery to the top room above the flat. Here, in amongst the scratching and canoodling sounds of London pigeons, he made regimented order out of Owen Zeigler's accounts, keeping meticulous details of every pound. He had no interest in art – the sale of a Vermeer was irrelevant – all that mattered to Nicolai was the money, and the accounting of it.

So when the first episode of instability hit, it caught everyone off guard when Nicolai's sweet control had plummeted into confusion, then a bizarre fury directed at the order of his attic world. And with his loathing of what he usually so admired, came his obsession with his brother. *He would find him*, he told an astonished Owen the first time he lost control. *Luther was still alive. He had to return to Poland, he had to go home* . . . And then the doctor was called, and Nicolai was medicated. Slowly, he became calm, but with the sedation came a helter-skelter fall into depression. His mania gone, Nicolai sat with his muzzled brain, his head in his hands, staring at the London panorama. He saw goblins in the chimney pots, and heard the rain cursing as it flushed out the drainpipes. Clouds slid against his window and made faces at him; a watery opal sun grinning like a demon. In amongst roof tiles and car horns, his brother came calling. Up the stairs and around the cellar corners, he told Nicolai his history and begged to be found.

When the despair lifted, Luther was gone, and Nicolai was left feeling foolish and embarrassed. For a number of days he would apologise, and blush behind his heavy glasses, making clicking sounds with his tongue as though he disapproved of his own thoughts and wanted to disown them. Kindly, Owen would shrug off the event, realising early on that any invitation to talk could send Nicolai back into his waxy confusion. And so Nicolai Kapinski would put aside his mania, his anger, his confusion – even his brother – and return to his tiny, gentle self.

That gentle self who was now regarding Owen steadily.

'Is this all of it? Nothing else you're hiding from me?' Nicolai asked again, his Polish accent evident in the vowels. 'Mr Zeigler, is this all?'

Owen nodded. 'That's it.'

'Why did you hide it from me for so long?'

'I thought . . .' Owen sighed. 'I was wrong, I should have asked for your help a while back, but I thought I could manage. I couldn't, of course.'

'You're ruined.'

'I know.'

Upset, Nicolai gazed at his employer, then looked back to the ledgers, making an indecipherable doodle on the corner of his notepad.

In silence, Owen watched him, then touched his shoulder. 'It's all right—'

'No, I don't think so. I don't think this is all right at all.'

'It is,' Owen insisted, passing Nicolai his coat and brief-case. 'Go home now.'

Nicolai stood up, hardly reaching Owen's shoulder, desperate to offer comfort and yet lacking the words.

'We . . . we . . .'

'You'll be all right,' Owen said quietly. 'I have an idea, something that might work.'

'You have?' His tone was pathetically hopeful.

'I think so.'

'What is it?'

'Something I should have done a while back.' Owen looked round the neat room under the eaves. 'If you need anything, ask Teddy Jack. I may have to go away for a while—'

'*What?*'

'Hear me out. The salaries are accounted for, in the safe. I've put a little extra aside for you, Nicolai, for your loyalty. You have the keys to the safe, pay everyone. If I *do* go away, reassure the staff, the porters and the receptionist. I should be able to keep this place going for another two months, maybe three. If you need help, ask Teddy.' He smiled, almost light-hearted. 'I like it up here. In fact, it's the nicest part of the gallery, I've always thought so. It's inviting. When we were living here as a family, I used to think I'd make this into a den.' He glanced round, taking in the blackened fire grate, the treacle- coloured rafters and the window frames, bellied with age. 'But it's too late now . . . I've been here too long, Nicolai. There are too many memories. Too many ghosts.'

Nicolai nodded. 'We all have those.'

A moment of understanding passed between them. 'But your ghost is real.'

'Every man's ghost is real to him.'

Smiling, Nicolai moved towards the narrow stairs, pulling on his coat and then turning.

'If I can help you in any way . . .'

'I know.'

'You've been a good employer, Mr Zeigler,' he said gently, putting out his hand and taking Owen's. 'And a valued friend.'

Twenty minutes later Marshall was driving into Albemarle Street. He would pick up his father and together they would leave for Thurstons. The evening had come into play, shaking out the tourists and the collectors alike, pushing the buyers along Piccadilly, into the lure of yellow taxi lights or the white belly of the underground.

Finally parking across from the Zeigler Gallery, Marshall looked at his father's achievement. The window was dressed with a Pieter de Hoogh painting, nothing more.

Never overcrowd, Owen always said, *let the painting breathe* . . .

Slowly Marshall's gaze moved up to the flat above. He couldn't imagine the building belonging to anyone else and felt a real dread of being banned from his childhood home. Memories, filled with the dust of poignancy, smoked around him. The sounds of the gallery porters, Gordon Hendrix and Lester Fox, reorganising the picture rails and hanging space, Owen cutting out newspaper shapes of the paintings, which he would hold up against the wall to judge where the originals would look best. Then he would start again, Lester muttering into his moustache, the morose Gordon dying for a cigarette in the backyard, but both men waiting for their employer's next instructions, knowing that in a couple of weeks it would have to be done all over again.

Down would come the paintings. Down from the walls, down into the cellar's belly. Dry down there, because heating had been put in. But unwelcoming nevertheless. The walls had been shelved for picture storage, and at the very back of the cellar was a partition, behind which Lester and Gordon ate their lunch, or played cards if they had a quiet half hour. In other galleries around the area, there were other stalwarts. But in some there had been an influx of young gay men, eager to work in the glamour of the art world, amongst the nearby exclusive shops, with the possibility of meeting powerful, homosexual collectors. Some got lucky, managing to hook a gallery owner and a rapid promotion from lowly gallery assistant to *in situ* lover. Others were caught out *in fellatio delicto* in the cellars, storage nooks, and crannies of their subterranean world. And then, when the Aids epidemic struck, a number of the beautiful lily-white boys died . . .

Marshall's thoughts moved on, his gaze travelling to the window of his old bedroom. He had looked out of that window throughout his childhood, scrutinising the hassle of shoppers, seeing his father's comings and goings. And at night Marshall would watch the lights make a Christmas card out of the London street. With no other children living nearby Marshall had been forced to make his own amusement. His one friend, Timothy Parker-Ross, was five years older than he, but as much an outcast. Poor Timothy, with his spectacular father, Butler Parker-Ross, one of the most admired – and respected – dealers in London. But he was too much for some, and definitely too much for Timothy. His father's bullish arrogance was not intentionally unkind, but he terrified his son. For a while Butler had convinced himself that Timothy would be trained up for the business, but his son had no talent or feel for paintings. He wasn't stupid, but thought in a slow, deliberate manner – a direct contrast to Butler's adrenalin-spiked behaviour. If asked a question, Timothy would consider his answer for so long his father would lose interest and move on. When Timothy was in his teens, Butler was so anxious about his son's shyness that he shipped him off to public school, where a reserved child is fair game for bullies. By the time Timothy was fourteen he had a stammer and had grown to six feet in height.

When he came back in the holidays, Timothy had developed a stoop to disguise his height and a shock of fair hair which fell over his eyes, blocking the world out. By the time he was eighteen, he'd just managed to scrape through his exams and was used to keeping quiet and out of trouble. But once back in London there was only one place he could go – the gallery. And under the kindly but forceful tutelage of his father, Timothy Parker-Ross tried very hard, but learned very little.

However, Timothy Parker-Ross had one talent – for friendship. He was constant and caring, and for a lonely child like Marshall, he was the ideal ally. Often the boys spent long afternoons at the British Museum, staring at the Egyptian mummies and telling each other stories about how No. 657 had been put away, out of reach. Because it was cursed. Everyone who had ever looked at the female corpse had died . . . And Marshall had let Timothy tell the story in his own time, responding with a tale of his own, about the soldier ghost in the Zeigler Gallery.

'D'you die if you see it?' Timothy had asked.

Bemused, Marshall had thought for a moment. 'I dunno. I suppose not, otherwise how could you tell anyone you'd seen it? You'd be dead.'

At other times the boys went to the cinema in Leicester Square, where Marshall developed an addiction to sci-fi and Timothy watched the screen with an expression of bland confusion. And afterwards they would catch the nearest bus, seeing how many stops they could go before the conductor asked them to pay. When they were caught out, they jumped off . . .

Marshall's thoughts slid on. When his father bought the country house and moved his family there, Marshall had missed London. Missed the smell of packing and sawdust. Missed the muttered curses as the delivery men tried to get larger paintings through the gallery doors, or round the back entrance. Missed the plane trees coming into leaf as the Ritz grinned its pillared smile at Piccadilly. Missed the newspaper seller at the end of the street who told him stories about the celebrities who had come to stay in the capital's finest hotels; told him about how he had been a chauffeur: *Oh yeah, I drove them all, when I was a chauffeur* ... Marshall had even missed the ghost. The lost faint shadow of the unknown soldier who had punctuated his dreams. But most of all he had missed his friend.

They had kept in touch, but it was never the same. Timothy had started to be trained up in the gallery business and when Marshall's mother died, life changed irrevocably. It seemed that within one summer Marshall lost most of the little family he had. Weeks after his mother died, his grandfather – the shadowy, slightly frightening Neville – had succumbed to a blood clot on the lung. Suddenly life shifted gear. There had been no more time for looking at mummies, for sci-fi, or dodging buses. He had grown up. Childhood had come to its end.

Marshall looked at the Zeigler Gallery, his gaze travelling down from the flat to the ground floor. The light was on in the porch doorway, but the blind was down on the door and he couldn't see in. If he was honest, he was dreading walking in and talking to his father. The thought shamed him, but it was there nevertheless. Owen had been so distracted, so desperate, and Marshall had never seen his father like that. Never seen the urbane Owen Zeigler out of control ... He sighed, opened the car door and got out. His father was getting older and he was in shock. He needed his son. The roles had suddenly shifted. As they did with all children and parents, and in all generations. Now Owen needed help. In the past, it had been Owen offering help to his son. This time, it was his son's turn to give support.

As he walked to the gallery door, Marshall considered what Samuel Hemmings had told him. He would ask his father about Rembrandt's monkey. Samuel was right, it would give them something to talk about, something to take Owen's mind off his problems. Marshall knocked on the door, listened, but there was no answer and so he unlocked it with his own key and walked in.

'Dad?' he called out.

No reply.

Looking round, he turned on a desk lamp and then flinched. Papers had been pulled out of shelves and files, drawers turned over, the main gallery ledger thrown onto the floor, its white throat of pages gaping open. Surprised, he stepped over the mess, imagining how his father had been panicking, going through the books.

'Dad?' he called out again.

Again, there was no response. But the mess was so unlike his father, it unsettled Marshall. Owen enjoyed order; reckless untidiness was uncharacteristic. He prided himself on keeping his papers meticulously. Surely, even in the state he was in, Owen wouldn't behave so out of character? Moving to the stairs which led up to the flat, he walked upstairs to his parents' old bedroom. There again, the place was in chaos, drawers pulled out and overturned, the contents scattered. By now seriously worried, Marshall moved out onto the landing and into his old room. That was untouched, as was the sitting room. Puzzled, he walked downstairs again, picking his way through the mess of papers as he headed for the back stairs which led down to the basement.

The light was off, so his father couldn't be down there, Marshall thought. But a moment later, he decided to go downstairs after all. He flicked on the light and went down the steep steps into the warren below. As he descended, he could feel the shift in temperature. The cellar wasn't damp, but it was always a few degrees colder than the gallery above. Dipping his head to avoid a low beam at the bottom of the stairs, Marshall passed into the cellars. He hadn't been there for a while, in fact not for some years. But when he was a child he had visited Gordon and Lester in the basement, watching as they mended the frames or packed up paintings to be shipped abroad. Sometimes he would sit on the steps and listen to their conversation about the old days, when they were Guardsmen, and hear them laugh and talk about some of the customers – many of whom they seemed to despise. They would talk about the dealers too, and Marshall would hear random titbits of gossip, which he knew they had gleaned from other porters and gallery assistants.

Curious, Marshall moved further into the cellar, past the wooden shelves where the Dutch interiors were stored, and past the segregated selection of church interiors. His gaze trailed over the edges of gilded frames and corners of paintings only half seen. He could remember the winter when a pipe had burst in the cellar and they had all – himself included – joined together in a line, passing painting by painting along the row until Marshall's mother lifted them to safety on the cellar steps. Afterwards she had made tea with whisky in it for the Guardsmen, and Owen had spent the rest of the night checking each painting for water damage.

Slowly Marshall moved on, past the old bins and the worktables, towards the partitioned-off portion where Lester and Gordon had their meals and the odd smoke out in the yard. He was just about to reach the partition when he heard a sound overhead.

He stopped and called out, 'Dad?'

Again there was no answer, and all Marshall could hear was the wind rap its knuckles on the back door. About to retreat, he decided he would check the lock before he left the basement. He moved forward to the partition and turned the corner, but in the place where Gordon or Lester would usually be sitting, was his father.

Owen Zeigler was tied to a cold water pipe, his arms suspended above his head, his body naked apart from his boxer shorts. His back was facing Marshall, the skin ripped from a beating, a piece of bloodied electric flex lying on the floor next to his feet. The wounds were varied; some little more than a scratch, but others were lashes which had torn into the flesh repeatedly, some slicing through the muscle beneath. There was barely an inch of Owen Zeigler's back that had not been lacerated. The blood had stopped flowing a while since.

Marshall took a moment to react, immobilised by the horror of what he was looking at. At last he moved towards his father, walking through a pool of blood and urine. His hand shaking, he felt for a pulse at his father's neck.

'*Dad? Dad?*' he said softly, stupidly.

It was obvious from the angle of Owen's head that he was dead, but Marshall kept talking to him, mumbling comfort as he reached up to try and release his father's hands. When he couldn't unfasten the bonds, Marshall stepped back, shaking uncontrollably, looking round for something to cut the rope. He could feel the blood sticky under his shoes, and feel the cold air coming through an open window, but he couldn't take his eyes off his dead father. His murdered father. Tenderly he touched Owen's face, then took off his jacket and placed it over his father's head. But as he did so, the body slumped, swinging from its tied wrists as it turned round to face him.

All the elegant charm of Owen Zeigler's face had disappeared under a coating of blood. His lips were drawn back from his teeth in pain, his scalp was split, his eyes stared out blindly, his rib cage caved in under the mottled flesh. And from the gaping cavern of his belly his intestines began, slowly, to slither to the floor beneath him.

Owen Zeigler had been gutted.

6

Rosella Manners stood by the door of the breakfast room of the Barnes house, watching her husband. She was standing barefoot, having kicked off her shoes moments earlier when she entered the house. It was a habit of long standing, a way to make her husband – shorter by three inches – feel less intimidated by her height. Her expression was unreadable, her coat unfastened, her bag on the hall table. Letting herself in, she had avoided any exchange with the housekeeper; keen that no one should overhear what she was about to say.

Mozart was playing, very quietly, the scent of the white lilies in the hallway was almost cloying. Fresh flowers twice a week. Rosella had insisted on it. Even when she was away. It was good chi, she would say mockingly, it keep the energy alive in the house. But looking at Tobar – who still had not noticed her – she realised that it was pointless to keep up any of the little pretences she had accumulated over the years. He was not a man susceptible to atmosphere. He was, she knew, immune to anything other than the materialistic. Rosella might try for an imitation of married life, but that was all it was – emotional costume jewellery.

She glanced over to the carpet under the coffee table. They had bought it in Tangiers, Tobar haggling with the dealer, flirting with him to get the price reduced. And she had stood in the background, silent behind her sunglasses, and suspected she had been taken for his secretary or a sister. Never a wife. Her gaze moved to the mantelpiece; to the cherubs nestling together amorously. Only both *putti* had male genitalia and their marble perfection was a frozen moment of homoeroticism. Everywhere was the language of the boy. Of her husband's preference, of the late-night conversations in the study and the two separate mobile phone numbers.

It both distressed and amused Rosella that she might be pitied, that people would think her wasted. Why be a wife to a man who had no need of one? But then again, she thought, why be a wife at all? Motionless, Rosella kept staring at the back of her husband's head. Gossip had tracked their marriage as day followed night, but she was a clever woman: she was well aware that to be perceived as a victim was her protection. Her own mock morality.

Throwing her copy of the *Evening Standard* over to Tobar, she watched as it struck him on the shoulder.

Irritated, Tobar turned round. 'What the hell—'

'Read the paper,' she said, her mouth a thin line of disgust under the patrician nose. 'See what your handiwork has done.'

Immediately he snatched it up, read the passage she had marked, and lost colour. 'Owen Zeigler killed . . .? What the fuck happened?'

'You cheated him with that Rembrandt—'

'Now, look here—'

'Don't lie to me, you little bastard. I know you, remember? I know every rotten thing about you.' She sat on the edge of a chair, facing him, swinging one of her stockinged feet. 'You cheated him when he needed money. If you'd sold that painting as a Rembrandt, it would have saved Owen's business—'

'But not his bloody life.'

'How d'you know? Maybe he took a risk, borrowed too much, got mixed up with the wrong people. God knows, there are enough sniffing around the galleries at the moment, scenting blood.'

Tobar was reading the paper hurriedly. 'It was a robbery that went wrong—'

She snorted. 'Odd that no paintings were taken. Mind you, the most valuable one had already gone, hadn't it?'

'I was told that it wasn't a Rembrandt!'

'You bloody liar!' she spat. 'I remember what you said when Owen Zeigler first bought that painting – *Lucky bastard, that will ensure a rich old age*.' She leaned towards her husband, her expression taunting. 'You wanted that painting for decades. And then you got it, but the novelty soon wore off, didn't it? You had to make Owen look like a fool, like a third rate dealer, to compound your triumph. So you sold it on. And he trusted you. If he hadn't

72

have been so desperate, do you think he would have believed you?'

Tobar shrugged. 'I was told it wasn't by Rembrandt. I lost money too—'

'I don't believe you,' Rosella replied. 'I've seen your work, and I've not liked what I've seen. Why do you think I spend so much time away from you?'

'We both know you have another man.'

'I have *one* man. You never counted as a man in my eyes,' she replied, with withering scorn. 'I was your *beard*. That's what you call it, isn't it, Tobar? When a homosexual needs to look married, the *faux* wife is his beard.' She smiled bitterly. 'Well, it's time you were clean shaven.'

Stung, he turned his pale eyes on hers, his expression flat. 'Stop being so fucking melodramatic. You need me.'

'Not any more,' she replied. 'I used to, but not now.'

'We have an arrangement.'

'We *had* an arrangement,' she corrected him. 'But now I couldn't live in the same house with you after what you've done.'

He was thin with spite. 'I don't know why you're being like this. It's business. I'm sorry Zeigler's dead, but I didn't kill him.'

'You ruined him, you made him desperate. God knows what chances he was taking—'

'And that's *my* fault?'

'You cheated him when he needed money. You know damn well you were his last resort.'

'He could have gone to someone else! I didn't force him to come to me.'

'You were his *friend*!' She sighed, her expression repelled. 'I've watched you for years,' she said. 'I've watched you sell fakes for the real article. I've heard enough to piece together what you do, Tobar. What underhand dealings you enjoy so much. While pretending to have no interest, I *did* still listen.' She could see her husband's face tighten. 'But business was business, and I liked the money you made. And frankly, judging by most of them, I thought the dealers were fair game. If you won a few more times than some, it was because you were a bit more ruthless.'

'So what's the problem now?'

'Owen Zeigler thought you were his friend. That's the problem. You acted like his friend, you behaved like his friend. You went to his house and invited him to ours, *like a friend*. We talked like friends, laughed like friends. And now, finally, I see that nothing you say or do is genuine. If you could cheat your oldest friend, what couldn't you do to me?'

Unnerved, Tobar pushed the newspaper away from him. 'Owen Zeigler's death has nothing to do with me.'

'Are you sure?'

His eyes cold, he studied his wife. 'Were you and Owen Zeigler lovers?'

She smiled, her hands going to her face momentarily before she replied.

'No ... But out of all the dealers you know, all the people you mix with, Owen was the most honourable. He cared for you, and yet you could still ruin him.' She stood up, smoothing down her skirt. 'I'm leaving you—'

'Don't be bloody silly! Because of Owen Zeigler?'

'No,' she replied, walking to the door. 'Because if his death didn't matter, I'd be as bad as you.'

7

'He never liked these places,' Marshall said, without turning round. He had heard the door open and had recognised the footsteps and the slight pressure of her hand on his shoulder. 'He'd have said that I should just have put him in a box – one of those earth-friendly things that break down naturally – and buried him in a field somewhere.'

'I'm so sorry.'

He turned and looked at his ex-wife. 'Aren't you going to say something funny?'

'It wouldn't be the right place.'

'That's why it would be funny. You always said the wrong thing in the wrong place,' Marshall replied affectionately, his voice low, as he reached for her hand.

Georgia pulled up a chair next to him, both of them sitting beside Owen's coffin in the Chapel of Rest. She didn't look at her ex-father-in-law's face. Couldn't bring herself to – not yet. As soon as she had heard about Owen Zeigler's death she phoned Marshall, and been there for him – on and off – over the next forty-eight hours. Talking, but mostly listening.

Taking the scarf from around her neck, Georgia flicked her long curly hair from her face. Lying hair, Marshall used to call it. Always changing. Chestnut in the morning, fire-red in fluorescent light and amber coated in sunshine. But her eyes were constant, dark and steady, always alert.

'They patched him up,' Marshall went on. 'He doesn't look too bad now.'

Slowly Georgia turned from Marshall and looked into the dead face of Owen Zeigler. The scalp wound had been closed, leaving only a faint scar line running vertically down his forehead. Puzzled, she then realised that the ochre tinge to Owen's skin came from make-up, applied thickly to cover the wound and the bruising. Steadily she studied his closed eyelids, the long line of his nose, his mouth. Unrecognisable, fixed into an undertaker's idea of a beatific smile.

'It's not like him.'

'No,' Marshall agreed. 'Someone said that they always make the dead smile so that they're less frightening, but that grimace looks odd, sinister. My father would've hated it.'

He reached out, then realising that he couldn't change his father's expression, he withdrew his hand. Marshall stared at the red carnation in Owen's buttonhole, taking in the light grey suit and the white shirt which he had brought into the undertakers the previous night after his father's body had been released to the Chapel of

Rest; after the pathologist and the police had done with it; after Owen Zeigler's scalp had been stitched together again . . .

'How long have you been here?' Georgia asked.

'All morning.'

'Have you eaten?'

Marshall shrugged. 'I'm not interested in food.'

'You have to eat. I'll take you for some lunch.'

He didn't move. 'People have been coming and going all morning.'

'Your father was popular—'

'Not with his killer.'

Her hand tightened over his. In the corner of the small, clean room candles burned, a stained glass window depicting a Biblical scene. The glass was thick, and coloured darkly enough to prevent anyone from seeing in – or out. Georgia looked at the dead man, noticing minute, pointless details. Like the pristine way the pale blue silk lining of the coffin was pleated; was this a grim echo of birth, she wondered? Blue for a boy, pink for a girl?

'The funeral's tomorrow. I'm burying him in the church near Thurstons,' said Marshall, quietly. 'Only a few people will travel that far, but the reception in London will be for everyone else. My father would have preferred that, I think . . . I don't know, he never said. I don't know what he would have wanted. He didn't leave a will either.'

'He didn't expect to die.'

'Nicolai Kapinski said my father had never even thought

about death. Well, in a way, why should he? He wasn't *that* old a man, but still, you'd have thought it would have come into his mind now and then.'

'I think people fall into two categories – half think about death too little, the other half too much.'

He turned to look at her. 'Which are you?'

'I'm superficial, I only want to think about life.'

'You were never superficial,' he replied.

Leaning forward, Marshall's eyes fixed on the coffin. Varnished wood, with brass handles that looked pseudo-French. The undertaker had shown him numerous brochures of coffins and brass plaques and handles – so many bloody handles – as if the handles mattered. And Marshall, still deeply in shock, had studied the brochures and chosen everything carefully, with thought, as though he was planning a menu. And all the time he was remembering how he had found his father; reliving the same hot fear as details of the murder scene intermingled with the coffin handles. He saw again the rope which had bound Owen's hands; recalled the hot, iron smell of blood, as the overhead light had dimmed and flickered, and the swollen insides sliding to the floor. He had wanted to pick them up, to push them back into the cavity of his father's stomach, to hold them in, and somehow make him whole again . . .

'Marshall?'

Distracted from the memory, he became aware that he had been grasping Georgia's hand so tightly her fingers were white. 'Sorry,' he said, letting go. 'I was just thinking.'

Nodding, she glanced through the small round glass window in the door. Someone was passing and paused, looking in and smiling a kind, professional smile. She responded, wondering how anyone could work in an undertakers' office, where there was only one ending – death. As a teacher, Georgia was involved with children; little humans for whom life was beginning, not ending. With luck, none of them would die too young, and she hoped that, in twenty years time, they would seek her out and tell her what a difference she had made to their lives.

It was a familiar daydream, which Georgia already had when she was married to Marshall. They had met at a private view at the Zeigler Gallery, Georgia invited there by friends and finding herself quickly bored. Rescued by Marshall, she had been amused at how little he was interested in his father's illustrious business. He could so easily have slid into ready-made affluence but, as he told her later, his heart wasn't in the art world. Georgia had liked that about Marshall Zeigler. Liked a man who didn't take the easy way out.

Their marriage had fallen apart after six years because they were both too young and too independent to settle into domesticity. Friends yes, lovers certainly. But a married couple? No. That hadn't been written into either of their charts, so their decision to separate had been amicable, their divorce good natured. Georgia had quipped to her friends, 'I was very good to my husband. I left him.'

In time they both found other people. When Georgia had had her heart broken, she had turned to Marshall, and when the heady intoxication of his affairs fizzled into flat champagne, they had always commiserated. In fact, they had remained fixtures in each other's lives, and their bond was such that they could talk every day for a week, and then have no contact for two months without it being a problem. When they spoke again, they picked up where they'd left off, and if one of them needed the other, they were always there.

'You never think your parents will be frightened, do you?'

Surprised, Georgia glanced at her ex-husband. 'Was Owen afraid?'

'Terrified, the last time I talked to him . . . He was supposed to be spending the weekend with *me*, not lying in a bloody coffin.' He stared angrily at the corpse. 'They made him look like a ghoul.' He fiddled angrily with his father's tie. 'And he never tied it like that! They've done a crap job. I told them. I told them *exactly* how it had to be, how everything had to be. You'd think they'd have listened. You'd think that, wouldn't you?'

Georgia put her arm around him.

'Jesus,' he said. 'I never said goodbye.'

'Say it now.'

'What?'

'Say goodbye now.'

'He's dead. I don't believe in life after death.'

'I'd still say it, Marshall. You never know.'

Georgia got to her feet and walked out of the chapel. She

leaned against the wall in the corridor, took a few deep breaths, and then looked in through the porthole in the door. Marshall was standing at the head of coffin, looking down. She could see his lips move, but could only decipher the last six words: *I'll make someone pay for this.*

8

Dressed in their heavy overcoats and black armbands, Gordon Hendrix and Lester Fox stood in the gallery doorway and watched the street. Next to them, Vicky Leighton, the gallery receptionist, was crying softly. They could see Marshall talking to a dealer, and Lester nodded respectfully to Samuel Hemmings, who had come up to town for the funeral of Owen Zeigler. Off to one side, on his own, stood a tiny, shaken Nicolai Kapinski, drained of all colour, his balding head a pale orb against the dark collar of his winter coat. Tufts of other people dressed in black clustered like barnacles on the bow of the London street. Faces, pallid from emotion or cold, exchanged murmured remembrances of a dead colleague. And at the corner of the street, the pinched figure of Tobar Manners watched. Surrounded by a bevy of his cohorts, his metallic eyes flicked from the mourners to Marshall, and back again.

Rosella had kept her word and left him, but no one knew. Everyone thought it was just another of her holidays. And Tobar would leave it like that . . . His face turned slightly against the wind, he stared at the back of Marshall's head, only half listening to what someone was saying. Of course there had been talk about the Rembrandt sale – a good deal of whispering behind Tobar's back. Some people had even intimated that he had cheated Owen Zeigler, and implied that he was indirectly responsible for his friend's murder.

And now, suddenly, the stakes had been raised even higher. Now there was a murderer in their midst.

He wouldn't admit it, but Tobar Manners had been struggling too. Not as much as some of the less successful dealers, because his coup with the Rembrandt had protected him. Of course he had lied to Owen; of course he had arranged for a second party to sell on the painting, then share the proceeds with him. His wife might know, but no one could prove it.

Pulling up his coat collar, Tobar turned, watching as Samuel Hemmings approached in his wheelchair.

'Manners,' Samuel said, his tone unreadable as he sat, leaning his chin on his stick, his driver waiting in the car across the street. In the dropping temperature, Samuel looked frail; whippet thin, muffled in a coat and scarf with a fur hat pulled down low over his forehead.

'You look like a fucking mushroom.'

'Good to see you too, Tobar.'

'I didn't expect you to make it up from Sussex, I thought you'd died.'

84

'Oh, no. After all, it wasn't me you robbed,' Samuel countered deftly. 'How are you sleeping?'

Shuffling his feet, Tobar glanced at his companions, then looked back to the old man, his voice low. 'Don't go throwing around accusations, Mr Hemmings. Although you're old and most people would put it down to senility, I'd still be careful.'

'You look thin,' Samuel went on, unperturbed. 'Your food not going down well? Must be all that bile in your gut, Tobar. Or a bad conscience. It shows on your face—'

'Shut up!' Tobar hissed, leaning down towards him. 'Owen's death has nothing to do with me.'

'He was in trouble.'

'Well, that much is obvious now,' Tobar replied, pulling his collar up further against the cold.

'Owen needed money, and you could have helped him out.'

'You were his bloody mentor, why didn't you do something?'

'He didn't come to me.'

'Well, that says it all, doesn't it?' Tobar replied peevishly. 'Go home, old man. You can rattle all the sabres you like there, but stay away from me.'

'Your wife told me she'd left you.'

Paling, Tobar flinched, guiding Samuel's wheelchair a little further away from the group.

'She's on holiday—'

'I know Rosella,' Samuel replied, his voice quiet but steady. 'And she told me she'd had enough. Apparently what you did to Owen finished your marriage. Rosella has always talked to me, Tobar, about all kinds of things. She's basically an honourable woman. Materialistic, certainly, likes her comfort. But she has a conscience, and living with you and seeing the things you did . . .? Well, it was too much for her, and she needed a confidant.'

'Are you threatening me?'

'With what, Mr Manners?'

'That's what I want to know.'

He was breathing more quickly, staring at Samuel and realising that he had a real enemy. And worse, that this enemy not only hated him for cheating Owen Zeigler, but for his treatment of Rosella. In that moment Tobar realised that he had underestimated the old man, believing him grown mute and toothless in Sussex.

'Now if I told you that, you'd be as wise as me,' Samuel retorted. 'You think you've got away with it, but you haven't. I want you to know that, Manners. I want you to think about that, and worry—'

Moving behind the art historian's wheelchair, Tobar suddenly flipped off the brake with his left foot. Samuel sensed the movement and gripped the wheels.

'What the—'

'You're an old man, Mr Hemmings.'

Samuel wasn't about to show fear. 'I'm old, but I have a long memory.'

'Too long for your own good,' Tobar replied, flicking the brake back on. 'I'd start forgetting things, if I were you.'

Samuel could still feel Tobar Manners' hatred as his driver pushed him towards the Zeigler Gallery. Not that he would have allowed it to show to anyone present, but he was aching with the cold and longing to be home. But nothing, he thought, taking in a ragged breath, would have prevented him from paying his respects to his protégé.

Glancing round, Samuel took in the empty gallery space, remembering what Marshall had told him about the night he found his father. The police had decided that it was a burglary gone wrong, that the gallery had been broken into and the thieves – for there had had to be more than one – disturbed; the violence intimating a drug-fuelled attack. It was further assumed that Owen had been tortured for the combination to the safe, but Samuel didn't believe it. Owen would have handed over the money rather than die – Samuel didn't believe his old friend had been given the choice. Leaning his hands, then his chin, on the top of his cane, Samuel looked ahead at a Jan Steen painting on the wall opposite. Why hadn't they taken that? It was worth good money, why leave it? Why leave the Epstein bust in the back gallery? The Dutch parquetry cabinet?

Quietly a door opened in the back and Marshall walked over to Samuel. He seemed diminished; listless with shock.

'Are you all right?'

Nodding, Marshall stared around the gallery. His actions were strained, as if the slightest movement was exhausting to him.

'I need to talk to you.'

'About what, Marshall?'

'Someone was looking for something. This wasn't a burglary, too little was taken. It wasn't just that my father surprised them and was killed by accident . . .' He paused, then closed the entrance door of the gallery and clicked the lock. 'I don't believe that. And neither do you.'

'Don't I?'

'They were looking for something very specific.'

'What?'

'I think they were looking for the letters. The Rembrandt letters.' Marshall stared at the old man. 'I can see from your face that it's already occurred to you too. When we talked about them you said they were dangerous, that they could cause a scandal—'

'But I was only telling you about your father's theory. I could be wrong—'

Infuriated, Marshall cut him off. 'Where are the Rembrandt letters?'

'I don't know.'

'But you do think someone was looking for them?'

'I think it's a possibility. The letters are important.'

'Why? You told me part of the story, but not all of it. What do the letters say?'

Samuel was discomfited, shifting in his seat. 'Your father never confirmed he'd found them—'

'If he *hadn't* found them, how could he know what was in them?' Marshall countered. 'How could he have told you his theory, with all the details, the names and dates you gave me? My father *must* have found and read those letters.'

Samuel hesitated, Marshall's voice rising. '*You* know what was in them, don't you?'

'I only know that they were letters which could damn Rembrandt forever – *and* prove that many of Rembrandt's paintings were not by his hand, but painted by someone else.'

'Rembrandt's monkey?'

'Yes.'

'Who was . . .?'

'Carel Fabritius, Rembrandt and Geertje Dircx's illegitimate son.'

Marshall leaned against the door. 'So it wasn't just the scandal of Rembrandt having a bastard son, but the fact that he faked his father's works?'

Samuel nodded. 'Many of them. When he left Rembrandt's studio, Fabritius lived in Delft, away from Amsterdam. Overworked and greedy, Rembrandt farmed out commissions to his most gifted student—'

'The letters prove this?'

He nodded again. 'Your father said so.'

'And if he'd released the letters . . .?'

'All Rembrandt's paintings would have had to be reassessed. It would involve galleries and museums all over the world. Not to mention the private collectors and independent experts.' Samuel paused. 'The letters would undermine the art market, which relies on the Old Masters. It would be little short of a catastrophe. If a single Rembrandt portrait – which could sell for upwards of forty or fifty million – was exposed as the work of his pupil, it would undermine his whole catalogue.'

Marshall looked at the old man. 'I get it. The letters were dangerous . . .'

'The letters *are* dangerous.'

'Enough to make someone kill for them?'

Samuel folded his hands on his lap, his expression stern. 'Yes, I believe so.'

A chill fell between them.

'Why did Fabritius act as Rembrandt's monkey?'

'The full explanation is in the letters. Geertje Dircx makes it all clear—'

'So tell me!'

'I can't!' Samuel snapped. 'I didn't read them, I only know what your father told me.'

'Would my father have confided in anyone else?'

'No, I doubt it.'

A car drove past the window, sounding its horn once, the noise eerie in the gloom of the gallery. The light was fading, rain coming on, the London sky morose over the crouching roof tops.

His voice expressionless, Marshall stared at the historian. 'Where are they? The letters?'

'I don't know.'

'I hope you're not lying to me.'

Angered, Samuel's expression hardened. 'I was your father's closest friend—'

'Which puts you in danger, doesn't it? Because who-ever's after them might think *you* had them.'

'Or you. You're his son, Marshall.'

The words cracked around them, the old historian amazed to find himself in the spotlight of Marshall's blatant mistrust.

'You know as well as I do, Samuel, that I knew nothing about the letters until you told me about them.'

'That's what you say.'

'And it's the truth!'

Shaken, Marshall took in a breath. His father's death had devastated him, and knowledge of his suffering had compounded the shock. According to the coroner, it had taken Owen Zeigler a long time to die and the beating had been protracted to cause maximum pain.

Tempering his tone, Samuel continued. 'Have you considered the fact that your father might have handed over the letters and *then* been killed? If his murderers got what they wanted, no one else is in danger.'

'But we *know* about them,' Marshall replied steadily. 'Knowing is almost as good as having them.'

'Knowledge is not proof.'

'Are you sure you haven't got them?'

'*How many times!*' Samuel asked, his face flushing. 'No, I haven't got them. I would love to say I have, but no, Marshall, I've never seen them. Never touched them. Never read them. Stop suspecting me, you're looking in the wrong place.'

Still unconvinced, Marshall stared at the old man. 'My

father wouldn't have told Tobar Manners about the letters, would he?'

Samuel flinched. 'No. For some reason he liked Manners, but he didn't trust him. Why d'you ask?'

'Because if Manners knew about the letters he was preparing the ground very cleverly.'

Confused, Samuel shook his head. 'What ground?'

'My father had been duped into believing that his Rembrandt picture was, in fact, only the work of a second rate painter. He was cheated out of a fortune . . . Doesn't say much for his reputation, does it?'

'Manners duped him.'

'I know. But how easily could it be made to look like my father didn't know what he was doing? People would only have to point to his failing business to undermine him. He would have lost his credibility, and if he had *then* revealed the Rembrandt letters, how easily they could have been discredited. They could have been written off as a hoax, or worse, a way for him to get publicity.'

'Your father wasn't like that.'

'You didn't see him at the end, Samuel. He wasn't like himself, he was panicked. The more I've thought about it, the more I think he knew he was in trouble. Real trouble. Not just money trouble. I spoke to Nicolai Kapinski earlier.

Samuel thought of the dapper little man who had been Owen's business ally.

'And?'

'Nicolai told me that only yesterday – only hours before he was killed – my father had been ringing everyone for help. No one gave him the time of day. The bank wouldn't even let him remortgage the gallery. He'd been a blameless customer for decades, and the first time he really needed help, they closed ranks.' Marshall paused. 'Nicolai said that my father had exhausted every possibility of help. No one came to his aid—'

'I would have done.'

'Yes, I know that,' Marshall replied, wary. 'So *why* didn't he go to you? You were his mentor, his trusted adviser. You'd known each other for years. So why *didn't* he turn to you, Samuel? I've been thinking about that a lot, why didn't he?'

'You told me yourself, he was ashamed.'

'Ashamed? Yes.' Marshall stared at his hands for a long moment. 'But if you were so close, would shame have been enough to prevent his asking you for help?'

'Are you intimating something?' Samuel asked, hoarse with outrage. 'Because if you are, come out with it, Marshall. I'm too old for games.'

'I don't think you'll ever be too old for games. I think they keep you alive,' Marshall replied curtly. 'My father was desperate. He had nowhere to turn. There was only one route left open to him – to reveal the Rembrandt letters. The letters many people would want destroyed. And others would want to own.'

'Or steal.'

'Yes, or steal. That was the risk, wasn't it? That instead of leverage, the letters became a death sentence.'

'*If* they exist,' Samuel said, steadily.

'I wasn't sure they did. Until now. Now I know for certain that those letters are still around. No one would destroy them, because then there would be no proof, no concrete evidence of Rembrandt's bastard. The letters *have* to be preserved so that someone can use them. That someone might have been my father – only he was beaten to it.'

Uneasy, Samuel stared at the younger man. He felt very tired, his astute brain stalling, letting him down. He wondered if it was because Tobar Manners' aggression had unsettled him, or if he was still shocked by Owen's death.

Wearily, he looked at Marshall. 'So what are you going to do?'

'Find them.'

'*Find them?* You think they're still here?'

'The pathologist said that my father held out for hours under torture. They said that finally he was lowered onto the floor and they stamped on his ribs, punctured his lungs, and then his chest was cut open. The pathologist said he was kicked and beaten with such savagery it could only be pure hatred and uncontrollable rage.' Marshall held the old man's gaze. 'Now, you tell me something. If his killers had got what they wanted, why would they be that angry?'

9

As he touched the outside railing leading to the basement, he felt the cold iron through his glove and winced. He had to be quick; the gathering of mourners outside the Zeigler Gallery would disperse soon and people would start coming back indoors. Gordon Hendrix and Lester Fox might try and get down into the basement, even though it was cordoned off with police tape, and at any moment someone could want to take a furtive, curious look at the murder scene. Ducking under the tape, he moved towards the back door, unlocking it, and moving into the porch which separated the outside from the basement.

Through the glass top half of the door he could see the darkening blood stains on the floor, the surfaces dotted with malign Easter Bunny markings of fingerprints powder. Above him, he could hear talking and paused, recognising the voices of Marshall Zeigler and Samuel Hemmings. Noiselessly opening the inner door, he passed into the basement, skirting the blood stains and made his way towards the shelved area by the stairs. He could hear loud footsteps above, but they faded as the person went upstairs.

Time was short, he knew that, as he moved along the shelves where the paintings were racked up, sandwiched between stored frames and unexhibited canvases. He gazed carefully over the storage. Where were they? Owen had never been obvious in his actions, so he was hardly likely to have chosen an obvious hiding place. Breathing quickly, the man tensed as he heard the voices above suddenly raised. A moment later, they dropped and he relaxed a little, his heart beating less violently in his chest.

Observing the police tape wafting slightly in a winter breeze from the half opened door, he wondered again why Owen hadn't told him exactly where he'd hidden the letters. Why? Suddenly angry, his hands sweated in the gloves. Or maybe Owen had been *about* to tell him. After all, they had been supposed to meet that night, but he hadn't kept the appointment. Owen Zeigler had been killed at the same time that *he* was sitting in a bar across London, waiting for him ... Another sound overhead made him jump. Was the inner basement door locked? Jesus, if it wasn't and someone walked in they would catch him red-handed.

Quickly, he made for the stairs, thinking he would slide the bolt on the door and lock it from the inside to give himself more time to search. But just as he reached half way, a scuffle of footsteps sounded outside the door and he hurtled down the steps again and hid under the stairs.

Breathing laboriously, he heard the door open and then saw a pair of feet descending the stairs. Was it the police? The feet stopped moving. He could hear his own breathing and was sure the stranger would hear it too, but after another moment the feet retraced their steps upwards and the basement door was closed again. And locked.

Then the light was turned off. Surprised, the man tried to remember where the light switch was in the basement and felt his way towards it. He was just about to flick it on, when he paused. Was someone waiting for him to do just that? Would someone see the light from outside? Or coming from under the door? His hand dropped from the switch as he took a torch from his pocket. Turning it on, he ran its subdued beam along the rows of shelving. Owen had been talking about a painting he had just sold – a small Pieter de Hoogh – and the torchlight fell on the second shelf, half way along, where the painting had been stored. But the space was empty. Hurriedly, the man felt around in the emptiness, but there was nothing. No painting, no letters, only dust.

Frowning, he stepped back, trying to remember what Owen had ever told him about the Rembrandt letters. He knew they weren't in the safe. They had been once, but not lately. No, lately Owen had intimated that the letters had been moved, hidden somewhere else on the premises. *But where?* he thought, with frustration. It would take days to search the gallery thoroughly, and even though he had managed to look around the main display rooms, he had not had a chance to hunt properly. And after today, how likely was it that he would get another opportunity? The gallery would soon be closed, the staff laid off, with none of them having access to the crime scene. Within hours the premises would be sealed off for God knows how long. Suddenly the front door of the gallery slammed violently. The vibration sounded in the basement, the anger behind the action obvious.

Silence fell again, but he could sense a nervous change in the atmosphere and, wary, flicked off his torch. Hardly breathing, he shrunk into the space under the basement steps, watching the back entrance as the police tape started to flutter manically in the draft from the opening door.

House of Corrections,
Gouda, 1651

It's long past one in the morning. I heard the clock chiming and counted the footsteps of the guard as he passed from the cells to the outer door. He will wait for one of the kitchen staff – I don't know her name – only recognise the mewling, cawing sounds she makes as he fumbles with her, her wooden heels rapping against the wall by the outside pump.

We had a pump in the walled garden of Rembrandt's house, under the window with the stained-glass picture of a sailing ship. Like the one my husband went to sea in. As a carpenter and – in his spare time – the ship's trumpeter. He tried to impress me with that when we met, saying he'd bought the trumpet off a man who'd died in Germany. I remember asking him what the man had died of, because I'd hoped it was nothing catching, and he'd looked at the trumpet and then at me, laughing, as though I'd made a joke. He'd seemed like an honest enough man back then, and my brother knew him. But then again, my brother seemed to know everyone. It would cost me that. My brother's friendliness.

Sssh ... the guard's moving off again now and I can keep writing. He'll go for his pipe and lean against the wall and puff rusty, grey smoke up to the moon like he was a burgomaster with the whole of Amsterdam to answer to him.

Amsterdam, even writing the name takes me back there. I remember the mute cold of Rembrandt's house in the winter. How the main staircase whistled with the wind, and how the smell of the canal came in sour in the summer. Boys used to pee in the still water, aiming for the ducks, their urine making quick citrine rainbows against the Amsterdam sky. Rembrandt always scolded the boys, although he would often piss in a pot in the studio. Once he even urinated in a pail of gesso. The smell lingered, sour and acrid, even more than the stink of raw umber and charcoal. But no one complained.

Certainly I never did. Even though his hands made paint smears on my petticoats and sometimes his hair was matted with grease. I would fill a bath for him by the fire – it would take a long time, half an afternoon – and once I ducked him under the water, washing his hair with the same soap the whores use. But I didn't tell him that. When I rubbed his hair dry it crackled like kindling. He trusted me. Even trusted me to shave him, the blade against his neck, the skin pock-marked in the creases, the razor slipping like an ice skate over his chin.

After I had been with him for over a year he caught me looking at his books. He was never a reader, not like some of the academics that sat to him. Rembrandt collected books as he collected armour and metal ware, for their beauty, not for their content. Yet although I would rub the silver trays with lemon and salt to clean off the tarnish; although I would check my smile in their reflections – keeping my mouth closed for my teeth were not good – I was not fascinated by silver.

But I loved the books and wanted to read. All the time that I was growing up, working in a tavern where they think you a whore for being there, I wanted to read so he taught me. Sometimes he was patient, mostly quick to anger, shouting out the words as though I should have mastered them as he said them. But I was a ready learner and that pleased Rembrandt. And when I had shown such promise, he said he would teach me to write. It took over a year, because he was busy, not because I was slow to learn.

He would push the writing slate over to me, nodding at the letters I had made, making me write a name over and over again. Not my name, his. I think of those days as I write. I think that he would regret teaching me if he knew what my letters would finally say. If he knew how I would use those syllables and vowels against him.

I was never stupid.

I wanted to write I love you, but never got the chance.

In the daytime I was always turned away. Whilst he worked I pushed Titus in his wooden walking stool, or held him up to the window to see the canal below. When the boy slept, I emptied the fire grates or went to the market and bought fish, because I could cook herrings better than anyone. Or so he said. Sometimes I would hear Rembrandt's voice coming from the floor above, irritably squabbling with his students. I would smile, because later I would rub his back in bed and feel his thick legs under me and take the bear out of him. He would tell me about the country, and Amsterdam. About how there was a headstone in one of the city churches that people were warned about.

'You must never stare at it for too long,' he told me.

'Why not?'

'Because if you stare too long you'll see the date of your own death.'

I never told him that, years later, as a broken, lonely woman, I went to that gravestone and I stared and I stared at it. But it told me nothing. Not my death. Or his.

Rembrandt loved me back then. Painted me, once. He gave me the picture, but when I ran out of money I sold it. Someone said they had seen it hanging in a baker's shop in The Hague, invoices clipped to the frame. Yes, I sold it, along with his late wife's ring. Saskia's ring. The one Rembrandt gave me as a betrothal ring. But later he denied it. Denied it when he fell from love and turned away, letting them lock the door on me . . . The clock is striking the quarter hour, in another moment the guard will knock out his pipe and start to walk the passage of cells. He will look in and listen, hoping to hear crying, hoping – if is he lucky – for some woman to offer him relief for a guilder.

I keep these letters hidden, somewhere no one will ever find them. Until one day they're read and people will know my story . . . When I came to Rembrandt's house in Amsterdam that day, that very first day, he looked at me and nodded. I would do. He did not recognise me . . . We had been very young, I know that, but progress had pushed us further apart than any years could do. He told me that I was being hired as a dry nurse for his son. He had no remembrance of my younger self; that shadow of the lover who had carried another, earlier child.

The boy who became Rembrandt's monkey.

BOOK TWO

10

Amsterdam.

Wrung out from travelling, Marshall walked into his flat, flung his suitcase on the floor, and turned on the light. The faint drift of dampness reminded him that he had left the heating off. A stack of mail lay on the rush mat. Picking it up, he recognised – with a shift to his heart – his father's writing. Locking the door and bolting it, he moved into his main room and sat down with the letter on the coffee table in front of him.

Marshall knew at once what the envelope contained. The Rembrandt letters. Just as he knew that once he opened the package and read them he would be committed to his father's cause. And, more importantly, closer to the reason for his father's death. Marshall leaned back in the leather chair, his gaze fixed on the package. These were the letters for which Owen Zeigler had been killed. The letters for which his murderers had tortured him.

His thoughts turned to his last conversation with

Samuel Hemmings. He had been wary of the old man, mistrustful, probing.

'. . . people would pay a lot to own these letters.'

'Or steal them.'

'Or steal them,' Marshall agreed. 'That was the risk, wasn't it? That instead of leverage, they became a death sentence.'

'If they exist,' Samuel said steadily.

Oh yes, they existed. Marshall stared at the large brown envelope, in which his father had sent them to him for safekeeping. Possibly Owen had panicked, had wanted the letters out of London, away from his circle, the people he knew. But which people? Who was his father afraid of? Strangers? Or someone close, intimate? He considered who had been close to his father – close enough to be a confidante, close enough to learn of the letters. Samuel Hemmings . . . Nicolai Kapinski . . . Teddy Jack . . . Marshall kept staring ahead, wondering how people he had liked and trusted had so quickly become suspects.

Again he thought of Samuel Hemmings. How could he be wary of the man who had been such a part of his childhood? His father's mentor? But then again, Samuel Hemmings was very ambitious – and old. Perhaps he wanted to die with a flourish, and exposing the Rembrandt letters would certainly do that. What better epitaph for a mischievous iconoclast than evidence which would undermine one of the world's greatest painters? How much pleasure would Hemmings have got from seeing attributions overturned and reputations publicly sabotaged?

What better revenge would there be than to ridicule the art world, to reveal the truth about Rembrandt's bastard, the monkey in the works who had made apes of them all.

But despite his ambition, or the temptation, would Samuel Hemmings *really* have hurt his father? Marshall kept on staring at the brown package, thinking of the accountant, Nicolai Kapinski. A gentle little man, sweet natured – except for those sinister lapses. Perhaps Nicolai had sat too long up in the eaves, seen too much of the money Owen Zeigler had earned. Perhaps jealousy had brooded, curdling with the sound of the cooing pigeons until, one day, the dark imp inside the Pole struck out.

Of course there was also Teddy Jack, a man he had met only once. The man Marshall knew least about, except that his father trusted him implicitly. Had that been wise? Had he perhaps confided too much in the Northerner? Perhaps Teddy Jack had learnt of the letters and found a buyer . . . Or maybe he had just killed Owen for them, for *him* to use? Tobar Manners' face flashed in front of Marshall. For all his denials, people knew that Manners' gallery was struggling as the recession bit deeper. The Rembrandt letters would have been catastrophic for his business, which relied on Dutch art sales. If Manners' attributions were discredited, his reputation would be obliterated. As soon as the letters came to light and the art world started questioning every Rembrandt painting, Manners would stand to lose a fortune.

Remembering what his father had told him, Marshall

realised that if the letters were exposed it would not be the first time Rembrandt's work had been reassessed. In 1969 the Rembrandt Research Project had been set up in the Netherlands to look at every available painting and, using the most sophisticated methods, determine once and for all which were painted by Rembrandt and which by his pupils. As a result, a number of previously authentic works had been demoted and the number of authentic Rembrandts swelled – if not in number, certainly in value. Then, in 2004, four oil paintings which had previously been attributed to Rembrandt's pupils, were declared to have been painted by the Master. Three were in private American collections, the last was owned by the Detroit Institute of Arts. Other rediscoveries of Rembrandts included a self-portrait, estimated to be worth £34,000,000, which was recovered by the Danish police nearly five years after its theft from Sweden's National Museum. And, in addition, several of the Rembrandts which were reattributed in 1969 had been promoted again.

Could the art world shoulder another attributions scandal about Rembrandt? Could museums, collections, galleries and private buyers accommodate such a catastrophic hit? Marshall knew that one of the only areas which was fireproof was the Old Masters, especially Rembrandt. They alone could hold their value, because of their rarity and the esteem they had built up over centuries of trading. A Rembrandt could always command respect and a huge sale. But a *demoted* Rembrandt was another matter. A Rembrandt which had been painted by a pupil was an auction also-ran. Even if that pupil happened to be Rembrandt's bastard . . .

Marshall picked up the package and weighed it in his hand, turning it over and scrutinising the envelope. Everyone in the art world be desperate to get hold of its contents, to use them to destabilise the market, or to make certain that they were destroyed in order to protect their interests. *And he, Marshall Zeigler, had them in his hands* . . . After another slight hesitation, Marshall opened the envelope and shook out the contents onto the table in front of him. The sheets of paper were of differing sizes and yellowing with age, the writing on them clumsy but not uneducated. The ink had faded in parts, but the script was still decipherable and, for Marshall, who was fluent in Dutch, easily readable.

Yet before he began to read, he looked back into the package, hoping to find a note from his father. But there was nothing there, and he felt oddly cheated. He had longed for a communication, something to blunt the horror of Owen's murder, but the package had obviously been sent in haste.

Carefully Marshall laid out the pages on the table in front of him, trying to work out their order. The letters were in a square hand, careful, but in places uncertain, as though written in difficult circumstances. The slant of the writing varied too. Sometimes it was even on the page, sometimes it sloped to one side, the words veering off towards the edge of the paper. At last he began to read, and he knew instinctively that the letters were genuine. He realised that he was bearing witness to a crime from centuries earlier.

Gradually, as he read on, the long dead Geertje Dircx was present in his flat, talking to him, her world coming alive as Marshall read about her incarceration. He could imagine the dread of being thrown out by her lover, the shock at being deceived by her own family, giving evidence against her. And her horror at having to face a twelve-year sentence in the Gouda House of Corrections – a sentence which could well mean dying in prison. From being Rembrandt's mistress, Geertje had become his ex-lover, labelled as an aggressive hysteric and locked away, silenced.

Turning to the next page, Marshall found the first mention of Rembrandt's monkey, and then paused, unnerved, as he noticed a piece of recent, clean paper clipped to the top. The note was written in a hurried, urgent hand:

I have had these letters checked out thoroughly, Owen. They are genuine. The paper and ink are from the right period, the watermark accurate. The ageing is also in line with what you believe. The tests were redone three times. To the best of my knowledge, and that of another leading expert, these letters were written by Geertje Dircx in 17th century Holland. They stand witness to a moral crime and an artistic deception, the fallout from which – I don't have to tell you – could be disastrous.

*Be careful with these letters, old friend. They could be
lethal in the wrong hands. They are certainly dangerous
and I advise caution.*

The note was signed Stefan van der Helde.

The light was fading. Marshall went over to the window
and pulled down the blind, flicking on a lamp to illu-
minate the chilly room. Pouring himself a drink, he
returned to the notes. The name Stefan van der Helde
echoed dimly in his head for a minute or two, then fell,
like a Bagatelle ball, into the forefront of Marshall's
memory: Stefan van der Helde. Murdered in Amsterdam
the previous year. Sodomised and tortured, forced to ingest
stones – a macabre detail which had made the unsolved
case even more memorable . . . Marshall felt the hairs rise
on the back of his neck. *Stefan van der Helde had read, and
authenticated, the Rembrandt letters.*

   And – like Owen Zeigler – he had been murdered.

Hearing a door slam closed below him, Marshall gathered
the letters together, and the note from Van der Helde,
and put them back into the envelope. He would have to
hide them but, where? He wondered suddenly why his
father would have endangered him deliberately, then
realised that Owen probably had had no choice. He had
had to get rid of the letters, and sending them out of the
country, to his translator son, must have seemed the only
alternative.

But two men had already been killed for them and Marshall fought panic as he remembered his last conversation with Samuel Hemmings:

'I was your father's closest friend—'

'Which puts you in danger, doesn't it? Because whoever's after the letters might think you had them.'

'Or you, Marshall. After all, you're his son.'

'Christ,' Marshall said out loud, snatching up his coat and making for the door. He would go to his bank and put the package into a security box, then hide the key. Tucking it into the inside pocket of his coat, he ran down the two flights of stairs towards the entrance, but as he reached the main door it opened and a woman walking in blocked his exit.

'Marshall? Marshall Zeigler?'

He paused, then nodded. 'Yes. Who are you?'

Without answering, she moved past him into the entrance hall. She was a woman around fifty, elegantly dressed, her hair just brushing her shoulders, her hands fiddling, agitated, with her car keys.

'I need to talk to you—'

'Who are you?' Marshall asked again.

He could feel the package pressing against his rib cage, could almost sense the words burrowing under his skin, wriggling into his bloodstream. Perhaps the woman had been sent to identify him. To point him out . . .

Marshall reached for the door handle. 'I'm sorry, but I have an appointment—'

'But I have to talk to you,' she cut in, urgently. 'Before

you leave here or do anything else. We have a great deal in common.'

'Maybe we do, but I'm not talking to you until I know who you are.'

'I'm Charlotte Gorday,' she replied, her intelligent eyes fixed on his. 'I was your father's mistress.'

11

When he opened his eyes, Teddy Jack found himself in a dark, enclosed, confined space, his hands automatically reaching up and banging against a lid only ten inches above him. Panic rose immediately as Teddy made himself feel along the lid over his head. He was in a box. Not a coffin, it was a box, about the size of a coffin and as confined, but he could feel nail heads on the inside and slats against his back. Suddenly he realised that he was in a packing crate, one of the boxes used to ship paintings abroad. Sweating, he felt along the lid, the nail of his index finger trying to lever it open. But instead his nail broke, and screws held the lid tightly in place.

All right, Teddy told himself, think, be calm. Think . . . He could feel the sweat running down his back and between his buttocks, and resisted the temptation to call out because he didn't know whose attention he would attract. Slowly, he breathed in, smelling the air around him. Wood shavings, and something familiar: rabbit size. It was one of the materials they used to prepare, or restore, picture frames. So, he was in the basement of the Zeigler Gallery. Someone had seen him break in and followed him . . . And now he remembered the blow to the back of his head, the soft squelch of his scalp as it split, and then nothing as he pitched into unconsciousness.

And woke up in a box . . .

His ear pressed against the wood, Teddy listened for sounds, but the basement was silent. The funeral wake was over and the people who had visited the gallery seemed to have gone. God, how long had he been here? He didn't know if it was day or night. Certainly there were no noises or footsteps, no sliver of light coming through the lid. And then another thought occurred to Teddy Jack – a thought which made his stomach heave. The packing cases were built to withstand any amount of rough handling – after all, the shipment of a valuable painting was a serious matter – so the crates were constructed to withstand being accidentally dropped, or any violent movement in an aeroplane or a ship. A series of wooden slats and leather straps held the painting inside, and the space between the work and the sides of the crate was bolstered by packing materials, kept separate from the surface of the picture but offering additional cushioning. In such a way the painting would be protected from any damage in transit, and the box was sealed tight against any water damage.

In other words, the crate was *air tight* . . . Teddy began to shake, clenching and unclenching his now sweating hands. He knew – because he had made and packed many of them – that there would be steel straps around the outside of the crate. Vertical *and* horizontal. Straps so strong they could prevent the crate being smashed to pieces if it was dropped.

So strong they could keep a man inside without any hope of escape.

Feeling uncharacteristically depressed, Samuel Hemmings wheeled his chair over to the fire his housekeeper had lit for him. The chill he had caught at Owen Zeigler's funeral had seeped into his bones, into his feet, aching in their slippers, and his hands clumsy with rheumatism. He thought fleetingly of how he had once promised that he would retire abroad, in the heat. But the years had passed like days and he had stayed in Sussex until he was too old to consider travelling any further than London.

Grasping his pen, Samuel opened the notebook on his lap and tried to turn his attention to an article he was writing on the National Gallery, but no words came. His brain was soggy with unease. Had he been right to lie? he asked himself, thinking back. He was an old man and had seen much in his life, but perhaps he had become too remote from the world, too busy with theories and opinions to confront reality. It was simple to take a stance over a dead painter; easy to pass judgement over what had long gone.

For many years, giving exclusive, intimate dinner parties had been a pleasure to Samuel, who would invite a handful of influential people to his Sussex home where they exchanged ideas. And gossip. Sheltered from financial anxiety, he enjoyed the gathering of competing intellects, and had encouraged younger dealers and writers who sat around the oval dining table, talking until the early hours; enjoyed listening to the bristle of ambition and the flutter of creativity. Excellent food, expensive wine, and comfortable sleeping arrangements had been provided for his guests, nothing changing as the years passed and the guests came and went. Even when the dog died, his bed still stayed in the corner, unmoved.

Rubbing his knuckles, Samuel stared into the fire and thought about Owen Zeigler. He had not wanted to know the details of the murder, but on his return home, he had searched the Internet and read everything he could about his friend's death. The details were shocking, terrifying, bringing overdue reality into the Sussex house. His friend had been tortured and killed. Dear God, Samuel thought, if Owen, why not him? Nervously he sipped at his tea, his hand unsteady. Verbally brave, he was mortally afraid of death – and pain. He knew all about pain. Rubbing his knuckles again, Samuel tried to imagine what Owen had suffered and wondered how his protégé had faced death . . . but he didn't believe for one moment that the killers had found the Rembrandt letters.

Certainly Samuel had hoped that he might convince Marshall that they had, and that therefore they were both out of danger. But he was lying to Marshall *and* himself. His mind turned to paintings he had studied over the years, portraits and visions of martyrs' deaths. Flayings, decapitation, all borne with fortitude and the knowledge of a reward after sacrifice. A spiritual lottery win. But Samuel knew he had not the makings of a martyr. In print, he could challenge and parry, but in reality he was old, crippled, and he wanted to live.

His tea finished, Samuel wheeled himself into the hall and set the burglar alarm, watching the flashing red light flicking thirty times until it went out, to indicate that the outer doors of the house were secure. As ever, he would be alone at night. Mrs McKendrick only came in at nine in the morning and stayed until seven p.m., having made his dinner. She left it on a tray in the kitchen, within Samuel's reach, and for the remainder of the evening he would usually work, or talk on the phone. Conversation fascinated Samuel, and his phone bills were a testament to the extent and length of his calls. Not only that, but during the last year he had extended his interest to the Internet and was now an active member of several historical and antique sites. To Mrs McKendrick's astonishment, pieces of unexpected machinery had started to arrive – pieces Samuel had bought on Ebay. Like the extra large, extra complicated microwave and the industrial washing machine with the built in dryer. Faced with alarmingly complex machinery, Mrs McKendrick would fold her arms and refuse to use them, leaving them wrapped in their plastic in the garage, although Samuel was convinced that before long he would manage to get them indoors and in use. As he said, people had to get used to change. Only the psychotic couldn't adapt.

Or the very old.

He sighed to himself. He had never thought of himself as old, but he was feeling old now. And lonely. Wheeling himself down the corridor, he headed for his sleeping quarters downstairs, next to a bathroom which had been altered to accommodate his disability. Upstairs was off limits to him now, and the rooms closed up except for when guests visited. Samuel had thought of getting a lift installed, but had decided against it. Until now. Now he was wondering about upstairs, remembering the rooms which were barred to him, the landing and attics as remote as Dubai. The house was too big, of course, but he would never leave it. Could never imagine having to uproot himself and his books, or readjust his thinking and habits to a new, convenient home. He could adapt his ideas, but his lifestyle? No.

And yet . . . Gripping the sides of his wheelchair Samuel patrolled the downstairs rooms, checking the front door, which had already been locked. With the windows curtained, and the alarm set, he should have relaxed, but Samuel Hemmings felt nervous. He was crippled, frail. Vulnerable. His house was outside the village, out of sight and earshot. Anyone could approach without being seen. Anyone could watch from the bushes in the day time and break in when darkness fell. For the first time in his life he felt afraid of living alone. The evening seemed to expand before him interminably, its usual pleasures dimmed. Unable to read or think with clarity, Samuel moved back to sit in front of the study fire, with the phone on a table next to him.

*

Would they come for him? If they had come for Owen Zeigler they would come for anyone else who knew about the Rembrandt letters . . . He thought back, to a summer day, hot with flowers and bees humming manically around the high trees.

'Let Stefan van der Helde look at the letters,' he had said to Owen. 'He's caught out every forgery in the last twenty years.'

Owen had been very serious that day. Well dressed as ever, he had sat with Samuel in the garden, under the arch of bay trees. Waving aside a wasp with one manicured hand, he replied, 'He's seen them.'

Samuel had paused, surprised. 'Really?'

'Yes. He says they're genuine.'

And how the sky had seemed to change in that instant. The bay trees cast a darker shadow, the sun listless behind the summer house, the birds watching from the tops of leafy trees. For an instant Samuel had been jealous, wanting to be young again. In the running. Wanting to share the uproar which would follow the exposure of the letters. Envy had inclined him to spitefulness. 'Is Van der Helde sure they're authentic?' he asked, in a tone that implied disagreement.

'One hundred per cent.'

'Then you must take good care of them, Owen.'

Owen had nodded, obviously thoughtful. 'I will. I always have.'

Taking a long, slow breath, Samuel's mind went further back. To the first time he had ever heard about the

Rembrandt letters. It had been in the summer of 1973, not long after the death of Neville Zeigler, when an excited Owen had come down to Sussex in a great hurry. He brought a package, which he put down and unwrapped on the table in the study. It turned out to be a sturdy medium sized casket, set with brass decoration, standing defiant in the sunlight.

'What is it?' Samuel had asked, almost amused. 'It doesn't look worth much.'

'The casket isn't valuable. It's what's inside,' Owen had replied. 'When my father was alive he used to tease me about knowing something which could "bugger up the art world good and proper". I asked him what it was, but he'd never tell me. Then a few years ago, he started to elaborate. He said there was a scandal about Rembrandt, some sordid secret – and he had *proof*.' Owen shrugged his shoulders. 'I still thought it was a joke. Then his solicitor gave me this.'

Both men had looked at the box, Samuel frowning. 'Go on.'

'With the casket was a letter from my father. After the war, being Jewish, he settled in the East End of London, where he married and started a business. As you know, he dealt in bric-a-brac, all sorts, but he had a good eye and sometimes he bought well.'

Owen had paused, apparently still in some form of shock, then said, 'Not long after the war, in 1953, there was a sale in Amsterdam of Jewish religious artefacts and my father went over to have a look. There had been a fire at a synagogue and they were selling off anything which could raise money for the repairs. My father saw the casket, and although it was blackened, burnt at one corner and he couldn't open the lock, he bought it. Thought he could clean it up and sell it on as a jewellery box.' Owen ran his finger along the casket lid. 'He said in his letter that it took him a long time to restore it, and when he had, he realised it was rather well made. Not worth a fortune, but very old. Naturally, he then began to wonder if there was anything inside it worth having.'

'Was there?'

'My father writes that it took him four hours to finally wheedle open the lock without damaging the casket. When he did, he found a lot of old bills, receipts and letters . . .'

Samuel could sense the muted excitement in his protégé's voice. 'Were they dated?'

'Yes, from the seventeenth century.'

Samuel's eyebrows rose. 'Any signatures?'

'Yes, on the invoices and on some legal papers. The names Titus and Rembrandt van Rijn.'

Raising his eyes Heavenwards, Samuel smiled. 'You don't believe—'

Owen had cut him off immediately. 'The papers hadn't been disturbed for a long time. Just put away, forgotten, the documents of Rembrandt's bankruptcy and overdue loans, and Titus's agreement to take over the running of his father's art business.'

'But if it was genuine why would this casket have ended up in a *synagogue*?'

Sighing, Owen had faced his mentor. 'Rembrandt was close to the Dutch Jews, he painted them many, many times. He was also friendly with the rabbi of that particular synagogue. Titus actually explains what happened in a note he pinned to some contract. There was an agreement between him and the rabbi that the latter would keep the casket hidden in the synagogue in return for one of Rembrandt's paintings.'

'Which one?'

'I don't know. It was probably destroyed in the fire.'

Gripped, Samuel had leaned towards Owen, his concentration intense.

'But why did Titus go to such lengths to hide this casket?' His clever eyes narrowed. 'What else was in the box?'

'A series of very personal letters.'

'Whose letters?'

'Geertje Dircx.'

'Rembrandt's *mistress*?' Samuel had replied, awestruck. 'Jesus, you have letters written by Geertje Dircx? What do they say?'

'No one knows much about Geertje, do they? Just rumours about her and what happened to her.' Owen paused, grabbed at a breath. 'Well, these letters were written by her from the asylum to which Rembrandt had committed her. They are her testament to the violence she endured, of the treatment meted out to her by the world's greatest painter. For loving Rembrandt she was given twelve years hard labour.'

Staggered, Samuel had leaned back in his seat. 'I thought it was a rumour.'

'The letters are the proof.'

'Titus must have read them . . .'

Owen had nodded sadly. 'Yes.'

'So why didn't he destroy them, I wonder . . .'

'Titus loved his old nurse, Geertje. He would have felt some loyalty to her and wanted to preserve her testimony. At the same time he would have wanted to hide his father's culpability.'

Sighing, Samuel had said, 'You think *Geertje* gave Titus the letters?'

'No . . . I think she turned to the church after she was released. After all, where else could she go? She had no home, no job. She couldn't go back to her family who had betrayed her. In my opinion, I think Geertje gave the letters to a priest.'

'So how did they end up with a *rabbi*?' asked Samuel. It seemed obvious that Owen had given the matter considerable thought.

'What if the priest, having read the letters, was scared and thought he should return them to the famous and powerful Rembrandt? Then the painter, relieved, would have put them away with his mass of other paperwork and his personal letters – history tells us he was a compulsive hoarder who seldom threw anything away. Then, over time, perhaps Rembrandt forgot all about them. He'd moved on, the court case was over, and Geertje was to all intents and purposes dead to him. Rembrandt presumably just got on with his life.'

'Until?'

'Until he was older and in real money trouble and hounded by his creditors. Only his son could get him out of it by having his father declared bankrupt and taking over the whole business. Titus would then have had to trawl through all the mountains of paperwork to do with his father's work, and personal correspondence too. I believe *that* was when Titus found Geertje's letters, and *that* was when he hid them. He knew how dangerous they were.'

'And your father left the letters to you?' Samuel said, hiding his unexpected, and unwelcome, envy. 'What did Neville want you to do with them?'

'He didn't say.'

'No suggestions?'

Owen smiled. 'My father writes that at first he thought of them as my inheritance; that I could sell them for a fortune one day. That as long as I had them, I would have a nest egg. Then, as the years passed, he realised I'd never sell them.'

'Never?'

'Never.' Slumping back in his chair, Owen had shaken his head, his expression incredulous. 'Jesus, Samuel, I wake up in the middle of the night and think about what I've read. I see her, Geertje Dircx, in that House of Corrections. Incarcerated, forgotten, scribbling away at those notes, and praying that someone would read them one day and know what happened to her.'

He turned to Samuel and held his gaze. 'She said that Rembrandt painted a portrait of her. I've been looking at

125

his pictures around that time, trying to work out which one it is.'

'Any luck?'

'Not yet,' Owen had admitted. 'But some people believe it's her likeness in *Susannah and the Elders*. I look at the painting, look into her eyes and I think about her, Geertje. About her son, about the tragedy of it all. And I think about how the world would view Rembrandt if they knew her story.'

Samuel brought his thoughts back to the present. Subdued, he moved over to the nearest bookcase and took down a volume, searching out the reproduction of *Susannah and the Elders*. When he found it, he looked intently at the young woman, with a bland, oval face, staring out at him. She had been painted as Susannah at the moment she was about to bathe – suddenly surprised by the old men watching her and holding a cloth to hide her nakedness. Her eyes were darker than the water under her feet . . .

Samuel stared into those eyes. Was he looking at Geertje Dircx? Before she was ill, and abandoned. Before she was imprisoned. The Geertje Dircx who was painted while she yielded to her lover and cared for his son. The woman whose words from the grave could ruin a reputation and undermine an industry.

Closing the book, Samuel's thoughts went back to that summer day in the garden. He had watched Owen carefully – then asked if he could see the letters.

'Of course you can. I thought you'd want to, once they'd

been authenticated,' Owen had answered, passing Samuel a package. 'They'll make you cry, I warn you.'

And they had. They had made Samuel cry, and excited him, and fascinated him. They had left him wrung out with emotion and – as he touched them – he had been aware that he was among the very few people on earth who had ever been privy to this secret part of Rembrandt's life. The story was incredible, and yet unfinished ... Samuel had wondered about that many times over the last year. It had seemed to him that the letters had ended abruptly, without a proper conclusion.

He had said as much to Owen, who had agreed. But something in the *way* he had said it made Samuel suspect that he had not been allowed to see all the letters. A possible last letter and the agreement between Titus van Rijn and the rabbi had perhaps been withheld from him. Perhaps Owen hadn't wanted to keep everything together; perhaps he had divided the papers up and hidden them separately for security reasons. Either way, Samuel's protégé was keeping something back. The thought had piqued Samuel at the time, since it seemed to indicate a lack of trust on Owen's part, but he had duly returned the letters after he had read them.

Turning his rheumy eyes towards the corner of the room, Samuel stared at the dog's bed. It was never moved, never disturbed, his housekeeper not daring to enter her employer's room or touch anything. So the dog's bed had stayed in the same place for years, long after the dog had gone. Dust had drifted underneath the bed, particles of fluff had sidled into the dark space. But there was something else in that darkness, under the empty bed. An envelope taped to the underside of it. An envelope containing a copy of the Rembrandt letters.

A copy Samuel had taken without Owen Zeigler's knowledge.

A copy which could well cost him his life.

12

Amsterdam

Walking to the back of the restaurant on Warmoesstraat, Charlotte Gorday took a seat at a table in a booth. Marshall sat down opposite her, facing a fly-spotted mirror through which he could see the premises behind him. The place was hushed; only a few customers sitting at the bar in that morose little period between the end of office hours and the evening rush. Without being obvious, Marshall scrutinised the woman as she rummaged in her bag. *His father's mistress* . . . It had never occurred to Marshall that Owen Zeigler would have a lover. Hadn't he seemed the resigned widower, content to live with the memory of his dead wife rather than the reality of a living woman? But here she was, his father's mistress. Charlotte Gorday.

The name meant nothing to him, had just added to his confusion. It seemed that everything he had believed about his father had been a smokescreen, hiding the truth. What else didn't he know? What else was there to find out about someone he had thought he knew? The shocks had come one upon another, with no preparation, stripping away the respectable image of Owen Zeigler and revealing a completely different persona. And now this woman, sitting in front of him – his father's lover.

She looked up, her eyes grey, freckled with hazel. Her steady gaze was contradicted by the shaking hand that held her coffee cup.

'You didn't know about me, did you?'

'No.'

'I'm sorry, but your father was a very private man.'

'Even more than I thought,' Marshall said cryptically. 'As every day passes I'm finding out things I didn't know.'

He paused. She wasn't what he would have expected from the word 'mistress'. Nothing vulgar or garish about her appearance; she was not overly young or overly blonde. Indeed, she had a faintly timid elegance, a refinement which reminded him unexpectedly of his mother and made her usurpation the greater blow.

'Do you know why he was killed?' she asked, her tone wavering.

'Do you?'

'No, why would I? I was just told it was a robbery that turned into a murder. At least, that's what the police said when they talked to me, but I don't believe it.'

Surprised, Marshall studied her. 'Did you see the police in London?'

Charlotte nodded.

'But you live in Amsterdam?'

'No. I came over here to talk to you. I missed you in

130

London, so I came here. I called by your flat yesterday, but there was no reply. Someone – one of your neighbours – told me you were travelling, but that you were never away for too long, so I thought I'd just wait until you returned. I know the city well.'

'Did my father – did he tell you about his circumstances? He was facing ruin before he died. Did you know that?'

She held Marshall's look for a long instant, embarrassing him.

'I wasn't dependent on your father, if that's what you think. I have my own income. For God's sake, I was helping him!' she burst out, her lips trembling for an instant before she regained her composure. Slowly she touched her throat, her skin fragile, a gold chain showing at the open collar of her silk shirt. 'I loved your father, I didn't need a meal ticket.' She reached for her bag, flushing with annoyance. 'You're not like him.'

'I'm sorry if I offended you,' Marshall said, putting out his hand to stop her leaving. 'I was just taken aback, that's all.'

'And I used the wrong word. I should have said *lover*, not mistress. But English isn't my first language and even after so long I sometimes make mistakes when I'm upset.'

'Where were you born?'

'I'm Swiss,' she said, hurrying on. 'I loved your father more than any other man.'

'Why didn't you marry him?'

She snorted, colouring slightly. 'Because I'm already married.'

Caught off guard, Marshall repeated.

'Married?'

'My husband works and lives in America. Philip didn't want a divorce so we kept up a respectable front, and in private we lived our own lives. It's not uncommon. Besides, we have a strong bond ... But not like I had with your father, that was special.'

She paused, as though the words had come out too quickly and were perhaps ill judged. Folding her hands on the table between them, Marshall noticed that she wore no wedding ring, only a large signet ring with a seal. Her nails were short and groomed, but across her right wrist was a faint scar. Before Marshall could check her other wrist, Charlotte tucked her hands under the table, out of sight. Her expression wasn't combative, but wistful, almost sad.

'I suppose I shouldn't have just turned up like this, unannounced. But I had to speak to you about your father.' She smiled suddenly and became unexpectedly beautiful; giving a hint of what his father had loved. 'There's no one else I can talk to, no one else who knew about us.'

'How long did you know my father?'

'We were lovers for eighteen years.'

Marshall stared at her incredulously. '*Eighteen years?*'

'We were always discreet. It was the way your father wanted it. And he was very protective of you. I think he believed that you would never accept anyone after your mother's death—'

'That's not true.'

'It's what he thought.'

'He should have talked to me about it.'

'He said he tried.'

Stung, Marshall said, 'I didn't know him at all, did I?'

'I wouldn't be too hard on yourself. How much did he know about your life?'

'Only what I told him.'

She smiled generously.

'Maybe you two *are* similar, after all.' A moment passed before she spoke again. 'I don't believe it was just a robbery. That's what I wanted to talk to you about. The police interviewed me but I couldn't tell them anything, except that I knew Owen was in trouble and owed a lot of money, but I have to tell you something now, something which won't put me in a good light. When we realised how bad everything was with the business, I wanted your father to run.'

'Run?'

She nodded.

'I told him that we could leave the country, go to Spain, South America. Switzerland. I had enough money for us to live quite well. The Zeigler Gallery and the paintings would be sold in absentia, the staff paid, any other profits passed over to his creditors.' She sighed, fighting despair. 'I just wanted him out of London, away from that gallery. I wanted him safe.'

Alerted, Marshall leaned towards her. 'Why wasn't he safe?'

'He wouldn't tell me, but I just know he wasn't only

worried about debts. There was more to it than money worries. I *knew* the man, there was more.' She took a breath, then hurried on. 'Owen told me everything about his work, his dealings. I knew about his finances. I was the only one who did. Even his accountant didn't know the truth until the end. But despite everything we shared – and it was a lot over eighteen years – I knew your father was keeping something from me. What was it, Marshall?'

'I don't know,' he replied, keeping his voice expressionless, the package in his inside pocket resting against his heart. 'All he told me was about his business. He said he'd lose the gallery, that's what was panicking him. That place was his life, his pleasure. He loved his work, and his reputation meant so much to him—'

'No, there was more!'

'Not that I know of.'

'I *know* there was more to it than that,' Charlotte said, looking away, fighting tears.

Swallowing, she struggled to compose herself. Marshall was tempted to confide in her, but resisted. Apparently his father had loved this woman for eighteen years, but if that was true, why hadn't he confided in her? To protect her? Or because he didn't trust her?

'I don't know how I'll live without him,' she said simply, getting to her feet. For a moment she stared ahead, then turned back to Marshall. He thought she was about to be angry, but her voice was quiet, resigned. 'I thought you'd be able to explain, to give me closure. To tell me something that would make his death bearable. I'm sorry, it was too much to expect.'

His breathing laboured, Teddy Jack felt the warm trickle of urine snake between his legs. He didn't know how long he had been in the crate but guessed it to be several hours, and all his frenzied shouting and kicking had attracted no notice. No longer caring whose attention he caught, Teddy pummelled the lid and, frantically moving his body from left to right in the tight confines, tried to turn the case over. He knew from the start that it was a wasted effort which would use up much precious oxygen, but simply lying still and waiting to die was unthinkable.

Exhausted, he finally stopped kicking, his hands clutching his head, his fingers raking at his beard. The Zeigler Gallery had been cordoned off, no one would come by. Not even the cleaner. It might be days before anyone returned and found him. And by then he would be dead . . .

Panting, Teddy closed his eyes, thinking of his past. If he had stayed in the North it would have been so different. He might not have made money, but had it been worth it? How much better might an uncomplicated life have been? A boring life . . . He thought desperately, longingly, of his ex-wife. Unaccustomed self pity made his eyes well up – how would she hear of his death? Would it matter to her? Probably not, she had moved on long ago. As for his parents, they were both dead, so who was left to grieve for Teddy Jack up North? And who would grieve for him in London? Just the working girls, and the woman at the café who made his tea the way he always liked it. In the final analysis, Teddy Jack realised that his closest friend had been Owen Zeigler, the man who had hired him and had come to confide in him. The man whose secrets he had carried for so long. And would now carry to the grave . . .

He should have walked away, should have resisted the temptation, but Owen had been persuasive and Teddy had always had something of the rogue about him. It had begun years earlier, not long after he had first come to work at the Zeigler Gallery. Owen had approached him in the basement, when the other porters were out having a smoke in the back yard.

'Could you watch someone for me?'

Surprised, Teddy had glanced at his boss. 'Watch someone?'

Coming from Owen, the request had seemed somehow less worrying. If Teddy had been asked the same by one of the working girls, he would have been wary, but his employer was a man with integrity. Teddy had seen how well he treated the other members of staff, how he made allowances for Nicolai Kapinski's lapses and the receptionist's bad time keeping. Owen Zeigler was fair in his dealings, a popular man, good natured and courteous.

And yet . . .

'Why would you want me to watch someone?'

'I told you when you first came here that the job might change a little,' Owen had replied, picking up a book of gold leaf which was lying on the work bench. Carefully he had touched one of the gold leaves, the metal clinging greedily to his index finger like a fish going for bait. 'I'm worried about one of the dealers. Timothy Parker-Ross. I knew his father, but now he's dead I think Tim might be struggling.' Casually, Owen had shrugged. 'I just wondered if you could see what he does after hours. When his gallery's closed. I'd like to know who he's dealing with.'

And that had been it. A simple task, with a philanthropic intention, for which Teddy had been offered a generous fee . . .

The air in the box was turning sour now and Teddy was sweating profusely, his knuckles bleeding from where he had rapped against the lid. Fitfully he called out, but his voice sounded small even in his own ears and he knew it would hardly travel beyond the crate. His eyes closing, he allowed his mind to wander, his thoughts going back . . .

Timothy Parker-Ross had been something of an enigma. Well over six feet, he had lost most of his hair by the time he was in his thirties, and his nails were bitten to the quick. The perfect victim for the bully boys of the public school system, Tim had graduated to the extended bullying of the London art world. While his father was alive, he had been protected, brought in to work at the gallery because he lacked the confidence to seek an occupation elsewhere. So for years lanky, nervy Tim had followed his father around to the auctions, and sat in on private sales. With his lopsided smile and hesitant manner, he had impressed no one and commanded no respect. But he was liked. And he was trusted. And he made that enough.

When his father died unexpectedly Timothy Parker-Ross inherited the Parker-Ross Gallery, dealing in German and Dutch art. Within six months the gallery manager had left, taking the secretary with him. By paying exorbitant wages, Tim had managed to secure the sneering loyalty of the porters and the receptionist, but his overblown bids for indifferent works and his unshifting backlog of paintings had left his accountant exasperated. He wasn't stupid, merely limited. In a less ruthless environment, Tim might have made a good living, but he was ill-equipped to deal with the bull pit of the art world and desperate to escape. So when another gallery owner had offered to buy him out, he had been tempted. Until Owen heard about their meetings.

Coughing hoarsely, Teddy scratched at the lid above him. Spittle was forming at the sides of his mouth, his skin was clammy, and his panic veered between indifference and terror. Stay calm, he told himself, breathe slowly, don't use up the air . . . Again, he thought back in time to his surveillance of Parker-Ross. When he had reported his findings back to Owen, his employer had nodded.

'So Tim's been seeing a lot of Tobar Manners, has he? He's out of his league there.'

'You can say that again,' Teddy had agreed. 'I used to work for that bastard, remember?'

'Has Tim been talking to anyone else?'

'Not that I've seen. Not in the evenings anyway. Just

Manners. They went to the Ivy on Tuesday night. Manners was courting the idiot like a prospective bride, and Parker-Ross was fiddling with his food.'

'Poor Tim.'

'Poor fool.'

'An orphaned fool with a sly stepfather in the making. I don't think we can have that.'

Teddy frowned. 'But you're friends with Tobar Manners.'

'Yes, we're friends – because he's never tried to cheat me, and he's a good dealer. We've done some profitable business together and I have no personal reason to dislike Tobar. But I know what he's like, and with certain other people he can't resist going in for the kill.' Owen had sighed, passing Teddy some money. 'You did well.'

'You don't want me to watch Parker-Ross anymore?'

'No. I know what I need to know.'

The following week Timothy Parker-Ross had been made an offer for his gallery from a dealer in the USA. A dealer Owen Zeigler personally knew and had introduced to Tim. Convinced by Owen that the proposition was exceptional and that he would have to move fast, Parker-Ross had signed on the dotted line and retired abroad. It took an enraged Tobar Manners months to get over it and he never knew the hand Owen had played in the matter.

Owen Zeigler had acted like a good man. *A good man*, Teddy thought. But was he really? There had been other occasions he had spied for Owen Zeigler, times which had not turned out so fortuitously and results which had been ambiguous. But Teddy had always given his employer the benefit of the doubt, and in return, he had been privy to Owen's secrets. Which was why he was now lying, gasping for air, in a box. In a gallery which was closed, in a basement which was cordoned off, within yards of where his employer had been murdered only days before.

He was dying too, slowly and agonisingly. Death, he thought, wasn't quick enough.

13

Following the children out into the playground, Georgia pulled on her gloves and wrapped her scarf around her neck. God, she thought, was it ever going to warm up? The winter seemed to be going on interminably, the trees still sullen without any hint of green, summer years away. Or maybe that was just typical of life. When you were planning for something and waiting, time the hare became time the turtle. Tempted to go back indoors, Georgia suddenly spotted the figure by the railings and frowned, surprised to see her ex-husband.

They had talked many times over the past days, Georgia mentioning that the police had been round to see her in her home in Clapham. Just routine, Georgia had reassured Marshall when he reacted violently, nothing serious. Then he told her that he'd been interviewed just after the murder. They had wanted to know if Owen Zeigler had had any enemies, because even though they were sure it was a bungled robbery, they had to ask. After another few minutes conversation, Marshall had rung off.

But now, here he was, standing at the gates of the school where Georgia was a teacher. Almost as though he was waiting for her, like he used to when they were first married.

'Hey, Marshall,' she said simply as she walked up to him. 'How are you doing?'

His hand was wrapped around one of the school railings, white flesh against black metal.

'I wondered if we could talk.'

'*Now?*' she asked, jerking her head towards the children behind them. 'I have to make sure that all the kids have been collected before I can leave. We lose about three a week to kidnappers.'

He smiled, relieved by her humour. 'Okay if I wait?'

'Fine,' she agreed, 'give me about ten minutes.'

When she came out fifteen minutes later she was buttoning up her coat, her red hair tucked into the collar, her blue eyes steady.

Casually, she slid her arm through his. 'How are you bearing up?'

'I saw you at the funeral service, thanks for coming. Why didn't you stay on afterwards?'

She shrugged. 'There were a lot of people there, Marshall, you didn't need me hanging around.'

Together they walked onto Fulham Palace Road, stopping at the lights to cross.

'How's Harry?'

'Fine.'

'So it's working out between you two?'

'Yeah, it is.'

'I'm glad you're happy.'

'Come on, I'll buy you a drink,' she said, steering him towards the Golden Compass. Inside the pub it was quiet, the tables empty. 'We should have booked,' she joked, sitting down at a table by the fire. Marshall brought their drinks and took a seat opposite his ex-wife. He held out his hands towards the warmth of the fire and Georgia could tell that he hadn't been sleeping well. She wasn't surprised. The death of a parent is a shock to anyone, but Marshall had found his father's butchered corpse and he looked haunted by it.

Taking a sip of her orange juice, Georgia studied her ex-husband. 'Are you working at the moment?'

'I was, but not now,' he admitted. 'In fact, I've just come back from Amsterdam. I was only there a few hours, had to come back to London.' He smiled awkwardly. 'Can't really think straight yet ... But I'll be working again soon.'

'You don't have to hurry.'

'I can't sit around doing nothing.'

'You never could,' Georgia replied, tapping his knee. 'D'you want to stay with us for a few days?'

His eyebrows rose. 'You think that would help?'

She shrugged. 'Maybe not. I just don't want you to be on your own. Why didn't you stay in Holland?'

'I couldn't. Well, I *could*, but I thought I should get back here. I felt as though I was turning my back on my father, just going home as though nothing had happened. And there are other reasons . . .' He trailed off, staring at her. 'You're the only person I can trust, Georgia. And I need someone to trust, need someone to talk to.'

'So talk.' She took off her coat and looking directly into his face. 'You can tell me anything, you know that.'

'I know.' He downed his drink and said, 'Jesus, I don't know what to do.'

Uneasy, Georgia looked around them. But there was only the barmaid nearby and she was talking to the other customers in the place.

'Tell me what's worrying you,' she said, keeping her voice low. 'Talk to me, Marshall.'

'Maybe I shouldn't—'

'Maybe you should! I'd come to you if I was in trouble, you know that. God knows, I've relied on you enough in the past. So tell me what's going on.'

'I think my father was murdered because of something he found.'

'What?'

Marshall paused, then – slowly and painstakingly – told her everything about the Rembrandt letters, Georgia's eyes widening as she listened. As though feeling a sudden chill, she drew her coat around her shoulders, then picked at a loose thread in the lining. For a moment Marshall remembered the smell of her skin against his when they had made love, and the way she read the papers on a Sunday morning, giving him her own hilarious résumé of the week's news. He also remembered how easily she could cry at a film, and how tough she was when her back was against the wall. And he realised how glad he was to have her on his side.

'So where are the letters now?' Georgia asked, then shook her head, her eyes widening. 'Don't tell me *you've* got them?'

'I've hidden them.'

'Where?'

He gave her an incredulous look.

'All right, don't tell me,' she said, 'but shouldn't someone else know where they are?'

'In case something happens to me?'

Her expression shifted with unease. 'Don't say that.'

'My father was murdered, Georgia. He was *killed*. And his killers didn't get what they were looking for. They won't stop searching for the letters now. They'll come after anyone who might know about them—'

'And you told me. Thanks.' She was teasing him.

'That's why I'm not telling you where they are.'

Shivering, Georgia moved closer to the fire to warm her hands. The barmaid had stopped talking and was wiping the end of the bar listlessly; the logs were shifting in the fire grate; reflections of the pub interior and its occupants flickered on the decorative copper pans and kettles, the gold tops of the optics winking blindly in the firelight.

Unusually anxious, Georgia felt the shift in atmosphere and realised that her life had changed within minutes. And, to her shame, she resented it. Resented her contentment being so summarily dethroned.

'Go to the police, Marshall,' she said at last. 'Tell them about the letters.'

'I daren't—'

'Why not?'

'Because – say they even believed the story – it would become public knowledge and then everyone would know. That would only make these people even more reckless and dangerous.'

'Depends on who *these people* are,' she replied, with a tinge of irritation.

His expression hardened. 'I found my father's body. I know what they're capable of.'

She stared at the floor, thinking about everything Marshall had told her. 'I don't suppose Stefan van der Helde's murder was just a coincidence, was it?'

'No.'

'So who else knows about the letters?'

'My father's mentor, Samuel Hemmings. Maybe my father's employees, Teddy Jack and Nicolai Kapinski. And possibly someone else – my father's lover.'

Georgia paused, her glass half way to her lips. 'You never said anything about your father having a girlfriend—'

'I didn't know about her. Until she turned up today. She said they had been lovers for eighteen years.'

Putting her glass down on the table, Georgia ran her finger down the condensation, writing the initial G. 'I never thought Owen was the type to keep secrets.'

'Well, he obviously was. I didn't know about Charlotte Gorday *or* the Rembrandt letters.'

'Makes you wonder . . .'

'What?'

'How well you know anyone.' She shook her head. 'It's like a chest of drawers—'

He smiled, bemused. 'What is?'

'Your father. It's like there was this big, handsome piece of furniture, which everybody admires. It's a chest of drawers. Simple. Obvious.' She paused. 'But when you look more closely, all these drawers are *hiding* things. A drawer with his debts, a drawer with his lover, a drawer – a *big* drawer – with the Rembrandt letters.' She shrugged. 'Yeah, I know, it's a basic simile, but I work with kids, remember.' She was silent a moment, then asked, 'What are you going to do?'

'I'm not sure. There's something I want to check out tonight, but after that I don't know.' His voice dropped. 'If I'm honest, a part of me wants to just go back to my old life, but I can't. I found that out today. I *have* to know who killed my father and I want to make sure they don't get hold of the letters. Exposure could bring down the art market.'

She looked at him incredulously. 'But why would that matter to you? You always hated the business.'

'A little while ago I'd gladly have seen the art world brought to its knees. I can understand why people hate the dealers' greed, how the huge profits stick in the craw.' He held her gaze. 'But when my father was killed I realised that good men could get caught up in the backlash too. That for all the bastards trading there are some honest

147

men who couldn't survive a bloodbath. The Rembrandt letters are worth millions because they could rock the market. They can't be allowed to get into the wrong hands.'

They were both silent a while.

'I'll help you any way I can,' Georgia said finally. 'But I won't tell Harry about any of this. I don't want him involved.'

Marshall nodded. 'No. Nobody else must know.'

'Is there anything I can do?'

Touched, Marshall shook his head. 'I don't know how to thank you.'

'Well, you could buy me another orange juice,' she said simply. 'That would be a start.'

An hour later they parted, Georgia making her way home alone through the London streets, brushing off Marshall's offer to accompany her home. It was quiet, mid-week, and as she walked along she was aware of her heels echoing on the pavement and her shadow extending in front of her. Uncharacteristically nervous, she thought about Marshall's revelations, and found herself glancing round a couple of times to check that she wasn't being followed. But the street was empty and Georgia shook her head, exasperated by her own nerves. Putting her bag over her shoulder, she walked beyond Clapham Common, passing under the streetlamps towards home.

At first annoyed at being involved, Georgia was pleased that Marshall had come to her. She had been thinking about him recently, wanting to hear from him, to confide her own news. But when she had been told of Owen's death, she had stayed quiet, and although she had been tempted to speak up earlier, the time was out of sync. She wondered fleetingly if she was still in love with Marshall and hoped she wasn't ... She turned into her road as a car suddenly rounded the bend, startling her, causing her to jump back from the kerb.

The car drove on, disappearing at the end of the street. Taking in a breath, Georgia calmed herself. What the hell was the matter with her? The car hadn't been coming for her. It had been taking someone home – picking up a daughter from dance school, perhaps, or a husband from squash. Surprised by her own unexpected nerviness, she walked resolutely up the front steps of her house and then slid the key into the lock.

'Hi, darling,' Harry called from the back. 'Where have you been?' He came out to the hallway, wiping his hands on a kitchen towel, and skirting round a mountain bike propped up at the bottom of the stairs. 'I should move that.'

She raised her eye heavenwards. 'And the hiking boots.'

'I thought you liked them there,' he replied, kissing her forehead. 'You used to say that it reminded you that you had a real live action man in the house.'

'Along with real live action mud.'

'Hard day?'

'I had to throw one child out of the window, but otherwise quiet.'

His head cocked over to one side. 'You look different.'

'It's the beard.'

He laughed. 'No, you do look different. Nothing worrying you is there?'

'No, Harry,' she said lightly, taking off her coat. 'Nothing's wrong.'

'Good. I made curry.'

Closing the door behind her, Georgia smiled, and dismissed all thoughts of Marshall and the Rembrandt letters.

14

'Marshall!' a voice called suddenly, 'I thought it was you.'

The tall, gangling figure of Timothy Parker-Ross, came towards Marshall in Albemarle Street.

He ambled over, then clasped Marshall in a sloppy hug, his long arms wrapped around his friend until he pulled back, embarrassed. 'Sorry, Marshall. I was just so pleased to see you . . . I'm sorry about your father.'

'I'm pleased to see you too,' Marshall said, and meant it. 'I thought you were abroad.'

'Came back. You know how it is, I always liked travelling.'

'I remember. When we were young you said you wanted to go to every country in the world. And learn every language.'

'Well, I don't have the brain to learn all the languages. Never was much of a scholar,' he laughed, his long arms folding and refolding as though they were in his way. 'But I do travel a lot. I have the time, and the money helps. I've got lots of money now, from selling the business.' He looked around the empty street. 'Are you staying in London?'

'I don't know,' Marshall replied honestly. 'I don't know what I'm going to do.'

'It was just that if you – er – if you, well, felt like it, we could – er – have dinner. Catch up.' Timothy paused, acutely aware that he was floundering. 'I tried to get back for your father's funeral, but the flight was delayed . . . my father always said I was late for everything.'

Smiling, Marshall touched his arm. He himself had grown up, thickened out and hardened, but Timothy had stayed soft and boyish. He had never married. Never had the confidence, his shyness making him a social hermit. He might travel the world, but he would never relax anywhere, and Marshall realised that he was probably still Timothy's only friend.

'We'll have dinner, I'd like that. I have to sort out my father's things, but after that we could meet up.' Marshall paused, staring at the friend of his youth. The lad who had jumped on and off the Piccadilly buses, the boy in the British Museum, the misfit cowering under his father's blistering ambition.

'Are you working?'

Timothy shuffled his feet. 'No . . . don't know what to do really. I suppose I *should* work, but at what? I thought I might go into property. You know, in Spain perhaps, lots of English people there so I wouldn't have to learn the language.' He laughed. 'Mind you, I helped organise a couple of charity balls this summer. Phoning people I knew, raising money, but lately I thought I might build a house in Switzerland.'

'Can you ski?'

He put his head on one side. 'No. D'you have to?'

Marshall smiled. 'It's not compulsory.' He reached into his pocket and scribbled down his mobile number. 'I have to go now, but we'll meet up again soon. Give me a ring, will you?'

Timothy took the number and nodded. When he walked off Marshall stood watching his etiolated figure move away, pausing only once to kick a tin can into the gutter at the end of the street.

Turning his attention to the gallery, Marshall stared at the police tape then glanced up to the windows on the first floor. He looked around him. Albemarle Street was deserted, London rain falling disconsolately on the street and running down the barred gallery windows. On the front door of the Zeigler Gallery was a notice: CLOSED DUE TO BEREAVEMENT. For a moment he wanted to rewrite the note to say CLOSED DUE TO MURDER -- but what would have been the point? Every one in W1 knew what had happened to Owen Zeigler.

Ducking under the blue and white crime scene tape, Marshall unlocked the gallery door and walked in. The damp eeriness of the place affected him, his shadow falling along the gallery floor as he moved further inside. Turning on the desk lamp, he looked about him. Everything was as he had last seen it, Nothing tidied up or moved; the papers still scattered, the frantic scrabbling search obvious. He wanted so much to tidy up, put the gallery to rights, to make it as his father would have wanted it – presentable, elegant, ordered. But he knew he couldn't because the police would be back. What for, Marshall wasn't sure. They had taken forensic evidence and fingerprints, had tramped up and down the floors until any clue would have been ground underfoot by sheer weight of numbers. But still they had cordoned off the gallery, allowing no one inside for the last twenty-four hours.

Yet *something* had drawn Marshall back. He had put the package in a security box in an Amsterdam bank as intended, but had kept a copy of the letters with him. In his case, hidden amongst his working translation of Dante's *The Divine Comedy*. After his conversation with Charlotte Gorday, Marshall had wanted to leave Holland fast, his return to London prompted by a desire to see his ex-wife, and a need to revisit the scene of his father's death. But as Marshall moved to the back of the gallery space, he found himself pausing, uncertain, in front of the door which led down to the basement. Did he *really* want to go back down there? Down into the dark underbelly of the gallery? To the place where Owen Zeigler had been tortured and strung up? Did he really want to remember . . .

He closed his eyes for a few seconds, then opened them again. The police, he told himself, had searched the area repeatedly; what could he really expect to find? But they were looking for clues, evidence. Marshall was looking for something a father might leave for a son to find. Some hint, some note ... Still hesitating, he saw the basement in his mind's eye, walked the space in his head. He had looked around after the murder. There had been nothing there. *Nothing.* There seemed no reason to go back downstairs, he told himself. What could he possibly gain from reliving such a hideous event ... Changing his mind, Marshall let go of the door handle and turned, retracing his steps back to the front entrance.

The gallery seemed crammed with memories, haunted with his recall. Out of the corner of his eye Marshall even thought he caught a glimpse of his mother, coming down the stairs to a private viewing, resplendent in 1970s finery. Without trying he could hear the chatter of past conversations, hear a phone ringing in the distance ... The memory of the burst pipe came back in that instant, Lester Fox and Gordon Hendrix up to their knees in water, passing the paintings from hand to hand. Lester to George to Owen to Marshall, and finally to his mother. Standing on the top step of the basement stairs.

And then Marshall thought of the ghost, the dead soldier, who had skirted his childhood dreams, but a muffled sound under his feet snapped him out of his reverie. At first he thought he was still daydreaming, that he was about to see the dead soldier finally materialise. But the noise seemed real to him and, curious, he retraced his steps to the basement door. He paused, listening. Nothing. And yet he knew he hadn't imagined the sound. Silently, he turned the handle and opened the door. The basement steps were in darkness and hardly any light was coming through from the back window at the far end. The dampness seemed to have intensified, and underneath it the smell of blood. Marshall moved down the first steps cautiously, and again heard a sound, a slight thud.

He wondered whether the boiler been left on accidentally. Perhaps it was the pilot light making a thunking sound as it lit. But no – it couldn't be the boiler, the building was too cold. Warily, he continued down the steps; another couple of feet and he would be able to reach out for the light switch. The musty air gathered in his nostrils as he descended, the partition wall coming into view at the far end – a huge black shape crouching in the eerie cellar.

There it was again.

The dull thump.

Marshall jumped and flicked on the light.

He hadn't known what to expect, but it certainly hadn't been the huge packing case in the middle of the basement floor. Mystified, he moved towards it, then realised that it was where the sound had come from. *Someone was inside the box.*

'Hang on!' he said urgently, 'I'll get you out.'

Taking a hammer off the worktable, Marshall tried to use the claw-footed end to jemmy up the lid, but the steel straps were holding it tight and gave no leeway. Desperately, he tried to break the straps, then ran to the wall and took down a pair of wire cutters. His hands clenched around the cutters, he put all his effort into breaking the top strap until, finally, the steel gave way.

'I've nearly got you. Can you hear me?' he called.

There was no sound.

He was too slow! Jesus, he was too slow! He scrabbled at the strap at the head of the box, tugging at it, pulling at it until it cut into his hands. Then finally he snapped it, jammed the claw of the hammer under the lid, and used all his strength to prise it up. With a crack, the wood split, the lid lifted a couple of inches, and Marshall peered as best he could into the dark box.

'Christ!'

Teddy Jack was grey, motionless, spittle around his mouth, his lips drawn back over his teeth. But as Marshall levered the lid open further the big man's eyes fluttered and, with a rasping intake of breath, he drew in a gasp of clean air.

15

'It makes you think . . .' Rufus Ariel said smoothly. 'Who would have killed Owen Zeigler?'

Leon Williams fiddled with his cuff links, fingering the smooth gold orbs with his bony fingers, his eyes wary behind tinted glasses. He had been shaken by the murder, coming so close to home. His wasted figure, dressed in a pristine navy serge suit, twitched with restless energy, his bony hands clasping and unclasping, finally finding some rest tucked deep in his trousers pockets. Always a nervous eater, Leon had barely managed to keep anything down in the last week and his gut was now rumbling with acid.

Rufus stared at the area of blue serge which was emitting noises. 'Why don't you eat something?'

'I can't keep it down,' Leon replied, looking at his colleague with admiration.

He was impressed by Rufus Ariel's calmness. Everyone was talking about the murder, wondering if it had been personal. Or if it had been a botched robbery – and they might be next. No one left their galleries unattended for long, and every night a ribbon of alarm lights blinked nervously over Albemarle Street.

'My secretary left yesterday,' Leon went on. 'After all, we're only two doors away from the Zeigler Gallery. She said her husband was worried and didn't want her working in W1 any more . . . Are you listening, Rufus?'

Nodding, Rufus glanced up.

'Why would anyone want to kill a secretary, even a bad one?' he said. 'Everyone knows that gallery secretaries are the stupidest women in England, just filling in time before they marry some wanker from the Home Counties.'

Rufus had a long-term, personal dislike of the upper class girls who worked in the galleries. But although he had never stopped flirting with them, he'd never managed to seduce one. Perhaps they were not that stupid, after all.

'You know what I mean!' Leon replied tightly. 'Why would anyone want to kill Owen Zeigler? I heard he was gutted. Blood everywhere . . . I mean, it was odd how quickly he was buried, wasn't it? All such a rush.'

'His son had to organise it when he was in London. He doesn't live here, remember.'

'But I saw him yesterday—'

Suddenly alert, Rufus looked at Leon, his puffy face no longer bland, his fat hands clenched across his stomach.

'*Marshall Zeigler*? I heard he'd gone back to Amsterdam.'

'If he did, he didn't stay there. I tell you I saw him yesterday.' Leon's voice rose, as it always did when he thought he was being challenged. 'I know what he looks like! I tell you, I saw him. He was going into his father's gallery. It was pretty late.'

'What was he doing at the gallery? I thought it was cordoned off, the police said no one could go in.'

'Well, it was his home once, wasn't it?' Leon countered, feeling cornered. 'I suppose he thought no one would mind. Can't say I'd fancy it, going back to where you found your dead father. D'you think the police will catch him?'

'Who? Marshall Zeigler?'

'The man who killed his father!' Leon replied petulantly, taking a seat on one of the gilt chairs positioned perfectly under a still life. His thoughts were speeding up, his words blundering on. 'Or should I say *men*? They think it was more than one, don't they? Could be two, even three. Could be a gang of them,' Leon went on, his agitation increasing, stomach acid burning his gut. 'You hear about it all the time, these gangs roaming around with knives, guns even . . . I should get my alarm checked again, maybe change the locks. Why did they do it? Why would they do that to anyone? Why? I mean, it could have been *any* of us.' He stood up, pacing restlessly. 'Do you ever think about Stefan van der Helde?'

Shaken, Rufus gave Leon a cold look. 'Van der Helde? What made you mention him?'

Something in his tone made Leon flinch, and his voice faltered as he spoke. 'It was something one of the dealers was saying at the club. Van der Helde worked in New Bond Street a long while back, before he moved to Amsterdam, and when we were talking about Zeigler's death, someone remembered how Van der Helde was tortured and murdered. It was only last year. Surely you remember about the stones?' He paused, unnerved by Rufus's unreadable expression. 'They made him swallow stones before they killed him. And they disembowelled Owen Zeigler . . . Why would they torture two dealers if there wasn't a connection?'

'People get murdered all the time.'

'But both men were art dealers, and both were tortured . . .' Leon was beginning to wonder if he was saying too much – and to the wrong person. Rufus's expression was chilling. 'Oh Christ, I don't want to think about it.'

Just then a young woman came into the gallery and sat down at the front desk. After a few moments, she began typing on the computer, stopping to pick up the phone when it rang next to her.

Getting to his feet, Rufus pulled his waistcoat down over his extended belly and moved back to his office, beckoning for Leon to follow.

Rufus closed the door behind him. 'No point talking in front of the staff,' he said, easing himself into his chair. 'I don't want to lose my secretary too.'

Leon flinched. 'Has she asked you about the murder?'

'No, but then she knows Vicky Leighton who worked for Owen Zeigler, so no doubt she's heard all the gory details.'

Relieved that the conversation was benign again, Leon relaxed.

'What about Victoria Leighton? She'll be looking for a job now, won't she? Maybe she'd work for me—'

'Sort it out for yourself,' Rufus replied, cutting him off and returning to their previous conversation. 'About Stefan van der Helde—'

'I don't want to talk about it anymore.'

'I do.'

Cowed, Leon glanced down as Rufus continued. 'Did his killers steal anything from Van der Helde's gallery?'

'No. And the police never found out who did it. It could have been the same people who killed Owen.'

'Now, why would you say that, Leon?'

'Say what?'

'That it could be the same killers.'

He was sweating now. 'Well, it could be.'

'Why? What did Van der Helde and Zeigler have in common?'

Shifting in his seat, Leon stammered. 'They ... they knew each other.'

'How well?'

'I don't know how well!'

'Van der Helde was gay, Zeigler was straight,' Rufus replied thoughtfully. 'Zeigler dealt in Dutch art, Van der Helde dealt in Russian art—'

'Yes, but before that Van der Helde also dealt in Dutch paintings.'

Rufus's eyebrows lifted, his mouth tight. 'He did? I didn't know that.'

'My father told me. It was years ago. Van der Helde went into Russian art in the 1970s – before you opened your gallery . . .'

Piqued, Rufus Ariel let the barb pass. Few things rattled him, but he despised any reference to some of the more privileged backgrounds of some of the dealers. Their happy inheritances irked him; he had spent twenty years grafting before he even obtained a toehold on the London art scene. Lazier, more stupid men had come by their galleries by luck and birth, and Ariel had had to cajole and smarm his way into their ranks. And even when he had finally been accepted, any reference to his not having been born into the business pinched at his ego.

Knowing that he temporarily had the upper hand, Leon blundered on. 'Van der Helde dealt in Dutch interiors. He knew loads of dealers at that time. My father told me once that he discovered a Vermeer, but I think that was a rumour. People are always lying about their successes. Only the other day Tobar Manners was going on about—'

Rufus cut him off.

'So Van der Helde was an expert on Dutch art and he knew Owen Zeigler.'

'Yes.'

'That's it?' Rufus sneered. 'That's all they had in common?'

Leon looked pained. 'They were both murdered—'

'I meant, was that *all* they had in common when they were alive?'

'I don't know!' Leon replied, his voice rising again. 'Why are you interrogating me, Rufus? I was just thinking aloud, thinking it was odd that two dealers were brutally murdered.

I'm not implying anything else, I don't *know* anything else! I don't *want* to know anything else. It might not be wise.'

'For whom?'

'For us! For all of us!'

'Jesus,' Rufus said cruelly, 'you *are* a coward.'

'I am, yes. I don't pretend otherwise. I'm not a brave man, never have been, but I liked my life until recently. I had it good, we *all* had it good round here, but everything's changed. People you thought would be there for life are leaving, businesses closing, marriages are breaking up. You walk around this place at night and it's like a ghost town. I thought depressions happened up North, in those bloody mill towns, not down here, not in the art market. It's not *supposed* to happen here.'

Delighted to have rattled Leon so thoroughly, Rufus assumed a sympathetic expression. He might not have been one of the chosen few on his arrival in Albemarle Street, but the naive dealers weren't going to be able to handle the hard times as well as he was. Now was the time when it paid to be streetwise.

'It's bad enough wondering if you can keep your business going,' went on Leon, 'but now to have to worry about being killed; worry about every person you let into your gallery; wonder about who's walking in and what they might do . . .' He shuddered. 'You know what I think?'

Rufus shook his head.

'That the bloody country's ruined, and no gives a shit! I ask you, what the fuck is going on?'

164

Rufus's expression was inscrutable. If he knew something, he certainly wasn't going to pass the knowledge on.

16

After the first shot of whisky, Teddy Jack felt his body begin to relax. His muscles started to loosen and the panic in his chest had subsided when Marshall offered him another drink. Which he accepted. The glass felt cool between his sweating hands, but Teddy's head still hummed with the silence of the enclosed box and his nose was still filled with the scent of wood shavings – and of his own sweat and urine. With Marshall's help, he had got out of the crate, then turned and smashed his foot down through the lid, his heart pumping, his eyes watering. *Watering*, yes. Not crying, no. Not crying to have been rescued from suffocation.

Shrugging off any further help, Teddy had gone with Marshall to the flat above, a place he had often visited in the evenings when he and Owen would talk – sometimes about business, sometimes work, sometimes even women . . . But not now. Now Teddy sat and nursed his second drink, staring at the man who was sitting opposite him. Marshall Zeigler, Owen's son. Marshall, who had got him out of the crate.

'How are you feeling now?' Marshall asked.

He looked down at his trousers, mortified. 'Jesus, I wet myself . . .'

Marshall said nothing.

'I didn't have much longer to go, you know,' Teddy went on, coughing, his bass voice hoarse. 'How d'you know I was there?'

'I didn't. It was just luck that I came back to the gallery.' He stared at the big man. 'You know my father always spoke well of you.'

Teddy's head bowed, the whisky taking effect. In his head he could hear silence under Marshall's words and even in the light he could still imagine the stifling darkness. Jesus, he thought, Jesus . . .

'Who did it?' Marshall asked finally.

'I don't know.'

'All right, *why* would someone do that to you?'

'Why would someone murder your father?'

Marshall paused, wondering how much he dared say. Teddy Jack had been his father's confidant, after all . . . Surely he could trust this man? This man who would have been killed without his intervention. Surely he had no reason to suspect Teddy Jack?

But he couldn't be sure.

'I don't know why my father was killed. Do you?'

Teddy's hazel eyes blinked under their pale lashes, but when he looked back to Marshall his gaze was steady.

'No.'

'Maybe my father had something they wanted?' Marshall asked, feeling his way, trying to test out what Teddy Jack knew.

'Maybe he did.'

'But you don't know what?'

'Should I?'

Patiently, Marshall took in a breath. 'We're on the same side, you know.'

Expressionless, Teddy studied the man in front of him. Marshall Zeigler was nothing like his father in appearance, but in manner there was a similarity. A linking of blood.

'Which side is that?'

'The right side. Think about it. If you were in any way responsible for my father's death, you wouldn't have been left to die in that box. And if I was any way responsible, I wouldn't have got you out.' Marshall paused, impressively composed. 'Now – what do you know?'

Shaking his head, Teddy Jack glanced away, trying to order his thoughts. Wouldn't Owen Zeigler have wanted him to keep his son safe by keeping him in ignorance? He thought so, but then again, they had had no time to discuss tactics. No time to plan . . . Taking in a breath, Teddy finished off his drink.

'I don't know anything about your father's death.'

'I don't believe that. My father confided in you, didn't he?'

'Sometimes.'

'So you must know why he was killed—'

'It was a robbery.'

'Did they get what they wanted?'

'I don't know what they wanted.'

'The Rembrandt letters.'

Shocked, Teddy looked directly at him. 'You *know* about them!'

'Yes.'

'After your father was killed, I looked for them but I didn't find them,' Teddy admitted. 'I was looking when I was jumped. I never got the chance to have a proper search. The letters are either still hidden somewhere here, or they've been stolen.'

It was Marshall's turn to pause.

'Did you read them?'

'No.'

'But you know what was in them?'

'Your father told me,' Teddy replied, adding hastily, 'Look, Marshall, I've told no one. Not in all the time I've known about them. I've never let one word slip. Never have, never will, even now.' He paused, thinking of the suffocating darkness of the box, his mouth drying. 'Don't ask me anything else about the Rembrandt letters. The less you know, the better. Stay out of it. You were never involved in your father's world, so don't start now. I don't understand what it's all about, but I'll find out.' He smiled curtly. 'Thanks for doing what you did, for saving my life, but you should get away now, Marshall. Go back to Holland, forget what you've found out and put all this behind you. It's what your father would have wanted.'

'Somehow I doubt that.'

'Why?'

'Because he sent me the Rembrandt letters,' Marshall said, his tone resigned. 'I have them. There's no way I can get out of this now.'

17

Breaking his long-held rule, when Teddy returned to his flat in Beak Street he invited one of the working girls in. Pleased, she accepted, rubbing her hands in the chill of the evening air, her face waxy, hollows under her eyes, her hair tucked behind her ears. In a short skirt and denim jacket she stood with her knees knocking as she leant towards Teddy's gas fire, a worn red friendship ribbon round her bony wrist, one of her earrings missing.

'Cold, hey?' she said.

He nodded, moving into the bedroom to change his trousers. But before he had time, she had followed him in, pushing him back onto the bed, his trousers round his ankles. Being so close to her, Teddy could see the sweat on her top lip and guessed that she had recently had a fix.

'Hey, just a minute!'

She grinned, holding onto him, her arms wrapped around his neck, her body curled against his. 'I've been waiting for an invitation for a long time, Teddy. The girls said you never had anyone up here, but I knew you'd ask me one day.' Her voice held a peculiar and misplaced triumph.

'What's your name?'

'Shelly.'

'Pretty name.'

'My mother said I was named after someone famous.'

'Yeah,' Teddy agreed, nuzzling the top of her head. 'He wrote poetry.'

'Is that right?' she asked, impressed. 'Imagine that! A poet!'

'Love poetry.'

She wriggled against him, satisfied by the thought, reading some romance into it.

From outside the window came the muffled sounds of Soho, a cab horn sounding, a shop's alarm going off in another street. The doorbell from the chemist below chimed in, out, in, out, shadows floating across the ceiling as Teddy stared upwards and put his arm around the girl's bony shoulder. He felt an unaccustomed affection for her, a need for closeness, for comfort. And yet even though he had invited her in for sex, he felt his intention shifting.

'You're around a lot of the time, Shelly.'

'Yeah,' she agreed. 'Busy this time of night. We all like you, you know.'

Surprised, he glanced at her. 'What?'

'All the girls. We think you're a great guy. One of the older women said you'd sorted someone out for her. You didn't have to do that, she said, but she was pleased. Anyone could see that. Mind you, that was a while ago.' She snuggled against his bare legs, her knees resting against his. 'You work at some art gallery, don't you?'

'Yeah.'

'So why live here?'

'I like it here.'

She laughed, making a face. 'If I had a good job I'd live somewhere nice. Not here. I wonder how you can sleep at night with all the noise.' She yawned; the room was warming up. 'You want to have sex now?'

'No,' he said simply, tightening his arm around her.

'You're not shy?'

'No.'

'Are you married?'

'I was. Once.'

'Kids?'

'No. You?'

'One, a boy. My mother looks after him.' She picked at something in the corner of her eye. 'I tell her that when I'm off the drugs I'll come for him. You know, get a little place, out of London. Be like a family. Maybe meet someone. Someone all right . . .' She paused, surprised to find that Teddy had taken hold of her hand and was holding it gently. 'Can't get on with those rehab programmes. I tried twice, but it didn't feel right. You know? You know what I mean? Like they were going to make me into someone I'm not. Oh, I know what I am is pretty skanky, but I *know* it. Feels all right. Being all clean and clear, what's that about? You can't go back, can't never have been an addict or a working girl. You can never go back . . .'

She moved her other hand towards his thigh, Teddy sighing. 'I'm good at this, why don't you let me? No charge, honest. And it's not a mercy fuck.'

He stared at her, bewildered. 'A what?'

'You know, when you feel sorry for someone. But I don't feel sorry for you, I like you. It'll be a pleasure, honest. It'll be a pleasure.'

Her mouth moved over Teddy's, her tongue finding his, and he responded, holding onto her, rolling over so that she was under him. Pulling up her skirt, he entered her and began to thrust. But as he did so, his excitement suddenly faded and the room shrank. He felt suffocated as his breathing speeded up, until he fell back onto the bed, gasping.

Startled, she stared at his face.

'You all right? You sick?' she asked, sliding off the bed and getting him a drink of water. 'Here, luv, drink this. Go on, have a little sip.'

Tenderly she held it for him. And, as he sipped at it, tears rolled down his face like those of a child.

Tobar Manners clicked off the phone in his study. On the desk in front of him lay the Sotheby's catalogue, together with an invitation to a private view at the Fine Art Society and a note from Rufus Ariel inviting him to dinner at the weekend. Tobar wondered why Ariel would suddenly be

so sociable: dining at Le Gavroche? How extravagant ...
They had known each other for years, but Ariel had made
no secret of the fact that he suspected Tobar's hand in
the Rembrandt scam, and for the past two weeks they had
not exchanged so much as a nod.

Wondering fleetingly who else was invited, Tobar
thought of phoning Rufus Ariel, but resisted. No point in
looking too interested; the dealers were all jittery at the
moment, after Owen Zeigler's murder, yet Ariel wasn't
the jumpy type. Too smart, the fat bastard, too smart by
half. Tobar thought of Rufus, of his podgy hands, of his
white hair framing the smooth, plump face. Fat as a spoilt
baby, Rufus had limited his Old Masters and bought into
the Brit Art market, making enough money in the Eighties
and Nineties to expand his gallery and indulge his culi-
nary greed. But where Rufus Ariel had been really clever
was in spotting the *end* of the Brit Art boom. Cutting back,
he began to court dead painters, advising his customers
to buy into eighteenth-century French art. So when the
crunch came, his backside – always amply cushioned –
was covered again.

It was obvious to everyone that Rufus Ariel was astute
and adept at the long game, but his arrogance had made
him enemies. He could never resist accusing others of stupidity. The secretaries were stupid, the dealers, the customers, all were stupid. But he had one weakness – his
vanity. Rufus Ariel knew he was not a good looking man.
He also knew that a rich man might be forgiven a great
deal, but women seldom fell for a fat man who made

clumsy advances. Because he paid well, he kept his staff, giving the secretaries and the receptionist enough perks to endure the hand on the lower back, or the imbecilic tweaking of a bra strap. He might call them all darling and bring back cakes from Patisserie Valerie, but he despised them for despising him. Everyone hoped that it was just a matter of time before Rufus Ariel hit the buffers. It might not be the recession which downed him, but a claim for sexual harassment brought by some wily upper-class girl he hadn't been able to pay off.

Tobar tapped his front teeth with his finger nail. Maybe Rufus Ariel wanted to talk business. A deal, perhaps? Still pondering, Tobar looked around him. He liked this room, liked the thick beige carpet, the rich, embossed wallpaper, the drapes from Colefax and Fowler. When he had called the interior designer in, he had told her, 'Make it look like an English country drawing room; one owned by a lottery winner.'

He was paying the woman enough to comply. Cleverly, she had blended faded English elegance with the brashness of the naked bronze figures which flanked Tobar Manners' desk, and with the showy mirror behind him, which had had to be screwed to the wall for support. Complete with intertwining snakes and sinuous, gilded reeds, the mirror was topped with a coronet, a smirking nod to the fact that Tobar – although self-made – was married to a member of the Venetian aristocracy.

But at that moment Tobar Manners wasn't thinking about the recession or his absent wife; his whole attention was focused on a rumour he had just heard about two Rembrandts which were apparently coming onto the market for sale in New York. Was that what Rufus Ariel wanted to talk about? Tobar sensed an opportunity presenting itself. Apparently they were portraits of a Dutch merchant and, the companion piece, his wife. Two Rembrandts for sale in New York? How fucking convenient was *that*, he thought cynically. Two Rembrandts being sold by a private collector in a recession. Two Rembrandts which had never come onto the market before.

Of course, it could be merely a rumour, he thought, making a note to ring the collector as soon as possible. He had brokered for the Japanese man before, so why hadn't he been approached this time? And why was the sale in New York rather than London?

'Excuse me, sir . . .' His thoughts interrupted, Tobar looked up to see his secretary standing by his desk. 'Mr Langley wants a word with you.'

'I'm sure he does.'

'Shall I put him through?'

'Did I say that?' Manners replied, his tone biting. 'Did I say – put him through?'

'No, sir,' she replied, a composed woman in a light suit, her expression unreadable.

She had worked for Tobar Manners for nearly two decades and was immune to his rudeness. Loathing him, she told her husband, was just a perk of the job. Manners was too careful to let her see too much, but she had overheard many innuendos about his dealings, and had had to put off a number of dissatisfied clients. When paintings were sold as one artist and then discovered to be by another, lesser, painter, Tobar Manners always affected an injured stance. Good Lord, of course he hadn't known. What would it do for his reputation? Would he have honestly risked his good name selling something he did not believe to be genuine?

In the 1980s there was gossip that he had been involved in trading forgeries; then he was suspected of stomping up the bidding on a Flinck, but it was never proven and Manners had his lawyer on speed dial.

'You don't put Mr Langley through to me. You don't *ever* put Mr Langley through.'

'Shall I tell him you're out?'

'Tell him I'm fucking water skiing, for all I care.'

Nodding, she turned to go, then turned back to him. 'Mr Langley said that unless you took his call he would feel obliged to visit you.'

'And when he does, I'll be fucking out,' Manners replied, staring at his secretary. 'Have you changed your hair?'

'Yes, sir.'

'Looks good.'

Fuck you, sir, she thought, smiling sweetly as she walked out.

He had overreacted, Samuel thought, angered by his own nervousness. It had been two weeks since Owen Zeigler had been killed and there had been no more instances of burglaries or murders in the capital. Taking off his reading glasses, Samuel heard the sound of his housekeeper walking past the study door. He waited, counted to five, then smiled as she knocked.

'What would you like for your dinner this evening?' Mrs McKendrick asked, walking in and keeping her head facing forward, as though to see the mounds of books and clutter would unnerve her. 'I thought chicken might be nice.'

'Would be lovely,' Samuel replied, glancing up at her and making a mental note to leave her some little inheritance. She had been a loyal employee, and even if her cooking was erratic, she was willing. 'My solicitor is coming to see me at three o'clock tomorrow, I wanted to give you some warning. Perhaps we could have some tea?'

'I'll see to it,' Mrs McKendrick replied, pleased at the chance to bake and garner the usual compliments. 'Will he be staying for dinner?'

'No, not that long. Just afternoon tea.'

'Perhaps scones?'

'Good.'

'Or a Battenberg?'

'Or both?'

She smiled, the answer was the right one.

'The newspaper, sir,' she said, passing it over to Samuel and pointing to the front page. 'Gets worse everyday. Unemployment rising again. I voted Labour, but now I wonder . . . There's two families in the village selling up and going, can't pay their mortgages. Both men been working at the local garage and laid off.' She looked at

Samuel, as though daring him to contradict her. 'It's the kids I feel for the most. Fancy being moved from your home *and* school friends. It's not right.'

Pausing, she realised that Samuel wasn't going to respond and turned away, opening the window half an inch to freshen the room. She knew about her employer's reputation in the art world. The articles in *The Times*, the *Observer* and the foreign papers had all caught her eye, but she had never read them. As she said to her husband, art wasn't her thing. Art was for the toffs. Art was what people talked about when they wanted to sound cultured. Art was a joke to the common man.

Turning back from the window, Mrs McKendrick looked at her employer. 'About four o'clock be all right for your tea, sir?'

Samuel nodded. 'That would be excellent, thank you, Mrs McKendrick.'

Nodding, she left the room. Oh no, Mrs McKendrick thought, her employer was a kind man, and generous, but he had no idea of the realities of life. No idea at all.

18

New York

Charlotte Gorday returned to New York alone. Dreading the long flight, she sat in first class and stared out of the window until it was dark, and then pulled down the blind. She hoped the engine's incessant murmuring might help her sleep, but sleep proved impossible. Her food remained untouched. Trying to engage her mind, she glanced at the magazines she had bought, then spotted an article that would be sure to interest Owen ... But Owen was dead and, remembering this, Charlotte found herself shaking uncontrollably. Embarrassed, she pressed herself against the window, but she was trembling so much she couldn't control, or disguise, it.

'Are you all right?'

Charlotte looked up into the air hostess's face. 'Yes, fine. Thank you ...'

'Are you a nervous flier?'

No, she wanted to say. No, no, no. Go away. I'm shaking because I'm in shock; I'm shaking because I've just left my dead lover behind. I'm shaking because it's natural, normal. And if you knew what I felt, you'd shake until your teeth rattled.

But she only said, simply, 'I've just lost somebody . . .'

I've just lost somebody. Not misplaced them. Not forgotten where I put them, but lost them. How careless was that? How little interest did that show?

'I'd been in love with him for eighteen years,' she went on numbly, feeling the air hostess's hand on her shoulder. And then Charlotte pulled herself together. She certainly wasn't about to fall apart on a plane, in public. That wasn't her style. Her sense of decorum made her straighten herself up. Controlled elegance helped her to stop shaking. There would be a time to let go – but not now, not here.

'I'll be all right,' she said calmly. 'Perhaps I should have a little something to eat after all.'

When Charlotte finally arrived at the Manhattan apartment she shared with her husband, Philip, she was surprised to find him at home, waiting for her. In fact, he had cried off a previous dinner engagement.

'Don't change your plans for me, Philip.'

'No problem,' he assured her. 'I'd have picked you up from the airport if you'd told me which flight you were coming in on.'

'I should have rung you. Thoughtless, wasn't I?' Charlotte said numbly.

But her husband sat down on the window seat without replying. Several photographs, and a contemporary portrait

182

of Charlotte, stamped her joint ownership on the apartment, but in reality the place lacked her spirit and was mostly her husband's abode. Newspapers and business books were piled around the room; Philip's mobile phone lay next to his lap top; an open cigar box had been left on another chair, and his reading glasses stared at her quizzically from the mantelpiece.

'It was terrible news about Owen Zeigler,' Philip began, glancing at his wife. 'I'm so sorry, Charlotte. I want you to know that.'

She turned to him, her expression unravelling, her vulnerability obvious.

'Thank you . . . thank you.'

'Is there anything I can do?'

'No,' she said after a pause.

'I know you loved him,' Philip went on, a reasonable man who loved his wife, but loved others too. A man who had made no secret of his tendencies, and in Charlotte had found a woman who had also been committed elsewhere. 'We could go on holiday somewhere . . .'

She nodded absentmindedly.

' . . . a change of scene might help you,' he went on, getting up and walking over to her. They had not made love for many years and he found it awkward to be close to her. Nevertheless, he sat down on the sofa and put his arm around her shoulders. He could smell her perfume, gone stale from long hours of travelling, and noticed the puffiness around her eyes. 'I liked Owen Zeigler,' he said.

'I loved him.'

'You know, sometimes I thought you'd leave me for him,' Philip said, Charlotte leaning her head against his shoulder. 'Stay in London, move in with him permanently. I thought I'd lose.'

'I never thought I would,' she said honestly, taking her husband's hand and looking at the wedding ring on his third finger. 'I don't know what to do now, Philip. How to live. I don't know if it was all worthwhile, now that I've lost him . . . I should be grateful for you, Philip, grateful that you're still here, and I am. But . . .' she gazed at him, lost. 'Why don't I know what to do?'

'No one knows what to do at a time like this.'

'Maybe we should have had children.'

'We never wanted them.'

'No,' she agreed. 'It wouldn't have been fair on them.'

'Or us.'

'Or us,' she echoed, then asked, 'Was *I* fair on you, Philip?'

He took a breath, looking into her face, did not know how to answer her.

'Maybe I wasn't fair on you,' he admitted slowly. 'I always had other women.'

'I only ever had Owen. I never wanted any other man.'

'I didn't know that.'

'I would have told you, if you'd asked.' She paused, her voice dipping. 'Owen was murdered, you know?'

'Yes, I read about it. Do they have any idea who did it?'

She shook her head. 'No.'

'Do they know why he was killed?'

184

'They say it was a robbery that went wrong.'

'It happens.'

'No, it doesn't. Not like that, Philip. They left the paintings, all the valuable objects they could have taken. Why would they leave them?'

'I suppose they were disturbed.'

'They were looking for something.'

'What?'

'I don't know, *I don't know!*' she said. 'I keep imagining what Owen must have suffered. How he looked, what he was thinking. I keep wondering why I wasn't there . . .'

'Thank God you weren't.'

'I'd gone to the country to visit some friends,' Charlotte went on. 'I *never* usually did that. I'd spoken to Owen on the mobile earlier that night and he was worried, I could hear it in his voice. I rang him later to say goodnight and he was surprised because it was so early, until I explained that there was going to be a dinner party and it might finish late. He was always a bad sleeper; he would take pills and then he was out cold for hours. I should have called him when I went to bed, but I didn't. Then my phone went in the early morning and I picked it up without looking at the number and I said 'hello, darling, did you sleep,' but it wasn't him. It was the police . . .'

Philip held her tightly, burying his face in her hair.

'I *should* have called him when I went to bed,' Charlotte said again. 'He might have answered the phone, and it might have stopped him going down into the basement.

He might still be alive if I'd called. I could have saved him!'

'No,' Philip said firmly. 'It wasn't down to you to save him. His death had nothing to do with you, or what you didn't do, or could have done.'

'How do I live without him?'

'You've still got me,' Philip answered, knowing that he would never be enough.

She wept quietly, hardly making a sound, Philip holding onto her and looking at her portrait hanging over the mantelpiece. It was Owen who had organised the sittings with a celebrated artist he knew, and Philip had agreed to it. And over the years, he had grown to like his wife's lover; not that he *knew* Owen, but he approved of his behaviour. And Philip could enjoy his affairs, feeling less guilty knowing that his wife had someone. He never suffered the misery of jealousy when she wore an outfit or a piece of jewellery he did not recognise. Phone calls and letters that came to the Park Avenue apartment didn't disturb him; he saw them, instead, as another indication of how remarkable Charlotte was. She had inspired love in two men, constant, unwavering attention – which was something Philip had never managed. Aside from his wife, no woman had loved him enough, which was why Philip Gorday felt it was only right that he support Charlotte while she grieved. Right that he didn't ignore her distress, or believe – selfishly – that it diluted her affection for him.

It was almost ten o'clock when Charlotte finally fell

asleep, Philip having given her a sleeping tablet. When he was sure he couldn't wake her, he lifted his wife off the sofa and took her into their bedroom. Gently he laid her on the bed and tucked the covers around her. She moved, troubled, murmuring under her breath, but she didn't wake.

House of Corrections,
Gouda, 1652

I've been ill, coughing up blood. A lot of the women do that here because the work's hard, it's always cold and the food isn't good. No fresh fish from the market, or new bread. No thick yellow cheese that you have to chew on your back teeth . . . An old friend came to see me yesterday. She brought some sweetmeats, smuggling them under her apron, cackling like an idiot when she was confronted. The guard thought she was just another mad old mare, and let her in . . . Women gamble with their looks. When you're young you can play a full hand, but when you're older the stakes get tougher, the face cards showing your age . . . I used to love cards, and skittles.

When I was a kid, when I was at home, my brother played with me in the back yard, with the skittles my father had made us. My mother was busy, a midwife, always coming home or leaving home, never seeming to stay long. She carried a bag with her which she made me promise never to look into. But I did. One day when I was six I saw the steel instruments and the tubing and snapped the bag closed, because I hoped I'd find a baby in it.

I had a baby once . . . Sshh . . . I'm back now, shuffling these papers. I had to stop writing for a while until it was safe again. Where was I? Oh yes, I had a baby when I was very young. Too young, they said, but it wasn't true. They took my baby away . . . Listen to me. They carried him off in the middle of the night whilst I slept and when I woke I felt the bed next to me and there was nothing. Not even a warm spot where his body had been . . . When I wouldn't stop crying, my father struck me. My brother locked my bedroom door and whispered that I was a whore and what else could our parents do?

My baby had been such a pretty baby. Too pretty for a boy.

One, two, three . . . there goes the guard. One, two, three. I can hear him pissing up against the outside wall . . . I was supposed to forget my baby. They'd called me names, so I acted them out. Promiscuous, that was the word. Promiscuous, the same word Rembrandt used all those years later in court. The word my brother and my neighbours used to back him up, to get me put away. I gave evidence, but I also argued. A coarse woman who was more than capable of lying and making trouble for a respectable man – or so they thought . . . Rembrandt looked at me in that courtroom as though he wanted me dead.

Putting me away would have to be enough.

I never thought he would have done that to me. Not even after I'd played my last face card and I reminded him of his son. Of Carel. I told him, that is your child. Your child . . . He pretended I was lying, but he knew. Remembered being that clumsy lout, groping a neighbour's girl . . . Remembered when he was nudged to remember. Then realised that under his roof was his old lover and his bastard son.

I thought the knowledge would protect me, but it sentenced me . . . Ssssh, here we go, here we go . . . The guard's feet, the *pissing . . . I can see out of the high window that sliver of the world they've left me with . . . I cut myself when I came here first. Rubbed my wrist against the iron bedstead where the metal had worn sharp. Went through the flesh, but not deep enough.*

I would like to have chosen my own death.

19

New York.

Coming in from the park, Philip Gorday unfastened the lead from the dog's collar and walked back into the apartment block. When he had gone out earlier, Charlotte was still deeply asleep, the pill he had given her working overtime. He suspected that it was the first time his wife had rested properly since Owen Zeigler's death, and he'd stayed out for over an hour, unwilling to disturb her.

The doorman looked up from his desk. 'Morning, Mr Gorday.'

'Morning.'

'No mail for you or your wife.' He paused, looking at the sturdy lawyer as he moved towards the elevator. 'How *is* your wife? She seemed very tired when I saw her yesterday.'

'She had a bad flight, I'm giving her a lie-in,' Philip replied. 'I'll tell her you asked after her.'

Entering the elevator, he pressed the button for the seventh floor, stroking his dog's head absent-mindedly.

Perhaps he should call their family doctor, get some sedatives prescribed to see Charlotte through the next few days. And then, maybe, they would take a trip. He could afford to take time off, even a month if she would agree to it. Thoughtful, Philip opened the apartment door, hushing the dog to be quiet and letting the animal into the kitchen. The drapes in the sitting room were still drawn, a light blinking on the answer phone. He played the message, wrote down a name and reset the machine. Going back into the kitchen, Philip put on some coffee and looked at the headlines in the *Times*, then checked his shares in the financial pages. The dog, tired from its walk, slumped beside the radiator, breathing rhythmically as Philip sat down to read.

He finished the paper and his second cup of coffee, put everything on the counter and went out into the passage. There was no sound from the bedroom, which meant that Charlotte was still sleeping. For a moment he wondered if he should simply leave her a note to explain that he had left for work, but thought better of it and moved to the door. As quietly as he could, Philip entered the darkened room, moving towards the windows to partially draw the drapes. But as he passed the bed he felt something brush against his leg and jumped, reaching down to feel his wife's hand.

'Charlotte? Charlotte!' he said urgently, snapping on the bedside light and then turning back to her.

She was lying across the bed, one arm over the side,

almost touching the carpet. Through the pale peach silk of her negligee, a large dark stain spread across her ribcage, a tear in the fine material dark with thickening blood. And in her right hand she was still holding the knife she had used to kill herself. The knife which had slid so accurately and so desperately into the vessels of her heart.

20

Having checked with the police that he could return –
and stay – at the gallery, Marshall took his case up into
the flat where he had lived as a boy. Oddly, he was not
afraid, because he felt both obliged and compelled to be
there. He was fully aware that some people, not least
Georgia, would be surprised, but as he moved into his old
room he felt a strangely comforted. He was back home.
That his father had been murdered in the basement below
did not prevent him from staying; neither did fear for his
own safety. The premises were alarmed, and Marshall had
realised that if he was going to be watched, he would be
watched anywhere. What point would there be in moving
to Amsterdam? Or New Zealand. Or France. He had the
Rembrandt letters, and if they knew that, and if they still
wanted them, nowhere would be safe. If he was under
threat, he would be under threat everywhere, so why not
stay in the place he called home?

   Or was it that he hoped to draw someone out? Marshall
would never have taken himself for a brave man, but he

was a good son. He had admired his father, and now felt the kind of guilt only offspring can feel on the unexpected death of a parent. Sighing, he unpacked his case, pulling open the drawers in the cabinet he had used as a child. Inside one was a newspaper, dated 1978, on top of which he now laid some clothes.

He was relieved that the original Rembrandt letters were in the Dutch bank, out of anyone's reach but his. Then he thought of the copies, secreted in his half completed translation of Dante, and decided that he would hide the copies after he had read them again. Marshall had always had a redoubtable memory, and he was relying on that ability to memorise the letters, detail for detail. When they were safely lodged inside his head, he would destroy the copies, leaving only the originals in Amsterdam.

He plugged in his mobile phone to charge it and noticed that he had missed two calls. He listened to the messages. One was from Teddy Jack:

I wanted to say thanks again. I don't know how much your father told you about me, but I was in jail, long time back, and I did some jobs for him . . . Watching people and the like. I just thought you might like to know, because I think you might need me.

Listening to the message again, Marshall found himself baffled. *I did some jobs for him. Watching people and the like . . .* Why would his father have hired an ex-convict to spy on people? For what reason? And *which* people? Not for the first time Marshall realised how little he knew of

Owen Zeigler. He had seen his father as a charming, urbane man in an elegant business. Cultivated, respected, respectable. But the other part of Owen Zeigler – the man he *didn't* know – had a former criminal as a confidant. That Owen Zeigler had debts, secrets, enemies, and a lover. And if Marshall was going to find out who had killed him he had, first and foremost, to find out who his father had really been.

Moving to the second message on his mobile, Marshall was surprised to hear the well modulated tones of Charlotte Gorday:

I rushed off without explaining what I needed to see you about. I thought I could return to New York and just go on as normal. But I now know I was wrong. Please return my call.

Glancing at his watch, Marshall decided that it was too late to phone and he would call Charlotte the following day. Then he thought better of it and entered her New York number, waiting for her to pick up. It rang out several times before it was answered, but not by Charlotte.

It was a man's voice, American, that said a curt 'Yes?'

Thrown by this, Marshall took a moment to answer. 'Is Charlotte there? Charlotte Gorday?'

'Who's this?'

'My name's Marshall, Marshall Zeigler.' He paused. 'Is she there?'

'Are you any relation to Owen Zeigler?'

'His son,' Marshall replied, feeling uneasy. 'Could I speak to Mrs Gorday now?'

'She's dead.'

'*What?*'

'My wife is dead,' Philip Gorday said, his voice flat. 'She committed suicide.'

No, Marshall thought, not suicide. No one left a phone message saying that they needed to talk urgently if they were about to end their life.

Cautious, he said, 'I'm so sorry.'

'She was depressed about your father's death. She couldn't handle it. I didn't realise how hard it had hit her . . .' Philip Gorday paused, surprised to be talking to the son of his wife's lover. Surprised to be talking at all. 'She stabbed herself.' He repeated the words, as though by repetition they would make more sense. 'Stabbed herself. Right in the heart . . . I would never have suspected that. An overdose, yes, but a knife? She was elegant, always perfectly turned out, stabbing seems too ugly for her.'

Uncertain of what to say, Marshall hesitated. 'I'm sorry, really sorry.'

'Did you know Charlotte?'

'I only met her once. She was—'

'Extraordinary.'

'Yes,' Marshall agreed, trying to keep the call going. 'Is there anything I can do?'

'You're like your father. He was always kind,' Philip replied, his voice trailing. 'It's all right, you know.'

'What is?'

'Charlotte killing herself. I wish she hadn't, but she

loved him very much, you see.' Philip faded on the other end. 'He won in the end.'

'How's that?'

'He got her. Your father – he took her with him. Even when he was dead, she loved him more than she loved me.' Philip took a slow breath. 'It was not his fault. I have only myself to blame, Mr Zeigler. I have only myself to blame.'

The call ended and Marshall listened to Charlotte's message again. And then again, memorised it before he wiped it. His father's lover had killed herself out of grief over Owen's death. It was feasible, believable, even likely, in a woman who had lost the man she most loved. People did react badly in grief. They behaved out of character, because they weren't really themselves at that time. Everyone knew that shock could change a person, made a good person vicious; a clever person dull; a well-groomed, elegant woman violent. No, Marshall thought, it wasn't right. He agreed with her husband; it was too much out of character.

The woman Marshall had met in Amsterdam had been poised. Deeply upset and troubled, but still with enough pride in herself to apply her make-up and perfume. Not out of vanity, but habit. A way of carrying on with normality, in order to *preserve* normality. Charlotte Gorday could have taken an overdose. Might, in a moment of blurred sanity, have thrown herself off the top of a building, making a graceful angel out of her dying fall. But drive a knife into herself? Risk mutilation? Butchery? Risk pain and failure? Not even on the strength of one short meeting did that seem like something Charlotte Gorday would have done.

Stabbed. Eviscerated. And then there were the stones in Stefan van der Helde's stomach. The stones no one had ever understood . . . Marshall stared ahead, his mind running over the facts. The first victim had been Stefan van der Helde, with the stones. The second, Owen Zeigler, disembowelled. The third, Charlotte Gorday, stabbed through the heart . . . *Was* it a suicide? Or had she been killed too? *Had Charlotte Gorday been murdered?* Marshall paused, asked himself why. Because of her closeness to his father, or because she might have known about the Rembrandt letters . . .?

'Jesus,' Marshall exclaimed aloud, and ran downstairs into the gallery, turning on the lights.

He could half remember something from his childhood, but the memory was faint and needed jolting back into focus. What *was* it, he thought, making for his father's office at the back. What was it he was trying to remember? Stones. Evisceration. Stabbing.

Looking round Owen's study, Marshall wrestled with his memory. He was suddenly a child again, bored with sitting still. Owen had been busy that weekend. They had been going to Thurstons, but his father had been detained by a customer who had come in to see him unexpectedly. As an hour had dragged on, Marshall had slid off his chair and gone to the window to look out, down into Albemarle Street.

It was winter then, dark coming early, the flat shaded behind him. Wait for me, Owen had told him, this is an important customer, just wait. Preoccupied, he hadn't noticed Marshall slipping out of the office and making for the flat upstairs, where he had opened the window and felt the chill of that December afternoon, snow promised before nightfall. Looking across the street to the offices opposite, he had stared at a group of typists working at their machines, noticing how one of them kept fiddling with her glasses. His attention had then moved to the street below, where the spindly shape of Timothy Parker-Ross was coming into view.

Leaning out, Marshall had called down to him.

''Lo there!'

Startled, the lanky Parker-Ross had looked up, waving a gangly arm.

Hearing footsteps coming upstairs, Marshall had then closed the window and hurried out, meeting his father on the landing.

'Are we going now?'

'Not yet,' Owen had replied, 'it's important, Marshall, you have to be more patient.'

He had been sulky, out of temper. If his mother had still been alive, she would have kept him company, but his mother was dead and the days seemed full of his father's business, and waiting. Always waiting. No cooking in the kitchen, no music playing from his mother's radio. No television even, because somehow when she died the sound and colour of everything had died too. Bereft, he had longed to leave London that day and go to the country where the house was still welcoming, still carrying something of his mother in its walls. But instead he had been told to wait, and keep waiting . . .

As he recalled the day, Marshall could feel the rage as clearly as he had then; feel the hot swell of temper that flushed his face as he had stood up to his father.

'Why do I have to stay here? Why? I hate the gallery—'

'The gallery pays for your schooling—'

'That's all you ever talk about! The gallery, the gallery! You and your customers and the bloody paintings!' He had struck out, childishly petulant. 'I hate pictures! I'll never work here, never! If I never saw another painting as long as I lived, I wouldn't care!'

Without warning, Owen had slapped him and Marshall, his eyes stinging, had fought not to cry. It had been the first and last time Owen ever hit his son, and when he spoke, his voice had been uncharacteristically hard.

'You've never been interested, have you? Never looked at a picture, not once.' He had paused, all anger gone, something much worse in its place – disappointment. Disappointment and resignation. 'I'm sorry, Marshall, I shouldn't have hit you, or expected you to be like me.' He had turned away, walking to the door. 'I won't be long, I promise. And then we'll go to Thurstons, all right? Maybe go fishing tomorrow, would you like that?'

Marshall had nodded, dumbly miserable. 'Thanks, Dad.'

'Yes, we'll go fishing,' Owen had concluded, walking out.

And Marshall had known in that fraction of a second that his future would never be in the art world. He had no passion for it. The thrill his father felt at proving a picture's provenance, of making a sale, had never interested him, no matter how exciting. Taken to auctions, Marshall had been a bored observer, unimpressed by the glamour and money, just smiling to please.

His thoughts went back to that winter day, reliving his father's disappointment. The matter was never referred to again, but it was accepted that Marshall would never follow his father's profession. The Zeigler Gallery might survive, but it would not be run by Owen's son, and all the triumphs of scholarship and dealing would peter out. In this manner, father and son had split. Until now. Now that Owen Zeigler was dead, Marshall was suddenly, indelibly, drawn back into the world he had so long avoided. *But he still couldn't recall what he was trying to remember . . .*

Exasperated, he looked around his father's office again. Examined the desk, the books, the photographs, the paintings on the wall. Nothing. Was it something to do with the photographs? No. The paintings? No. Marshall turned back to the shelves, to his father's books. It was something in the books, perhaps. Something Marshall had read, or been told, many years earlier when he would have been only half listening, that bored, truculent kid. He reached for the first volume on Vermeer and flicked through it, then put it down on the desk, none the wiser.

All right, Marshall said to himself practically, think about everything that's been going on. Consider what the facts were. Stefan van der Helde and his father had both read the Rembrandt letters. Charlotte Gorday had been his father's lover. She had told him that she knew everything about Owen, so *had* she known about the letters? Perhaps she had, but had not thought them important, not realised they were the reason for two men's deaths. And now her own.

Think, Marshall told himself, think . . . Once again he was back to being a child in this same room. But this time it was hot, stifling summer in the middle of London, and he was standing on a chair, reaching for a book on the top shelf. The memory came back with burning clarity. Marshall could see himself on the chair, reaching for the book, that beautiful, glossy volume with its gilt lettering on the spine. So big, so heavy. He had overheard his father say that it was magic, that the book held magic, and Marshall had to look, hadn't he? Had to see the magic for himself. So he had reached for the book but, when he pulled it off the shelf, it had been too heavy for him, and he had dropped it.

It had fallen onto the floor with a crash which had echoed around the building so loudly that Marshall was sure everyone in Albemarle Street would know what he had done. And what *had* he done? As though still looking through his child's eyes, Marshall stared in his mind's eye at the split book, its spine broken, the frail, aged paper damaged. And then the images came back to him, staring up at him hotly from the page: two colour plates, facing each other, one of a corpse with its stomach emptied, the other a close-up of the cadaver's head, the scalp split open.

'Oh, my God,' Marshall whispered and turned hurriedly back to the shelves. He pulled out one of his father's many books on Rembrandt. For the first time in twenty odd years he searched the reproductions, finally coming across the painting of *The Anatomy Lesson of Dr Joan Deyman*. The corpse had been disembowelled, the scalp split. Just as Owen's had been. Frantically Marshall turned the pages, pausing as he saw an image of a man being stoned. Underneath it read *The Stoning of St Stephen*. Stephen . . . Stefan . . . Stefan van der Helde had been forced to swallow stones . . .

His heart racing, Marshall kept turning the pages. Image after image passed, all painted by Rembrandt, and then Marshall paused for the third time at the painting of Lucretia. *The Suicide of Lucretia*, depicting a woman stabbing herself through the heart with a knife.

Marshall stared at the last image, then looked again at all three reproductions, one after the other. He could see suddenly what was happening. Someone was interpreting Rembrandt, copying his works, but not on canvas, in real life. The killer – the person searching for the Rembrandt letters – was reproducing deaths the Old Master had painted. He wasn't killing at random, he was killing in a very controlled, artistic manner. No doubt one which gave him some intellectual pleasure. A cultured killer, trying to find the letters, and, when he failed, mimicking the masterpieces with his victims' deaths.

Slumping into his father's chair, Marshall stared ahead. The deaths were connected – and they were all murders. Rightly or wrongly, Charlotte Gorday had been killed because of her association with Owen Zeigler. She hadn't killed herself, Marshall knew that now. Because the killer had spelt it out for him, reproducing Rembrandt's Lucretia. His hand shaking, Marshall pushed the book away from him. The reason for the deaths was obvious. The victims had all been involved with the Rembrandt letters. Systematically the killer was going to pick them off – until he found the letters, or destroyed them.

Troubled, Marshall wondered who else knew of the incriminating documents. Certainly Teddy Jack did. As did Samuel Hemmings and possibly Nicolai Kapinski. And he himself . . . Below him Marshall could hear the pipes banging as the central heating system began coming on as the temperature dropped. He thought of the copies he had made, and wondered if he should go to the police – knowing full well that he wouldn't. If he informed them, the Rembrandt letters would enter the public domain – the one thing his father would have avoided at all costs. With their revelations the art market would stagger globally and one of the world's greatest painters would be reviled.

But was keeping the letters secret worth further deaths? Marshall was very tempted to give them up. Go to the newspapers, get them published and expose Rembrandt's bastard. But if he did, how many businesses, collections and museums would suffer from the fallout? And more than that, if he told the police, the case would be taken over by them and he would be excluded, become just a relative of one of the victims. And Marshall wasn't going to allow that. He had chosen from childhood not to be involved in his father's world, but now a clammy guilt was nudging him and forcing his hand. Perhaps in life he had failed Owen Zeigler, but he wouldn't in death.

An unwelcome thought which had persisted for days came back to him. If he had been closer to his father, closer to his work, closer geographically, would Owen have confided in him? Told him of the problems which had eventually overwhelmed him? If Marshall hadn't made it so clear that he wanted nothing to do with the art world, would his father have turned to him? Samuel Hemmings was right, a parent shouldn't force a child into following in their footsteps, but Marshall had been stubbornly averse to Owen's profession.

Guilt, unnerving and potent, troubled him. He could hardly blame his father for keeping so much of his life a secret. After all, he had confided little himself. They *had* been closer for a while, when Marshall was married to Georgia, but when the marriage disintegrated and he moved to Amsterdam, their bond had weakened again. There had been affection between father and son, but little common ground. Owen might well have been proud of Marshall's work, his obvious and impressive cleverness, but he could no more be involved in his son's profession than Marshall could in his.

I owe you, Marshall thought suddenly. I owe you. Regret,

poignant and troubling, moved him, and in that instant he made a promise to himself: he would find his father's killer, and he would protect the Rembrandt letters, a memoir so valuable it had cost Owen Zeigler his life. After all, what was the option, Marshall asked himself. Destroy the letters? Never. They were of tremendous importance – *which was why someone was prepared to go to such lengths to get them*. The killer knew what they contained, what a hold he would have over the market if he used them to blackmail dealers.

Pay me to keep quiet and no one will know that the paintings you're selling aren't original Rembrandts . . .

With such knowledge and proof, the killer could gain a stranglehold and wield phenomenal power – but only if he got hold of the letters. He knew they existed; the one thing he didn't know was who had them.

Sitting in his father's chair, in his father's study, Marshall Zeigler felt the hairs rise on the back of his neck. Stefan van der Helde hadn't had the letters; Owen hadn't given them up; apparently Charlotte hadn't even seen them. But there were a handful of other people who knew about them. Teddy Jack, who had already been attacked. The crippled Samuel Hemmings, his father's mentor. Were they under threat? Were they innocent? Or were they somehow involved? Would they turn out to be victims, or predators? And perhaps there were others, people that Marshall didn't know about. Maybe Tobar Manners or Nicolai Kapinski . . .

The enormity of the situation struck him in that

moment, along with the realisation that he didn't know who he could trust anymore. Not only was he in danger, others were too. People that might be under threat simply because they knew him. Like Georgia. He had to warn her, Marshall thought hurriedly, and stay away from her. And he had to warn the others too ... He struggled to stay calm. Only one thing was certain: the killer wanted the Rembrandt letters. The letters he, Marshall Zeigler, now had.

Somewhere, on the street outside, or in his father's country house, walking down Piccadilly, or in an airport lounge, *somewhere*, someone was waiting for him. He could be the man in the queue next to him, or sitting in the opposite seat on the Underground. He could be a cab driver, a delivery man – anyone. And he was coming for him, Marshall. Maybe tonight, maybe tomorrow, maybe next week ...

Maybe it was someone he liked, knew, trusted.

Maybe, God forbid, someone he never expected.

BOOK THREE

House of Corrections,
Gouda, 1654

I have been here so long. Not writing because I was ill and couldn't put my thoughts down clearly. Couldn't put down any thoughts, because it all became a mêlée of times and dates ... But I am better now, and I have visitors. Neighbours from my old town, come to see me. Say they will talk to the authorities because I'm not well.

Am I dying?

Shame to be dying so young. Well, in my forties anyway. I dream of him. Of my son, our son ... I had been in Rembrandt's house for over a week before I saw him. Carel had been a pupil of Rembrandt's for nearly two years, along with his brother, Barent, but it was two weeks, fourteen days, before I caught the first sight of the child I had lost. I'd been cleaning copper when I heard his name called. I put down the pan and went to listen at the door. Someone was talking to Rembrandt, offering 100 guilders for him to take on a new pupil. Ferdinand Bol.

Rembrandt was listening, then turned to the young man next to him.

'What do you think, Carel?'

I heard the name and knew it – Carel Fabritius. The name they gave my son, Rembrandt's child ... Breathing fast, I stood on my tip toes, struggling to see through the high window in the kitchen which looked into the hallway. His shadow fell on the black and white tiles as he walked in and took off his hat, his hair thick and dusty from the road, nodding to Rembrandt as the visitor continued talking . . .

I bit my lip because I hadn't seen my son for eighteen years. Bit my lip because I wanted to cry out, but I didn't. Instead I bit down on my own flesh and felt the blood coat my tongue. I stayed on my tip toes and watched Rembrandt make a guttural sound as he looked at the prospective pupil . . . 100 guilders, he said . . . 100 guilders? The boy's good, very good, his companion answered. He'll be a credit to you . . . I'll be the judge of that, Rembrandt replied, winking at Carel, and then looking at the boy's hands . . . 100 guilders, I'll try him out. Has he been with another teacher? No, we came to you first . . . And Carel was standing straight-backed as the town hall flagpole, with his wide mouth and dark eyes. My son. Rembrandt's son.

He had my eyes . . .

All my family had told me was that my son had been given to a couple, the father an amateur painter. Strange that . . . No one suspected anything when Carel was made a pupil of Rembrandt's. He had talent from his father, they said. Yes, he did – but not his adoptive father . . . For days after that first sighting of Carel I waited for another, but it was only when Rembrandt called me to the studio to sit that I saw my son again. I was placed on the dais, in the old Roman chair Rembrandt always used for his sitters. He took my chin in his hands and jerked my head left and right, until he was pleased with the light. Then he told his pupils to draw me . . . Charcoal sticks scraped on the thick vellum paper, breaths blown to clear the sooty dust, fingers smearing the outlines to make shadows. Sometimes a huffing of disgust as the paper was turned over and the pupil began again.

I stole a look at my son and caught his eye. I waited. But he didn't know me and I had no right to be disappointed. I was the master's housekeeper, sometimes model. No more to him . . . I doubt he even saw me. I was just something to be copied . . . It wasn't a hot day, but Carel was soon flustered, red about the ears. Rembrandt came over and stared at his work and then, irritated, made changes. But I had seen his surprise, that flutter of envy . . . You didn't know it then, van Rijn, but you felt it. Here was a rival. Very young, crude, untutored, a lad with dusty hair. But a rival none the less . . .

When the day faded you told me to get down off the dais and light the candles, and I walked past the drawing my son had done of me and saw nothing of myself . . . That night I didn't sleep. I lay next to Rembrandt and heard the students moving about in the upper part of the house. Fancied I already knew Carel's footsteps above the others. I lay, dry- eyed with excitement that my son was near me. And near his father. Even if he knew neither of us. I lay, dry-eyed, and listened to Rembrandt's breathing.

Then I whispered Carel's name in his ear, so his soul would hear it and know who he was.

21

Nicolai Kapinski arrived at the gallery and rang the entrance bell three times before Marshall came down from the flat above. Nodding a welcome as he opened the door, Marshall watched the diminutive Pole enter. He was obviously disturbed, his tie loosened, the top button of his shirt undone, and moving his briefcase from under one arm to the other. Then back again. Taking off his glasses, Nicolai breathed in slowly, as though trying to compose himself. But the action didn't have any effect, and when he spoke his voice was rapid, intense.

'Did you stay here last night?'

'Yes.'

'Alone?'

'Why not?' Marshall asked. 'It was safe with the alarm on.'

'It wasn't safe for your father,' Nicolai said hurriedly, walking past him and making for the stairs. Surprised, Marshall followed the accountant to the top office. He watched as Nicolai took off his coat and sat down, then asked, 'Did you come in to work?'

'Of course.'

'But the gallery's closed.'

'You're here.'

'It's my home,' Marshall replied, noticing the nervous jittering of Nicolai's right leg. 'There's nothing for you to do.'

'I have a job!'

'Not at the moment,' Marshall said calmly. 'I don't know what's going to happen, what I'm going to do with the gallery, but for now, Mr Kapinski, the place is closed.'

Kapinski blinked slowly behind the thick glasses smeared with his fingerprints and his hands gripped the briefcase, leaving sweat marks on the leather.

Troubled, Marshall studied him. He knew of the Polish man's manic episodes, but had never been witness to one. He chose his next words carefully.

'Are you all right?'

'Fine.'

'I'm afraid there's nothing for you to do—'

'I can do the books.'

'Mr Kapinski—'

'*I can do the books!*' he snapped, his voice rising. Just as quickly, it fell again. 'I'm not ill, not this time. Don't worry, I'm fine . . . I just need to be here. I can help you, Mr Zeigler—'

'Marshall. Call me Marshall. Mr Zeigler was my father.'

He nodded. 'Nicolai.'

'Nicolai.'

'I can help you, Marshall,' he said again, his glasses catching the light as he looked over the rooftops. 'I know what happens here. I know about your father, and his business. I know things no one else knows.' His accent intensified, his hands still clutched his briefcase tightly to him as he glanced back to Marshall. 'I know more than you think.'

'About what?'

'Your father was a very worried man.'

'I know that. What was he worried about?'

'Money. Or the lack of it,' Nicolai said, standing up and putting the briefcase on his seat. Then, oddly, he sat down on it. A comical gesture veering on the tragic.

'Was that all? Just money?'

'He was going to lose the gallery.'

'I know, he told me,' Marshall admitted, watching Nicolai. 'Look, I wasn't going to do this for a while, but seeing as you're here we could take an inventory today, work out the value of our stock, and then sell it as best we can to pay back my father's creditors.'

'Who were they?'

Taken aback, Marshall stared at him. 'I don't know. Don't you?'

'No. Your father only confided in me at the end. I have some information, but not all of it by any stretch.' Nicolai jiggled his leg again, restless, agitated. 'I left a message for Teddy Jack to come here for a talk.'

'You did *what*?'

'I want to see him, talk to him. But I don't think he's coming.' Nicolai glanced at his watch. 'It's past nine now, he should have arrived.'

'And what if I *hadn't* been here?' Marshall asked, his tone sharp. 'How would you have got into the gallery then?'

'With my key.'

'You have a key?'

'Yes, so does Teddy Jack. And the porters.'

'So any of you could have got into the gallery at any time?'

'No. Only I know the code for the alarm.'

Suspicious, Marshall looked at the little man.

'If you knew how to turn off the alarm, and you have a key, why didn't you use it this morning? You didn't know I'd be here to answer the door, so why didn't you let yourself in?'

Nicolai blinked. 'Because my key was stolen a few days before your father was killed.'

'Did you tell him?'

'Of course! He wasn't worried, he said he would get another key cut.'

'He didn't think to change the locks?'

'He had no reason to.'

'He was murdered,' Marshall countered. 'He had reason.'

'He couldn't have known that. Your father didn't expect to die.'

'How d'you know that?'

'Because I knew him,' Nicolai replied. 'The last time I

217

spoke to your father he said he had an idea, a way to get out of trouble. He said he was going on a trip—'

'Where?'

'I don't know.'

'You didn't ask?'

'It wasn't my place to ask,' Nicolai replied, ill at ease. 'Why are you talking to me like this! I'm not your enemy. I cared for your father, I was with him from Monday to Friday, every week of God knows how many years. We became friends . . .' He paused, pushing his glasses on top of his balding head. 'Your father was closer to me than anyone – outside my own family. Did he ever tell you about my brother who went missing?'

Marshall nodded. 'Yes, he told me.'

'Did he tell you that he tried to find him, all these years later, when everyone else thought I was just crazy. But not your father. He set Teddy Jack on it.'

Stunned, Marshall stared at the agitated man. *Teddy Jack?*

'He did a lot for your father, and your father was a complicated man. He got involved in different circumstances, with different kinds of people. Sometimes he relied on Teddy Jack,' Nicolai said, jiggling his leg frenetically. 'He watched people, or tried to find out where they were. Like Luther. Teddy went over to Poland and investigated the disappearance of my brother. Found out some things no one had ever known before – that Luther had been abducted.'

'By whom?'

Nicolai shrugged. 'There was a paedophile in our village, but it wasn't him. Everyone thought it was, but Teddy Jack found evidence that Luther had been taken to a children's home in Warsaw. It happened back then, sometimes. Children from remote villages were kidnapped and passed on for adoption. I wondered if my father had organised it . . . they paid good money, you see. They paid well for a male child.'

'What else did Teddy Jack find out?'

'That Luther had gone to live with adopted parents called Levinska, but they left Poland and the trail ended.' Nicolai stopped jiggling his leg, his eyes now huge with distress. 'There was nothing more after that, nothing more to find.' Nicolai could see Marshall's amazement. 'You're surprised by all this, aren't you? But you didn't know your father like I did. All his kindnesses. He wanted to help. If he cared about you he wanted to help. So when I got my depressions he sent me round to his doctor on Harley Street, paid the bill. Paid all the bills for my treatment, even when I said he should take it out of my wages. He had money, he always said, more than enough . . .' Nicolai shifted his position on his seat. 'I would have done anything for your father . . . You should have got to know him more.'

'Yes,' Marshall admitted, sitting down beside the attic window. 'Every day I hear things about him, things I never knew. Like his involvement with Teddy Jack – and Charlotte Gorday.'

Instinct made him throw out the name, the little man's head shooting up. 'You know her?'

219

'Yes, I met her.'

'When?'

'A few days ago. Why?'

Restless, Nicolai took the briefcase from underneath him and hugged it to his chest. 'Your father didn't want you to know about her. He thought you wouldn't approve of their relationship. That's what he told me, anyway. She was very good for him, at first. Very kind, always considerate. She used to travel between New York and London, take your father away when he needed a break.'

'I'm glad he had her in his life—'

To Marshall's amazement, Nicolai laughed. It was a high pitched sound, bitter and unexpected.

'What did she say to you when you met?'

'She was very upset about my father's death.'

'What else?'

'She said that he had told her he was worried about business, but she was insistent that there was something else worrying him – but she didn't know what it was. She asked me a few times if I knew.' Marshall paused, watching the little man. He was leading Nicolai Kapinski on, trying to draw him out. 'I told her I didn't know anything other than that my father had money troubles.'

'What did she say then?'

'Nothing. She accepted it. That was the first and last time I saw her.' Marshall paused. 'D'you know she's dead?'

'Yes.'

Wrong-footed, Marshall stared at the accountant. 'She committed suicide.'

'That's what I heard.'

'Lost her mind because of grief over my father's death,' Marshall went on. 'I spoke to her husband – he was shattered, but he accepted it.'

'And what about you?'

'*Me*?' Marshall replied. 'Why would I doubt her suicide?'

'Because your father was murdered. Perhaps Charlotte Gorday was also murdered?'

Needled, Marshall stared at the little man. 'Why would she be killed?'

'For the same reason your father was.'

A draft of cold air drifted around them. It seemed to come up from the floor below, as though someone had walked into the gallery. Off balance, Marshall felt suddenly threatened. Not by the accountant, but by the palpable malice that was in the room. The abrupt shift into suspicion. Both men knew more than they were admitting, but each was waiting for the other to be the first to confide. Glancing towards the staircase, Marshall thought he heard footsteps, but when he looked back to Nicolai, he was composed.

'My father was killed because a robbery went wrong,' Marshall said, finally answering the accountant's question.

But the explanation didn't satisfy the little man. Instead he muttered under his breath and began to jiggle his left foot impatiently again. His short fingers rapped on the top of the oversized desk, a sheen of sweat appeared on his forehead. Still nursing his briefcase, his eyes became watery, his confusion intense.

'I kept many secrets for your father,' he said at last. 'It was my way of rewarding him for all he'd done for me. But now, now I wonder if you should have been told more, if I should tell you more. Would it be breaking my word . . .? This is very difficult for me, very hard. You see, your father kept all of us apart, without appearing to—'

'Who are you talking about?'

'Charlotte Gorday, Teddy Jack, and me,' Nicolai said. 'I know your father confided in Teddy sometimes. I know he must have confided in his lover, but he never made it clear. Left a little bit of suspicion between us – his way of making sure we would always be on our guard with each other.'

Frowning, Marshall stared at the accountant. 'I never realised he was so manipulative.'

'He wasn't – at first. It got worse in the last few years,' Nicolai explained. 'Then, in the last year, your father trusted none of us completely. He thought I didn't know why.'

'But you did?'

'Tell me the truth, Marshall – *do* you know why your father was killed?'

The question jangled in the stuffy air between them. When Marshall didn't answer, Nicolai sat down again, close to tears. Reaching for his handkerchief, he wiped his eyes and then put his glasses back on, the Adam's apple in his throat bobbing as though he was about to choke. And then he spoke again: 'He would have been all right if he hadn't found those letters.'

'What letters?'

The little man exploded, all control gone. 'Don't *lie* to me, Marshall! There's no time for this. You know what I'm talking about – the Rembrandt letters, the letters your father believed would make his reputation. The letters he guarded so assiduously. The letters which changed everything. As soon as they came into his life his luck altered.'

'How?'

'Owen couldn't resist letting a little information slip, and word got out, rumours about Owen Zeigler's theory. That stupid theory! His father – old Zeigler – had put the idea in Owen's head a long time ago, but when he left the Rembrandt letters to his son, it wasn't a theory anymore, it was fact. Before that, it had been just one more art theory, one more ludicrous hypothesis the dealers indulge in all the time. Their pet theories about their pet artists, always trying to prove a new artistic Eucharist. The art world everywhere – London, New York, Amsterdam – is populated with conjecture. But most theories are unproven.' He held Marshall's gaze. 'But when Owen inherited the letters he had *proof*.'

Marshall took in a breath. 'Did he tell anyone?'

'He told me. And I imagine that he told Samuel Hemmings. Hemmings was his mentor, after all, they'd talked about the Rembrandt theory for years, on and off. I suspect Teddy Jack knew as well, and I *know* for certain that Charlotte Gorday knew.' Nicolai glanced away from Marshall. 'She was lying to you.'

'What?'

'When she said she'd no idea what your father was worried about, she was lying. Testing you, trying to discover whether you knew about them. Trying to find out if you had them.' Nicolai paused, ill at ease, sweating. 'Did you tell her you had them?'

Marshall paused, seeing the trap. 'I never said I had them.'

'I posted them to you! I know you have them,' Nicolai replied, his voice rising, then falling into a monotone. 'After your father died, I mailed them to you in Amsterdam. I used an old envelope your father had addressed to you, but never sent, so you would be sure to open it. I didn't know what else to do. I didn't know what your father would have wanted. I just wanted to get them rid of them ... I'm sorry,' he said at last. 'I panicked. I hadn't the courage to burn them.'

Transfixed, Marshall stared at the frightened man. 'Before you sent them to me, did you read them?'

Exasperated Nicolai threw up his hands. 'How could I? I don't speak Dutch. But I knew *you* could read them.'

'What about Charlotte Gorday?'

'She spoke the language, as does Samuel Hemmings. He speaks and reads it fluently, as your father did. Probably better than your father did. I know what was in the letters only because your father told me. I imagine he told Teddy Jack too. After all, *he* couldn't read them.' Nicolai sat up in his seat, perched uneasily. 'You *can't* suspect me, Marshall! Not now. I had those letters in my hand, I could have kept them, used them. Not told anyone.

Think about it. If I'd wanted them, I had them. There was nothing to stop me from keeping them, but I sent them to you. Maybe it was the wrong thing to do, maybe I shouldn't have involved you – but you're Owen's son, and there was no one else I could trust.'

'What about Charlotte Gorday? She'd been in my father's life for eighteen years. She loved him. Why didn't you trust her?'

'Why?' Nicolai asked wearily.

'Yes. Why didn't you trust her?'

'Because she was blackmailing your father, that's why,' Nicolai replied, turning to the window and looking out onto the London skyline. 'And now she's dead.'

22

Before Marshall could respond to Nicolai Kapinski's revelations, he heard footsteps coming up the stairs and turned to see Teddy Jack walking into the office. He didn't seem surprised to see Marshall and nodded, glancing over to Nicolai. The difference between the two men was marked; the accountant small, nervy; Teddy Jack in a denim shirt and jeans, casual, relaxed. He seemed completely altered from the disturbed man Marshall had rescued; his physical size all the more impressive against the diminutive stature of the accountant.

'How are you?' Teddy asked Marshall. 'I was hoping to see you.'

'I'm good, thanks.'

Settling himself in one of the old armchairs, Teddy looked around him, seeming at ease as someone can be only when they know their surroundings well. For a moment Marshall was the one who felt out of place.

Waiting to hear what else Nicolai was going to tell him,

Marshall said, 'Well, go on Nicolai. What were you saying about Charlotte Gorday?'

'You know about her?' Teddy asked.

'Yes, and apparently you must have done too. You don't look at all surprised.'

'Your father wanted to be discreet—'

'For eighteen years? That's a lot of discretion.' Marshall leant on the desk and looked from one man to the other. He felt uncomfortably cornered, as though they were accomplices in something from which he had been deliberately excluded – and he was unexpectedly angered. His father's secrets seemed to be a link between the two men, and their complicity exacerbated Marshall's growing guilt. To find himself cut out of his own father's confidences had been hard – but he knew he had no right to expect otherwise. After all, they had not shared an intimate bond. But to find himself begging for crumbs of information was humiliating.

'Did anyone else know about her?'

Teddy shook his head. 'No. Only us.'

'But you heard what happened to her?'

'She's dead.'

It was a statement of fact, without emotion, and seemed chilling to Marshall. How did Teddy Jack know about Charlotte Gorday's death so quickly? And Nicolai?

'She committed suicide.'

Marshall could hear Nicolai clear his throat, and a look passed between him and Teddy Jack. After a moment, the big man shrugged. 'I don't think it was suicide.'

'You think she was killed?'

'We both think she was killed,' Teddy replied, glancing over to the accountant for confirmation.

'Because she was blackmailing my father?'

This time it was Teddy Jack's turn to look surprised. Leaning forward in his chair, he stared at Marshall.

'Who told you that?'

'Nicolai did. Just now.'

Slowly he turned to the accountant. He seemed almost hurt to have been excluded. 'Why was she blackmailing him?'

'I don't know—'

'Of course you know!' Teddy snorted. 'Unless you've just made it up – which wouldn't surprise me. You were always trying to make out that the boss preferred you, that he confided in you more than he confided in me.' He rubbed his big hands together sheepishly, moderating his tone. 'He would have told me if Charlotte Gorday was blackmailing him.'

But Nicolai wasn't going to back down. Instead he laid his hands flat on the desk in front of him, a smudge of triumph in his voice.

'I wondered if you knew. Sorry to spring it on you,' Nicolai said lightly.

'I don't believe it.'

'It's true.'

'But *why* would she blackmail him?'

Marshall studied Teddy Jack as Teddy waited for his answer. His eyes closed for an instant then opened again, fixing on Nicolai. 'I'm not playing fucking silly games.'

Nicolai coloured. 'Neither am I! The only person who played games is dead. Charlotte Gorday blackmailed Owen because of the letters.'

The words were out, Marshall watching the interplay between the two men.

'She'd known about the letters for a while,' Teddy countered. 'Why would she suddenly blackmail him now?'

'Charlotte Gorday wanted him to sell them and use the money to clear his debts,' Nicolai replied, his tone even. He seemed almost smug that he had been privy to the confidences of the dead man. 'She badgered him about it, said they could find a buyer, raise a fortune, but Owen wouldn't have any of it.'

'How d'you know this?' Marshall asked.

'I overheard an argument they had,' Nicolai replied. 'I'd known about the letters for months. I advised your father not to tell her about them – I thought it would be dangerous.'

Angered, Teddy Jack lashed out. '*He trusted her!*'

'And look where it got him!' Nicolai retorted. He turned back to Marshall. 'Charlotte loved your father, but she didn't understand what the business meant to him, what his reputation meant. Your father would *never* have exposed those letters – and never ever for money. He'd been looking for them for years; it was like a pilgrimage, the Holy Grail. He would have protected those letters with his life.'

'He did,' Marshall replied coldly.

'Yes . . . he did.' The emotion suddenly drained from Nicolai's voice. 'I think Charlotte believed that she had found someone to buy the letters. Maybe when Owen didn't agree to sell them she had to disappoint the buyer and go back on her word.'

'And was killed for it?' Marshall said.

'I don't know for sure. Maybe.'

Shaking his head, Teddy smiled knowingly. 'You've got it all wrong. Charlotte Gorday could have sold the letters any time she wanted to – because she had them.'

That certainly surprised Marshall who, out of the corner of his eye, saw Nicolai look over to him. Marshall had been hearing many things about his father's intricate relationships, but now, finally, he was seeing the results of Owen Zeigler's mendacity. His father had told everyone *part* of his story, never confiding fully in anyone, so that each person ended up with their own version of the truth. He thought back on Nicolai's earlier words: *Your father kept all of us apart, without appearing to – left a little bit of suspicion between us – his way of making sure we would always be on our guard with each other.*

Marshall stole a cautious glance at Nicolai. He could see he had been wrong-footed, and wondered which way he would jump; whether he would tell Teddy that the letters were now in Marshall's possession or stay silent and keep the knowledge to himself.

'So where are the letters now?'

Teddy's expression gave nothing away. 'Whoever killed Charlotte Gorday must have them.'

'And who killed her?' Nicolai asked him.

Teddy Jack didn't answer immediately. Marshall stared

at him, registering the huge hands, the thick shoulders, the muscled forearms. A powerful, dominant man. A man capable of violence, indeed once imprisoned for it. But murder? Marshall, less certain of that, recalled how he had found Teddy Jack almost suffocated in the packing case. Was it a real attempt on his life, or a set-up? Something he had organised to throw suspicion off himself?

'How would I know who killed Charlotte Gorday?' Teddy asked, staring at the accountant. 'You think *I* did?'

'I never said that, I—'

'Jesus, you fucking prat!' Teddy shouted. 'You pen-pushing, shiny-arsed bookkeeper. You think that you knew what went on in Owen Zeigler's life? You knew what he *wanted* you to know—'

'I knew more than you did!'

Teddy laughed. 'Owen didn't trust you, Nicolai. He told me that many times. He liked you, felt sorry for you, but he didn't trust you.' Teddy paused, deftly positioning the final blow. 'He thought you were crazy, did you know that? He used to send me to Poland to find that brother of yours, and sometimes laugh about it behind your back – *there's no brother*, he'd say. *Poor Nicolai, not right in the head. But we have to be seen to be doing the right thing.* He pitied you.'

His eyes bulging, Nicolai stared at the big man. Marshall stepped between them. 'Stop it. Let it drop.'

But Teddy Jack ignored him. 'He thought you were a good accountant though,' he continued. 'A creepy little shit, but good with the books—'

'Shut up!' Marshall shouted, as Nicolai looked away, clearly shaken, breathing heavily. He stared out over the rooftops, hardly moving, and Marshall expected him to turn back to Teddy Jack at any moment. To tell him he was wrong. That Charlotte Gorday didn't have the letters, that *he* had sent them to Marshall. He could feel the shudder of injury come from the Pole, but – to his impressed surprise – Nicolai kept his counsel.

'I have to go,' he said finally, getting to his feet. He picked up his briefcase and swiftly made for the stairs.

Marshall ran after him, finding Nicolai already out in the street when he caught up with him.

'Wait!' he called out, catching the little man's arm. He could see that Nicolai was close to tears, fighting emotion, desperate not to make a fool of himself. 'I don't believe my father said any of those things. I know he relied on you, Nicolai, and I know for certain he liked you.'

Dumbly, the Pole nodded

'Why didn't you tell Teddy Jack that I have the letters?'

'Because I wanted him to think the letters had been taken. Because I wanted to keep you safe,' Nicolai said finally, his voice wavering. 'You see, there's something you have to understand. It wasn't me your father didn't trust – it was Teddy Jack.'

23

Waking early, Samuel Hemmings reached for his glasses on the bedside table, put them on and watched the bedroom come back into focus. Outside the window, he could hear a blackbird, the spare branches of a winter tree just visible from where he lay. He seemed surprised at first that he had not been disturbed, then amused, pleased that no one could see his embarrassment. Slowly, Samuel sat up, struggling to move his legs over the side of the bed and get himself into his wheelchair. He still had some little use of his lower limbs, but preserved it as much as he could, preferring to be out of the wheelchair only when necessary – or when he needed to seem younger. People, he knew only too well, could be bigoted. Look, sound and act like an old man, and no one listened to you anymore.

And Samuel liked to be listened to. It tickled his vanity that people admired him; appealed to his personal ego that he could still command respect or incite an argument. Wheeling himself into the hall, he turned off the alarm, hardly believing how nervous he had been the previous night. But then that was what the dark did to everyone. When the light faded, no man was completely brave. At the front door, he unbolted the main locks, leaving only the Chubb on so that Mrs McKendrick could let herself in. Reaching into the wire letter tray, he took out the papers and two letters, wheeled himself into his study and shut the door behind him.

His gaze moved over to the dog bed and then back to his post. Nothing of any importance caught his attention, so he turned his thoughts to what had been occupying them the previous night – his solicitor's visit. Never before had he thought of making preparations for his death: his funeral, the partitioning of his assets. But since Owen's murder, Samuel had been determined to put his affairs in order as soon as possible, hence the visit from his solicitor that afternoon.

He had decided that he would leave the bulk of his estate to charity – half to The Art Fund, the other half to the local church and school. Now that his protégé was dead, his valuable book collection would go to the British Library and his few paintings to the local art gallery. After a lot of thought, Samuel had bequeathed several impressive pieces of silver to Marshall, as well as his old, and long unused, Austin car. He thought it would amuse him. As for Mrs McKendrick ... Samuel paused, mentally increasing the sum he had first decided on. After all, no one made a Battenberg cake like his housekeeper. He wondered fleetingly if his gift would be enough. After all, what *would* be recompense for her finding her employer's body? Either dead from natural causes, or murdered and, worse, mutilated.

Disturbed, Samuel tried to shake off his sudden melancholia. The previous night he had been anxious, but it was daytime now. He could see his surroundings and the first timorous stirrings of spring. And after spring, summer would come lush and laughing into the garden, warming the house and mottling the walls with sun . . . Two weeks had passed, Samuel told himself, over two weeks since Owen's murder. Perhaps it was over. Perhaps the whole terrifying business would simply end . . .

He opened a second letter and was reading it hurriedly when the phone rang next to him.

'Hello?'

'Samuel, it's Marshall.'

He took in a breath. 'How are you?'

'Fine, and you?'

'All right.'

'Did you know that my father had a girlfriend?'

'No!' Samuel replied, genuinely taken aback. 'Owen never said anything about a woman.'

'Her name was Charlotte Gorday. They knew each other for eighteen years.'

Taking off his glasses, Samuel rubbed his eyes, then wheeled himself over to the window. 'I didn't know anything about her. Does it matter?'

'She's dead. Committed suicide the day before yesterday.'

Down the lawn Samuel could see the gardener arrive and take the mower out of the shed. Ponderously the man then walked up and down the grass, cutting it close to the earth.

'She killed herself? Why?'

'Doesn't it seem odd?' Marshall pressed him. 'My father's girlfriend dying?'

'Should we be talking about this over the phone?'

Marshall laughed without humour. 'You think someone's listening?'

'I don't know, someone could be.'

A silence, then, 'I want you to move into a hotel,' Marshall said.

'Don't be stupid.'

'Samuel, listen to me—'

'Don't say you're worried about me, Marshall,' Samuel replied, acidly. 'Last time we spoke you seemed to think I was the devil incarnate. In fact, you even intimated that you didn't trust me.'

'I'm sorry, Samuel, really. It's been difficult.'

'For all of us.'

Marshall kept his voice even. He didn't want to frighten Samuel Hemmings, but he wanted to make sure that the historian was safe. And living alone, handicapped, in a remote house was inviting trouble. If Stefan van der Helde, Owen Zeigler and Charlotte Gorday – all able-bodied and fit – had been overpowered and killed, Samuel Hemmings would stand no chance at all.

'You have to go to a hotel.'

'No.'

'Samuel, please!'

'What about you, Marshall, are you going to hide in a hotel?'

'That's different—'

'Because you're able-bodied?'

'Yes,' Marshall admitted. 'And because I have no choice.'

'Since when?' Samuel countered. 'What's changed?'

'I need to find out who killed my father.'

'Forget it,' Samuel replied, trying to sound nonchalant. 'If you ask me, it's over. I think the killer has the letters.'

'No, he doesn't. I have them.'

Samuel could hear the mobile phone connection crackling and presumed that Marshall was on the move.

'*You* have them?'

'They were sent to me.'

'Where are you now?'

'In London. I'm coming down to see you,' Marshall replied. 'I just want to make sure you're safe—'

'Where are they? The letters?'

Marshall ignored the question. 'You *did* read them, didn't you?' he said.

Samuel glanced over to the dog bed, remembering the copies taped underneath.

'Yes, I read them. All but one. Apparently your father didn't trust me any more than you do, Marshall. I didn't say anything to Owen at the time, but the letters ended too abruptly. One, at least, was missing. I don't know how Geertje Dircx finished her testimony.'

Surprised, Marshall stopped walking. He was on the Embankment, opposite Cheyne Walk, looking out over the blank eye of the Thames. A chill was blowing, making scuffs on the water; a tug boat was passing yards away, churning up a baby tide.

'Who sent the letters to you, Marshall?'

'Does that matter?'

'All right, look at it another way – *why* did they send you the letters?'

Marshall stared into the dark water. 'Like you said, Samuel, I'm Owen's son. I suppose I was the natural person to send them to.'

'But you know nothing about the art world, or about Rembrandt. You would be easy to dupe.'

'Would you rather they'd been given to you?' Marshall parried. 'No, I don't think you would, not really, not now. My father died for those letters and I want to know who killed him. And I want to make sure that they don't get hold of the letters, because otherwise my father's death means nothing.'

'You don't know who you're up against.'

'Do you?'

'No,' Samuel said truthfully. 'I can't help you, but I can warn you, Marshall. You're out of your league. If you don't go to the police, you don't know what you'll bring down on your head.'

'We both know I'm not going to the police, Samuel,' he said coolly. 'Are you in your study?'

'Yes, why?'

'Get one of your books on Rembrandt.' He paused, waiting. 'Ready?'

Struggling, Samuel opened a volume on his desk, the phone tucked under his right ear.

'Now, look at the painting of *The Stoning of St Stephen*.' Marshall said. He could hear Samuel turning over the pages, then pausing. 'Stephen ... Stefan. Stefan van der Helde's stomach was full of stones ...'

There was a sharp intake of breath from the old man.

'Now, turn to *The Anatomy Lesson of Dr Joan Deyman* ...'

Samuel hurried, through the pages while Marshall waited, until the image was looking up at him. 'Yes, I see it ...' he said. His gaze moved over the picture, stared at the split scalp, the emptied-out belly of the corpse. 'Oh, Jesus, your father ...'

'Yes,' Marshall said softly. 'You see it. Now look at *The Death of Lucretia* – and remember what I told you. Charlotte Gorday stabbed herself. Or rather, she was stabbed. *Now* d'you see why I want you to get out of your house?'

Transfixed, Samuel stared at the images, looking from one to the other in shock.

'I have to see someone this afternoon, I have to keep an appointment—'

'You have to leave.'

'*I can't leave here!* This is my home, Marshall. I'm an old man in a wheelchair; if anyone wants to catch up with me they won't have to try very hard.' His humour was strained. 'I can't leave this place. This is all I have, no one's driving me out. Anyway, Mrs McKendrick's here. She'll be here until my lawyer leaves.'

'And tonight?'

'I can't change my life now. It's too late—'

'You might not have a life to change if you don't watch out,' Marshall said firmly. 'I'm coming down tonight.'

'What for?'

'I need you to help me with something.'

Puzzled, Samuel frowned. 'What can I help you with?'

'I'll tell you when I see you,' Marshall replied. 'You need to get someone in the house. Someone able-bodied, someone around after Mrs McKendrick leaves for the day. You can't be on your own at night.'

'I don't know anyone,' Samuel said stubbornly. 'I can't just ask someone to come here and babysit me—'

'Yes, you can. You're handicapped, it would be a perfectly normal thing to do.' Marshall replied. 'Or get a male nurse.'

'A nurse! I'm not having some bloody nurse around me, fussing and taking my pulse every half an hour.'

Patiently, Marshall took in a breath. 'All right, don't get a nurse – but get someone. There must be someone in the village you could pay to stay over. Get a man who looks capable of handling himself, there must be someone looking for a job.' He paused, his tone serious. 'Don't brush this off, Samuel. Three people have died already – don't be the fourth.'

Leaning against the counter of the village bakery, Doug McKendrick bit into the hot meat pie and winced as the gravy scalded his tongue. On a cold day there was nothing like a meat pie, he thought, wiping the gravy off his chin with the back of his hand. Hearing the door open, he turned, and nodded a greeting to his brother-in-law Greg Horner, the part-time driver for Samuel Hemmings.

Always critical, Greg looked at Doug sourly. 'Why don't you try to get some of that pie into your mouth?'

'Ah, stop moaning. That's what you need, a good meal,' Doug replied, taking another bite and refusing to acknowledge that his mouth was on fire. Ruddy-faced, he stared at Greg. Miserable sod, he thought, never a smile. 'What,' he said, after swallowing the mouthful, 'are you doing here today? The old man want you?'

'He does now.'

'It's Thursday, Mr Hemmings never wants you on a Thursday.'

'Get off the counter and talk outside,' the owner said, pushing Doug's elbow off the glass and pointing to the door. 'You're dripping gravy everywhere.'

Outside on the pavement, Doug took another bite of his pie, Greg nursing a cup of black coffee. It was well known in the village that Greg Horner had once had a business of his own, but had lost it. Something he could never get over. Working as a part-time handyman and chauffeur had made his already bitter nature curdle. When he looked at Samuel Hemmings he thought of all his ambitious plans which he had been certain would bear fruit. He would be successful, that much had always been obvious to Greg. But not to anyone else, and he took his failure as a mark of his bad luck, rather than of his own doing. His natural surliness had not encourage custom at his garage, and as the business faltered and his wife started an affair with the landlord of the Crown, Greg's grudge against the world had hardened.

What irked him more was the happy contentment of Doug McKendrick. When he had first married Greg's sister, Doug had been an oily-haired rocker with a motor bike. Thin as a garden hose, winking at the girls. When Lily got pregnant Doug had done the right thing, wearing his greased quiff to the wedding. Greg had sneered at his sister's choice, and he'd never stopped sneering over the years which followed. Making sure he married a snobbish widow from the village, he opened his garage and lorded it at the local pub and round the shops. Every atom of his being was puffed with conceit – until another garage opened nearby and provided the locals with a choice. No one needed to go to Greg Horner any more, and within two years his business had failed. Forced to take work as a handyman, Greg managed to salvage some respect by working part-time as a chauffeur, but his demotion rankled with him and his wife's infidelity had succeeded in finally curbing his ego.

And all the time Doug had been a happy man. Still living in the same place he had taken his wife when they married, he hadn't changed or progressed in life, and seemed to feel no need to. The child which had necessitated their bond ended up a rather dull, round-faced girl who worked as a nanny for the local solicitor. When her charge grew up she took a job at the Co-op in the village, then married and moved away. With amazement Greg

Horner had observed his sister and brother-in-law, wondered why they didn't rebel against the boredom of their lives, their lack of status. He never realised that they pitied him.

'So,' Doug asked, finishing his pie and screwing up the brown paper bag, '*are* you working for Mr Hemmings today?'

Greg paused to make the answer seem more important. 'I've just collected his solicitor from the station.'

'Solicitor, hey? Wonder what he's come for. It'll cost money, whatever it is.'

'He's up from London,' Greg replied, eager to embellish the tale. 'Mr Hemmings said he was coming for a meeting this afternoon. Said it was important. Lily's made a cake.'

'*Cake?*' Doug repeated. 'She never said.'

Greg was about to move away, but couldn't resist passing on his news. 'Mr Hemmings has asked me to stay at the house for a bit.'

'*You never!*'

'True,' Greg replied, nodding. 'Asked me to come on in the evenings, when Lily goes off. I reckon he's not feeling up to being alone anymore. You know, being in that wheelchair most of the time must be a struggle. I suppose he wants company.'

God, Doug thought, the old man must be pushed if he had chosen his brother-in-law for company.

'What are you supposed to do?'

Greg could see that the news had irked the usually

equable Doug, and the thought pleased him. 'Nothing much, just be around. There's a flat over the garage where Mr Hemmings said I could stay. He wants me to be in the house until he goes to bed, but after that, my time's my own.' He paused, the idea hadn't appealed to him at first, but now that he could see Doug's unexpected discomfort, it was growing on him. 'You should see it. Nice little bathroom, bedroom, sitting room. Really comfortable.'

'He never asked *me* to stay at the house.'

'You never worked for him!'

'My wife does.'

'Yeah, well, maybe he thinks we'll get on better.'

Miffed, Doug stared at Greg, his tone sly. 'Well, I suppose it's all right – if you don't mind fetching and carrying for an old man.'

'He's paying me well enough not to mind.'

Smiling stiffly, Doug nodded. 'Like I said, being a nursemaid might not be everyone's cup of tea, but I hope it goes well for you. You could do with some excitement in your life.'

Turning into the garage of the Sussex house ten minutes later, Greg was surprised to see a car in the driveway. He had collected the lawyer from the station, so who was this? Parking, he stared over the hedge, but couldn't see anyone. He lifted his suitcase out of the car boot, then climbed the steps to the room above the garage, where the stuffiness smelt warm from the heating. Greg glanced out of the window towards the house. From this vantage point he could see anyone approaching – or leaving. He liked the idea. His insomnia had plagued him most of his life and made the nights elastic. He had lost count of the hours he had spent staring out of windows into empty streets. At least, living at Samuel Hemmings' house it would be a different view, if nothing else . . . He sighed, glanced over the mature garden and the long drive, then turned back his suitcase. Perhaps Doug was right. Perhaps he *was* just going to be a babysitter for an old man.

After all, what was likely to happen here?

Preoccupied, Samuel looked past his visitor into the garden. He had just seen Greg Horner arrive and was unexpectedly relieved. Perhaps it *would* be comforting to know that there was someone else on the premises, someone more than capable of handling themselves. Greg wasn't a friendly kind of man: bitter enough to be mean, and big enough to make any burglar think twice.

'Samuel?'

He turned at his name, smiling an apology. 'Sorry, I was day-dreaming. You do that a lot at my age.'

Jonathan Henderson nodded, eager to get on with the discussion and catch the last train back to London. With luck he could be home by six-thirty, before it was really dark. Then again, if he couldn't get his client to concentrate, the whole meeting might drag on interminably.

'You're now happy with the contents of your will?'

'I think so,' Samuel said, looking at the notes he had made. 'How quickly can you get this drawn up and legalised?'

'Within the week.'

'Good,' Samuel replied, liking the idea of his life being sorted.

He wouldn't care to be caught out, dying before everything was organised. He shifted in his wheelchair, wondering again why Marshall was coming to see him that night. Surely he wasn't that worried? Or did he know something else?

'I'll just need your signature.'

'What?'

'When the will's drawn up, Mr Hemmings. You need to sign it.'

'Yes, of course,' Samuel agreed. 'Get it done as quickly as you can, will you?'

'You're not ill?'

'No,' Samuel replied, smiling. 'Never been better.'

24

Irate, Tobar Manners slammed the front door of his home in Barnes and went into the drawing room. A vase of dying lilies was on the window ledge, three days' worth of newspapers lay on the coffee table. Glancing at the answer phone, he was further irritated to find no messages. Rosella had left him, as she had said she would. Without another word. Obviously she had been preparing her departure for some time because, although she used to receive mail regularly, nothing had come to Barnes. Wherever she had gone, she had made sure her post followed her.

The thought irritated Tobar even more than her leaving. He had never suspected Rosella of being premeditated and was stung by her indifference to him. Their marriage had lasted ten years. Surely, even for a façade, that was a sign of commitment? He went into the kitchen, looked in the fridge. There was a dying lettuce, a pint of milk and a slab of hard yellow cheese. He found some bread in the cupboard and toasted a couple of slices, then piled cheese on top, pushing the toast back under the grill. The smell was inviting, more so than the lunch at Le Gavroche, which had stuck in his craw. Or perhaps it hadn't been the food to blame for his lack of enjoyment, but the silky, puffy smugness of Rufus Ariel . . .

Moving back into the drawing room, Tobar ate his cheese on toast, letting crumbs fall on the Aubusson carpet and then discarding the empty plate on the floor by his feet. He felt a perverse pleasure at being a slob. He might even watch television with his feet on the coffee table, or order a pizza. Anything which Rosella would have abhorred. Yet there was little pleasure in undertaking actions – however satisfying – which would not be seen. What good was it annoying his wife when she wasn't there? What use provoking a phantom? Tobar's thoughts turned back to Rufus Ariel, and the way he had hinted, without actually saying anything specific, that there may well be two companion Rembrandt portraits *possibly* coming up for sale in the summer. In New York. Fuck you, Tobar had thought, watching Ariel's manicured pink hands break into a bread roll, you know something I don't.

'Who's selling the Rembrandts? A Japanese collector?'

Ariel had paused, rosy-cheeked in a pale blue suit. A little like Goering, in the wrong light. 'I don't know. It could be a rumour.'

'Who has two Rembrandts to sell?'

Ariel had shrugged, staring lovingly at his lobster. 'Maybe it's only one.'

'You said they were a pair.'

'I said I'd *heard* about a pair. I don't know, Tobar.' He

had paused, picking up a lobster claw and sliding it into his mouth. He made a sucking sound, then withdrew the decimated limb. 'It could just be hearsay.'

'So why tell me?'

'You deal in Dutch art. I thought you'd be interested.' He had paused again. 'Especially after you were so badly treated over the last Rembrandt.'

The sarcasm was vicious.

'I was told it was really by Ferdinand Bol,' Tobar replied, reiterating the old lie. 'I lost a fortune.'

'So did Owen Zeigler. He ran out of luck in the end, didn't he? Shame that, when he'd been so successful for so long. And to be killed in such a brutal way . . . God, it makes you think.'

'Yes,' Tobar agreed. 'It makes you think.'

'I said to Leon Williams the other day, no one can be too careful. London is getting to be a violent place.' His toffee-coloured eyebrows had risen at the thought. 'Aren't you worried?'

'About the Rembrandts?'

'About the murder?'

'No,' Tobar had said, surprised. 'Should I be?'

'Leon – and other dealers – have been talking. Wondering if there's some kind of set-up, some game plan. You know, if the killer or killers might break into other galleries. I mean, there *were* two thefts last autumn, but then again, theft isn't the same as murder. Leon mentioned Stefan van der Helde.'

Tobar had put down his fork. 'Who?'

'You remember, last year. He was murdered in Amsterdam. The man who was forced to eat stones.'

'Oh yes,' Tobar said, his tone dismissive. 'What about him?'

'Leon was saying that Van der Helde and Owen Zeigler had both been tortured and then killed.'

'So?'

'He wondered if there was a connection.'

'Why should there be? People are murdered every day. It was terrible about Owen, but Leon panics. Always has, always will.'

'But murder *is* something to panic about, isn't it?' Ariel had said, pausing with the other lobster claw in his hand. 'Perhaps he has a point.'

'Galleries are always getting robbed. Mind you, I wish someone would rob me. Then I could claim on the insurance.'

'Not if you were dead,' Ariel had replied, sucking his fingers and then wiping them on his napkin. 'We thought we might form an organisation, like Neighbourhood Watch.'

'*Neighbourhood Watch?*' Tobar had repeated, with incredulous amusement. 'We have a fucking Neighbourhood Watch, it's called the Metropolitan Police. Anyway, I don't understand why everyone's so jumpy. There was one murder last year, in Holland, and one in London. Hardly an epidemic, is it?'

'So why didn't they take any of Zeigler's paintings?'

'Presumably because they were disturbed,' Tobar replied,

pushing away his plate and impatiently beckoning for the waiter to come over. 'Coffee, please. Strong.' He had then turned back to Rufus Ariel, trying to change the subject. 'These Rembrandt portraits – is there anyone I could talk to?'

'Oh, I don't know, Tobar. I just heard a rumour and thought I'd pass it on. Just to keep you in the picture, if you'll forgive the pun.'

Smug bastard, Tobar thought, remembering the conversation. Why *would* there be a connection between the murders, he wondered, walking back into the kitchen and musing about Owen Zeigler. He had last spoken to his old friend three weeks before he died, at a private view that Owen held for a newly acquired Gerrit Dou. And, it was suggested, a possible Carel Fabritius. Very few paintings by Fabritius had survived, and so the viewing had been well attended and the small portrait of a sleeping maid attracted much attention. Impressed, Tobar had gone up to the canvas and studied it, noticing the silvery tones, typical of the artist, and the understated realism.

'So, what d'you think?' Owen had asked, coming up behind his friend.

Tobar had smiled warily. 'A Fabritius? That's pushing it a bit, isn't it? I didn't think there were any left to find.'

'I can't prove it, but I will,' Owen replied. 'It might be the start of a change of fortune for me. Not before time. Fabritius was a fine painter, better than we give him credit for.'

Curious, Tobar had put his head on one side. 'He died too young to make a splash.'

'Who knows what he could have done if he'd lived longer? He lived nearly as long as Caravaggio.'

'Oh, come on, Owen, he wasn't in that league.'

'He was an original.'

'Well, maybe. After all, he was the only one trained by Rembrandt who didn't copy his tutor.'

'Rembrandt referred to him as his most gifted pupil.'

'Doesn't fetch Rembrandt's prices though, does he?'

Owen had paused, and for a second Tobar had thought he was going to tell him something. But the moment passed and Owen was soon preoccupied with a customer, while Tobar drank his free champagne . . . It had been the last time Tobar had seen Owen Zeigler alive, and now, apart from when he glanced at the picture of them fishing up in the Lake District, he would never see his friend again. He would have to make do with a photographic image, which would fade and lose colour as quickly as his memory.

Melancholy, Tobar poured himself a glass of wine and mentally toasted the only real friend he had ever had; the one person who had made excuses for his low dealings and greedy, avaricious ways. As Owen had advanced in business through skill and charm, Tobar had wheedled and plotted his progression. Friendships with Lebanese businessmen and East End hard men had put money in his pocket, but for every rent boy reward, Tobar had wallowed a little further in the mire. And now he was alone, his wife gone, his guilt a dark puddle in the middle of his gut.

He should never have cheated Owen Zeigler, he knew that. He should have given him the money for the Rembrandt painting, not lied about its provenance. The coup had pulled in a greedy profit for Tobar, and – using an intermediary – he had hidden his deception. No one knew that the Rembrandt was back with Tobar, that the one possession Owen Zeigler had relied on to save his business was now lounging in Tobar's bank. Every so often he tried to convince himself that Owen Zeigler would have found a way out of his financial difficulties, but he knew he was lying to himself. Owen had needed the money – the fortune every Rembrandt painting reached. Tobar thought again of the rumour about the pair of Rembrandt portraits coming up for sale. He *had* to find out who was organising the sale, and where. He had to ensure that he was the broker. After all, everyone knew that Tobar Manners could get the highest prices for Dutch art. Even if he *did* take the biggest percentage.

Hating the silence, Tobar put on a CD of Mendelssohn, then changed it, choosing Mahler instead. The house was hideously quiet, his thoughts loud in the stillness, his guilty conscience singing like a trapped bird.

Lillian Kauffman got out of the taxi, paid the driver and tipped him well. Her late husband, Albert, had always told her to be generous – *people rely on tips*, he'd said. Looking up at the entrance, she read KAUFFMAN GALLERY on the door; in the barred window a fine painting of a Dutch interior was on display, the one Lillian had put there three weeks earlier, before she had gone off to Florida for a vacation. Although over seventy, she was as sparky as a thirty-year-old. She was slightly built, but oozed a kind of chutzpah which made people cautious about taking her on. Her hair was carefully arranged, the highlights blonde to cover the grey, and she always wore a pair of very large pearl earrings, mounted in gold. Everyone knew they were worth a fortune. Just as everyone knew Lillian never took them off, even though the weight of them had made her ear lobes droop. Lillian and the earrings were inseparable.

'I don't care if my ear lobes stretch down to my bloody kneecaps,' she had told Owen frequently, 'the earrings are my trademark.'

A very shrewd woman, Lillian Kauffman had learnt the trade from her husband, and after his death twenty years earlier she had taken over the gallery and made it a third more profitable within eighteen months. Business acumen was not the only reason for her success; Lillian also had a ferocious appetite for gossip. And she remembered everything. About everybody. If there were hidden skeletons, Lillian knew why, where and how. So revered and feared was she that other dealers gave her gifts, or invited her to their country homes, hoping to curry favour with the art world's Hedda Hopper.

Enjoying her power, Lillian understood that the business was pretty much like any other. Her ability was not so much in her artistic appreciation, but in her skill at understanding the market. She had been one of the first to buy into Brit Art.

'I hate the bloody stuff,' she would say defiantly, 'but it means I can make money to buy what I want.'

And so she started buying Damien Hirst when he was just beginning and showed conceptual art when the movement first emerged. Smoking handmade cigarettes in a tortoiseshell holder, Lillian would stand at her gallery door, watching the art world go by. Terrified of her power but conscious of her influence, dealers passed the time of day with Lillian, and also passed on rumours and news. Wearing Chanel suits and Hermes shoes, Lillian was an elegant rodent, exuding an aura of Bal à Versailles perfume, and wearing an expression which daunted most men.

Standing outside her gallery, looking down the street, instinct told Lillian that much had changed in the time she had been away. Her holiday routine was always the same: she was not to be bothered. No news was to be given her, no interruption to her time of rest. By sticking to this, she found that when she returned to London it was with renewed zest and her instincts heightened. She was hungry again, curious. Almost sniffing the air on Albemarle Street, she sensed a change in atmosphere; something had happened. She glanced across the street, surprised to see that the Zeigler Gallery was closed. That was unusual, Owen Zeigler never closed. Opening the door of her own gallery, she left her bags inside and then crossed the road.

Outside the Zeigler Gallery, she peered in at the window, surprised to see someone looking back at her.

Unfazed, Lillian rapped on the window, and Marshall opened the door.

'My God,' she exclaimed as she walked in. 'What happened here? And where's your father?'

She could sense the tension as she rummaged in her bag for a cigarette and lit up. 'Marshall, where's your father?'

'He was murdered—'

'He was *what*!' Lillian snapped, as though it was a personal insult to her. 'I've been away. What happened?'

Undaunted by her reputation or her manner, Marshall told her the details – without, of course, mentioning anything about the letters. Alert, and with something close to excitement in her eyes, Lillian listened, puffing on her cigarette, her eyes narrowed.

'So who did it?'

'No one knows. The police haven't caught anyone.'

'The police couldn't catch a cold,' she responded. 'I'm so sorry. Your father was a friend of mine.'

'I know.'

'One of the few men I had time for around here,' Lillian went on, knowing that Marshall was holding back and wondering what he was hiding. Her instincts leapt into action, her brain was galvanised. 'Mind you, he had some mad theories.'

Marshall said nothing.

'There was some wild tale about Rembrandt.' She

flicked her ash into a waste bin and paced the gallery. Her expensive shoes were too tight, her ankles puffy from the plane journey. 'We used to talk about it, make up stupid stories about painters. Once, when we were drunk, we spent half the night trying to outdo each other. I believed that Leonardo's boyfriend, Salai, was his bastard, and your father said he thought that Rembrandt had a son.'

'He did,' Marshall replied, unmoved. 'Titus.'

'Oh, your artistic education *is* improving,' Lillian replied, now certain there was something to be uncovered. 'There was a time when you thought Duccio was a brand of condom.'

He smiled, but refused to be drawn. Lillian sat down and crossed her short legs. Although Marshall had been warned from childhood about Lillian Kauffman, he admired her intelligence and, despite her acid tongue, knew her to be honest.

'Are you staying here?'

'Maybe,' Marshall replied. 'I've not made my mind up about what I'm doing.'

'What about Teddy Jack?'

The question caught him off guard. 'What about him?'

'Was he questioned?'

'You think Teddy Jack had something to do with my father's murder?'

'I think Teddy Jack was devoted to your father,' she replied, smoothly. 'He did many jobs for Owen. You see, living above the shop, as I have done for over twenty years,

I can see people's comings and goings. Mr Jack used to visit your father at very odd times.'

'It must be useful having insomnia.'

She didn't even blink. 'Then again, Tobar Manners was also a frequent visitor. Is *he* still alive?'

'Very.'

'Pity,' Lillian replied. 'I was hoping your father's murderer might turn out to be a serial killer.' She looked around the gallery, then back at Marshall. 'What aren't you telling me? Oh, I know people say what a cow I am, and it's true. But I was fond of your father and know a lot about what goes on around here. You don't, and I could help.'

'The police—'

'Are arses,' Lillian cut in. 'The art world is as enclosed as a monastery. You have to work here, or be born into it, to understand it. No outsider can penetrate this world. You can't afford to be ignorant here.' She paused, then said, 'Your father was looking for those letters, the Rembrandt letters' – her eyes narrowed fleetingly – 'Oh, I see a response! Very good, Marshall, no one else would have caught it. So you know about the letters, do you?'

'No.'

She ignored him. 'I knew your father had them—'

'Really? Where?'

'I don't know that,' she answered blithely. 'I just know he had them. Now – speaking metaphorically of course – if there *were* Rembrandt letters, and if they proved that Rembrandt had a son, why would that matter?' she asked

258

herself, putting out her cigarette and pacing again. 'It wouldn't matter. Unless there was something about the son which was important . . . Am I warm?'

'I don't know what you're talking about.'

'Before Owen found the letters he would talk about Rembrandts being faked en masse. So is there a connection between the fakes and the son?'

Marshall shrugged.

'Of course there are forgeries discovered everyday. Fake paintings, fake sculptures, fake letters – but then again, no one would kill for *fake* letters, would they?' Lillian asked, not waiting for a reply. 'But if the letters contained something dangerous, or something which could affect the art market then, yes, people *would* kill for them.' She raised her eyebrows. 'You have to tell me, Marshall.'

'No, Lillian, I don't have to tell you anything. There's nothing to tell,' he replied, his face impassive.

'Don't be fucking stupid!' she retorted. 'You need help. And I can help you. Do you realise how many people would be after those letters? Either to destroy them, or use them? Owen used to talk to me about it – oh, this is a long time ago, when he'd bang on about his bloody theory every time we had a few drinks. He'd say that if Rembrandt had had a son who was proved to have created many of his father's works, the value of Rembrandts would topple. I can see Owen now, drinking a pink gin, leaning back in that chair' – she pointed to one beside the empty desk – 'He never seemed to tire of talking about it. Then suddenly, around a year ago, your father *stopped* talking about

Rembrandt. He was struggling with money at the gallery, sales were down. He kept it quiet, but he let a few hints slip.'

Marshall could see her clever mind working, drawing on everything she remembered.

'I noticed his silence on a subject with which he had previously seemed obsessed. The fact lodged in my brain.' She tapped her left temple. 'Your father could be obvious at times. His sudden reticence spoke volumes.'

'Maybe he just went off the idea.'

'Oh, yes, people do that,' Lillian said sarcastically. 'They just drop an obsession which they've been chasing for decades. And around that time that your father "went off" the idea, I remember noticing that Samuel Hemmings was visiting a lot.'

'He was my father's mentor.'

'Did he authenticate the letters?'

'Why don't you ask him?'

'Don't get snotty with me, Marshall,' she said coldly, 'I'm trying to help.'

'Really? How could you help me?'

'Have you got the letters?'

He thought of them sitting in the Amsterdam bank. 'No.'

'All right,' she said, taking in a breath. 'Let's play a bit longer, I love a good game. I've had a marvellous holiday, my brain's just burning to work. So, shall we take it from the beginning? Are the Rembrandt letters authentic?'

Marshall shrugged, watching Lillian.

'Samuel Hemmings could have authenticated them, I suppose. But then again, maybe he's not enough of an expert in Rembrandt. *So who is?*' She paused, her back suddenly rigid. '*Stefan van der Helde was murdered last year in Amsterdam*. Van der Helde would have been the perfect person to authenticate the letters.'

Marshall realised that Lillian Kauffman wasn't going to let go. She had fixed her bite on her prey and wasn't going to give it up. Her mind was filtering everything she knew, drawing on information she had collected, old information which had seemed trivial but was now beginning to gel together into a sensational whole. Marshall watched her, her eyes brilliant, her logic at work, and was impressed.

'I'd say Van der Helde was murdered because of the letters, so they must be authentic. My God,' she said urgently, 'what do they say? Tell me, Marshall, what do they say?'

Standing up, he walked to the door. 'Thank you for coming over, Lillian, but I've some work to do—'

'You have those bloody letters, don't you?' She looked up at him fiercely. 'Christ, Marshall, if you do, watch your back. And remember, I'd be a bloody good ally.'

He was tempted, but decided against talking to her further. He remembered the mistake he had made in confiding in Georgia. Anyone involved in the Rembrandt letters was under threat.

'Honestly, I don't know about any of this. I don't know what my father was talking about. We never spoke about his business,' Marshall replied, his voice steady. 'I really do have to go now, Lillian—'

'You need me. Don't throw my offer in my face!'

'I don't mean to offend you, Lillian.'

'Mrs Kauffman to you, boy,' she replied, her tone auto-cratic. 'You haven't earned the right to familiarity yet.'

25

Rinsing her hair in the shower, Georgia paused, thinking she heard the phone ringing. Grabbing a towel, she moved out into the bedroom and then realised that the answer phone was picking up the message. Or, rather, the lack of message. Annoyed, she moved back into the bathroom and turned the shower on again, putting her hand under the water to check the temperature. The water was slow to heat up, she thought, wondering if she should turn the boiler on again, but then stepped gingerly under the tepid stream. Her teeth chattering, she danced from foot to foot, the blind drawn over the bathroom window shifting slightly behind her.

Feeling the water temperature rise, Georgia relaxed, the heat soothing her shoulders and back. She would phone Marshall later, give him an earful for not returning her calls . . . Her thoughts drifted as she wallowed under the warm water. Only six more months, she thought excitedly, six more months and she would be a mother. Smiling, she bit her lip. When she was married to Marshall they hadn't wanted children; they were too young and too full of plans to settle down. But Harry was another type of man. Reliable, loving, a father in his pram. Made to be the head of a family.

Georgia shook her wet hair, then placed her hands on her stomach and pushed it out, arching her back. She wondered fleetingly what she would look like when her stomach swelled further, and made a mental note to get some Bio Oil to rub in to prevent stretch marks. Gazing at her fuzzy reflection in the tiles, she could see her arched back and rounded belly, see herself languidly soaping her skin . . . Behind her the blind shifted slightly, while Georgia sang to herself under the warm water and turned the HOT tap higher. But the water went suddenly cold and, cursing, she jumped out of the shower. Wrapping the bath towel around her, she made her way into the kitchen and stood in front of the boiler, staring at the timer knob and twisting up the temperature.

Suddenly, from above her head, came the crashing sound of glass. She jumped and looked up, then realised instantly that it came from the bathroom and was about to run back upstairs to see what was happening when she saw the shadow of a figure on the landing. Backing away, she scrambled for the front door handle – and then she ran, half naked, into the Clapham street.

Parking outside Samuel Hemmings' Sussex home, Marshall was just turning off the engine when he noticed someone watching him from the steps on the side of the garage.

A thin, morose man was smoking a roll-up, his jacket over his shoulders, his eyes curious under beetling brows. Carefully pressed trousers and shined shoes gave him a kempt look, but his face was heavily lined and sour.

Nodding, Marshall called over to him. 'Is Mr Hemmings in?'

'Who wants to know?'

'I'm Marshall Zeigler. Who are you?'

'Greg Horner,' he replied, flicking some ash off his smoke. 'I'm staying here for a while. Keeping an eye on the place – and who comes here.' He walked down the steps, over to where Marshall was standing, his glance resting admiringly on the car. 'Nice.'

'Didn't you used to have the garage in the village?'

'Yeah, sold it,' Greg replied, lying and putting a more positive spin on the truth. 'I remember your father. He used to spend a lot of time up here. Sorry about what happened to him.' He dropped the fag end onto the gravel and ground it out with the heel of his polished shoe. 'He was a gentleman. I bet the old man's taken it hard?'

'Yes, he has.'

Greg dropped his voice, although no one could possibly have heard him from the house.

'Mr Hemmings never used to mind being here on his own. But now . . .' he let the inference trail. 'You don't think about it, do you?'

Marshall blinked. 'About what?'

'Being able-bodied. No, you don't think about it, but it must be hard, not being able to get around and do for yourself. I don't suppose,' Greg went on, his tone authoritative, 'that Mr Hemmings will want to go back to being on his own. Not after having me around. Looking out for him.'

'I don't suppose he will,' Marshall replied, moving into the house.

Samuel was bent over a book at the round table under the window when Marshall walked in. Looking up, he raised his eyebrows.

'Have you met the guard dog?'

Marshall nodded. 'Got the teeth marks to prove it.'

Smiling, Samuel leaned back in his wheelchair. 'I thought you'd be impressed. You wanted me get someone around the place.'

'Well, he certainly won't be inviting company,' Marshall replied, sitting down at the table and flicking over the pages of a book. Tired, he yawned and then rubbed his eyes, Samuel watching him carefully. In the short time since his father's death, Marshall's face had gained a wary look, but despite his obvious exhaustion, his eyes were alert, his deep voice stable.

'Did you look at the paintings I told you about?'

Samuel nodded. 'Very carefully.'

'It's a pattern, isn't it?'

'Yes, it looks that way.'

'I need some help.'

'Yes, you said that on the phone. What kind of help?'

'I need you to teach me.'

Surprised, Samuel stared at his visitor. '*Teach* you? Teach you what?'

'About Rembrandt.'

Laughing, Samuel leaned back, his jumper spotted with gravy, his eyebrows raised.

'What the hell for?'

'Because I don't understand what's going on,' Marshall confessed. 'I've read the letters, but I don't really know why they're so important. I don't know how the business works. Or how Rembrandt lived. I'm reading his mistress's letters and I've only half the picture.'

'Dear God, if your father could hear you now,' Samuel said, flicking crumbs off the tartan rug which covered his knees. 'He had to die to get you interested in art.'

Marshall smiled wryly. 'Yes, ironic, isn't it? But I have to know what I'm talking about. Look, I've inherited these bloody letters and the responsibility. People are dying because of them, so shouldn't I know what I'm doing?'

'Your father studied for a lifetime, and it didn't save *him*.' Reaching for the bell, Samuel rang it vigorously and Mrs McKendrick came in a few moments later. 'Could we have some tea, please, Mrs McKendrick?'

'Cake?' she asked simply, wiping her hands on a tea towel.

Samuel nodded. 'Oh yes, and cake.'

Smiling, Mrs McKendrick left the room and Marshall turned back to the old man.

'Just tell me what I need to know, Samuel.'

Wheeling himself over to the fire, Samuel poked the flames into life, then looked over his shoulder towards his visitor.

'Why are you suddenly trusting me?'

'Because you told me about the letters,' Marshall said frankly. 'I knew then you weren't lying.'

The door opened, and both men watched in silence as Mrs McKendrick laid down a tray on the table in front of the fire. When she had left the room again, Marshall poured the tea and passed a cup to Samuel, saying, 'This is very civilised.'

'When life is in chaos, the civilised things matter,' Samuel replied enigmatically. 'This is very serious, Marshall.'

'I know.'

'And I understand why you don't want to go to the police, but you should think about it. Something could happen to you—'

'No, Samuel, I'm not going to the police. Don't ask me again. This is something I have to do myself. For myself and my father . . . I thought he'd sent me the letters, but it wasn't him after all. It was Nicolai Kapinski. *He* sent them to me,' Marshall paused for an instant. 'Funnily enough, that's made me more determined, not less. I was chosen to sort all this mess out.'

'But you don't have to get killed to prove it.'

'I don't intend to get killed,' Marshall retorted. 'But the more I hear about my father, the more I realise he wasn't a happy man. He didn't really trust anyone around him, and that's a sad way to live, Samuel. I should have been closer to him.'

'You had your own life.'

'Yes, and I was so determined to prove the point. I didn't

want to know about the art world, I wasn't interested, and I made it very clear I wanted to follow my own career, but I realise now how much that must have hurt him.' Marshall paused, regretful. 'My father couldn't share his interests with me, because I didn't want to know. The only thing I remember about his books is dropping one when I was a kid and getting shouted at because I broke the spine. Oh, I know my father had friends, people around him, but the more I hear the more I realise his life was not ideal. I told you about his girlfriend?'

Samuel nodded.

'Well, Nicolai Kapinski told me she was blackmailing him.'

'What!'

'And Teddy Jack, the man who was apparently my father's closest confidante, believes the letters were in Charlotte Gorday's possession and now her killer's got them.'

'So he doesn't know you have?'

'No, and Nicolai Kapinski hasn't told him either,' Marshall replied. 'I was watching them both this morning, wondering who was lying and who was telling the truth. It's like they were still competing for my father's attention, even after his death. When he was alive, it seems that he was always pitting one against the other.'

'Divide and rule,' Samuel said thoughtfully. 'Perhaps I shouldn't say this, but I will. Your father had many good qualities and a brilliant mind, but he had one major flaw – a total inability to trust anyone. I'd known him for years, shared all my research with him, my private thoughts and feelings, but he still didn't trust me.' Samuel thought about the Rembrandt letters, and the fact that Owen had kept one back. 'I believe that if your father had trusted someone he wouldn't be dead now. Don't you make the same mistake.'

'My problem isn't so much trusting, as knowing *who* to trust,' Marshall replied, holding the older man's gaze. 'I'm sorry if I offended you before, Samuel, I should have known you'd never do anything to hurt my father. And I don't want anything to happen to you.'

'*I* don't want anything to happen to me,' Samuel joked, but his expression was serious.

'I really do need your help, Samuel,' Marshall repeated. 'You're the only person who can tell me what I need to know.'

'All right,' Samuel agreed, finishing his tea and setting down the cup. 'I haven't lectured for a long time, Marshall; you'll have to bear with me until I get in my stride again. Now, let me see. You want to know about Rembrandt?'

'Yes. I want you fill in the gaps.'

'Then you'll need some background . . . Like other artists of his time, Rembrandt took in students. He was very successful when he was young, so he had a studio early in his career. And pupils.'

'He taught them how to paint?'

Samuel blew out his cheeks. 'Well, it wasn't quite that simple, they were first taught the basics then trained up. An important artist would take in students to live on the premises, if there was room. And there was, because Rembrandt's house was plenty big enough.'

He scooted over to the round table and came back with two volumes, slapping one down on the low table in front of the fire, and opening the other at an illustration of Rembrandt's studio. 'This is a good example – *Interior of an Artist's Studio, possibly Rembrandt* – drawn by the artist himself. You see him looking over the work his pupil has done? See the apprentice at the easel and the others in the background, and all the paraphernalia that Rembrandt collected for his paintings – spears, costumes, caskets, helmets? And look at the sitter, a woman in traditional Dutch costume of the period—'

'Who could be Geertje Dircx. She wrote that she sat for Rembrandt's pupils,' Marshall said, staring at the drawing avidly. 'Could be her.'

Samuel nodded.

'Could be, or could be a number of other women. The artists paid some models to sit to them, others they found almost destitute and fed them instead. It was pretty low work – or that's how it was perceived anyway. Prostitutes often sat for painters, or relatives of the artists were sometimes used as models.'

'Did Rembrandt have any female relatives?'

'His wife was dead, his sister didn't live in Amsterdam, and at that time he didn't have a daughter. So no, if Rembrandt wanted to use someone close to hand, he might have had to use his housekeeper. After all, he wouldn't have had to pay her.'

'And he taught the pupils to draw first?'

Samuel nodded. 'To draw, and to mix paints, prepare the ground of an oil painting. The under-painting of Rembrandt's pictures was usually grey, or warm brown, or a yellow.'

'So why were they so dark?'

'If he had painted them on a dark background the colours would have faded back. Painting them over a lighter background meant that the lightness of the base came through. Especially if he was using glazes—'

'What?'

'A transparent colour mixed with oil. Linseed oil, or Venetian turpentine sometimes. There could be up to ten glazes laid one over the other transparently, each one with more oil than the preceding one.'

'Why?'

'Fat over lean,' Samuel replied. 'With every layer, you use more oil, or the painting will dry out and crack.'

'OK, then what?'

'The layers of glazes would glow against the lighter base, acting as a refractive index, so that the colours seemed to radiate. That's what took the time, waiting for each layer to dry before applying another. It took months, not weeks. When the ground was grey, Rembrandt taught his pupils how to intensify the shadows with warm colours, so that the greyness underneath gave cool half tones. If he used a yellow ground, half tones were added over. But he also used scumbling and glazing too, as I said.'

'But Rembrandt laid the paint on thickly sometimes,'

Marshall said. 'I remember the picture my father sold, there were chunks of cream highlights.'

'And that's what gave a three-dimensional effect. The contrast made the painting seem more real. But there were no ready-made paints in those days; every colour had to be ground up with a pestle and mortar for a long time, until it was smooth. No shortcuts. And then it would have to be mixed with more oil. Think about it – the smell of the ground paints, the linseed and the turpentine would have been overwhelming. In the summer, they left the windows open, but there wasn't much air because there was no proper ventilation. In winter it was cold, and the house would reek of the materials they were making – and using – every day.' Samuel paused, thinking back to his old lectures. 'Rembrandt didn't go in for training his students to draw much. But we know he used to get them to copy his preparatory paintings in order to learn. *Proeven van zyn Konst.*'

'What?'

'It means "put his skills to the test".'

'Then what?'

'Well, sometimes Rembrandt would do a painting of a theme he liked, say for example, the Head of Christ – and the pupils would create their own versions.'

'So there would be numerous versions?'

Samuel nodded. 'Varying in quality, of course.'

'How long would it take a student to learn all this?'

'Depends on the student. A good pupil might learn fast. Another might take three years. Three years was the usual time for an apprenticeship. Remember, some of Rembrandt's pupils had already been partly trained by other artists before they came to him. Ferdinand Bol, for instance. There's some evidence that he had been tutored by Jacob Gerritsz, Culp or Abraham Bloemaert.' Flicking over the pages quickly, Samuel passed Marshall a book, open at a page showing a *Portrait of Elisabeth Jacobs dr. Bas.*'

'But this is by Rembrandt, surely.'

'No, that's by Ferdinand Bol,' Samuel said, smiling knowingly. 'See how closely he mimicked Rembrandt. When Bredius – some say the most important art historian of the last century – declared this work to be by Ferdinand Bol and *not* by Rembrandt there was an outcry. It was owned by the Rijksmuseum and was one of their prize exhibits; they didn't take kindly to it being demoted.'

'Because it lost value?'

'A lot of value – and because they were trying to build up a collection of Rembrandts at the time.'

Marshall thought for a moment. 'Tobar Manners said that my father's Rembrandt was actually by Ferdinand Bol.'

'Many works have been attributed to Bol that were previously called Rembrandts,' Samuel replied, 'but that painting of your father's was genuine, and Manners knew it. He knew its worth from the first time he saw it – and he wanted it.'

'So why didn't *he* buy it?'

'That's where the luck comes in. It was a *sleeper*. A valuable painting no one else had spotted. Your father found it at an auction in The Hague, bought it, and it made his name. At the time Manners was also building his career and had made a few lucky buys. He spotted a Gerrit Dou in France and bought a Pieter de Hoogh from an American dealer. Both big names, but not *the* big name. He'd never owned a Rembrandt. Brokered them, yes. Dealt in them, but never owned one. That stuck in his craw.' Samuel laced his hands together. 'Manners has a very sound reputation in Dutch art, but what he wants most is a Rembrandt. He needs it now, needs a good sale to prop up his business—'

'*Manners* is struggling?'

Samuel shrugged.

'Everyone is struggling now. There isn't a dealer in New York or London who would want to see their stock lose value. But as for Manners, if he could handle a big Rembrandt sale, it would propel him back into the limelight. I told you, Rembrandts keep their value, increase it every day – that's why the letters would be lethal.'

'OK. Tell me more about Rembrandt.'

'He was a greedy man. Ambitious, quick to make money, a voracious collector. He was successful from the off, and that meant that he never had to struggle for recognition. He was the painter people wanted to commission; the favourite of the authorities and of the merchant classes. Remember, the merchants had suddenly been promoted in Holland. They were the ones with the money now, and they wanted to show it off. You remember the tulip trading?'

Marshall nodded. 'A fortune was paid for the bulbs.'

'Well, that was one way they showed their wealth. Other ways consisted of collecting silver ware, newly imported fabrics and furniture, but most of all, if you were anybody in seventeenth-century Holland, you had your portrait painted. And you had it painted by the best, the most expensive, the most sought after. That was Rembrandt van Rijn. He knew he could ask big prices because he would get them, and he became avaricious. You have to recall that Saskia, his late wife, had been rich, and she came with a good dowry. I don't doubt that Rembrandt loved her, but the money would have been a definite bonus.'

'So people would buy pretty much anything Rembrandt painted?'

'Yes,' Samuel agreed. 'And as everyone wanted work in the manner of Rembrandt, that was how his pupils painted. They wanted to be successful, after all. Especially someone like Govert Flinck, one of the best pupils. He realised early on that by adopting Rembrandt's style he would never be short of work.' Samuel passed Marshall another book, showing him a painting by Flinck of a man in a plumed hat. 'In fact, in 1675, Sandrart commented that Flinck's portraits were "*judged to be more felicitous in the exactness and in the pleasing quality of the portrayal*".'

Marshall raised an eyebrow. 'He was thought to be better than Rembrandt?'

'By some then, not now,' Samuel replied. 'In fact in the first half of the 1630s, when Flinck was working closely with Rembrandt, a great number of Rembrandtesque portraits and tronies – head only studies – were turned out.'

'Which they were *both* painting?'

'Yes. And which benefited them all, I imagine, particularly Rembrandt and his dealer, Hendrick van Uylenburgh.'

'So the dealers haven't changed much over the years,' Marshall commented drily. 'I suppose Van Uylenburgh knew these Rembrandts were actually by Govert Flinck?'

Samuel shrugged. 'How do I know? I imagine he guessed. There was a lot of money to be made. Rembrandt wasn't above getting colleagues to bid up one of his paintings at auction—'

'To make more money?'

Samuel shrugged. 'Rembrandt had expensive tastes. He loved to collect paintings, silver, armour, furniture, china. In fact anything. Many of his valuable antiques he used in his pictures, but it seems that he just loved to spend.'

Thoughtful, Marshall stared at the Flinck portrait, then asked, 'But if Rembrandt had people queuing round the block, how did he have time to undertake every commission?'

'And there you have it!' Samuel replied, leaning back in his wheelchair. 'Rembrandt trained his pupils in his manner. Nothing wrong there – Rubens did the same – but where Rembrandt differed was that he would allow the work of the best pupils to be passed off as his own.'

'You're joking,' Marshall said, feigning ignorance.

'No, there's evidence from the period. Houbroken, a

friend of Govert Flinck's son, says that Flinck's paintings were accepted as authentic Rembrandts – and sold as such.' Samuel replied. 'But we don't have any evidence which says conclusively that such and such a painting was by *Bol* or *Flinck* or *Fabritius*.'

'What about Fabritius?'

'He was Rembrandt's best pupil,' Samuel replied, showing Marshall Carel Fabritius's self-portrait of a young man. The face was strong, with a firm mouth and steady, level gaze. Intelligence shimmered around the features, but it wasn't painted like a Rembrandt and had a look which was unique.

Surprised, Marshall stared at the image. 'Fabritius didn't paint like his father.'

'No. Not when he was satisfying his own taste. Then he chose cooler colours, muted tones, like *The Goldfinch*, which is a masterpiece.'

'But Geertje Dircx says that Carel Fabritius was Rembrandt's monkey. That not only was Carel his son, but he was the chief assistant to Rembrandt—'

'His main *jonggezel*.'

'His what?'

'His collaborator.'

'His forger, you mean.'

'And how clever it was,' Samuel replied thoughtfully, 'to pick the pupil with the greatest talent – but the one least influenced by the Master. People would easily suspect Bol or Flinck, but not Fabritius. Besides, Carel Fabritius didn't stay in Amsterdam, he moved to Delft, away from the studio, apparently well away from his mentor's influence. To all intents and purposes, he studied with Rembrandt in the early 1640s and then left to run his own studio.'

'So if we hadn't read Geertje Dircx's letters we would never have known about any of it?'

'We wouldn't have known that Fabritius was Rembrandt's bastard, but over time there have been a few interesting attributions which have been reversed,' Samuel said. 'In Pasadena there's a *Bust of Rembrandt* which has now been attributed to Fabritius, and in the collection of the Duke of Wellington is a pair of portraits, a man and his wife, which were long considered to be by the master. But not now.'

'So people have suspicions?'

'There have *always* been suspicions, but without proof. As I said, Rembrandt wanted to turn out as much work as possible. Over the centuries his works have been attributed and reattributed, but as most of them are considered to be authentic the value of Rembrandts have held worldwide.'

'So the letter which name the paintings?'

Shaken, Samuel Hemmings stared at Marshall, his voice hardly more than a murmur.

'The letter which *name* the paintings?' He was alert in his chair, his eyes glistening, his expression shrewd. 'Do you mean to tell me that there's a list of the pictures Carel Fabritius painted for his father? A list of works which everyone thinks are Rembrandts but were actually created by his bastard son? *A list of fakes?*'

279

Marshall took in a breath. 'You didn't know?'

'No, I didn't bloody know! The list was in the last letter?'

Marshall nodded. 'Yes.'

'The one your father didn't let me see.'

'You didn't see that one?'

'No, and I always wondered *why* Owen didn't let me see it – but now I know,' Samuel replied, smiling ironically. 'That last letter is the key to the whole fraud, isn't it? Without it, it's just Geertje Dircx's word. The evidence of a mad woman.' Sighing, he wheeled himself over to the corner of the room, his cane extended and poked at the empty dog bed.

Baffled, Marshall watched him. 'What are you doing?'

'Come over here, will you?'

As Marshall did so, Samuel looked at him, then gestured to the basket. 'Turn it over.'

'Turn it over?'

'Please.'

Nodding, Marshall flipped over the dog bed, and saw a faded brown package taped underneath. Without looking at Samuel, he pulled the parcel free and weighed it in his palm.

'The letters?'

'A copy.' Samuel wheeled back to the fire, shivering although the temperature had not fallen. 'This is a greedy business, the art business. We're all ravenous for success, money, reputation. Reputation above everything. We want to make our names, so that people will remember us and our intellectual detective exposés.' He laughed sourly, his hands folded on the tartan rug over his legs. 'This copy was supposed to be my guarantee.'

'Of what?'

'My part in history,' Samuel replied. 'My guarantee that I knew about the letters, that I was in on it. That this incredible information *I* was privy to. When people talked about the Rembrandt letters in the future they would remember Owen Zeigler *and* Samuel Hemmings, because I would write about them. I would be in on it.'

'Only if my father revealed them.'

'But he would have done, in time!' Samuel snorted. 'Not now. I understood that, it would have been wrong for the truth to come out now. But in a couple of years, when the economy's recovered, when New York and London are back to their old greedy ways – *then* he could have published them. Blown the whole art market up. Boom!' He made a sound with his lips, his hands raised, palms upwards. Then he let them drop back into his lap. 'I was living for it, Marshall. It kept me alive. I could hold on, knowing that I had something to hold on for. I used to look over to that dog bed and smile, thinking about the packet taped underneath and know that I knew the truth.'

'You never felt tempted to expose them yourself?'

There was a pause. 'The time wasn't right.'

'And besides, you didn't have all of them, did you?'

The historian's head shot up, his expression defiant. 'Implying that if I *had* got them all, I'd have gone behind your father's back? Had them published and taken the credit for myself?'

281

'I didn't mean that!'

'Oh, yes, you did,' Samuel hurled back. 'You're not that different from your father, after all, are you, Marshall?'

'Think what you like—'

'I'll do just that!' he snapped. 'You come here, wanting to pick my brains, wanting to get a potted history of Rembrandt so you can understand the business. Well, you can't, Marshall,' he said fiercely, 'you *can't* – not until you've spent years and decades reading and looking, and caring. You can't learn a few facts and think you can go up against experts. You want the easy way and there isn't one. Your father knew that, he knew how much effort had to go into making a reputation.'

'I don't want a reputation in the art world—'

'No! And you never did!' Samuel replied, wheeling himself away towards the window and looking out. His face was white, and on his cheeks were two bright spots of colour which revealed how angry he really was. 'And you have the temerity to suspect me. To doubt me!'

'I'm sorry.'

'Of course you are,' Samuel replied, still staring out of the window at the empty garden. 'We're all sorry. To be honest, at this moment, I'm sorry I ever laid eyes on the Rembrandt letters.'

'You don't mean that.'

'You think not?' Samuel parried, looking over to his visitor. 'Three people already dead, Marshall. Because of those letters. *Three people dead.* And it won't stop there. I didn't want to spend the last of my days frightened, with some goon playing at being bodyguard. That wasn't the way I pictured my demise. Yes, I've been ambitious and ego-centric; yes, I've wanted the limelight and courted it. But essentially I'm not brave and I'm not up to this. You're young enough to want to fight. I understand that. You want to prove something, find out who killed your father. You feel almost excited by what you've learnt about Rembrandt and the letters. But I'm old and in a wheel-chair – fear is not the last emotion I want to feel.'

Subdued, Marshall stared at his hands, taking a moment before he spoke again. 'I always envied you and my father.'

'Envied?'

'Yes,' Marshall said, nodding. 'You had such passion. Such a fire for this business. Such commitment. I would watch you both and wonder why it was all so exciting. After all, the artists were dead, the paintings weren't as interesting as a movie. It was dry and over. Done with.' He sighed. 'Then my father was murdered and I realised that, no matter how insane it seems to the outside world, people kill, and are killed, for the reputation of dead artists. They kill for auction prices, to keep the market up, the name protected.

'I saw my father's body and there was nothing dull about that. It was fresh and venal. When the police said it was a bungled robbery, I knew they'd leave it at that, because you're right – no one understands the art world unless they're in it. No one realises the brutality of it, the ruthlessness, unless they're a part of it. No one can con-ceive of the lengths people will go to – unless they've moved in it and watched it.' His voice fell. 'And yes, Samuel, God forgive me, but for the first time in my life I *do* feel a kind of excitement. Because I want to find the person who did this to my father. And I want to make sure that they don't get the Rembrandt letters and destroy them. Or worse, use them, and profit by them. It's not because I give a damn about some dead Dutchman, but because I care about some dead Englishman.'

Impressed, Samuel stared at his visitor. 'You're putting yourself in danger.'

'Everyone who knows about the letters is in danger.'

'Yes,' Samuel agreed. He picked up his copy of the letters and to Marshall's amazement, he threw them into the fire. Both men watched them burn until, with little left of them but embers, Samuel turned back to Marshall, and said, 'You need help.'

'Yes, maybe I do.'

'You should have a plan. Know what you're going to do next,' Samuel went on. 'Have you anything to go on?'

'The killer or killers must be in the business, otherwise they'd never go to such trouble with the murders. Setting them out like Rembrandt reproductions – that's a specialised touch. They have a contrived look, artistic, eerily cultured.' He caught Samuel's attention and held it. 'I don't think the person who's behind all this is the actual killer. I think someone else does the killing. The person who's after the letters is clever, patient. He wants to show his *refinement*.'

'D'you know who he might be?'

'No. I just know that he'll come after me,' Marshall replied, reaching for his coat. 'He's found out that my father, Teddy Jack and Charlotte Gorday didn't have the letters, so now he'll be wondering who else would be likely to have them. And that leaves me.'

'Or me.'

Marshall shook his head. 'No, Samuel. You didn't have *all* the letters, you don't know everything, and now you don't even have a copy. And I'm certainly not going to let you read the last one, that would be fatal. Stay in semi-ignorance. You're not safe, but you're not able to give this person what they want. You don't know enough for them to kill you.'

'I hope you're right.'

'So do I. Don't let anyone too close, you hear me? Keep your housekeeper or Greg Horner with you at all times. Don't go out alone, don't *be* alone—'

'But what if the killer gets to you?'

Marshall stared at the old man, puzzled. 'If he gets to me?'

'Yes.'

'I don't follow you.'

Samuel shrugged. 'Think about it, Marshall. If you're killed, who'll stop him then?'

26

'Jesus, darling, what is it? God, God.' Distressed, Harry ushered Georgia into the sitting room, passing her a brandy and putting his jacket around her shoulders. She was wearing only a bath towel and she was shaking, but angry, her voice strident as she rubbed her bare legs to warm them.

'Bloody kids!' she snapped. 'I was just taking a shower and smash went the window! God, I just ran, and when I looked back, there was this man on the stairs. Our neighbours called the police and they caught the little sod in the garden on Littlejohn Road.' She pushed her damp hair back from her face. 'Apparently they break into houses when they think people are at work. And usually I would have been.'

'Are you all right?'

'Yeah, yeah,' she said dismissively. 'I'm fine. As fine as anyone can be, trying to take a bloody shower and then running out of their house half naked.' She laughed hoarsely, touching her stomach. 'Poor baby, all that excitement.'

Harry stared at her hand on her stomach. 'Is it . . .?'

'Fine,' she reassured him. 'Honestly, you do worry.'

'Well someone did just break into the house.'

'Did they steal anything?' she asked suddenly, getting to her feet and looking round. 'Have you checked?'

He laughed, holding her to him tightly. 'You're an ass, Georgia, what difference does it make if they stole anything? All I care about is you and the baby.'

'Me and the baby are fine,' she replied, 'but what about the cash in the desk drawer? Did you check?'

The phone ringing next to them interrupted their conversation. Harry answered.

'Oh, hi there, Marshall . . . Well, I can get her, but now's not the right time. We've just had a break-in—'

She snatched the phone out of her husband's hand. 'Marshall?'

'You had a break-in?' he asked nervously, his grip tightening on the phone. 'Are you all right? What happened?'

'It was just kids. Apparently they've burgled a few places around here. Nothing to worry about. Honestly, I'm fine. Harry's just panicking because of the baby.'

On the other end of the line, Marshall took a moment to respond.

'*The baby?*'

'I was going to tell you next time we met up,' Georgia said hurriedly. 'I'm over three months gone.'

'Congratulations,' he replied, a knot in the pit of his stomach.

He had told Georgia about the Rembrandt letters and

here she was, on the phone, telling him that there had just been a break-in at her house and that she was pregnant ... Jesus, he thought to himself, how could I have put her in such danger? What was I thinking? He could imagine her hair, her face – and for a second had an image of it mutilated and bloodied.

He struggled to keep his voice even. 'Georgia, you remember what we talked about last time we met? About the letters?'

'Yeah'

'You didn't tell anyone, did you?'

'Only the BBC—'

'Georgia, you *didn't* tell *anyone*, did you?'

She dropped her voice, making sure that Harry couldn't overhear. Behind her, she could just make out the sound of the kettle whistling in the kitchen.

'No, of course not! I said I wouldn't. Harry doesn't know. No one does.'

'Forget what I told you. It was all rubbish. I was wrong.'

'Hang on,' Georgia said, running upstairs with the phone and throwing it onto the bed. Then she pulled on a warmer robe and wrapped her hair in a towel before picking up the phone again. 'That's better, I was cold—'

'Cold?'

'It's a long story,' Georgia replied, hurrying on. 'Now, what are you talking about?'

'What I told you, the Rembrandt letters. They don't exist. It was a hoax.'

'Your father's death wasn't a hoax though, was it?' she

said, her intelligence as sharp as ever. 'What are you up to?'

'Nothing. I've told you, it was a hoax.'

'So your father was killed for nothing?'

'It was a robbery that went wrong. Just like the police said.'

'Have they caught the murderer?'

'No.'

'So how do they know?'

'Because there have been other break-ins around the area, in other galleries. Apparently they think my father was tortured to give up the combination of the safe.'

'Which he didn't.'

'No, Georgia, he didn't.'

'And Stefan van der Helde?'

'A gay murder, or just another break-in.'

'And both men tortured, and both galleries left intact,' Georgia said smoothly. 'Perhaps someone should tell these burglars that they're supposed to *take* something.'

'This is not funny—'

'No, Marshall, this is bullshit.'

'What?'

'Oh, come on, Marshall, I might teach kids but I'm all grown up and I know when I'm being fobbed off.' She paused, smiling as Harry came into the bedroom with a cup of coffee. 'Thanks, darling. I'm just talking to Marshall about something he's working on. I won't be long.'

Nodding, he left the room. Georgia waited until she could hear her partner's footsteps move into the sitting room and then turned her attention back to Marshall. 'You can't lie to me. I was married to you, remember? I can always tell when you're spinning a yarn. Honestly, Marshall, if you're worried about the break-in, it was just that. A break-in.'

'What did they look like?'

'Who?'

'The burglars?'

'I just saw one man.'

'What colour? Height? Weight?'

'Jesus, Marshall, he was on the landing, standing against the light, I couldn't see anything about him clearly!' She paused, keeping her voice steady. 'The police caught him in a neighbour's garden—'

They caught him?

'Yes, he was a kid. I told you, it's nothing important, and it has nothing to do with your bloody Rembrandt letters.'

Momentarily relieved, Marshall took in a breath. At first he had needed a confidante, but as time had gone on and the danger of the situation had become more apparent, he had felt guilty for involving his ex-wife. His *pregnant* ex-wife. His thoughts turned to Charlotte Gorday and he flinched, wondering how to warn Georgia without spooking her.

'Look, I just want you to be careful, that's all.'

'I know, I will be,' she replied. 'Is this because of the baby?'

'No, I was going to talk to you anyway.'

'So, it's serious?'

'No, it's—'

'Serious.'

He nodded. Then, realising she couldn't see him, said, 'Perhaps I should talk to Harry.'

'No! Don't involve him, I don't want him to know. He's a worrier. A great husband, but a worrier. I can't have you telling him, Marshall, not when I'm pregnant. It's not fair, and you shouldn't ask it. Look, if it makes you feel any better, I'll forget everything you told me.'

But he knew she wouldn't. She was too bright to wipe it from her memory.

'I won't see you for a while.'

Now she was worried. 'What?'

'I've a lot to do, Georgia. I'll be tied up.'

'So call me.'

'I will. If I get the chance.'

Gripping the phone, she found herself anxious for the first time. 'Marshall, you can't cut yourself off. I have to hear from you, know you're all right.'

'I'll be in touch,' he assured her, knowing that he would dump his mobile immediately he got off the phone. If Georgia didn't know how to contact him, it was one way he could safeguard her. 'Don't worry about me. Just look after yourself.'

She clung to the phone. 'Look, you stupid bastard, don't go getting into trouble, you hear me? You're a translator, not some vigilante.'

'I want to ask you something.'

'Go ahead.'

'How would you have described my father? Not in looks, in character.'

She paused to consider her answer. 'I loved him. Owen Zeigler had a brilliant mind. Perhaps he could be devious, but he also had a great passion for what he believed in.'

'That's right,' Marshall said. 'And I never had that passion. Until now—'

She cut him off, because she was suddenly afraid for him. 'You're not your father, Marshall. You're honest and smart, with a memory like a computer. You're a brilliant academic, Marshall, but you're only good in your own world. Stay in it – and stay safe.'

'How can I?' he asked gently, 'when I now know it would never be enough?'

House of Corrections,
Gouda, 1654

It is hard to write these words. But I want to give a true account of my history. I cannot alter anything; cannot better it, make myself more respectable. I am what I did ... When Carel had been working with Rembrandt for a while I would watch them and see likenesses. So much so I wondered that no one else had seen them too. Rembrandt's nose was a miller's nose, Carel's large, but finer. Rembrandt's mouth was not appealing, his teeth always giving him trouble. Carel's mouth was wider, his teeth even, like the painting outside the barber's. But their mannerisms echoed each other.

He was my son. Our son. Then, when Carel had been studying for a year, Rembrandt showed me something he had painted, and I saw it. I thought he saw it too and wanted to let me know. Wondered if he would suddenly remember me, remember the girl in the country who had had his child. But he was looking at the painting and thinking something else entirely. Not that this could be talent he had passed down, but that this talent could be used ... Greed was his weakness, did I tell you that already? I forget ... I've been ill again, shakes, and vomiting with the milk, which is rancid, the bread sour, crawling with weevils. They make you work, but not lately, not me. Rembrandt is still giving them money to keep me here, they don't want me to die ...

Is some love still there? No, I doubt he cares. I know he does not.

Greed, yes, he was greedy. Greedy like a pig at making love. All fingers and tongue, all heaviness, and greedy with his money, his love for painting. His colours, rags, brushes wiped down the side of the canvas, his shoes wet with oil, making slime patterns on the wooden floor. And the munching, harrumphing sounds he made when merchants came to the house to be considered for portraits.

I know – I doubt he did – that they looked down on him. We were country bred. He was a miller's son. Not upper class Dutch, not merchant arrogant. Van Tripp might sit for a portrait, but he thought the painter a boor. I could see it, Rembrandt could not.

In some ways, I was the clever one.

When he walked towards mirrors he would pause, adjust his head as though painting himself, and then admire his face. I wondered often what he saw. I knew he understood each open pore, each crease to the lip, every hair around his fleshy ears, and yet he used pigment to make an aristocrat out of the miller's son. The painting of him laughing, Saskia on his lap, hung on the stairs, high up, so you could only see it from the top landing. I used to stare at it, wonder about her ghost, if she still came around the house looking for him. Her breeding was a scold to Rembrandt, a reminder of what he was not . . .

I was bred like him. I was his natural wife. I was his son's mother. And the truth used to tickle my tongue . . .

Then one night I told him. But I told Rembrandt whilst he

slept and he heard nothing . . . Yet the day after he was different with me and stared at Carel longer than usual. His sleeping mind had heard me. Something was telling him. From then on, he gave Carel more time than his elder brother, Barent, or any of the other pupils. The creeping Govert Flinck might try to impress him, but Rembrandt encouraged Carel, held his elbow and guided his hand, passing down through his touch and blood the talent which we all watched grow daily . . .

I could clean out the grates, chop the wood, weary myself carrying pails of water that a horse would balk at – but did I care? Every callus told me of the time I had spent in the house, and in Rembrandt's bed. Every swollen vein, each bruise, reminded me that I was working for the man I loved, and our son was working too. Sometimes my pride would make my heart race. I would stop, touch my breast and look upwards to the wooden ceiling. And laugh, because I was the mistress of the house, of the master's heart, and the mother of Rembrandt's son – his finest pupil.

He must have known it. But the mind takes longer than the heart to understand . . . then one night I was washing and turned. Rembrandt was watching me, and his face shifted. He remembered. Later we made love as though we had never met before. As though we were strangers, and I told him – spoke the words – that Carel was his son. That I was the girl who had lain with the miller's boy . . .

He put his hand over my mouth, told me to keep it a secret, and never to tell Carel. Then he gave me a little trinket, something of Saskia's . . . I think she saw us. I think she came down from that painting on the landing and stood at the bedroom

door, and pulled back the drapes round the bed and damned me
. . . I believe she did. My life darkened from that night onwards.

And Rembrandt, knowing his son, made a knecht out of him.
His assistant, he said. Then a little later, his jonggezel. His collaborator . . . Govert Flinck was steeped in bile, up to his puffy
neck; Ferdinand Bol, quiet as a pastor, watching his companion
pupil rise like a summer moon. Rembrandt worked often into
the night with Carel, making him copy portraits and soon – how
soon it was almost shocking – he asked our son to paint a portrait of a sitter who was coming the following day.

That morning it rained so long the gutter overflowed and
some of the market stalls floated away . . . Rembrandt stood, his
feet apart, his hands on his hips, and told his client that Carel
was going to do a preparatory oil sketch, which Rembrandt would
then make up into a finished portrait. Sixty guilders he asked.
Sixty guilders . . . Carel painted the portrait, and his father signed
it. And the sitter paid the sixty guilders. Of which Carel was
given ten.

The master paying the pupil . . . Carel was so pleased he smiled,
which he seldom did. A serious lad, barely nineteen, smiling like
a monkey. And that's what Rembrandt called him, a monkey.
His monkey. Rembrandt's monkey . . . It was said with affection,
but I knew that monkey also meant someone who was a rogue,
a scoundrel, a wrongdoer. And I had made my son that . . . But
Carel smiled and took the ten guilders, never knowing that
Rembrandt was paying him cheaply. Giving him ten guilders,
instead of his name. Money instead of van Rijn. Guilders not
genealogy. Lies not lineage.

Carel didn't know Rembrandt was his father. He didn't know Geertje Dircx was his mother. He would find out, but never in the way I wanted or expected.

27

New York

Surprised, Philip Gorday looked through into the reception of his law firm and studied the diminutive man sitting with a briefcase on his lap. Surrounded by glass windows and steep glazed walls he seemed like a lost ship in the middle of Antarctica, some tiny freight overwhelmed by its imposing surroundings. Immaculately dressed, his shoes buffed to a high shine, the balding man jiggled his left foot restlessly, then coughed twice. Not as though he was clearing his throat, but his head.

He seemed familiar to Philip, but someone from a long time back. Curious, he moved over to his secretary.

'Who's that, Nicole?'

'He wouldn't give his name, sir. Just said he had to see you on a matter of extreme importance. He says he used to know your wife.'

'My wife?' Philip, thinking of Charlotte, flinched inwardly.

He had grown adept at segregating her memory from

his work. He could sometimes obliterate all thought of her for hours at a time – until he returned home and walked into their apartment, into the bedroom where he had found her body.

Everyone had expected him to move out. Charlotte's lifeless corpse, loaded into its body bag, was moved. The police, having decided that the death was a suicide, had moved on too. Everyone moved out or moved on except Philip. He stayed, because he felt a curious and belated loyalty to his dead wife. In life he had committed adultery frequently, and Charlotte had had her long affair with Owen Zeigler, but after her death – her suicide – no, not suicide, he could never quite take that on board – after she *died*, he lost his zeal for women. He thought it would come back in time. That after the grief had lessened, his guilt would subside too. But the grief was still as acute, the guilt beggaring.

One particular woman with whom Philip was involved had always held out a hope that she would take over from Charlotte. So when her rival died, she waited for Philip to turn to her, but he did not. He did not turn to his secretary, Nicole, either, although they had enjoyed a long on/off relationship which, miraculously, had never curdled their working life. In fact, Philip Gorday found that freedom from his marriage brought a glut of attention. And its very availability was its turn off.

Curious, Nicole watched him standing at the door of his office. She had to admit that the weight he had lost since his wife's death suited him, made him look younger.

Her gaze took in the speckled hair, the keen features, the now pared-down midriff, before she glanced over to the visitor still waiting in the reception area.

'Do you want to see him?'

'Should I?'

'Do you know him?'

'No.'

'He looks harmless.'

'He certainly does,' Philip said simply, moving away and calling over his shoulder, 'Show him in, will you, Nicole?'

Nervous, the stranger stood at the doorway of Philip Gorday's office, then moved a few feet in, closing the door behind him. His gaze – behind the thick lenses of his glasses – flicked around the room, taking in the sombre elegance expected of a New York lawyer. Hating travel of any kind, Nicolai Kapinski had passed the flight in a state of hyperventilating silence. All food had been refused, all conversation curtailed. Instead he had sipped at water and dozed intermittently, with his briefcase on his lap. On the back of the seat in front of him there was a screen on which he could watch the latest movies, but instead Nicolai had chosen to view the map which showed the route from London to New York: a little yellow plane marking its flight path achingly slowly as it inched across the Atlantic. Away from Albemarle Street, from London. From home.

Gesturing for Nicolai to take a seat opposite his, Philip smiled faintly. 'How can I help you?'

'I hope I might be able to help you.'

'Really. How?'

'I knew your wife. We had known each other for a long time.'

'Where did you know her from? New York?'

'London.' Nicolai paused. 'It was Charlotte who introduced me to Owen Zeigler and got me the job at the gallery, I was Owen's accountant. I thought you knew all about it.'

'About what?' Philip asked, baffled.

Nonplussed, Nicolai stared at the composed man. God, what was he doing? Had he made a mistake? Miscalculated? He had thought about it for a long time, then decided that he couldn't stay in London. They would find him there. They would guess he was involved in the Rembrandt letters. After all, they were working through everyone else who had been close to Owen Zeigler. Teddy Jack had disappeared, and when Nicolai phoned Marshall's mobile it had been disconnected. Feeling suddenly exposed, he'd panicked. The knowledge that Marshall had the original letters didn't console him. He was worried, anxious that Charlotte had made copies. That perhaps his theory of her disappointing a seller might be true, after all. Then he had decided that if Charlotte *had* made copies, he would have to get hold of them. That way he would have some bargaining power with whoever was coming after *him*.

So, in an effort to save himself, Nicolai Kapinski had made the trip to New York. His small hands gripped the briefcase tightly, his accent more pronounced. 'Your wife,' he said, then paused. 'Charlotte – you knew about her and Owen Zeigler? She told me you knew all about them.'

'Yes, I knew.'

'Good,' Nicolai replied, relieved. 'What else did she tell you?'

'Mr—?'

'Kapinski,' he stammered. 'Forgive me, my name is Nicolai Kapinski. I should have said that at first. I should have told your secretary, it was remiss of me. As I said, I worked for Owen Zeigler until he was killed.'

Philip was watching him.

'Go on.'

'Your wife died. I'm so sorry, I heard all about it. They said it was suicide, didn't they, but I don't think so.'

He now had Philip's full attention. Frowning, he leaned forward, his wedding ring catching the light.

'What do you mean by that?'

'I think Charlotte was murdered.'

'Why?'

'You have no idea?' Nicolai countered, trying to get some feel of how much Philip Gorday knew. 'You believe she committed suicide?'

'Why not?'

'Why would she?'

'She was very depressed about Owen Zeigler's death.'

Nicolai took in a long breath, as though he was about to dive underwater. 'She wasn't that type of woman.'

His eyes flickering, Philip's voice became hostile. 'Really?

302

Just what kind of woman was my wife? In your opinion?'

'I'm not giving evidence!' Nicolai said, his tone rising. 'I'm not in a court of law. This conversation is in confidence. I mean no disrespect to your wife, I just want the truth. I think she was killed.'

Expressionless, Philip moved behind his desk and sat down, pulling a notepad towards him. 'D'you mind if I take notes?'

'If you do, I'll leave.'

Nodding, Philip stared at the little man. 'All right. Why d'you think my wife was killed?'

'Because she was trying to blackmail Owen Zeigler.'

Philip flinched. 'What!'

'I'm telling you the truth. Not to hurt you, but to explain why she was killed,' Nicolai said hurriedly. 'At one time she possessed some important letters. She wanted Owen to sell them and get himself out of his financial trouble. She said that if he did nothing about them, *she* would make sure they were seen—'

'Were they?'

'What?' Nicolai asked, wiping his forehead with a folded handkerchief.

'Seen. Did Charlotte show these letters to anyone?'

'No.' Nicolai shook his head emphatically, trying to test out what he knew against what he was told. 'She had them, but she didn't do anything with them.'

'How d'you know all this?'

'Because if she had sold them to the person who wanted them, she would still be alive.'

Narrowing his eyes, Philip glanced away. There was something about the little man which made him compelling. His story should have sounded far fetched, the rambling of someone disturbed, but Nicolai Kapinski was clearly frightened and Philip had never been convinced that his wife had killed herself. The memory of her body, the way he had found her, the brutality of the stabbing came back to him and jolted his gut. In the bleak days after Charlotte's death Philip had gone over her belongings, doing the distressing job of the bereaved. But there had been nothing unusual. Just her will, a few possessions bequeathed to friends and relations, but no paperwork of note, and certainly no letters.

Still turned away from Nicolai, he stared into space. How much did he really know about his wife? From the first time they had met, Charlotte had impressed him with her chic composure. She had never been an adventuress, never a woman drawn to anything immoral or criminal. Sordid was not a word that had any relevance in Charlotte Gorday's life.

Yet she *had* been the long-time lover of Owen Zeigler, and as such there *had* been a part of her life completely separate from his. Perhaps there had been part of her character off limits too . . . But blackmail? Philip couldn't accept the idea. It was too low for Charlotte – unless she had been trying to force her lover's hand in order to help him. To lever Owen Zeigler into saving himself. That was feasible.

Or was it?

'What were these letters about?'

Nicolai shook his head. 'I can't tell you.'

'This conversation is in confidence.'

'Believe me, you don't want to know more. Charlotte was killed because she was involved, and she wasn't the first. There was a man in Amsterdam who knew about them, and Owen Zeigler. All the people who know about these letters are either dead, or likely to be—'

'*You* know about them.'

'Yes, and I'm terrified, Mr Gorday,' Nicolai admitted, wiping his forehead again, then the palms of his hands. 'Why do you think I'm in New York talking to you?'

'To be honest, I don't know.'

'I need any copies your wife made of the letters.'

'I don't have any.'

'Charlotte had them,' Nicolai persisted, 'so they must be with her things.'

'Mr Kapinski, there are no letters in my late wife's belongings.'

'Maybe hidden—'

'No!' Philip silenced the frightened man. 'And besides, even if there were copies, why would I give them to you? You come in here, a total stranger, and tell me you knew my late wife and that she was murdered. Then you ask me for these documents. If they're as dangerous as you say, why would you want them?'

'To stop the killings,' Nicolai blurted out, his composure rattled. 'Why should these letters be protected? Why *shouldn't* I give them up? They mean nothing to me, it's history, the past. Why should I care about what happens in the art market? It's a grasping business, perhaps it's time it was shaken up.' He paused, fractious, nervy. 'If they get the letters, it will stop. They'll have no need to come after me or anyone else.'

'I need to know what these letters are, Mr Kapinski.'

Shaking his head, Nicolai got to his feet. His skin was waxen, his hands shaking.

'I understand why you ask me this, but I can't tell you. I came to you for help, Mr Gorday. I want to live, you see. Not much of a life, mine. But I have a wife and son who I would rather like to see again.' He smiled faintly, hardly lifting the corners of his mouth. 'You see, I know what to do with these letters, I know where to place them. I can put an end to all of this. I'd like to do that.'

'But if you did expose them, would it hurt people?'

'It would rock the art world,' Nicolai said dully. 'Some dealers would be ruined, some might kill themselves, many would struggle. Fortunes would be lost. So, yes, Mr Gorday, if the letters came out, people would suffer.'

'And you think that's a good enough argument for me to pass them over to you?' Philip asked, his tone ironic.

'You have to ask yourself, what's the alternative? Another murder? Or would that be counted as collateral damage? Maybe two, three murders would be unacceptable? Oh, but there have already *been* three murders, Mr Gorday. Your wife's was the last. So far.' He leaned over the desk, his eyes wide behind the thick lenses. 'If you have copies of these letters, give them up. Not just for my sake, but for yours.'

'I'm a lawyer, I would need proof of all this,' Philip said. 'I can't take it on trust.'

'In the end you'll believe everything I've told you,' Nicolai replied, defeated. 'Can't you help me?'

Philip shook his head. 'If I couldn't help my wife, how the hell can I help you?'

28

London

'So it's true?' Tobar Manners asked, staring at Leon Williams, 'there *are* two Rembrandt portraits coming onto the market?'

His visitor nodded, but he was preoccupied. 'Shouldn't you get some more bars on the window?' he said. 'I mean, what with all these break-ins and murders.'

'*Two Rembrandts*?' Tobar repeated, 'Who's selling them?'

'Some Japan dealer—'

'Hokinou?'

'I don't know,' Leon replied. 'I wasn't really listening.'

'Well, where did you hear it?'

'Rufus Ariel was muttering about it. He's been in the London Clinic for some more Botox injections and—'

'Rufus Ariel has *Botox*?'

'Didn't you ever wonder why his face didn't move and was so shiny?'

'I thought that was just fat,' Tobar replied, and pushed on. 'So, what about the Rembrandts?'

'Rufus heard the rumour a while back, and then Lillian Kauffman came to see him—'

'While he was having Botox?'

'I don't know if he was having Botox at the time, maybe it was afterwards,' Leon replied thoughtfully. 'Anyway, Lillian Kauffman confirmed it. I think Rufus wants to handle the sale—'

'I bet he bloody does!' Tobar drummed his fingers irritably on his desk. No one was going to handle the sale but him. He needed it, and he had to get it. If the galleries couldn't pay the rents, they would be priced out. So much valuable retail property up for grabs. Not only that, but a sale to a German collector had fallen through and an exhibition Tobar had been planning to put on in the summer had been cancelled. Bloody Russians, he thought, all that Moscow Mafia money was running out, just like Arab money had in the 1970s. His confidence was nose-diving, his usual arrogant bluster faltering. If Leon Williams and others couldn't – or *wouldn't* – see what was happening, he could. Some dealers were even stupid enough to ignore the warning signs – that nervy Tim Parker-Ross, for example, opening up a new gallery off the King's Road although God only knew how long it would *stay* open.

Fretting, Tobar worried about his precarious future. Lillian Kauffman, he thought bitterly, that bitch would be trying to secure her position early. If he didn't make the big Rembrandt sale and preserve his reputation, he would join the list of casualties which was growing weekly.

A walk around Bond Street, Davis Street and Cork Street, once the preserve of galleries, with their private vews and parties, once the prime site for swathes of Brit Art, paparazzi and minor royals – was changing. Some of the windows were empty and 'To let' notices had appeared on premises which had flourished for decades. Where limousines once waited by the kerbside for their celebrities, discarded copies of the *Evening Standard* flapped round the empty gutters.

Only the previous week Tobar had put a Govert Flinck into an auction and it hadn't reached its reserve. Regretfully he had had to pull it and put it back into storage. No one was buying, and the few that *might* buy were only going for the biggest names. Like Rembrandt . . . Tobar realised that unless he managed to secure the Rembrandt sale he might well be fighting to find the rent in six months time.

'That wasn't *all* I heard,' Leon went on. 'There's a rumour going round that Owen Zeigler was killed because he knew something.'

'Like what? The time?'

Leon, missing the point, blundered on. 'No, no. I mean someone heard something about how he'd got some letters.'

Already unnerved, Tobar's patience was running out. 'What are you talking about?'

'Letters which prove that many Rembrandts are forgeries.'

'Oh, he was always blathering on about some bloody theory of his.'

'But there's proof.'

His eyes glazed, Tobar stood up and faced Leon. His expression was threatening, his tone hostile. 'What?'

'I heard—'

'From who?'

'Just a rumour, Tobar,' Leon said nervously, now sorry he had ever started the conversation. 'Just a rumour.'

'About Rembrandts being fakes?'

Leon nodded, wretched with misery. 'Apparently these letters are proof that paintings which have always been thought authentic are fakes. Done by a pupil of—'

'People have said that for centuries.'

'But there are *letters*, Tobar,' Leon went on, his thin face filled with panic as he watched his companion begin to sweat. 'Proof. The rumour goes that up to half of the pictures we think are by Rembrandt are fakes. It would be bad for the market—'

'*Bad for the market!*' Tobar exploded. 'It would bring *down* the fucking market. It can't be true.'

'There's a list.'

Tobar felt a hot flush of panic. 'What?'

'With the letters there's a list. A complete list of the paintings which are fakes.'

Tobar's legs lost their strength as he stumbled into his chair and loosened his collar. He could feel the sweat running down his back and puddling under his armpits. If it was true, these letters – this list – would destroy the market. He would never be able to broker the sale in New York and make the fortune he needed to prevent the collapse of his business. If the letters came out, with the list, every Rembrandt would be questioned, undermined. *And what if the Rembrandt portraits due for sale were proved to be fakes?*

With cold misery, Tobar thought back to the paintings he had sold to private collectors and galleries. If they were discovered to be counterfeit they would be worth a tiny percentage of the selling price. And his reputation, what of that? Tobar felt his breathing accelerate. It was a bitter irony that the Rembrandt he had stolen from Owen he had claimed to be painted by a pupil. But perhaps it had been; perhaps it was a fake after all. Perhaps it *had been* worth next to nothing.

He stared ahead, blind with shock, acutely aware he had cheated himself. 'Where are these letters, Leon?'

'No one knows for sure.'

'*Where are they?*'

'Someone said that maybe his son had them.'

'His son . . .' Tobar replied thoughtfully.

'It's just a rumour going the rounds, but everyone's talking about it,' Leon stammered. 'Is it bad for us, Tobar?'

Tobar ignored the question, unsettled. If it was true that Owen Zeigler had found the letters, was it possible he had been killed for them? A memory nudged Tobar, his recent conversation with Rufus Ariel. Something about the death of Stefan van der Helde . . . And then there was the suicide of Charlotte Gorday, Owen's lover. His hand shaking, Tobar reached for his glass of water. He sipped at it, tried to swallow. He had been close to Owen; if he had *kept* close Owen would have confided in him, told him about these letters. Given him insider knowledge.

And it was then Tobar realised that by cheating his friend he had inadvertently cut his own throat.

29

New York

Drenched by the heavy downpour, Philip Gorday ran into the entrance of the office building, taking off his coat and shaking it impatiently. Water flicked onto the polished floor, throwing flecks up onto the front of the reception desk. Philip smoothed back his damp hair with his hands as he walked to the elevator. Staring at the illuminated floor numbers, he watched them change, thinking of the conversation he had had with Nicolai Kapinski the previous day.

He wanted to dismiss it as a hoax, but the words had jammed in his head and rattled around his dreams that night. Charlotte was alive again, walking into the sitting room of the apartment and then laughing. But as she laughed, her portrait over the mantelpiece faded, dying back into a blank canvas until there was nothing left of her. Jerked awake, Philip had got up and padded into the kitchen, making coffee and petting the dog. He had known instinctively that what Nicolai Kapinski had told him was true. Charlotte hadn't committed suicide, whatever the police said. Which meant that someone had broken into the apartment and killed her while she was sleeping in their bed, alone. Philip had been out walking the dog that morning, so there had only been a short space of time for the killer to act. Uneasy, Philip wondered if he had been watched, if someone had waited for him to leave the building, before they broke in. But then again, the lock hadn't been forced, and Philip knew only too well he had not left it undone.

Which meant that Charlotte's killer had a key. Was it someone she knew? Philip paused, stirring some cream into his coffee. Was it someone they both knew, in New York? Or someone only Charlotte knew, from London . . .?

Sighing, he stepped out of the elevator and walked to his office. 'Any messages?' he asked Nicole.

'Just these.' She passed him a few notes. 'Nothing urgent.'

'Anything from Nicolai Kapinski?'

'No.'

Nodding, Philip sat down at his desk. If Charlotte had been killed, he wanted to find her killer. Wanted him brought to justice. Wanted him punished for taking away a woman he had loved so much. And missed more. Once again he wondered whether Charlotte had known her killer, and then his thoughts turned to Nicolai Kapinski. Kapinski said he had known Charlotte for a long time in London, but was he genuine? Had he come to confide in Philip or to try and trap him into handing over copies of these phantom letters? Had he been lying about being afraid for his life?

But if Nicolai Kapinski was Charlotte's killer, he would have already got the letters, Philip thought. *Unless Charlotte didn't have them.* Perhaps Kapinski had been bluffing, trying to discover if she had passed them over to her husband. Uncertain of everything, Philip took a note out of his middle desk drawer and punched the number into his phone.

'Hotel Melmont. Can I help you?'

'I want to speak to Mr Nicolai Kapinski,' Philip said, glancing back to the piece of paper. 'He's in room 223.'

'One moment, please.'

There was a long pause, during which Philip heard the phone ring several times before the operator came back on the line.

'No answer, sir. Would you like to leave a message at reception?'

'No,' he said hurriedly. 'No, thanks.'

It was after lunch before Philip had time to think about Nicolai Kapinski again. Pushing away his coffee, he stared at the phone and then decided that he would visit the man at the hotel. He strode out of his office, past Nicole, without uttering a word, and hurried into the street. The rain had stopped and a truculent sun pitted the shiny road. Hailing a cab, Philip gave his destination and then leaned back in his seat, staring out of the window until the car drew up outside the Hotel Melmont. He paid the cabbie and walked into reception, surprised to notice a number of people milling around, talking. Curious, Philip was about to get the elevator, when he decided to take the stairs instead. On the second floor he walked towards room 223.

As he turned into the next corridor he almost collided with a policeman who was standing at the half-open doorway. Craning his neck, Philip could just make out two other men inside, standing over a covered heap on the floor.

'Hey, sir. You can't go in there,' the policeman on the door said, putting out his arm to stop Philip.

'What's happened?'

Inside, one of the detectives turned to Philip. 'Why would you want to know?'

'Is Mr Kapinski all right?'

Noticing that the two detectives exchanged a glance, Philip raised his voice. '*Is Mr Kapinski all right?*'

'What's it to you?'

'I'm his lawyer,' Philip lied, and the policeman on guard dropped his arm to allow him into the room.

'Correction,' one of the detectives said flatly. 'You *were* his lawyer.'

The hairs rising on the back of his neck, Philip looked at the body covered with a sheet.

'Can I see?'

'Well, it's more than he can.'

Frowning, Philip looked questioningly at the detective.

'His eyes were gouged out.'

Tentatively, Philip lifted the sheet which covered the remains of Nicolai Kapinski. He was naked from the waist up and his eyes had been pushed in by some terrific impact or object, splattering blood outwards and coating his face and chest. His hands had been tied behind his back so tightly that the wire had been driven into the flesh, and in his struggle he had managed to sever a vein. Another repugnant detail lay on the floor around the tortured body. Nicolai Kapinski had had little hair, but now his scalp was totally bald. In places his hair had been pulled out, the roots still attached, while other parts of his skull had been shaven, white and eerie as a bone.

And in his left hand was his tongue.

BOOK FOUR

30

London

Hurrying down Beak Street, Marshall paused outside the narrow entrance of number 67, where several doorbells had names beside them. Lulu, Stacy and Kim all offered massage; but the very top bell was marked Teddy Jack. Somehow knowing that the Northerner wouldn't answer his bell, Marshall pressed all of them at once, and the door clicked open almost immediately.

As he rounded the stairs to the first floor, a girl came out, eating a cheese sandwich and smiling morosely.

'You looking for company?'

'I'm looking for Teddy Jack.'

Half heartedly, she jerked her head upwards. 'He's on the next floor. I think he's in. He's not been going out much lately.'

'Is he ill?'

'Nah . . . well, you'll see.' She went back into her room and closed the door and Marshall made his way upstairs in the fading light. The air was clammy with incense and an underlying sourness. When he reached Teddy Jack's door, he saw a handwritten note – DON'T DISTURB. He ignored it and walked in. The damp, mottled blind was drawn, the light shaded, and the thick odour of old food, stale beer and cannabis was cloying. On an unmade bed under the window lay Teddy Jack, dressed but dozing. His head was lolling over to one side, dry crusting sat at the corners of his mouth, his big feet were bare and dirty.

'Teddy,' Marshall said, leaning forward and shaking his arm. 'Teddy, wake up.'

He murmured in his sleep, but didn't wake.

Sighing, Marshall moved into the tiny cubicle which served as a kitchen. In the full sink, a cockroach scuttled for cover; a half-eaten tin of beans sat discarded on top of the hob. Throwing aside a slimy cloth, Marshall put some water onto boil and then made coffee before walking back into the front room and lifting the blind. Disturbed by the light, Teddy finally woke, while Marshall was opening the window and letting in some cold air.

'Fucking hell!' Teddy exclaimed, reaching for a blanket. 'What on earth . . .' He stared at Marshall in disbelief. 'What are you doing here?'

'Nicolai Kapinski's dead.'

Teddy's eyes registered nothing. No flicker, no emotion, just an empty, almost resigned, acceptance.

'He had the letters?'

'No,' Marshall replied, watching him rub his face with his ham-sized hands. 'Are you taking drugs now?'

'Why d'you care?'

'Cannabis?'

Teddy leaned forwards in his seat. 'Why d'you care?'

'Is that all you can say?'

'OK, try this. What's it to you what I do?'

Closing the window again as the room temperature dropped, Marshall leaned against the wall. 'You didn't strike me as the type to give up.'

'I was having a holiday,' Teddy replied drily. 'In my head.'

'Go anywhere nice?'

'Can't remember. Don't want to. In fact, I don't want to be talking to you. No offence, Marshall, you saved my life and I'm grateful, but you don't have to spend the rest of your time looking after me.'

'Aren't you surprised that Nicolai's been murdered?'

Reaching for the stump of a smoke, Teddy lit up and inhaled. His eyes were puffy and unclear, his red beard mottled with food and spittle. And he stank.

'Why should I be surprised? We'll all be killed in the end.'

'You think so?'

'Yeah. I think anyone involved with the letters is as good as dead.' He slumped back against the bedhead, his expression unreadable. 'I don't suppose they know who killed Nicolai?'

'No. In fact, if Philip Gorday hadn't told me all about it, I doubt I would have heard. You see, Nicolai was killed in New York.'

Finally interested, Teddy stared at Marshall. '*New York?* What the hell was he doing in New York?'

'Apparently he was trying to find the letters.' Marshall hesitated, wary, careful not to give too much away. 'Nicolai thought Charlotte might have had them, or copies of them.'

'So?'

'Philip Gorday said that Nicolai knew who would want to buy the letters. Where to place them.'

'In New York?'

Marshall shrugged. 'No, apparently Nicolai just went to New York to see Philip Gorday—'

'And save his own skin.'

'Can you blame him?'

Teddy's eyes narrowed as he inhaled again. 'I think *you've* got those fucking letters.'

Marshall ignored the comment. 'Why don't you put that out?' he pointed to the joint. 'You'll think more clearly.'

'Why do I want to think more clearly?'

'Because you could be the next victim.'

'Why? I don't have the letters.'

'Neither did Nicolai,' Marshall said pointedly.

'I didn't like the little creep. We never got on.' There was a long pause. 'How was he killed?'

'He was tortured. His eyes were put out. Nicolai was held down on the floor, and a sharp instrument blinded him. First one eye, then the other. Then they cut out his tongue.'

Wincing, Teddy stubbed out his smoke and got to his feet. Barefoot, he padded into the corridor. Marshall could hear a cistern flushing a few moments later and watched as Teddy came back into the flat and splashed water on his face.

'Why would anyone kill him like that?'

Because they were copying *The Blinding of Samson*, Marshall thought, because it was the fourth death which emulated one of Rembrandt's paintings. Teddy Jack wouldn't have understood, but Marshall had got the message.

'The last time we talked, at the gallery, I said some things I regret.' Teddy paused for an instant. 'I said Owen used to laugh about Nicolai behind his back, mock him about his missing brother. Well, that wasn't true. Your father *did* tease him about it, because Nicolai used to go off on these weird depressions, but there was more to it.'

'Like what?'

'I found Nicolai's brother.'

It was the last thing Marshall expected to hear.

'Nicolai didn't mention it to—'

'Because he didn't know. I only found Dimitri – as Luther now calls himself – a few days before your father was killed.' He rubbed his beard vigorously with the towel. 'I'd had no time to talk to Owen about it, ask him what he wanted to do, so I let it be. Anyway, after what I found out, I thought maybe Nicolai wouldn't want to know that his brother had been found. You know, maybe it was better if he remained lost.'

Marshall stared at the big man. 'Why?'

'Because he was no good. Dimitri Kapinski wasn't abducted. His father sent him away, paid for him to be taken on by another family. The mother never knew, but Dimitri was sent to work in a farm in the backwaters of Hungary. He was only a kid, and by the time he'd been there for a couple of years he'd been starting fires, and when he was seventeen he'd started thieving. He had some odd ways too. Wasn't all there. Moody,' Teddy went on, tapping his left temple. 'By the time he was twenty odd, Dimitri had spent time in jail and been married. Then he'd bunked off to London, worked there for a short while, selling drugs. He'd become pretty violent too, then he went back to Poland, and finally returned to his wife in Hungary.'

'Where is he now?'

'Last I found out, he was in jail abroad. Someone said Turkey. After that, I lost trace of him. I mean, Nicolai was a bit of a creeping Jesus, but he wouldn't have wanted to know that his brother turned out to be just one more East European scumbag.' He thought back. 'When Nicolai had one of his funny turns he used to talk about his brother constantly, obsessively, and make him out to be something special. You know, a kid someone *would* steal, like he was Merlin or something. Your father never stopped him, just let Nicolai talk. And he'd go off on one and start speaking to his brother – like Dimitri was in the bloody room with him! Weird, but then Nicolai was pretty strange at times. He wasn't a bad man, though. Not like his brother.'

'Perhaps it was better that Nicolai didn't know about him.'

'Yeah, that was what I thought.' Teddy took a breath and looked round the sordid room as though suddenly disgusted by it. 'Let myself go a bit, haven't I?'

'Understandable.'

'Is it?' He stared at Marshall for a long instant. 'Why did you come here?'

'I need your help.'

'You found *me* in the packing case, remember?'

Marshall laughed, then became serious. 'I'm being followed.'

'Are you sure?'

'Yes. I thought someone was behind me on the street, then I saw them reflected in a window. They went everywhere with me this morning.' He paused. 'And the gallery's being watched. There were two men last night who didn't belong in Albemarle Street.'

'You scared?'

'Yeah, of course I'm scared,' Marshall admitted. 'I don't want to die.'

'Well, we've got that in common.'

'Can you find out who it is?'

'That's following you?'

Marshall nodded. 'I have to go to Amsterdam as soon as I can, and I want to go alone. I'm not just worried for myself, but I'd like you to keep an eye on my ex-wife, Georgia.'

Surprised, Teddy raised his eyebrows. 'Is she involved?'

'I told her about the letters,' Marshall replied, hurrying on. 'It was just after my father was killed and I needed someone to talk to. Unfortunately I chose her. She's pregnant, and I don't— Well, just look out for her, will you?'

Nodding, Teddy pulled on his socks and shoes. 'When are you leaving for Holland?'

'Tonight. On the six o'clock flight.'

'OK.'

Marshall took in a breath. 'It might mean trouble.'

'It *always* means trouble.'

'I can pay you.'

'I could do with the money, no work around.' He shrugged. 'I thought about going back up North, but it's just as bad there, so I just decided to sit on the bed and get stoned for a while.'

'Did it help?'

'A bit maybe. I thought about your father. Kept going over what he did and said about those fucking letters, trying to think if there was something I'd forgotten. And I thought about the people he knew, and what I'd done when I was working for him, and I kept wondering who'd kill him like that – him, and the others. Killing someone, yeah, I can understand that. In temper, I can understand it. In the heat of the moment. But torturing someone? Making it last? No, I don't get that. And I'm not going to let them do it to me.'

Marshall nodded. 'Good, because we have to work together now, Teddy. I think it's the only way we'll survive.'

'Even though you don't trust me?'

'I never said that.'

'You didn't have to,' Teddy replied. 'Maybe if I was in your shoes I wouldn't trust anyone either.'

'I'm asking you to look out for my ex-wife. I must trust you.'

'How long are you staying in Holland?'

'I'm not sure, I'll keep in touch.' Marshall paused. 'But don't let Georgia know what you're doing. She's smart, she won't be easy to fool.'

Teddy nodded. 'And you know what you're doing?'

'Not really.'

'I thought not.' Teddy smiled. 'No plan?'

'Well, I know they'll come after me. I can draw them out that way. And if they're coming after me, they're not going after anyone else.'

'Which means that you're going to set yourself up?'

Marshall hesitated. 'They won't stop. That much is obvious.'

'Is there anyone else left – apart from you, Samuel Hemmings, and me – that knows about the letters?'

'Only Georgia.'

'*And then there were four . . .*' Teddy said quietly. 'Four down, four to go.'

'Don't let anything happen to her!' Marshall snapped. 'You keep her safe, you hear me?'

'I hear you. But who's going to do the same for you?'

House of Corrections,
Gouda, 1654

He hired a new maid, younger than me, called Hendrickje Stoffels. She came to help me out, and I hated her from the instant I saw her. Knew in her cat's eyes what she was after. Titus didn't like her, clung to me, but she wasn't going to be his nurse. Just keep house, help me. Jesus, she helped me. She helped me out of my master's bed. She watched, feline, plumply sleek, never once looked at the painting on the landing. Didn't believe in ghosts. I know that.

She will, when she hears them walk the house at night and sees Saskia's face at the window, looking in, or drawing back the curtains around the bed . . . I'm jumping in my story. Did I tell you that Carel became so clever? So very very skilled. I watched him work and used to creep back into the studio late at night, and lift the cover over his canvas. And wonder how the child – that had kicked me in my ribs as he grew in my belly – could paint so well. So well he impressed his father . . . Carel knew I admired his work and was kind. Never patronising or dismissive, like Gerrit Dou, with his round, bird's-eye glasses and his clever verbal barbs. Carel didn't know I was his mother, he was just kind. Because kindness became him.

He got that from me . . .

Then suddenly he was gone. Rembrandt hadn't told me he was sending him away. Didn't say a word. Carel was just there, and then not there. When I asked him about it, Rembrandt said he had set our son up in his own studio in Delft, where he was going to be a triumphant success . . . I had to let him go, without a word. What else could I do? His monkey, Rembrandt told me, was clever. So clever he would work for his father and they would make money. Fabulous amounts of money. Midas would have been envious. We will dupe all Holland, we will dupe the world, he said, nuzzling my neck with his thick lips.

We will dupe the world. But Rembrandt coughed when he said it, as though his throat choked on the words . . . Would Carel get into trouble? I asked, curled up against Rembrandt in bed. And he snorted, and told me to stay quiet, that no one knew about our son. And if – oh God – if I ever mentioned it he would deny it. Ruin Carel's career . . . Say nothing, he told me in the big bed. Stay silent . . . Carel must never know his real parents and no one must ever know of the work he was doing for his father.

Then Hendrickje came . . . I would have stayed quiet for the rest of my life. It would have been enough. I would have made it enough . . . Carel was out of my life, but he was successful, married, there was no reason to talk. What good would it do him to know his real mother? . . . But then Hendrickje came and soon she was raising her eyes behind me and making Rembrandt laugh. And he became impatient and scolded me, mocking me in front of the pupils and letting Hendrickje sit for them. I was being usurped. In his heart, in his bed, and in his studio.

But I kept quiet . . . I swept the black and white tiles and carried the water. I loved Titus and made herrings, and I waited for Hendrickje to leave, for this new passion of Rembrandt's to

wane. After all, I was his real mistress and the mother of his
son. He would come back to me. In time. I had a hold over him
through Carel. I just had to wait, that was all. I had the upper
hand.

It wasn't enough.

31

Hurriedly packing a suitcase, Marshall heard the bell ring in the gallery below. For a moment he considered ignoring it, then ran downstairs to find Tim Parker-Ross waiting in the doorway. He grinned shyly as Marshall let him in, ambling through to the back of the gallery and standing under the skylight.

'I was wondering if you'd like that dinner tonight,' he said, putting his head on one side, his expression curious. 'What's wrong?'

'I didn't say anything was wrong.'

'No, but I've known you since we were kids,' Tim replied kindly. 'I can always tell when you're worried.'

'It's just that there's so much to sort out. I don't know if I'm going to sell up the gallery or keep it running.'

'Keep it running?' Tim replied. 'Wow, that would be something. I mean, I'm not being rude, but you've never been into the art business. Bit like me really.'

'But I heard you'd just opened another gallery.'

Tim raised his eyes heavenwards. 'Worst time, hey? I've

no head for business, probably lose a fortune . . . So, you're not on for dinner tonight?'

'Sorry, I can't make it, Tim.'

He nodded, looking round. 'Well, maybe later in the week. By the way, I saw Tobar Manners this morning, in a terrible state.'

'About what?'

'He was talking about two big Rembrandt portraits coming up for sale in New York.' Tim scratched his nose thoughtfully. 'Tobar wants to broker the deal. Make a killing.'

'Yeah, well he's good at that.'

'You hate him, don't you?'

'He cheated my father,' Marshall replied flatly. 'I'd like to see him ruined.'

Embarrassed, Tim laughed, shuffling his feet. 'I don't like him either. He always talks to me as though I'm a fool. He confuses me, makes me stammer. I can never think when he's around.' His voice speeded up, then dropped. 'I heard Tobar Manners needs this big deal with the Rembrandts, or he'll be ruined.'

'Then let's hope he doesn't get it,' Marshall replied, changing the subject. 'I have to get on with some work now, Tim.'

'Oh, yes, yes, of course.' He nodded towards the bag at the top of the stairs. 'You going away?'

'Just overnight,' Marshall lied. 'I've a translating job to do. I'll be back before you know it.'

'We'll have dinner then,' Tim said, nodding and walking off down the street.

For a moment Marshall watched him go, a lonely figure with no home or family, but kind. Always kind. Deep in thought, Marshall returned to the flat, only to hear a loud banging on the gallery door moments later. Impatient, he went back downstairs and found Lillian Kauffman at the door.

As he let her in, her expression was confrontational. 'You're fucked.'

'No, Libra,' Marshall replied smoothly. 'I've things to do—'

'Look, you bloody idiot, I've told you, I can help. I don't suppose you noticed anything strange the last two nights?'

'Like what?'

'Like men watching your gallery,' Lillian said. 'And when you went out earlier, I could have sworn someone was following you.'

'You watch too much television.'

'I watch the *street*, darling, and I see what goes on,' she said, her tone curt. 'I don't need a television, I've been making my own entertainment for years. I don't suppose you knew that Leon Williams was gay, did you?'

'I don't know Leon Williams. And anyway, why would it matter if he was gay?'

She clicked her tongue. 'Gossip is important, darling. It pays to know everything about everyone. Leon Williams is a dealer. Used to be a friend of your father's. Rufus Ariel's little running mate.' She paused. 'Anyway, that's by the by. I've been thinking all day about what's been going on. And about those letters, and about the sale coming up in New York. Two Rembrandt portraits, set to make a fortune. Everyone's excited by it. It's going to make big money.'

'So?'

'But only if the Rembrandts are authentic, because if they're fakes, you're screwed.'

Marshall raised his eyebrows. 'How?'

'If you have proof they're not by Rembrandt, then their value will plummet.' She ran her tongue over her bottom lip. 'And everyone who was set to make a fortune will be seriously out of pocket. Unless, of course, they can suppress the information: stop the letters coming out.' She tapped her foot impatiently and lit a cigarette. 'I heard about a young man the other day who had knifed and killed another man for his mobile phone. Makes you think, doesn't it?'

'About what?'

'About how little someone will kill for. If a mobile phone worth – what? Twenty quid? – is worth murder, then killing for something which could lose someone millions and millions of pounds would be pretty much essential.' She paused, fiddling with one of her extravagant earrings. 'You can't hold onto those letters, Marshall. They'll kill you for them.'

'Who will?'

'Don't piss about! I can understand why you wouldn't want to go to the police. I can see you'd want to find out who killed your father, and deal with them yourself – and get your own back on Tobar Manners. But you're only going to get killed—'

'What if I don't have the bloody letters?'

'Don't insult my intelligence.' Lillian was curt. 'We have to talk about this. You can arse about with me all you like, but you must have thought of the alternatives, Marshall. You can make the letters public and bring down Rembrandt's reputation and undermine the art market; or you could sell them to someone who would pay you a handsome price so that they could keep them quiet. And keep the market stable. Or you could sell them to someone who could use them covertly, and blackmail the dealers.'

'I don't know—'

Her voice hardened as she cut him off.

'Perhaps you've even thought of that yourself, Marshall? I mean, you could crucify Tobar Manners, and get your revenge at the same time if you let it be known that some paintings he sold as authentic Rembrandts, weren't.' She drew on her cigarette, staring at Marshall intently. 'I can see you want to keep your cards very close to your chest. I don't blame you. But you have to do something, Marshall, or someone else will make the first move.'

He stared at her in silence.

'They've killed your father,' Lillian continued. 'And Charlotte Gorday, Stefan van der Helde, and now Nicolai Kapinski.'

Marshall's head shot up. 'How did you know that?'

'Philip Gorday is a friend of mine.'

'Jesus, does everyone know everyone else?'

'He's my lawyer. He represents my American interests.

Besides, Philip has collected paintings for years, and I knew Charlotte very well.'

'Apparently everybody did, except me.'

'Don't be defensive, Marshall, your father wanted to keep his private life private. After all, did he know who you were screwing?'

'You've got sex on the brain.'

'At my age, on the brain is the only place it can be,' she replied, tartly. 'I know that Owen wouldn't have wanted the letters to come out, especially not in a recession, and I know you want to honour his wishes. But you can't just sit on them, because they'll come for you, Marshall. You must know that. They're already watching you. God, isn't this getting through your thick skull?'

'I found my father's body, so yes, Lillian, it's getting through to me.'

She had the grace to look momentarily embarrassed.

'When they catch up with you, you'll have a choice: give them the letters, or they'll kill you.'

'And even if they get what they want, they'll kill me anyway. If I know who they are, they won't let me go,' Marshall replied, his stomach clenching. 'I'm not a brave man, Lillian. I didn't want to get involved in any of this, but I am. And I have to deal with it the best way I can.'

'Your father wouldn't have wanted you to get killed,' she said impatiently. 'Of course, there is one other alternative. You could destroy them.'

'I can't do that. They're history, proof—'

'Of Rembrandt's bastard,' Lillian said slyly. 'No, I didn't

think you'd go for that suggestion. It would be too much like betraying Owen, wouldn't it, Marshall?'

Nodding, he moved towards the back of the gallery, followed by Lillian, and sat down at his father's old desk. Above him the skylight let in the day; the pilot light on the boiler made a popping sound as the heating came on. On the desk lay a pile of unopened post addressed to Owen Zeigler, and the answer phone was flicking with several messages. For a moment it seemed as though Owen was simply out of the gallery and would return in an instant, pick up his mail and answer his calls. And in the office in the eaves Nicolai would call down the stairs, while the porters brought in frames at the basement door ... But they would never come back, not his father, nor the accountant. Not Charlotte Gorday. They were ghosts now, joining the murdered soldier at the bend on the stairs.

'Marshall?'

He looked up, surprised by his own melancholia. 'What?'

'The letters are not worth dying for,' Lillian said firmly. 'They were your father's obsession, not yours.'

He sighed, trying to read her face. 'Who's doing it?'

'What?'

'Who are the killers, Lillian? You should some have some idea. You know everyone, you hear everything. You've got a clever mind and a quick brain, much smarter than mine. Christ knows, you've told me that often enough. You know everything that goes on. So who's mad enough to being doing all this? Who's clever enough? Come on,

Lillian, even I know that the Russians have bought up some of the prime galleries. The rents getting raised again? Too high? Is someone putting pressure on?'

'The Russians are just bully boys.'

'Maybe. But you can't deny that they'd jump at the chance to get hold of the Rembrandt letters. Much less work to blackmail the dealers, rather than have to go around collecting all those rents.'

'I'd have heard something.'

'Of course, you are the eyes and ears of this neighbourhood. In fact.' He paused. 'What's to stop it being you?'

'Don't be fucking stupid! I might have stolen the letters, but I'd never torture someone I liked.'

Marshall smiled. 'But don't tell me you haven't thought about who it might be. There must be *someone* you suspect? I've suspected damn near everyone. I thought for a while it might be Nicolai Kapinski, then Teddy Jack, and even Charlotte Gorday—'

'A woman?'

'A woman could kill, with help. That's what the police said, anyway,' Marshall replied. 'She wouldn't be strong enough to do it on her own, but if she had an ally she could.'

'Charlotte wasn't capable of killing anyone.'

To her surprise, Marshall laughed. 'You know something? I even doubted Samuel Hemmings, and he's in a wheelchair, for God's sake!' He shook his head. 'I've suspected everyone. And now most of them are dead, and I'm no nearer to knowing who killed my father.'

'The police—'

'Have no idea! They've never even made the connection between the murders. Why should they? They don't know about Rembrandt or the letters, so why should they connect killings in Holland, New York and London? I've asked around, and in Amsterdam Stefan van der Helde was thought to be a gay murder. Charlotte Gorday's death was put down to suicide. As for Nicolai, they said he was just unlucky, that he was killed while being robbed, probably by some addict. For the police, there's no reason to connect the deaths – and I'm not giving them the reason.'

'Just making yourself bait?'

He ignored the comment. 'Sometimes I wonder if I could have known my father's killer. Spoken to them. Broken bread with them, gone to the same exhibitions. They could have come to the gallery, or even visited our house in the country, and I wouldn't have known. And that's what sickens me, that when I find out who killed my father, I'll have known them. Maybe even liked them.'

She snorted impatiently. 'Or then again, they could be complete strangers.'

'No,' Marshall said. 'There was no forced entry at Stefan van der Helde's flat. No forced entry here. My father let his killer in. *He knew them.* Charlotte Gorday was stabbed without a struggle. Someone got so close to her there was no disturbance in her bedroom. And as for Nicolai, poor little Nicolai, he let them into his hotel room. He was terrified, in a strange city, and yet he let them in.'

'Which means?'

341

'That the killers aren't threatening. He, or they, are known to the victims, they seems harmless, familiar.' Marshall rubbed his eyes. 'Which makes me wonder: will I let them in too?'

32

Impatiently, Georgia dialled Marshall's mobile again, and was told – again – that the number was not valid. Thoughtful, she returned to the kitchen and made herself a sandwich, wondering where Marshall was. Certainly not at the gallery. She had called and left a message on the answer phone, even dropped by early that morning. But no one came when she knocked on the door, and the sign read CLOSED DUE TO BEREAVEMENT. The only person whose attention she did catch was an overdressed, overbejewelled woman who was watching from across the street.

Her anxieties about her ex-husband had been growing, and were even keeping her awake at night. Beside her, Harry would sleep undisturbed while she stared into the darkness, thinking. Sometimes, in the small hours, she decided she would go to the police in the morning and tell them about the letters, explain what was going on. Damn what Marshall thought. *He wasn't safe.* But then daylight would come and Georgia would realise that it wasn't her decision to make. Besides, she didn't even know where the letters were . . . Taking another bite out of her sandwich, she thought about Owen Zeigler, remembering her father-in-law's effortless charm. Owen: so respectable, so safe. So dead.

She put down her half-eaten sandwich and picked up the phone again. This time, she didn't call the gallery or Marshall's defunct mobile. This time she dialled a number she hadn't used for many years, and waited patiently for Philip Gorday to pick up.

Struggling to hear Marshall's voice against the background noise from the airport, Samuel asked him to repeat what he had just said.

'Nicolai Kapinski's been murdered in New York.'

'Dear God,' Samuel said, shaken, and automatically glanced out of the window. Greg Horner was leaning against the garage wall, smoking, idle as a statue but oddly comforting. 'Where are you?'

'On my way to Amsterdam.'

'Why?'

'I have something to do,' Marshall replied. 'Don't be alone, Samuel.'

'I'm not. I'm fine. It's you that has to be careful. Has anyone approached you?'

'No, but I'm being watched. Or rather, I *was* being watched. I don't think anyone followed me to the airport.'

Samuel could feel his hand shake and gripped the phone tightly. 'You have to be careful—'

344

'I *am* being careful. The person who killed Nicolai was copying Rembrandt's painting of *The Blinding of Samson*.'

'They blinded him?'

'They blinded him,' Marshall said. 'And it's come out about the letters. It's all over London, everyone's talking about it.'

'*How* did it come out?'

'I don't know,' Marshall admitted. 'All of a sudden, my father's theory is fact. People know there are letters that prove which Rembrandts are authentic—'

'And which aren't,' said Samuel, finishing the sentence for him.

'Yes.' Marshall glanced warily around him. His gaze ran over the crowd in the departure lounge, where a few businessmen, one of them slightly drunk, were talking morosely in a group. Alongside them, a woman nursed a small child. Behind her, a gaggle of schoolboys in uniform chattered frantically, giggling at a good-looking woman across the aisle. Only two people were alone, one a scruffy young man reading a book, the other an elderly man watching the planes through the window of the lounge. No one seemed to be paying any attention to Marshall.

'Samuel, are you still there?'

'I'm here.'

'There are two Rembrandt portraits coming up for sale in New York—'

'The Issenhirst pictures.'

'Is that what they're called?'

'They've had a few names, because they've been re-attributed a couple of times.'

'They're not by Rembrandt?' Marshall asked.

'Oh yes!' Samuel answered. 'Yes, they are. At least, that's what everyone believes. They were re-authenticated around the same time that the Duke of Wellington's pair of Rembrandt portraits were attributed to Carel Fabritius . . .' He paused, sighing down the phone. 'You've got Geertje Dircx's letters *and* the list of fakes. Are they on it?'

'That's what I'm going to find out,' Marshall replied. 'I memorised the list, but I can't remember any paintings called the Issenhirst portraits.' He paused, listening to the overhead intercom that was calling for people to board the Amsterdam flight. 'Samuel, I have to go now.'

'Marshall, those portraits are worth a fortune. The sale's been put together very hurriedly, and it's supposed to be the biggest for a decade. It's meant to bolster the market. The Rembrandts are expected to make at least forty million. If they're not genuine, then—'

'I'm not sure yet. I have to check the list.'

'Dear God, be careful,' Samuel said, gripping the phone even more tightly. 'If they *are* fakes, people will do anything to stop it coming out. They'll be desperate to save the sale. You must watch your back—'

'I have to go, Samuel,' Marshall said hurriedly. He clicked off his mobile and walked towards the boarding gate.

He didn't notice the scruffy young man put down his book and stand up, keeping his eyes on Marshall; didn't notice him as he moved behind him in the queue.

33

Rosella Manners unlocked the front door of the house in Barnes and let herself in. As she moved through the hall she could smell stale cigarette smoke and opened the window. So Tobar was smoking again, was he? Well, who cared? He could kill himself for all it mattered to her. Looking around the immaculate, untouched kitchen, Rosella realised that her husband had been eating out and that he'd forgotten to put the rubbish in the bins. As usual. Lifting the bag out, she moved into the back yard and dropped the bin liner into the refuse, wrinkling her nose in disgust.

Her return had been prompted by her decision to divorce Tobar. After so many years Rosella had become used to his devious ways, but his treatment of Owen Zeigler had been the final straw, the lever between marriage and divorce. Rosella was back in London, but she wasn't staying. After the divorce, she would leave the city and never come back. There was nothing left for her in London; better to return to her own country and family and begin again.

She sifted through the post, extracting the letters addressed to her for reading later and glancing idly at Tobar's mail. An envelope caught her eye, Rosella picked it up, staring at the thick black letters, which read:

TOBAR MANNERS
Delivered By Hand

All through their marriage, Rosella had had no interest in Tobar's dealings, nor had she ever opened any of his post. Perhaps she hadn't wanted to be involved – or tainted. Or perhaps she had simply been uninterested. But this particular letter, with its demanding writing, fascinated her. *Delivered By Hand*, it said . . . Rosella went to the door and looked out into the smart front garden, with its gravelled drive and trim little walk to the door. But whoever had left the envelope had long gone.

Rosella went upstairs, the letter in her hand, and placed it on the dressing table in her bedroom. She opened the window to let in the cold air and started unpacking. She and Tobar had never shared a bed. Their arrangement had not included any sexual contact, and besides, Tobar wasn't interested in her. She knew that he had frequently indulged in homosexual flings, but none had led to a lasting relationship and none had ever impinged on the Barnes house. If Tobar wanted to have sex, he could do it in the gallery . . . Rosella took off her shoes, gathered up clothes from her suitcase, and placed them in the walk-in closet. Finally she laid out her make-up and toiletries in the en suite bathroom and mused at how quickly her life had shunted back into its usual routine. Only this time the routine would not endure. This time, when Rosella left again, she would never return.

Rubbing some moisturising lotion into her hands, she looked at the letter. There was a hot, nervy energy to it, almost as though the syllables were in a rage, that the writer had been bilious as he wrote the words. She knew – with her impeccable instinct for trouble – that the letter was not good news, and for a moment she was tempted to put it back onto her husband's pile of mail, unopened.

But then again . . . Rosella was going for a divorce. She and her lawyer would have to take Tobar on and her husband would be certain to fight dirty. Surely this was the time to gather any ammunition that could benefit her? God knows, she needed every bit of help she could get. Their finances were off limits to Rosella. Tobar had kept her in comfort certainly, but she had never been privy to his business dealings. Of course there had been times when Tobar had been rattled, even vulnerable; times he had crept into her bed and spooned up against her, resting his head on her shoulder. In the morning he would be gone and neither of them would refer to it, but Rosella knew how much her presence gave him comfort, albeit celibately. At such times Tobar had told her little dribbles of information, his guilt talking, his remorse making a midnight child out of the daytime tyrant. In such a way she had heard about his dealings with the United Emirates, how he shipped second-rate paintings instead of top quality portraits. And he had once, then again a year later, muttered about being threatened, the gallery broken into.

Then, only a few weeks earlier, he had talked in the darkness. Forming words that would have been too much in daylight.

'We're in trouble, Rosella . . . I need to make a killing . . . we're in trouble . . .' He had reached for her hand and she had let him take it, wondering if this presentiment of doom was just one of his nervous shudders, or something more serious. 'We might have to cut back soon . . .'

'That bad?'

'It might change,' he had replied, suddenly aware that he was making himself look vulnerable, and worse, like a man who might fail. 'Don't worry, I'll think of something.'

And with that he had slipped out of her bed, and in the morning he had been back to his cocksure, spiteful self.

Recession or no recession, *she* wasn't going to suffer, Rosella thought fiercely. If Tobar was going to fall, she wasn't going to fall with him. He hadn't earned that kind of loyalty. Her mind turned back to their last argument. She had meant it, she *had* been disgusted by her husband's treatment of Owen Zeigler, realising that his ruthlessness to his closest friend did not bode well for her. If he could cheat Owen Zeigler, he could just as easily betray her. Rosella might like the money, and the comfort of her life, but she didn't like the fact that she felt suddenly vulnerable.

Her attention moved back to the letter on the dressing table. Rosella reached out for it and tapped it against her chin. It had such an urgency. Maybe a lover's note? A hateful spurt of verbal venom? Another of the lily-white boys? Perhaps she should open it? Perhaps it would give her some interesting information to help her with the divorce. Perhaps some rent boy had put his feelings on paper – or maybe it contained something incriminating about Tobar's business. She knew that Tobar used some disreputable people – a letter that implicated him might be a valuable bargaining chip ... Slowly Rosella opened the envelope and slid out a sheet of paper. It was hand-written and brief.

> *Tobar*
> *The Rembrandt letters exist – and with them is a*
> *list of fakes. Maybe the two coming up for auction*
> *in New York?*
> *About time you got what's coming to you.*

Taking a long, slow breath, Rosella stared at the words. The Rembrandt letters – what were they? And what was the list of fakes? She paused, remembering what she had heard about the New York auction of the Rembrandts which was being arranged ... *Maybe the two coming up for auction?*

'My God,' she said under her breath. *Were they fakes?* Jesus ... She thought back a number of years. Owen Zeigler had been visiting them, with a group of other dealers.

After dinner, they had talked about Dutch art in general, and then about Rembrandt. And Owen, the charming raconteur, taunted them all with some vague theory about the artist having a bastard son who had supposedly painted many of Rembrandt's works. She could remember everyone laughing about it, particularly Tobar, who had said that anyone could *say* anything, that theories came ten a penny. That no one would worry *unless they had proof.*

The Rembrandt letters exist – and with them is a list of fakes . . .

And now there *was* proof . . . Pushing the note into her pocket, Rosella realised the enormity of what she had just read. And what it would mean to the art market – and to her husband's business. Tobar might well be ruined. Which, by extension, would mean that she would not come out of a divorce well. Damn it, she thought impatiently, padding around in her stockinged feet. Why would someone have sent Tobar an anonymous note about this? Just to gloat? But surely it would also tip her husband off about the upcoming sale? The sale Tobar would be desperate to profit from.

A clammy unease settled over Rosella. If he found out about these Rembrandt letters, what would her husband not do to get hold of them? She caught her breath. What would he do to make sure the facts stayed hidden – especially the list of fakes. She remembered the death of Owen Zeigler. Had he been killed for the letters? Oh God, she thought, beginning to panic. Maybe Tobar knew about it.

Maybe he had been involved. He was capable, she knew that. She might not have admitted it to herself before, but she knew it. Knew it the moment she realised that her husband had cheated Owen Zeigler – or worse.

Shaken, Rosella glanced over to her suitcase on the bed. She hurriedly brought back some of her clothes from the closet and put them in her case. She wasn't going to stay. Didn't dare to, not now. Tossing her underwear in the suitcase, she went into the bathroom and picked up her toiletries but, as she moved back to the bed, she heard the front door opening downstairs. Tensing, she listened. The cleaner wasn't due, and no one else had a key. Unless it was Tobar . . . Hearing the footsteps coming up the stairs, Rosella took the note out of her pocket, looking round frantically for somewhere to hide it. She noticed her discarded shoes on the floor, and was just cramming the paper into the toe of her left shoe as Tobar walked into the bedroom. Her heart was pounding, the pulse in her neck thumping as she turned to him.

'Rosella?' he said, surprised, but with a touch of pleasure in his voice. 'You came back.'

She was holding the shoe in her hand. Calmly, she bent down and picked up the other shoe, placed them both in the walk-in closet then turned back to her husband. Decades of innate breeding had made Rosella refined and circumspect. She hadn't endured years of unhappy marriage to jeopardise her chances now. Far better to hold back and review the situation before doing anything rash. If she could have left before her husband returned that would have been one thing, but now it would look suspicious for her to suddenly change her mind and go.

Instinct had prompted Rosella to open the envelope. Instinct now prompted her to stay her hand.

'I missed you, Tobar,' she said lightly. 'Florence was dull.'

His arrogance didn't allow him to question her words. Instead, sure of himself again, he leaned against the doorframe. 'You know, one day, Rosella, you might push me too far. You were talking about us to that bloody old fool Samuel Hemmings.'

'Samuel's an old friend,' she replied blithely. 'And he's always been very protective of me.'

'I didn't need his fucking interference in my home life!' Tobar snapped. 'He's never liked me.'

'You never liked him.'

'He lives in the past, doesn't understand that the business has changed. It's not like it used to be. People like Leon Williams and Timothy Parker-Ross are on their way out, bloody public-school pricks who got handed their galleries on a plate. I built up my reputation, grafted for what I've got.'

Her mouth was dry, but her composure was complete. 'That's what makes you an expert in your field.'

He nodded, pleased she was giving him credit. 'Yes, and that's why I'll *stay* an expert in my field.'

'Sometimes you have to be ruthless in business.'

'You have to fight to stay one step ahead.'

'You've always fought, Tobar,' Rosella said, her tone honeyed. 'We've had our differences, but I've always admired you for that.'

Slowly he looked her up and down, swinging the door key in his hand, his expression sly.

'You seem different, Rosella.'

'Just tired, it was a difficult flight,' she replied. 'You look tired yourself.'

'Yes, well, times are tough at the moment. Mind you, I've just had some welcome news.'

'About what?'

'About the sale coming up in New York,' he said, trying to sound nonchalant but failing. 'Two Rembrandt portraits are going to be auctioned. And I – I – have just managed to close the deal as the broker. I get fifteen per cent of the sale.'

He paused, luminously triumphant.

Rosella thought of the anonymous note. 'Are they important paintings?' she asked.

'Rembrandt at the height of his powers. Should reach forty, even fifty, million.'

'Good provenance?' she asked, trying to feel her way.

'Good enough,' Tobar replied. 'We know that the portraits were painted in 1653, and that they stayed in private hands in Amsterdam until someone sold them to a Japanese collector last century. Their names were changed a couple of times, and there's a gap for a while in the 1950s, but now they've been put on the market. The owner wants to stay anonymous.'

'But you know who he is?'

'Of course I bloody know!' he responded shortly. 'But anonymity is what he's paying me for.' He paused, self righteous to a fault. 'Everyone wanted this deal. That smug fart Rufus Ariel was provoking me about it, and I daresay there was lots going on the background to try and cut me out.'

'But you won,' Rosella replied, smiling and wondering how to phrase the next words. 'No problems with attribution?'

'*What*?'

'Well, you've talked enough about Rembrandt fakes coming on the market—'

'These portraits are famous! And have been famous since 1653. They're reproduced constantly. Every book ever published on Rembrandt has listed these, along with the Rijksmuseum pair of portraits of the same time. No one's ever questioned their authenticity.' He seemed suddenly put out. 'They aren't bloody fakes! Anyway, it's not like you to be that bothered.'

'I was just showing an interest.'

'Yeah, and fifteen per cent of a fortune is something to be interested *in*.' He glanced at the suitcase on her bed. 'You haven't unpacked yet.'

'I haven't been home long.'

He nodded, looked around the room, and then walked into the closet. Rosella could feel her hands begin to sweat, knowing that the pair of shoes – with the note hidden inside – were lying on the floor only feet away from her husband. Composed, she studied the back of him, the

356

thinning froth of hair, the sloping shoulders that even a good tailor couldn't disguise. And then she caught sight of his reflection in the dressing room glass and thought suddenly about Owen Zeigler.

'Some people thought the works were going to be sold in London,' Tobar went on, glancing at her rows of clothes. 'Some thought Paris, or New York.'

'Which is it?'

'New York.'

Leaning down, his hand moved to the shoes, then drew back, picking up a handbag instead.

'This new?'

'No, I bought that a while ago. In Milan.'

Sensing something in the atmosphere, Tobar glanced around the closet again, aware that his wife was unnerved, edgy. No one else might notice it, but he knew her. His antennae flickered for hints as to the cause of her uneasy mood. Perhaps some over-indulgence? Some affair? But there was nothing obvious – and Rosella was giving nothing away.

After another moment, Tobar walked out of the dressing room and touched his wife's shoulder.

'Don't run off again, Rosella,' he said plaintively. 'You don't know how rough things have been for me lately.'

'I'm sorry.'

'I've had to do some things I'm not proud of.'

She thought he was about to admit something, but Tobar censored himself in time.

'I've been losing money, the market's down. It's been

difficult, more difficult that you can imagine. I don't have friends, Rosella. People are out to get me . . . You're my only real friend.'

'You can rely on me.'

'Maybe,' he said quietly. 'But then again, maybe not. You might not like some of the things I've had to do.'

She nodded, holding her breath. What was he referring to? Her imagination danced on the edges of her nerves, making jolts into half formed suspicions.

'You're not in trouble are you, Tobar?'

'Let's put it this way – without this Rembrandt sale I'd lose everything,' he admitted, running his index finger down the length of her arm. 'But we don't have to worry anymore. You thought we were well off before? After New York you're going to be married to a very rich man indeed.' He slid his hand into hers, clasping her fingers as a child might. 'We have to stick together, Rosella. We need each other. I know I've been difficult, not the best husband, but I'll pay you back in full.'

'I know you will, Tobar,' she said, squeezing his hand affectionately. 'I know you will.'

34

Valkenburgerstraat
Amsterdam

Walking into the bank, Marshall was greeted warmly as he asked for his safety deposit box. Dropping into step behind the manager, he was shown into the vault beyond and then steered into a small anteroom. A few moments later he was handed his security box. Marshall waited until the door closed, then locked it and glanced around the plain, unadorned room, looking for hidden cameras. There were none that he could see. Satisfied, he slid the key out of his inside pocket, he unlocked the box, and he took out the Rembrandt letters.

He felt a thrill as he touched them, smelt the faint ageing on them, and gazed at the old Dutch writing. Although he remembered most of what she had written, Marshall paused when he came to the later letters. Slowly, he began to read them again, Geertje Dircx's voice coming down the years to him:

House of Corrections,
Gouda, 1654

My friends talk of getting me out. Surely I have been ill enough. They talk of seeing Rembrandt in the town. Not Gouda, Amsterdam. They tell me about her . . . She gave evidence against me, just as Rembrandt did. Hendrickje Stoffels stood in the court and told everyone how well Rembrandt had treated me and how ungrateful I had become. A madwoman, a liar, she called me, quietly, so everyone would believe her.

I was so stupid for a clever woman.

The court heard about how I had lived with Rembrandt for six years in the Sint Antoniesbreestraat. I told them I had become his lover and that he had given me several of his late wife's rings. One to count as a betrothal. Later I sold the ring. I'd had to, to raise the money and fund my cause when I took Rembrandt to the Commissioners of Marital Affairs on a charge of breach of promise . . .

Rembrandt swore at that, said he would never promise to marry me, or anyone, because of the dictates in Saskia's will. It wouldn't profit him, he said, to lose her inheritance.

In the end the court made him pay me 200 guilders annually, for life.

I'd hired a room over a seamen's bar. Which made me a whore, they said. My brother said, my neighbours said. She said. They all stood up in court, perjured themselves and made a slut out of me. Afterwards, people spat at me, talked about me, sneered at me. Me, who had been Rembrandt's lover. And the mother of his child . . . Once he came to see me in the room over the bar. In secret, wearing something ugly, because peasants lived there.

He warned me. Making his doughy face soft, as though he was sorry. He said I had to agree to his terms. But I argued, like the whore I was. The whore they'd made me. And then I said the name. Carel. Carel, I said, what of our son? I lost at that moment. Because he misunderstood me, thought me capable of blackmail. Thought I was like him, and would act out of spite. Tell everyone about his bastard, his secret, and how Carel had become his monkey. How he had painted pictures Rembrandt had been happy to pass off as his own.

My son had made him rich, the dealers rich, and when Carel wanted to stop working for his old master, Rembrandt had pressured him.

I didn't find that out until a while later. And it wasn't Rembrandt who told me.

I see Rembrandt now, as though he is stood in front of me, threatening me with his fleshy hands, telling me over and over, be quiet, be quiet. Say nothing . . . Sssh, listen, the guard is back on duty, pausing by the window and listening. I've put the papers under my skirt and pretend to sleep, slumped against the straw pillow which prickles your skin and houses the bugs in summer. We itch, in every place known to man, we itch. My hair was crawling with fleas when I was ill, they bit my scalp and sucked at the blood . . .

The argument we had was violent, and I struck Rembrandt, like a whore. I struck him and cursed her, Hendrickje Stoffels. And his heart turned to lead against me . . .

Moved, Marshall stared at the letter, then leaned back in his seat, looking around the blank walls of the ante-room. He wondered how it had felt for Geertje Dircx to not only be rejected, but imprisoned for twelve years by the man she had previously loved. The cruelty hit Marshall as hard as it had done the first time he read the letters, and he was just about to continue when there was a knock on the door.

Hurriedly, he put the letters back in the box.

'Come in.'

The manager entered, apologetically, his English fluent. 'Sorry to disturb you, Mr Zeigler, but there's someone asking for you in the bank reception.'

'There can't be, no one knows I'm here,' Marshall replied, looking over the man's shoulder into the bank beyond.

He could see a number of customers but no one he recognised, and realised that he had been followed – and was now effectively trapped. Nervous, Marshall calmed himself. What could anyone do in the ante-room of a bank vault? They could hardly attack him. And even if they wanted to steal the letters, they couldn't take them away from him while he was on the premises, in full sight.

'Who asked for me?'

The manager turned, then frowned as he glanced around the reception area. 'Oh, he appears to have left.'

'What was his name?'

'He didn't give one,' the manager answered, obviously embarrassed. 'I'm very sorry, Mr Zeigler, I hope this wasn't some kind of hoax. Perhaps I shouldn't have disturbed you, but he was very emphatic—'

'What did he look like?'

'Rough.' He paused, looking for the right words. 'A rather worn looking individual, sir.'

'Worn looking?'

'Not well dressed, casual. A working man. He seemed around thirty-five. Dark hair and eyes, clean shaven. And not Dutch.'

Marshall raised his eyebrows. 'Not Dutch? Was he English?'

'No, he had an accent I couldn't place, sir.'

'And he asked for me?'

'Yes, I told him you were in the vault.'

Marshall nodded. 'Then what did he say?'

'That he would like a word with you.'

'Nothing else?'

'No. I said I would pass on his message and when I last looked, he was waiting.'

'Do you have security cameras here?'

'Why?'

'Because I think the man who asked for me was the same person who broke into my home in London,' Marshall replied, thinking on his feet and watching the startled expression on the manager's face. He dropped his voice conspiratorially. 'I'd appreciate it if this could be kept quiet. You see, I think he might be a relative of my wife's. He's no good, into drugs, and he wanted to borrow some more money, but we were against it. So he helped himself, and now he's putting me under pressure, turning up at my bank.'

The man was suddenly sympathetic. 'Oh, I see. Family troubles.'

Marshall shrugged. 'What can you do? I'd be sure it was him if I could see the security tape. You know me well, I've been a client here for a long time. I'd appreciate some understanding in what is a very difficult matter.'

The manager nodded, but his tone was uncertain. 'I can talk to our security people. They couldn't show you the whole tape, obviously, but perhaps we could show you a still of the man?'

'That would be enough,' Marshall replied, turning back to the security box. 'I'll carry on here for a while.'

'I'll leave you to it, sir. Sorry for the interruption.'

Marshall, now taut with apprehension, relocked the door, then took out the letters again and rifled through them for the list. When he had it in his hand he read, slowly and incredulously – the names of the fakes, numbering almost a hundred paintings. Almost one hundred pictures which had been painted by a forger. And not just any forger, but Rembrandt's bastard son ...

Taking in a breath, Marshall could only imagine the furore which would greet such news, but as he studied the names again he could see no mention of the Issenhirst portraits. A hurried second conversation with Samuel after he had landed in Holland had given him the names of those two paintings – *Portrait of A Man and Wife*, 1653, and *Portrait of Abraham de Potter and his Wife*. The latter name had been queried and changed, then, in the 1950s, the pictures had temporarily been referred to as the Issenhirst Portraits. But there was no mention of the name Issenhirst on the list, only an entry – *Husband and Wife*, 1653. Marshall frowned at the paper, turning it round to read a tiny entry in the margin. Something indecipherable, in Geertje Dircx's hand, but impossible to read.

Holding the paper up to the light, Marshall began to see the words more clearly. They were written in the equivalent of an early Dutch dialect, hard to translate for a moment.

'*Man with beard*,' Marshall said finally, staring at the entry again. '*Husband and Wife, 1653 ... man with beard*. That should narrow it down.'

Excited, he made a hurried note and then turned back to the list. Slowly he read the names of the paintings, closing his eyes and repeating them over and over again. One after the other.

All his life Marshall had prided himself on his memory, his gift for vivid and detailed visual recall. Since childhood he could look at a page and remember it. As he grew older, he retained only matters of interest, erasing unimportant details from his memory. As a linguist, the skill had proved invaluable. Not only could he remember the grammar of languages, but also the version from which he was originally translating. For example, if he was translating Alexander Pope into French, he could mentally retain both the English and the French versions, together with the nuances of speech and phrasing. His ability had made him sought after, especially for the Classics, which demanded not only skill, stamina and sympathy but a prodigious memory.

And that memory Marshall was relying on now. Opening his eyes, his gaze went to the top of the list and he looked away, listing the names one after the other in the order he had read them. About half way through he paused, glancing back to remind himself of the next entry.

Another knock on the door interrupted him. Marshall rose and let in the manager, who seemed pleased with himself.

'I've organised everything with the security team, Mr Zeigler. When you're ready, I've got something for you to look at.'

'Thank you. I just need another fifteen minutes here.'

The man nodded, glancing at his watch. 'I'll come back for you then.'

Marshall returned to his seat, closed his eyes again, and began to recite the list from the beginning. This time he was word perfect. Again, he repeated the process, then tucked the papers into the security box and, placing the letters on top of the list, locked it. Then he paused, considering his options.

If he left the letters in the bank they would be safe, but he would have nothing to bargain with. If he kept them with him, he would have access to them at all times and could pass them on or even destroy them. Marshall hesitated. The letters were a death sentence, he knew that, and he realised suddenly how much he wanted to live.

How precious his life seemed now that it was under threat. His friends, his work, his flat, took on a poignant resonance with the knowledge that at any moment he might lose them all. And with them, his own life . . .

After a few moments, Marshall unlocked the box and took out the letters. He tucked them into the inside pocket of his jacket. As he left the room, he passed the box over to the manager and followed him up a flight of stairs and into a cramped office at the back of the building. A bored, corpulent man was sitting in front of a honeycomb of screens, showing every view of the bank. The lobby, reception, tellers and queues. And, interestingly, the manager's office.

The manager gestured to a single screen that showed an image of a man standing in reception – the worn looking man he had described earlier. Marshall studied the photograph. The man was unknown to him, and didn't resemble anyone he had ever known, yet there was something familiar about him . . .

'Is that your relative?' the manager asked, dropping his voice tactfully.

'It's him,' Marshall lied, memorising the image before turning away from the screen. 'Thanks, I appreciate it.'

'Don't mention it, Mr Zeigler. As you say, you're a valued customer, it was the least I could do. If your brother-in-law calls by again, what would you like me to tell him?'

Marshall thought for a moment before answering. 'I don't usually like involving people in family business, but you're obviously a man of the world, and you've been very understanding—'

'No problem, sir.'

'So, *if* he comes back, perhaps you could tell him that I deposited some documents in my security box. And that I mentioned that I was going back to London?'

Obviously delighted to have something to relieve the monotony, the manager smiled. 'I understand, sir.'

'It would stop him being a nuisance here. I'm just sorry I've put you to all this trouble.'

'As I say, sir, no problem. You can count on me.'

Shaking his hand, Marshall turned to go then turned back. 'Perhaps we could keep this between the two of us?'

He nodded, flattered to be the confidant. 'Absolutely,' he agreed, holding the door for Marshall to pass through. 'Absolutely.'

35

New York

Closing the door of his office, Philip Gorday picked up the phone and told his secretary to put the call through. An instant later, a woman's voice came down the line – a voice Philip hadn't heard for many years, a voice which brought back unwelcome memories. The past loomed up before him as he recalled a summer spent in Connecticut, with a mistress and her child. A daughter, only ten or eleven years old. With red hair and a smart mouth. A child who had been truculent and demanding.

'I had to bring her,' Eve had said, her tone injured. 'What else could I do? My mother's ill.'

'You've got a sister—'

'Christ, Philip, don't put yourself out, will you?' she had replied, turning away, her fair skin pink from the overheated sun.

Theirs had been an intermittent affair over the course of a decade. Philip was irritated but fascinated by her, Eve independent but sensually bound to him. While Philip

369

remained married to Charlotte, Eve had divorced one husband and married another, but that summer she was alone, without a husband but with a daughter in tow. A resentful daughter, embarrassed, and aware that she wasn't wanted by this amorous, quarrelling couple.

'You should have found someone else to take care of her.'

'It's only for a week!'

'Yeah, that's the point,' he had replied. 'Couldn't you have found someone to take her for seven days?'

And then, two nights later, the girl had gone missing. The police had been alerted, Eve panicked, Philip certain that the child had run off deliberately to cause even further disruption. They found her forty-eight hours later, sleeping on a beach, hungry and defiant.

She was using the same defiant tone now. 'Philip Gorday?'

'So it *is* you, Georgia.'

'You sound surprised.'

'I never expected to hear from you.'

'My mother *always* expected to hear from you. She spent her life expecting to hear from you,' Georgia replied curtly. 'I heard about your wife's death, I'm sorry.'

He was caught off guard. 'Thank you for that . . . Why have you called me?'

'Not to plead my mother's case, she's married again. Settled down.'

'I'm glad.'

'So am I,' Georgia replied, pausing to find the next

370

words. 'Apparently we have some people in common – and I don't mean my mother.'

'We do? Who?'

'My ex-husband, Marshall, is Owen Zeigler's son.' She could hear Philip take in a breath and continued. 'Marshall doesn't know that I ever knew you. I didn't like lying, but to be honest, I was glad you were out of my life and I didn't want you back. Anyway, he didn't even know that your late wife was his father's mistress, and I didn't think I should be the one to tell him.'

She paused, remembering how she had bumped into Charlotte one day in London, when she was coming out of the Zeigler Gallery. She had been a long time friend of Eve's and recognised Georgia immediately.

'My God,' Charlotte had said, smiling. 'I didn't expect to see you here.'

'I was visiting my father-in-law.'

The news had impacted Charlotte like a bullet. 'Your *father*-in-law?'

'Yes, Owen Zeigler. I'm married to his son, Marshall.'

With an effort, Charlotte had covered her surprise. 'I see . . . And how's your mother keeping these days?'

'She's fine.' Georgia had known at once what had been going through Charlotte's mind. 'Don't worry, she's not with Philip again. That affair's long been over.'

Behind Charlotte's eyes there had been a flicker of relief as she changed the subject. 'Owen never told me you were married to his son.'

'No?' Georgia had queried. 'Well, maybe he likes his secrets.'

Having lived with a promiscuous mother who was adept at lying, Georgia had a well-developed instinct for conspiracy. Although fond of Owen, she had sometimes suspected that he had kept things back – and time had proved her right . . .

'Are you still there?' Philip asked down the phone.

'Yeah, I'm here. I don't want Marshall knowing about our connection. He doesn't need to know about that part of my past.'

'It was just one week, Georgia—'

'For you, maybe! For me, it was years of my mother's obsession with you. Christ, Philip, you were a bastard with her.'

He said nothing. He knew it was true.

'Anyway, that wasn't why I called,' Georgia went on. 'Marshall's in trouble. Our marriage didn't work out, but we're still close. He's involved in something dangerous, and I think you might know something about it.'

'What?'

'The Rembrandt letters . . . Ah,' she said, counting the seconds of silence, 'I knew you would. Did Charlotte tell you?'

'It doesn't matter who told me. Let's just say that I've heard about them. And about Owen Zeigler's death, which was apparently connected.'

'I have to ask you something, Philip: you're not involved in this, are you?'

'What are you talking about!'

'Well, it would be one way to get revenge on Owen Zeigler, wouldn't it—'

'*For what?*'

'For being Charlotte's lover.'

Exasperated, Philip took in a long breath before answering. 'You really think I'd be capable of that? You really think it mattered so much to me? We led separate lives. Charlotte was free to have lovers—'

'That's what you said to my mother, but you still got into rages if she cheated on you,' Georgia said coolly. 'You don't like losing, Philip, you never did. Perhaps Owen Zeigler was a thorn in your flesh for too long.'

'Don't insult me.'

'Don't insult me either,' she replied, her tone testy. 'I'm worried about my ex-husband and I'm not going to be polite to save your feelings. I have to know if you're involved in this whole business.'

'Well, I'm not.'

'Thank God,' Georgia replied evenly, 'So you don't know about Stefan van der Helde?'

'No,' Philip said honestly.

'He was a Dutch dealer who was tortured and murdered after he authenticated the Rembrandt letters. He was killed for them. As your wife might have been—'

'And Nicolai Kapinski, your father-in-law's accountant.'

This was news to Georgia.

'I didn't know about that ... That makes four deaths, Jesus ... Last time I spoke to Marshall he tried to convince me that it was a hoax, told me not to worry – but how the hell can I not worry? He's got those letters, and people are killing for them.' Georgia hurried on. 'You can't repeat any of this, Philip, it's in complete confidence. It's just that I didn't know who else to ask for help. I *had* to come to you, Philip, you owe me – and besides, you always had connections in the art world. I remember how you used to talk to my mother about art. You always had an interest.'

Deftly, he changed the subject. 'Why doesn't your ex-husband go to the police?'

'He has his reasons.'

'Maybe he does, but I don't know how I can help him.'

'To be honest, I don't know either, but if he gets in really deep – I mean, if Marshall needs a lawyer—'

'I'll take care of it.'

'I don't want a bill.'

He grimaced down the phone. 'You were always charming.'

'You don't know the half of it.' She paused, thinking, then asked, 'How did you find out that Owen's accountant was killed?'

'Nicolai Kapinski came to see me a few days ago. He wanted to know if *I* had the Rembrandt letters.' Philip glanced over to the door, watching his secretary through the glass. 'Kapinski was an odd, nervy little man, but he was really scared and what he said played on my mind. He *also* thought Charlotte had been murdered . . . Anyway, I didn't have copies of the letters and I told him that, but something niggled about what he'd said, so I went to his hotel to talk to him. When I arrived, he'd already been killed.'

'Did the police catch anyone?'

'No. They've had no more luck in New York than they did in London,' Philip replied. 'You should try to convince your ex-husband to go to the police and tell them the whole story.'

'I've told you, Marshall won't do that. And besides, he's changed his mobile number and left the gallery. I've tried calling him at his flat in Amsterdam, but no reply. I don't where he is, or where he'll go next. I don't know what's happening, but if he's gone for the letters and they find him, God help him.'

Philip heard the imminent panic in her voice and tried to calm her. 'Where are the letters now?'

'Marshall lives in Amsterdam, so I reckon he'd have them there.'

'What's he going to do with them?'

'I don't know!' she said desperately. 'I've been trying to work out his next move. If the letters are made public they'll rock the art market, so Marshall won't publish them—'

'But someone else might? And they could control the market that way?'

'Yes. There's a list of fakes with the letters.'

'Christ!'

'I know. Can you imagine how valuable that would be?'

Frowning, Philip rummaged around on his desk, then moved over to the table by the window. Underneath the day's papers was a catalogue of the specialist auction coming up at the Museum of Mankind in central Manhattan: an auction of two Rembrandt portraits.

'If your ex-husband calls, you put him straight on to me.'

'Why, what is it?'

'I believe,' Philip said evenly, 'that he's in even more danger than you think.'

36

Wheeling himself over to the door, Samuel was about to leave his study when the phone rang. Hurriedly, he turned his wheelchair round, knocking it into a table as he did so and spilling some tea. Just reaching the phone on its last ring, he snatched it up.

'Hello!'

'Samuel, it's Marshall.'

Samuel sighed, wondering why he was so nervous. Outside the door, Mrs McKendrick began vacuuming; a moth beat its wings helplessly against the lining of one of the study curtains.

'Did you find out anything?'

'Geertje Dircx made a note about the paintings, a little memento to remind her that the portraits could be identified because the man had a beard.'

Quickly, Samuel scrabbled around the books on his desk and pulled a catalogue towards him. 'I have a reproduction of them now. The woman is wearing a typical Dutch cap; the man has a small ruff and a beard.' He flicked over the pages hurriedly, testing his memory against the facts.

'What are you doing?'

'Checking something.' Samuel went on, glancing over all the portraits Rembrandt painted in 1653. 'There are two other paintings of men with beards, but no companion portraits. These were the *only* pair of portraits painted that year.'

'So these are the ones on the list?'

'Yes. They're the only portraits we know that stayed in Dutch private hands for centuries, which narrows it down even further.' Samuel rubbed his eyes. 'Incidentally, I found out something else. The portraits *were* referred to as the Issenhirst portraits but only once, in an old 1957 catalogue. They were supposed to be put up for sale, but they never made it to the auction. They were withdrawn and—'

'Disappeared for a while,' Marshall finished for him. 'So the New York paintings *are* fakes. Rembrandt's monkey painted them.'

'Dear God!'

'How much would they make if it came out that Carel Fabritius was the artist, not Rembrandt?'

'About a hundred and seventy-five thousand pounds.'

Marshall, glancing around as he walked through Amsterdam and approached a bridge over a canal, was amazed. 'So little?'

'Fabritius isn't regarded as an Old Master, but as one of Rembrandt's many pupils.' Samuel dropped his voice. 'Where are you? Are you all right?'

'I'm fine,' Marshall replied, glancing behind him again. This time he was suddenly aware that he was being followed and paused, looking into the cloudy water of the canal. 'I have to go, Samuel.'

'What are you going to do?'

'What my father would have wanted me to do,' Marshall replied, looking around again. 'If I get the chance.'

Before Samuel could reply, he clicked off his phone.

Scratching his beard, Teddy Jack looked into the rear-view mirror of his van and watched Georgia walking up to her house. He had been keeping an eye on her since Marshall left. As she opened her front door and walked in, Teddy sighed and took out his mobile, running through the images he had captured on the camera. The first was of Tobar Manners hurrying around Albemarle Street with Rufus Ariel; two further images were of Georgia, but the last photograph was the one which made him smile wryly.

On the evening Marshall had left for Heathrow, Teddy had trailed him. And at the airport, he had snapped the person who was following Marshall. Teddy recognised the man. In fact, he had known him for a while, had even tracked him once . . . Georgia's door opened again, and Teddy saw an athletic, wiry man enter the house. Georgia's husband, Harry Turner. After waiting for another few minutes, Teddy drove off, parked in a side street and called Marshall on his mobile.

It rang out several times before Marshall picked up.

'I've got a photograph of the man who's been following you in London.' he began, without so much as a greeting. 'Are you all right?'

'Someone's following me now,' Marshall replied, obviously rattled.

'Go to a public place, don't stay out on the street,' Teddy advised him. 'Keep in crowds, with people.' He guessed that Marshall was walking fast, heard his breathing speed up. 'You'll never guess who's been following you in London.'

'Probably the same person following me now. Who?'

'Dimitri Kapinski.'

Marshall stopped walking. The street was deserted, slicked from a rain storm, and empty. *Too empty.* Moving into the nearest bar he ordered a beer. He then stood, tense, by the counter with his back towards the wall, scanning the faces around him. The sudden realisation that he was afraid hit him with a jolt.

'Did you hear me?'

'You said Dimitri Kapinski,' Marshall replied, understanding coming fast. 'Nicolai's brother?'

'The same.'

Marshall dropped his voice. 'Why would *he* be involved in any of this?'

'Especially as his brother was murdered,' Teddy said evenly. 'Perhaps they were working together?'

'Nicolai? No,' Marshall replied, 'not him. He wasn't the type. He wouldn't have hurt my father.'

'You never know who's the type and who isn't. People

change type when they're under pressure.' Teddy could hear the sounds of the crowded Amsterdam bar in the background. 'Have you got the letters with you?'

'No.' Marshall replied, wanting to add – *only in my head*. He knew that he didn't need them on his person as every word was committed to memory. The actual letters were to remain in the bank for safekeeping, with no one but himself able to get at them. As for the key, Marshall had put that in an envelope and posted it to the Zeigler Gallery, London.

'There's been a break-in at a gallery on Dover Street.'

'Another?'

Teddy sighed. 'Lillian Kauffman was burgled too. She called the police.'

'Did you talk to her?'

'Yeah, she said nothing to them about the letters, just said she'd been burgled. And then she asked me where you were. Said I should help you out, because you'd make a crap hero.'

'That sounds like her,' Marshall said, scrutinising the drinkers around him. Suddenly he noticed a man watching him across the bar, and put down his drink. The man regarded him levelly, without blinking. Marshall looked away, and when he looked back, a woman had joined the man and they were laughing. God, he thought, calm down.

'What now?'

'Keep an eye on Georgia,' Marshall said firmly. 'Make sure she's all right, you hear me? Look after her until I get back.'

'She's fine.'

'Don't let them get to her,' he said urgently, thinking of his father's violent death, and of Nicolai Kapinski. 'I should never have got her mixed up in this, Teddy.'

'I'll see she's OK, I promise,' Teddy reassured him. 'Trust me. What are you going to do now, Marshall?'

'I'll be in touch—'

Teddy butted in quickly. 'Before you go, I saw Tobar Manners today. He interrupted me when I was talking to Lillian – he thinks the peasants are deaf – but he was in a panic and he was talking about the letters.'

'What did Lillian say?'

'Told him to fuck off and grow up.'

'How did he take that?'

'Badly. He said that she'd take it more seriously if the letters turned up. Then she asked him if he was worried that the paintings coming up for sale in New York would turn out to be fakes. He looked like he wanted to slap her, but you know Lillian Kauffman. She just fiddled with one of those doorstop earrings of hers and smirked at him. Said it would be justice for cheating your father.'

'God, she doesn't care what she says, does she?'

'Nah, but Tobar Manners was really shaken, I could tell. She went on to say that it would be a blessing if someone got hold of the letters, a favour to the business, and then she said that if anyone had them it would be Rufus Ariel.' Teddy paused. 'Tobar Manners looked stunned, like maybe he hadn't thought of that. Then he let it slip that a person

382

could be in real trouble if they tried to hold on to the letters. Even killed.'

'*He said that?*'

'He said it.'

'And Lillian?'

'Said that she was looking forward to seeing two fake Rembrandts being exposed, and how it was a shame, seeing as how Tobar was acting as broker. But then again, what goes around, comes around.' Teddy laughed. 'She cares about you, said if you got strapped for cash, she'd help. I think she's excited by the whole affair, wants to be in on it.' Teddy paused for a moment, then took a shot in the dark. 'You're going to New York, aren't you?'

It was Marshall's turn to be surprised. 'What makes you think that?'

'Because of the sale. Because if there's one place on earth you should be now it's New York,' Teddy replied. 'They'll try and stop you, you know that, don't you?'

'I know.'

'Are you up for this?'

'Hell, no,' Marshall replied frankly.

'All the dealers will be in New York for the sale. The people after you will be there too. It could be any of them.'

'I know that.'

'So how are you going to find out who it is?'

'I'm going to flush them out,' Marshall replied evenly. 'He – or they – will have to show their hand. They want the letters, so they'll have to try and get them off me.'

'Then what?'

'I don't know.'

'Like I said, keep to the crowds,' Teddy warned him, hearing the mobile connection breaking up. 'Keep to the crowds.'

Turning off his phone, Marshall left the bar and moved over a bridge. The sun was high, but giving little warmth, the bare trees were reflected in the canal below. He found himself thinking about his father, remembering. Many years earlier they had gone on a weekend to the Cotswolds, just after his mother had died. Owen had been rigid with grief and totally ignorant of how to cope with a young boy, and Marshall had been withdrawn. His memory shuddered as an image came back to him. One evening father and son had sat in the plush dining room of an expensive hotel, eating dinner, Marshall in his public-school uniform, Owen in a business suit. Their conversation had been forced, Marshall refusing to eat his fish, Owen embarrassed, his charm only working on the waitress.

Refilling his wine glass, Owen had finally looked across the table at his son and said, 'We could go for a walk tomorrow.'

Almost as though it was happening to him at that moment, Marshall could feel the dessert spoon in his hand, the metal cool and heavy . . . He thought of what to say, what he *could* possibly say, wishing that the following day would disappear, simply pass without the excruciating walk and intermittent silences. He wanted to throw the spoon at his father and ask him why he was even bothering to try, because it was obvious he didn't want to be

384

there. In that old-fashioned dining room. With his resentful son.

'Marshall, what d'you think?' Owen had persisted. 'About having a walk?'

He had let go of the spoon in that instant. The resounding clatter as it hit the plate had made Owen jump, the surrounding diners turned to stare and the waitress watched from across the room. And then Marshall had looked into his father's face and realised that his mother's death wasn't *his* fault. That he was as lost and wretched as the child in his care. As sick to the heart with the beef stew and the apple pie and the blathering conversation of diners who had no inkling of his crucifying grief.

In that moment Marshall had pitied his father. 'I'd like a walk,' he had said at last. 'A walk would be good.'

And some kind of empathy had passed between father and son, a complicit understanding which would have to do in place of comfortable companionship . . . Time would change them, mellow them. Time would make Marshall sympathetic and Owen comfortable. But in that dining room, that dusty summer evening, they had made a form of truce.

Still staring into the murky canal water, Marshall then remembered finding his father's body, and shuddered involuntarily. No one should have died like that, he thought, and especially not Owen Zeigler. Dying in war was bad enough, dying with cancer, with dementia, with the crumble of old age was bad enough. Dying to protect something was another matter. Dying for another person's story, another human's trust, was noble. And that was how, finally, Marshall became close to his father. The letters didn't mean anything to him personally, but Owen Zeigler had died for them. And in his dying, they had become precious.

Marshall turned his head, staring at the pedestrians walking past, wondering if one of them was watching him; if one of them had already broken into his Amsterdam flat, or followed him to the bank; if the man in the bank – Nicolai Kapinski's brother – was coming after him. Oddly, Marshall found himself smiling. He was so out of his depth that he felt the fleeting bravery of many desperate men. He had no real idea who to trust. He was trusting Teddy Jack because Teddy had been attacked; because he had been close to his father; because he had offered help. And because he was tough enough to protect Georgia. His guilt pricked like a needle in his skin. Jesus, why had he told her? Why put her in danger? Of all people, Georgia would have been the one person he should have kept safe . . .

Consoling himself with the thought that Teddy was watching over her, Marshall suddenly found himself outside the Waterlooplein Flea Market and remembered the advice to *keep to the crowds*. Moving into the overcrowded arena, he felt the press of people and paused beside a stall selling cheap tourist mementoes. Pretending to be

interested, he picked up a book. Underneath was a reproduction of Rembrandt's *The Night Watch*.

'You want to buy that?' a stout woman asked, leaning
towards him over the stall and raising her voice. 'You
English, right?'

'How did you know?'

She smiled, benign in a headscarf. 'You're pale and
you're looking at tourist stuff.'

Out of the corner of Marshall's eye he could see a man
glance at him. He moved on, the stall owner calling after
him, 'Make me an offer! I can do a special price for the
English!'

Moving down the aisle between the stalls, Marshall could
smell the scent of fruit mixing with the dry cement chalk-
iness of reproduction statues. Men with vacant eyes sat
on low stools behind their stalls, some smoking, some
just watching the shoppers pass. Behind a worn-down clock
stall, three men played cards, one smoking a Turkish cigarette, the tobacco pungent. Everywhere Marshall looked
people seemed to be looking back at him. When he turned,
there always seemed to be someone pressed up against
him, or brushing into him, their eyes catching his, their
expressions furtive. Everyone seemed suddenly suspicious,
untrustworthy, dangerous.

His anxiety increasing, Marshall bought himself a coffee
from a nearby stall and sat down to drink it. He had to
control himself. A woman bumped into his seat and he
jumped up, accepting her apology as she moved past with
a child's pram. He felt as though he was illuminated by

some incandescent light, marked out, and obvious to everyone. As easy to spot as a coffin in a bread tin. Around him the voices and footsteps echoed eerily, rising into the high, glassed roof of the market.

Why was Dimitri Kapinski following him? Marshall thought, sipping his drink. Why him? Then he remembered what Teddy Jack had said about the man.

'Wasn't all there. By the time he was twenty odd, Dimitri had spent time in jail and been married. Then he'd bunked off to London, worked there for a short while, selling drugs. He'd become pretty violent too . . .'

But why was he involved? Marshall's glance moved to a middle-aged man who had sat down at his table. The man nodded at Marshall, then began to read his evening paper.

Was Dimitri Kapinski working alone? Or working with someone else? The names spun like a roulette wheel in Marshall's head: Tobar Manners, Rufus Ariel, Dimitri Kapinski, God knew who—

'Sugar, please.'

Marshall stared at the man across the table. 'What?'

'Can you pass the sugar?'

Nodding, he pushed it towards the man, watching him curiously. 'You spoke English to me. How did you know I wasn't Dutch?'

'I heard you order your coffee in English,' the man replied reasonably, turning his attention back to his newspaper.

Marshall looked around, surprised that he had made such an elementary mistake in using his own language.

'Waar woon je?' he asked the man, watching as he put down his paper.

'Plantage Middenlaan,' he replied, offering up the street where he lived. He then asked, in English, 'Do you know it?'

'Yes, I've lived in Amsterdam for a while,' Marshall replied, wondering if the man was watching him or merely taking time out to read his newspaper. 'Hoe heet je?'

'Gerrit Hoogstraten.' He put out his hand, Marshall shaking it as Hoogstraten asked, 'And what's your name?'

'Marshall Zeigler.'

He nodded, smiling. 'You seem . . . nervous.'

'A little, yes.'

'Are you in trouble?'

'Why would you ask that?'

'You seem like someone with problems, and you keep looking around as if you expect someone to be watching you. And you obviously suspect me of something . . . Are the police after you?'

'No.'

The man put down his newspaper, looking steadily at Marshall.

'I used to be in the police myself, before I retired. I was a detective in the Amsterdam force.' He sipped his drink. 'Perhaps you need help?'

'Why would I?'

'Well, I wouldn't turn round now, Mr Zeigler, but there's

389

a man staring at you. He has been ever since you sat down. I noticed him because he wasn't interested in the stalls, just in you.'

Marshall stiffened in his seat. 'What does he look like?'

'Around thirty, clean shaven, very short hair.'

'I think I know him. He's been following me for a while.'

'I would say – looking at you and looking at him – that perhaps he is not the injured party here?' Gerrit Hoogstraten said perceptively, smiling again as though they were having a light-hearted talk about the weather. 'Perhaps I could help?'

'Why would you want to get involved?'

'Why not? I've a good instinct for people, and I don't like the man who's following you.'

Marshall finished his drink, then glanced over to his companion. 'How could you help me?'

'If you want to get out of the market, just tell me when, and I'm sure I can hold up the man who seems so interested in you.'

'Why would you do that?'

'Why not? You can trust some people, you know, Mr Zeigler.' He glanced around idly, as though merely talking and passing the time of day.

'Is he still there?'

'Yes.'

Marshall nodded. 'I'm going to get up in a minute and head for the door.'

'Excellent,' Gerrit Hoogstraten replied. 'I'll make sure he's delayed.'

Saying goodbye, Marshall rose from his seat. Then, without looking round, he headed for the nearest exit onto the Waterlooplein. As he left the table, the man followed him, passing Gerrit Hoogstraten who immediately put out his foot. Tripped up, the man fell, Hoogstraten apparently trying to help him to his feet, but delaying him instead.

'Zorgig! Zorgig!' he said, trying to brush the man down as he struggled to get away.

'Piss off!' he replied, breaking free and running towards the nearest exit.

But Gerrit Hoogstraten had seen Marshall head for the same exit and then turn at the last moment. Wrong footed, his pursuer ran out and paused, frantically looking round the churning street and knowing he had lost all sight of his prey.

37

As she folded some laundry, Georgia glanced at the kitchen clock, then turned to Harry.

'Aren't you going to the gym tonight?'

He nodded, picking up his case. 'Yes, I'm just running late. Unless you don't want me to go. I could stay in.'

'Oh no, out you go!' she teased him. 'I've got my evening planned. When I've done all this, I'm having a bath, then watching a DVD.'

'Which one?'

'It's a romance, with men and women in it. Talking about their feelings,' she said drily. 'You wouldn't like it.'

He kissed her on the cheek. 'Lock the door when I've gone, won't you?'

Waving, she watched Harry leave, then slid the bolt closed. For a moment Georgia considered trying Marshall's phone again, but realised it would be a waste of time. He would contact her eventually; she just had to wait for news. Finishing folding the laundry, she put it in the airing cupboard and went into the bedroom, where she undressed. She ran a bath, but found herself too uneasy to enjoy a long soak, and a few minutes later, got out and dried herself. Suddenly Georgia was startled by a ring at the front doorbell.

Moving into the hall, she called out, 'You see, Harry, if you didn't tell me to lock the door, you could have let yourself in.' Smiling, she slid open the bolt but, instead of Harry there were two policemen on the doorstep.

Pulling her robe around her tightly, Georgia knew it was bad news. Marshall . . . ?

'Mrs Turner?' asked one of them.

'Yes. What is it? What's wrong?' she replied.

'Perhaps we could go inside to talk—'

Panicked, she quickly waved them inside. 'What is it?'

'I'm afraid that—'

'What!'

'Your husband has been knocked down by a car—'

'Harry! No! Where is he?' she asked, making for the door.

'In the Chelsea and Westminster Hospital—'

'How bad is it?' There was a protracted pause. '*Tell* me! How bad is it?'

'It's not good, Mrs Turner,' one of the officers said gently, taking Georgia's arm and guiding her back into the house. 'If you get dressed, we'll take you to the hospital.'

Twenty minutes later, her hair still damp from her bath, Georgia stood in the Intensive Care Unit, looking in at the inert form of her husband in the hospital bed. She had been told that it was a hit and run, and that Harry might have sustained serious brain injuries. Trying to stay calm, she thought of the baby she was carrying, and asked to talk to a doctor. After being kept waiting for another half an hour, the doctor appeared; the prognosis, he told her, was grave – but there was some hope. They would know better in the morning . . .

Clutching her hands together, Georgia watched Harry. He was hardly recognisable with his face swollen to twice its size and his nose bloodied to a pulp. His hands were scratched where he had struck the road, and the index finger of his right hand was torn half way down the nail bed. He was unconscious, breathing on a ventilator.

'Are you all right?' the nurse asked Georgia.

'I'm pregnant.'

'I see,' the nurse said. 'Perhaps we'd better have you checked out by—'

'Who did it?' Georgia asked, cutting her off.

'The police said it was a hit and run. I'm afraid they don't know who the driver was.'

'Why are *you* afraid? He's not *your* husband,' Georgia snapped, distraught.

Numbed, she continued to sit by the bed. Disconnected images fluttered like dry moths in front of her: Harry coming in with his running shoes, leaving mud on the hall floor; the children at the school, playing in the yard and yelling at the tops of their voices; and Marshall in the pub, talking about the Rembrandt letters . . .

'My father was murdered, Georgia. He was killed. And his killers didn't get what they were looking for. They won't stop

searching for the letters now . . . I have to know who killed my father and I want to make sure they don't get hold of the letters . . . there are some honest men that couldn't survive a bloodbath. The Rembrandt letters can't get into the wrong hands . . .'

Georgia remembered only too well what she had said next.

'I'll help you any way I can. But I won't tell Harry about any of this. I don't want him involved . . .'

But he *was* involved, she thought, her mouth dry as lint as she looked at him. A hit and run accident. A hit and run. Poor Harry. Harry, who had never done anyone a bad turn but was now the victim of something he didn't even know about. Or would care about. Rembrandt. Art. None of it meant anything to her husband, so why hurt him? *Why?* But Georgia knew the answer. To warn her, to make her realise that she was now alone. Pregnant, vulnerable, unprotected.

A touch on her left shoulder made Georgia turn nervously. A tall, well-built man was looking down at her, his beard fire red, his expression serious.

'I'm—'

'Teddy Jack.'

He nodded. 'How did you know?'

'Last year Owen sent me some photographs of an exhibition opening at the gallery. You were in one of them.'

'Don't ask any questions, or make a scene, please, but you have to come with me.'

'Are you joking? I'm not leaving my husband!'

'You *have* to leave him,' Teddy said, his grip tightening on her shoulder. 'You're in danger, Georgia. Marshall asked me to look out for you, but neither of us thought they'd go for your husband.'

'I'm not leaving Harry,' she said firmly, looking at the figure in the bed. 'I'm not afraid of anyone.'

'You should be,' Teddy replied, drawing up a chair next to her. His voice dropped to barely a whisper. 'They won't do anything else to your husband, they just wanted him out of the way . . .'

She made a small, catching sound in her throat.

'You're vulnerable, Georgia, you have to come with me. I can keep you safe. I have to do this, I promised Marshall—'

Her eyes widened. 'He knows about Harry?'

'No, I haven't spoken to him since this morning. I don't even know where he is.'

'Why doesn't he just give up those bloody letters!' she snapped. 'Nothing's worth this.'

'Georgia, come with me, please,' Teddy persisted. 'I have to look after you. I'm going to take you somewhere safe. Somewhere I can keep an eye on you until all this is over.'

'All *what!*' she hissed. 'Until what? Until Harry dies?'

'He isn't going to die. He'll recover.'

'And what about Marshall?' she asked, her eyes blazing. 'What if they get him? Will they just injure him or will they kill him? How many is it now, Teddy? I know of four deaths, and now Harry's accident . . .'

'Which is why we're not going to add to the numbers,' Teddy said, his voice implacable. 'Come with me—'

'Sod off!'

'Come with me!' Teddy commanded her. 'You think being here with your husband will help? You can't stay here, and you can't go back home. You can't be alone. You're in danger. Don't you get it?' His expression was hard. 'Stop fucking around and help yourself. That way you'll help everyone else too.'

Slowly, Georgia stood up, pulling on her coat. The nurse came over to the bedside. 'Are you all right?'

'I'm fine, just tired. I thought I'd go home and get some rest.'

'Good idea,' the nurse said. 'Your husband's stable now. You can afford to relax a little.'

'Will they keep him on the respirator?'

'Until he's breathing on his own, yes.'

'And he *will* breathe on his own, won't he?' Georgia asked, her voice shaky.

'Yes, he will. He's making progress, believe me. He'll recover. We'll look after him. You just have to look after yourself now.' She smiled encouragingly. 'And the baby.' She glanced over to Teddy. 'Are you family?'

'Cousin,' he lied, and the nurse smiled as she took in the red beard and hair. 'Of course, same colouring,' she said.

Clumsily, Georgia fumbled with her handbag and buttoned up her coat. 'I'll be back tomorrow.'

'Good,' the nurse replied cheerfully. 'But get some rest first, all right? Your husband's going nowhere.'

In silence Teddy and Georgia walked down the back stairs to the corridor which led to the hospital car park. He walked quickly; Georgia was withdrawn, uncertain of where she was being taken.

'Why can't I stay at home?'

'I've told you, it's not safe,' Teddy replied, moving over to his van and unlocking it. 'You can trust me, Georgia, honestly you can. I promised Marshall I'd look after you.'

Nodding, she slid into the passenger seat, suddenly cold. She wanted, above anything, to go back home. To make something to eat and then sit and watch the DVD she had promised herself. She wanted to see Harry and listen to him tell her about the gym, bragging about the weights he had lifted, and most of all she wanted to curl up against her husband in bed and feel warm and safe. Instead, she was sitting in some uncomfortable van, on a cold plastic seat, having just left Harry in Intensive Care.

After stopping briefly to allow Georgia to pack a bag, Teddy turned out of London and headed for Sussex. In silence, Georgia sat beside him, staring at her reflection in the window. As the miles passed, she thought she might doze, and then realised she would probably never doze again. Until it was over.

'Where are we going?'

'You know Samuel Hemmings?'

'The art historian?' she asked, surprised. 'Owen's mentor?'

'Yeah, him. We're going to his house. I can keep an eye

on both of you there,' Teddy replied, driving carefully as they moved onto the unlit roads. The van jerked over the uneven surface, then the road smoothed out again and they entered a village.

'What about Marshall?' she asked suddenly. 'Where's he?'

'I don't know.'

'So who's looking out for him?'

'No one – at the moment.' Teddy was obviously irritated. 'Your ex-husband plays his cards very close to his chest. Like his father for that.'

'You were close to Owen, weren't you?'

Nodding, Teddy kept his eyes on the road as it began to rain. 'He was a good employer and then he became a friend. And before you say it, I already feel guilty for what happened to him.'

'It wasn't your fault.'

'No,' Teddy said curtly, pulling into a drive and turning the car into a garage beside a large property. Shutting off the engine, he looked at Georgia. 'There's a man called Greg Horner here. He's living over the garage part time, but he's going to move into the house. God knows, there's enough room. He's a surly bugger, but he can handle himself, and he's big enough to make anyone think twice.'

'You think someone will come here?' she asked, startled.

'No,' he lied, 'but if anyone did, I've got it covered. You're not going to be on your own, and neither is Samuel.'

Her eyes fixed on him, unwavering. 'You think they'll come for me—'

'I just—'

'Think they'll come for me,' she interjected. 'Well, you better be bloody good at your job, Teddy Jack, because I'm not about to die. And neither is Harry, or our baby. So you look after me, you hear? You bloody well look after me, because I didn't ask to get involved in any of this.' Angry, she slammed her hands down on the dashboard, her voice wavering. 'It's not my bloody war!' Then, more calmly, she said, 'I want my family back, and I want my life back. So you make sure I *get* them back, you hear me?'

Teddy nodded, smiling faintly. 'I hear you.'

'And you can find Marshall too,' she added. 'Find him – before they do.'

House of Corrections,
Gouda, 1654

Winter arrived early, or maybe it just seemed that way . . . News came, the guard called me out of my cell, and together we walked down the corridor towards the asylum. The House of Corrections. The Asylum. So close they could be the same. You hear the noises at night of women barking like dogs. Some crying, some imitating the lascivious lip-smackings of sex, some clucking like mad ducks at little duckling children . . . Mad, sad. Different. And the same. Like me . . .

God made us that way, in His image.

The guard walked me to the Governor's room, which was soft like the inside of a robin's egg, all yolky yellow fabric, the desk black as a coalface. And a mirror which distorted you, making your body huge at the belly, your head and legs small as an ant's. Or maybe that was how I looked after years here . . . He stared at me and said I had a visitor and I thought it might be Rembrandt, but when they took me into the little greeting room there he was.

They say larks sing when they see Heaven. I do not doubt it.

Carel. Carel, my son . . . He stood there, his hat in his hands, not dusty now. Older, almost handsome, smiling as though he found it difficult. But he was so kind, and asked me to sit down. Asked me, taking a seat for himself afterwards. As though I was come for a portrait . . . I couldn't think of what to say, sat on my hands like a fool, and his head went to one side because I believe he was sorry for me.

He said he knew I was his mother.

My lips were so dry they cracked when I tried to make an answer. They cracked and a little blood salted my tongue . . . He said van Rijn had let the truth slip, when he was drunk. Sloppy with wine and talking about the past, and how sometimes he couldn't sleep for the bad he had done . . . I said nothing, waiting, not wanting to add anything until I knew what my son did. But when Carel spoke again he spoke of Rembrandt as his teacher, his mentor − not his father.

So the breech truth was only half delivered, half born, wedged into my pelvis, dragging at my innards until I felt the pushing of the years stop somewhere, half arrived. He said he was sorry that he had not been kinder to me and I told him he had never been anything other than kind. Not like the stoat-faced Gerrit Dou, or the lumbering Jan Victors. And then his head bowed like a child come late for confession, certain to be judged. He whispered about the paintings, and I told him I knew. There was a slow nodding, as though it was right I should know. I told him I remembered Rembrandt calling him his monkey, and he smiled. Rembrandt's monkey. Yes, Carel said, he had been pleased to be called that. Once.

Ssssh . . . A door bangs outside. I will write when it is quiet again. Now the silence comes like a dead skin over me . . . When Carel saw me that day he told me he would do everything to get me released. He cared, I saw it in his eyes, and dying would have been sweet that moment . . .

I took his hand. Yes, I took his hand.

402

Rembrandt was merciless, Carel said, speaking of what had been done to me. Then he told me of how he had been made to continue working. Painting portraits for Rembrandt, who would sign them, then give them on for selling to his agent, Hendrick van Uylenburgh. A man with a cold, soft voice and a hat brushed blue-black as a magpie's wing ... We are creating a king's fortune, Rembrandt had said to Carel, keep quiet. Keep quiet. Remember, I made you, I can unmake you also ... keep quiet.

All the keepings quiet. All the silences muffling the facts like the drapes round the old bed ... Then Carel said he had met Rembrandt's mistress, Hendrickje Stoffels, and my heart twitched at the name.

Go away, go away, I told my son. Leave Delft, Holland. Go abroad, go to another country ...

I would have pushed him, if I could have. Would have taken him into the courtyard and prayed for his back to arch and wings the width of a cathedral to lift him up and take him from Amsterdam.

Take your wife, your children, I urged him. Take them and go whilst you can. Whilst there is time ... You owe me nothing.

I took his hands and kissed them. He let me. I kissed him for calling me his mother and for recognising me as such.

Get away, I told him, get away ...

The clock of the Gouda House of Corrections was striking seven, booming the dead, brass notes into the flatlands. When he left he turned at the gate and raised his hand to me. For a second his fingers were silhouetted against the setting sun and they looked like the spokes of a Catherine Wheel.

403

38

Having shaken off Dimitri Kapinski, Marshall ducked into the doorway of an abandoned shop. On the windows were advertisements for the Moscow State Circus and the Rijksmuseum, and underneath, in smaller letters some joker had written 'dyslexia lures, KO?' Glancing round again, Marshall took out his mobile, thought for a moment, then dialled a London number. It was a number he had known for many years; a private number few people had, outside the business. A number Owen Zeigler had used many times.

'Hello?' a querulous voice answered.

'Tobar Manners?'

'Who's this?'

'Marshall Zeigler.' He was certain he could sense an intake of breath at the other end. 'You cheated my father, you bastard, and I'm going to make sure I ruin you.'

'Now, look here—'

Marshall could feel the pulse thumping in his neck. He was flinging caution to the wind, trying to provoke a challenge. 'The portraits you're selling are fakes.'

'What!!?' Manners exclaimed, then tried to bluster his way out. 'Look, Marshall, perhaps I did a bad thing with regard to your father. It wasn't meant—'

'You fucking liar!'

'All right, all right.' Tobar pushed his free hand through his dandelion hair. 'I cheated him. OK, so you want to get your own back, fine, I understand. I can pay you.'

'No, you can't. I don't want money.'

'So what *do* you want?'

'I want to see you disgraced and penniless, that's what I want. And I have the means at my disposal to do it.'

'You have the Rembrandt letters?' Tobar asked, his voice barely a whisper. *'They're real?'*

'Indeed they are.'

'Look, Marshall—'

'No, Tobar, *you* look. I've got the letters and I've got proof that the Rembrandts going up for sale in New York are fakes.'

'Are you going to expose them?' Tobar asked, his voice thin. 'I mean, if you were, why haven't you already done it?' His confidence percolated. 'You *don't* have them, or you would have acted already. You're bluffing, Marshall. You should be careful who you piss around with, this isn't amateur night.'

'After four murders, no, it's not amateur at all,' Marshall answered, pushing him. 'Who are you working with?'

'Jesus Christ!' Tobar snapped. 'You think *I* killed those people? Your father? The rest? Are you insane?!' he slumped into his seat, loosening his collar. 'I had nothing to do with those murders.'

Marshall was inclined to believe him. He had never really thought that Tobar Manners was involved in the killings, he was just hoping that his father's old acquaintance would act as the town crier. By telling Manners he had the letters, Marshall knew it would be all over London within hours. And by telling him that he had proof the portraits were fakes he was effectively setting himself up as bait. The real killer would then be sure to come after him.

Him, and no one else.

'Where are you?'

Marshall laughed. 'Of course you'd be the first person I'd confide in. I bet you'd sell me out to the highest bidder without pausing for breath.'

'I'm sorry about your father, Marshall.'

'You don't know what sorry means,' Marshall replied. 'But you will, Tobar. When your portraits get laughed out of court. When you'll be lucky to get a hundred and fifty thousand pounds for them – instead of forty million.'

'Marshall, calm down, we can come to an arrangement.'

'Really? You know who's behind all this?'

'No,' Tobar said honestly. 'But between us, you and me, we could make a deal . . . You don't have to make the letters public, Marshall. You could just let the sale go through, and we could split the proceeds afterwards. Think what you could do with all that money.'

'What would you do with your half, Tobar?'

Manners ran his tongue over his dry lips before answering, quietly, 'I could save my business . . .'

'Hell of a business if you need twenty million to save it,' Marshall replied. 'My father could have saved his gallery with just half a million. My father could have saved his business with the proper proceeds from selling his own Rembrandt. But you cheated him, and now I'm going to cheat you.'

'Marshall, think about it! Think about what it would mean. You'd bring down the art market—'

'So I gather.'

'Hardly anyone would survive. You want that? And what about the letters themselves, Marshall? Proof that Rembrandt had a bastard who faked for him? If that poisonous little secret comes out it will undermine one of the greatest painters who ever lived.'

'Why should I care? Let the world see Rembrandt for what he was,' Marshall said shortly. 'You don't give a damn about his character, you just care about the money his works make. Even in the middle of a global recession, he's foolproof. People can always rely on Rembrandt to shore up the market. He's gold, platinum, bank-safe. The pound and the dollar might crumble, but not Rembrandt. As long as there are Rembrandts to sell, there are fortunes in the offing.'

Rattled, Tobar began to panic. 'How d'you know the letters aren't fakes?'

'They've been authenticated by Stefan van der Helde. Remember him? He was the first murder victim. The letters are real because people have killed for them. People don't kill for fakes, Tobar. They don't risk everything for a hoax. The Rembrandt letters exist, and they can ruin you, and your fucking business.'

'So why tell me?' Manners said. 'Why are telling me this, Zeigler? You want revenge for your father, fine, I get it. But why else are you telling me? Are you checking me out, is that it? Seeing if I *am* involved, seeing how far I'd go to shut you up and get hold of the letters?' He paused, staring ahead, aware that he was looking into his own destiny and was terrified by it. 'You want to make a deal.'

'No, I just want one thing from you, Tobar. The thing you're best at – I want you to talk. To gossip, to make sure that everyone knows I have the letters.'

'Surely you don't also expect me to tell everyone the paintings due for sale are fakes?'

Marshall shrugged. 'You'd stab anyone in the back, Tobar, but you won't cut your own throat.'

'*You can't expose the fakes!*'

'Yes, I can. And I can – and I *will* – ruin you.'

'But what if someone stops you, Marshall?' Tobar said viciously. 'What if someone fills up your belly with stones? Guts you? Blinds you? You want to be a fucking martyr, go ahead. But I'd think about it very carefully ... You might hate me, perhaps I deserve it, but I can help you. I can protect you, keep you safe. I can also make you a very rich man if you keep quiet about the sale. Look, you can keep the fucking letters, if you want. You could sell them later. Make a fortune when times are on the up again. Or you could use them as a bargaining tool to get the art market over a barrel—'

408

'Like you are now?'

Biting his lip, Tobar struggled to keep his composure. 'I know this business.'

'I don't. But I know what's right.'

'Jesus, you don't think you're honouring your father doing this! Or do you? . . . God, I think you do.' He laughed bitterly. 'Owen Zeigler wasn't quite the hero you think he was. He was very cunning, in his own way.'

'He lived for the art world—'

'Because he learned how to work the strings. His sleight of hand was always impressive. Even more so because no one suspected the depth of his ingenuity.'

'Don't talk about my father like that!'

'You didn't really know him! You should have invested more time with your father when he was alive. Dead men – even the undeserving – become ready heroes.' His voice hardened. 'You don't know what you're letting yourself in for. You think you have the upper hand? There are no upper hands. There's just a continuous game of pass the parcel. We do a favour, we return a favour. We drop a word in the right ear, and forget a fact. We put alarms on our windows and gallery doors to keep out the bad men, but in reality it's to keep them in. Almost every gallery in these streets has a history of fake promises and lying. We all fill our bellies – not with the few big, genuine sales – but with the drizzling, petty diet of trumped up artists and overestimated Scottish cattle. For every Modigliani there are hundreds of sodden Lake District scenes, in Victorian frames, buffed up and regurgitated

409

for the gullible. Vermeer? Once in a lifetime, if you're lucky. But any amount of bilious indifferent Dutch interiors and fucking portraits of monks.'

He started laughing to himself, almost amused. 'People hate art dealers because we're pompous and patronising. They see the recession hit us and think we got what we deserved. Why? Because we're elitist, and frequently banal. And rich – and envied for it. But, by Christ, we earn our crust. I've sold dross as twenty-four carat gold, and pap as platinum. It takes a special skill to be an art dealer; mendacity is a prerequisite. Fakes? We're *all* fucking fakes.' He paused, his tone cooling. 'You need to think about this conversation, Marshall. Think very carefully. You've got this number, call me later when you've considered what I've said. Think about what you could do with a great deal of money. Then we'll talk ... But if you tell me we can't do business—'

'We can't do business.'

'Then start running, Marshall Zeigler. And don't stop.'

39

Due to the unprecedented media interest, the venue for the auction of the Rembrandt portraits was rumoured to be about to move, until confirmation that the auction would be held at the Museum of Mankind, New York. Handled by a leading auction house, the insurance and security was due to run into the hundreds of thousands; the front glass wall of the foyer was re-enforced with another wall of toughened glass. The paintings were being kept at an undisclosed location until the day of the auction, when they would arrive under police escort. The sale was publicly touted as being not only a way to raise money, but to revive interest in the plummeting art market.

Journalists from around the globe came to interview the director of the Museum of Mankind, and Tobar Manners, the broker for the sale. The owner of the Rembrandts was to remain anonymous, although, as Manners pointed out repeatedly, the history of the works was never in question. On camera he seemed a brusque, clever man, with a facility for words and an unexpected charm, as dazzling as a firefly. No one watching or listening to him would suspect the panic inside, the ever present fear that at any moment the paintings would be called out as fakes. And with proof.

It had taken Tobar only half an hour to decide what to do after he had finished talking to Marshall. He had waited in the dubious hope that Marshall might call him back, but as the thirty minutes ended, Tobar picked up the phone and began calling his associates. He said nothing about the Rembrandts coming up for sale in New York, and certainly made no mention that they were fakes. But he made very certain that everyone he spoke to knew that the Rembrandt letters existed. That the theory Owen Zeigler had had for so long was actually proven. Rembrandt had a bastard son who had forged for him. Rembrandt's son, by Geertje Dircx. The monkey was finally out of its cage.

The news was met with incredulity in some quarters, but as the rumour had been going apace lately, there was almost a sense of relief that the letters had actually surfaced. Then, after the initial relief, the facts slammed home. Without exception, everyone realised the importance and the danger of the letters. Leon Williams visited Rufus Ariel; Tobar Manners joined them a little later, all three men oddly reserved. The murder of Stefan van der Helde was understood when it was known that he had authenticated the letters. The murder of Charlotte Gorday came into focus too, because of her being Owen Zeigler's mistress. And when someone mentioned the murder of

Nicolai Kapinski in New York, no one was in any doubt that the killings were all connected. They spoke of Owen Zeigler, and of his theory. They spoke of a colleague and sometime friend who had found a smoking gun and had passed it on.

The barrel was now pointed at all of them – and in the hands of his son.

Flinging open the door of Rufus Ariel's gallery, Lillian Kauffman walked into the office beyond. Her expression was combative.

'When *exactly* were you going to tell me?'

'You already knew about the letters,' Tobar said, his tone surly.

'I didn't know that Marshall had them,' she lied, sitting down on a chaise longue and crossing her short legs. Her make-up was perfect at eight-fifteen in the morning, her voice flinty as she studied Tobar. 'Why put Marshall in danger by advertising the fact? I would have thought you'd done enough damage to that family.'

'He told me to tell everyone.'

'That he has the letters?'

'Yes.'

'But why? It would just mark him out.'

'I didn't ask why,' Tobar replied unpleasantly. 'He just asked me to pass on the message. Which I duly did.'

She regarded him for a long moment, taking in the unreadable expression and level voice. Was he lying? Difficult to tell, but if Marshall had wanted to set himself up, why? Fiddling with one of her earrings, Lillian glanced at the three men, each displaying different emotions. Tobar Manners, inscrutable; Rufus Ariel, pink and chilling; Leon Williams edging panic, his thin, long legs stretched out in front of him as he slumped in his chair, nursing an acid stomach.

'Maybe he wanted to flush out the killers,' she offered, watching them all turn to her. 'Well, it would, wouldn't it?'

'You really think one of us is a murderer?'

'No, Rufus, I think maybe all *three* of you are,' she replied blithely. 'Besides, the murders have a theme, copying Rembrandt paintings. How arty is that?'

'I didn't know about that!' Leon murmured, disturbed as he looked round at the other men. 'Who knew about that?'

'There've been rumours,' Rufus replied. 'In the last killing Nicolai Kapinski was blinded.'

Nauseated, Leon glanced away, and Lillian continued with her previous theme.

'I was joking, of course, but then again, all three of you *do* have contacts. You could arrange things, get someone else to commit the murders for you. Don't look at me like that, Leon! I remember that your grandfather was jailed for fraud. He could have made some useful contacts in Wormwood Scrubs.'

'That's a damn lie!' Leon spluttered. 'He was innocent.'

Raising his eyebrows, Rufus turned to Lillian, his baby face malign. 'What about you, Lillian? I imagine you could be as deadly as Medea.'

'But why?' she countered. 'I adored Owen and wouldn't hurt Marshall. And besides, I don't deal in Dutch art.'

'It wouldn't just affect Dutch art, it would rock the whole market. We'd all suffer.'

'We've all made fortunes, don't you have any savings?' Lillian replied, seeing them exchange glances. 'Oh dear, never put anything away for a rainy day? Or even a spot of drizzle, by the looks of it.' Her voice was amused. 'The recession was never going to happen to us, was it?'

'You needn't look so bloody pleased about it,' Tobar said testily. Lillian remained implacable.

'Of course those Rembrandts coming up for sale . . . If they did turn out to be fakes—'

'Fuck off, Lillian.'

She stood up, amused, and left, crossing over and walking to the Zeigler Gallery when she thought she saw a movement behind the window. Curious, she peered in, then rattled the door handle. No one answered, but Lillian wasn't satisfied and, pushing open the back gate, walked down the basement steps. Knocking at the basement door, she waited, then rapped loudly and imperiously on the glass.

A moment later, the huge figure of Teddy Jack came into view as he opened the door. He nodded, then stood back for her to enter.

'I've just seen Tobar Manners and his cohorts,' Lillian began, walking into the basement area.

The porters had long gone, the blood stain on the floor had dried to a raw umber, the window had been repaired.

Slowly she looked around, her gaze resting on the large waste pipe where Owen Zeigler had been tied. At the bottom of the pipe was a strip of police tape, and a scratching of sawdust.

'What d'you want, Mrs Kauffman?'

'Maybe I should ask what you're doing here, Teddy?'

Shrugging, he leaned against the bench, lighting a cigarette. 'I couldn't keep away.'

'Some say the murderer always returns to the scene of his crime.'

'So *you* did it, did you?' he asked, raising his eyebrows. 'You know, I still imagine Owen here. Think I can hear his footsteps overhead, or the phone ringing in the gallery above.'

'He was very fond of you.'

Teddy nodded. 'I know.'

'He relied on you,' she went on. 'I don't want to know the details, Teddy, but I know you did some unusual jobs for Owen ...'

He said nothing.

' ... and I know that Owen was never indiscreet, or injudicious about his confidants. Neither is his son.'

'No.'

'So why would Marshall Zeigler suddenly announce – via the odious vessel of Tobar Manners – that he has the Rembrandt letters?' She perched on a stool, her feet just brushing the floor. 'It's a bit like being spotted by a bear.'

'*What?*'

'Well, if you were camping with your family and a bear

burst out of the woods – if you were brave and wanted to protect the ones you loved – you would call attention to yourself. Then the bear would go after you, and not your family.' She paused. 'Is that why Marshall did it?'

'Of course that's why he did it.' Teddy agreed. 'Don't repeat this to anyone, but his ex-wife's husband was the victim of a hit and run last night.'

'Is he all right?'

'Harry Turner will live, but I don't know in what kind of a state. I've got Georgia somewhere safe, along with Samuel Hemmings.'

'Does Marshall know?'

'No,' Teddy replied, inhaling deeply on his smoke. 'Marshall asked me to watch Georgia, but it was obvious when Harry was injured that I had to get her into hiding, and ensure Samuel was safe too. I've got people with them now.' He regarded Lillian steadily. 'Trouble is I don't know where Marshall is. I don't even have a number to ring him on. He keeps changing his phones . . . Have *you* got a contact number?'

She shook her head. 'No.'

'He didn't tell you where he was going?'

'Not a hint.'

'D'you think he'd go to New York?'

'He might . . . for the sale.'

'Mrs Kauffman,' Teddy began steadily, 'I should warn you not to go around blowing your mouth off. You should be more careful what you say – and who you say it to.'

'I'm not scared!' she snapped. 'Besides, who'd believe an old Jewish broad like me?'

He paused, wondering how he might best phrase the next words. 'You should leave your gallery for a while. Until all this has been sorted out.'

'All this?'

'You know what I mean.'

'No, Teddy, I don't. And I'm not going anywhere. I live at the gallery. It's my home, and no one's scaring me out of it.' She tapped the back of his hand. 'I have an alarm system which would fry anyone who so much as touched the windows. I have a panic button direct to the police—'

'Both of which rely on electricity.'

She blanched. 'What?'

'Someone could cut the wires, Mrs Kauffman, and you'd be helpless.' He stared at her, unblinking. 'You know about the letters, that makes you vulnerable. Let me get you somewhere safe.'

She rallied fast. 'Do guns run on electricity?'

'*What?*'

'No, I thought not . . . I have a gun, Teddy, and I happen to be a very good shot. My late husband taught me how to defend myself. Trust me, I wouldn't think twice about shooting someone.' She smiled, her lipstick vivid. 'I'm not running away. I've never run away from anything.'

'I can't watch you here.'

'I don't *need* watching! Watch Georgia, watch Samuel Hemmings, poor bastard's in a wheelchair. And besides, he knows all about the letters. He was Owen's mentor—'

'But he didn't see all of them.'

Her pencilled eyebrows rose. 'He didn't?'

'No, he never saw the list of fakes.'

'How d'you know?' she asked, her tone suspicious.

'Marshall told me,' Teddy replied, stubbing out his cigarette. 'He said that Samuel Hemmings was safer because he didn't have all the information. You see, the only people who are *really* in danger are the ones who know everything.' He looked at her steadily. 'Have you seen the letters and the list?'

'No!' Lillian laughed, genuinely amused. 'I heard about them for years, but never saw them. To be honest, I never thought they really existed.' She slid off the stool and walked to the back door, then turned. 'Thanks for worrying about me, but it's Marshall who needs help now.'

And with that she walked out, her footsteps fading gradually on the street above.

'I can't stay here indefinitely!' Georgia said, pausing beside the fireplace in Samuel Hemmings' study. 'I want to see Harry.'

'Phone the hospital again,' he replied, 'they keep you in touch. You know what Teddy Jack said, we have to stay here.'

Sighing, she turned to the old man and folded her arms, watching him at his desk. He had aged considerably in the last weeks, an angina attack proving the strain he had been under. His hands were not shaking any more than usual, but the skin seemed stretched, the blue veins visible. As though desperate to keep his mind focused, Samuel was working on a paper, typing laboriously at his computer, his gaze moving from the keyboard to the garden, and back again repeatedly. Aware of how difficult the circumstances must be for him, Georgia tried to curtail her restlessness. But although she had called the hospital three times that day, and been assured that her husband was making steady progress, she was unable to cover her unease.

Luckily Samuel Hemmings was not a stranger to Georgia. They had met at her wedding to Marshall, and several times afterwards at the Zeigler Gallery. But the clever, sharp-witted historian she remembered seemed now reduced, shrivelled into a fallen leaf.

Walking over to the table, she stood looking at the reproductions Samuel had laid out.

'What are these?'

'Nothing important.'

'Try again.'

'It's the way the victims were killed.'

She slid out a chair and sat down. 'You mean that each killing mirrored a Rembrandt painting?'

He nodded. 'Nicolai Kapinski's was the last. His eyes were gouged out – *The Blinding of Samson*.' Samuel paused, taking off his glasses, and turned to her. 'You shouldn't be thinking about any of this. Teddy said you were pregnant. You should be resting.'

'How can I?' She pulled the reproduction of *The Blinding*

of Samson towards her. 'Each victim's death represents a painting?'

He nodded.

'How theatrical,' she said, although she had wrapped her arms around her body protectively.

The baby wasn't moving and she wondered anxiously if the trauma would injure the foetus. Then Georgia realised that if she was killed, the child would die too . . . Her mind wandered back to Charlotte Gorday, then Owen Zeigler, finally resting on the memory of a summer six years earlier. She had still been married to Marshall then, and they had fought – the subject wasn't important – and she had walked off. Defiant, she had stayed away for over six hours, knowing he would worry and knowing she was punishing him. Just as, when a child, she had punished her mother because she felt unwanted and resentful on that romantic holiday break Eve had planned with Philip Gorday . . .

Staring at her stomach, Georgia made a promise to herself that if she survived she would never walk away from anything or anyone again. Because it was so passively violent. So silently hostile. She might fool herself and say that she was avoiding confrontation, but by leaving, she had known full well that she would fill the beloved's head with terrifying anxiety. When all this was over, when she was home again, with Harry well and the baby born; when life was once more hers, and normal, she would never again walk away from anything.

A noise outside interrupted her thoughts. 'Where's Teddy Jack?' she asked Samuel.

Sighing, he looked up from his books and pointed to the garden.

'He's gone now, but Greg Horner's here and one of Teddy Jack's men.'

Curious, Georgia moved to the window. She could see Horner washing the car, his sleeves rolled up. He was soaping the headlights, rubbing a rag over them in curt, circular movements, his shadow mimicking the action. A little way off, across the garden, Georgia caught a glimpse of another man, someone she hadn't seen before, younger, with cropped hair. He was very watchful, looking around him, at the house, the garden, even at Horner. His alertness was the very detail which worried her.

'Who's he?'

'One of Teddy Jack's men.'

'A Northerner?'

'I don't know.'

'Have you spoken to him?'

Samuel looked up. 'No. This morning is the first time I've seen him.'

Pulling a jacket over her shoulders, Georgia moved out of the house, skirting the garage and heading across the lawn. It had been raining again, and the heels of her shoes sank into the turf as she approached the stranger. Seeing her, he straightened up, taking his hands out of his pockets. He smelt of cigarettes and there was something familiar about him which Georgia couldn't quite identify. A look she had seen in someone else's face, an echo of another person.

'Hello,' she said simply, seeing his surprise as he nodded his greeting. 'Do you want a cup of tea? Or coffee?'

He paused. His eyes were very pale, his skin pockmarked around his neck. 'Coffee.'

'You're not English,' she said, smiling. 'Where d'you come from?'

'You should go back indoors—'

'I need some air.' Georgia laughed. 'I have to stretch my legs. All that sitting around is boring.'

'Mr Jack said I shouldn't talk to you.'

'Really? How dull,' she said easily. 'So, what's your accent? Russian?' She put her head on one side, teasing him. 'I have two Russian children in my class.'

'No, not Russian.'

'Ah, you just sound Russian. D'you want sugar in your coffee?'

He blinked. 'Two spoonfuls, please.'

'What?'

'*Two spoonfuls, if you please*,' he repeated.

'Polish.'

He looked into her open, intelligent face and shrugged. 'Polish, yes.'

'I thought so. I'm usually good at accents,' Georgia replied lightly. 'I'll get that coffee now.'

Walking back towards the house, she paused beside Greg Horner, and, making sure she was not seen by the other man, tapped him on the shoulder. He turned his long-jawed face towards her.

'Aye?'

'That new man. D'you know him?'

'Nah, never seen him before.'

'D'you know his name?'

'Nah, Mr Jack just said he were here to help me out. Watching you and Mr Hemmings.'

'So you know nothing about him?'

Greg Horner squeezed out the rag he was holding and began to buff the car headlights. 'Not a thing. And Mr Jack said to keep it that way. Said he could be a funny bugger, so to keep my distance. He said he was good in a fight though.' He paused, straightening up. 'Has he been bothering you?'

'No. I was just wondering about him, that was all. He's Polish.'

'Well, that would account for it, wouldn't it?'

'For what?'

'Him being a funny bugger,' Greg Horner replied, turning back to the car and beginning to polish the bumper.

A little later Georgia called the hospital and was told that Harry was stable, then she rang the Zeigler Gallery, knowing as she did so that no one would pick up. Inactivity didn't suit her; her restlessness was only temporarily stilled when she took a late afternoon nap. But her sleep was disturbed by the image of a man with cropped hair climbing through the bedroom window and she woke, sweating, staring up to the unfamiliar ceiling, her breathing rapid. A lonely dread began to take shape in her brain, some insubstantial hint of menace. Against the drawn curtains she could hear a fly humming, even so early in the year, and the crunch of the gravel as someone walked over the drive. The day was beginning to turn down the covers to night, the light fading, as she struggled to her feet and moved out onto the landing.

Downstairs she could hear Mrs McKendrick in the kitchen and remembered cooking for Marshall. And then she thought back to another time, watching the waitresses struggling to prepare food in the cramped kitchen off the gallery space. It had been the night of a private view and she was attending with Marshall, before he had moved to Amsterdam. Owen was there, talking to a collector, another strange, little man hovering beside him. He was diminutive, bi-spectacled, holding a vol-au-vent in one hand and balancing a glass in the other. Feeling sorry for him, Georgia had struck up a conversation and discovered that his name was Nicolai Kapinski, Owen Zeigler's Polish accountant. He had been fretful, nervy, telling her about a breakdown he had had, and how kind Owen had been to him. Even confiding something about a missing brother . . . Another image flickered in front of Georgia: the pale eyes of the man outside, so similar to another pair of pale eyes. Nicolai Kapinski's eyes, Owen's *Polish* accountant.

She thought of the recent conversation she had had with Philip Gorday, and how he had told her of Kapinski's violent death in New York. And suddenly Georgia knew who the man outside was. Knew instinctively that he was Nicolai

Kapinski's brother . . . But why was he here? Why was he guarding them when his own brother had been killed?

From her room came the sound of her mobile phone ringing, She ran in and snatched it up.

'Hello?'

'Georgia, are you all right?'

'Marshall!' she said hurriedly, 'Harry was hurt—'

'I know, I've just spoken to Teddy. He told me where he'd taken you. He said you were safe, Thank God. Are you OK?'

She clutched the phone. 'I'm fine. But Teddy Jack's not here now.'

'No?'

'No. Greg Horner's here, and Teddy brought in another man. Someone he knows. Someone who works for him.'

There was a pause on the line, Marshall's voice anxious.

'What is it, Georgia?'

'He reminds of someone. Didn't Nicolai Kapinski have a brother who went missing?'

Marshall could feel his mouth drying. 'What about him?'

'Did they ever find him?'

'Teddy Jack found him,' Marshall replied, hardly breathing. 'He's called Dimitri Kapinski. He's a convicted criminal and up until today he was following me. But I lost him . . . I don't know where he is now.'

'I do,' Georgia said flatly. 'He's here.'

BOOK FIVE

40

As the flight from Heathrow to Kennedy Airport crossed the Atlantic, Marshall phoned Teddy Jack's mobile repeatedly. There was no answer and he left the same message every time – *Call me. Urgent.* Shifting position in his airplane seat, Marshall could feel his eyes were gritty from lack of sleep, his stomach empty. He was hungry, but couldn't eat because of the spasm of anxiety in his gut. At first he had thought of calling the police, then calmed himself down enough to reason that Georgia could be mistaken. After all, she had little to go on in order to positively identify Dimitri Kapinski as Nicolai's brother. And yet he knew Georgia was no fool, her intuition unfailing. So, Marshall asked himself, if it *was* Dimitri Kapinski, why was he now guarding Georgia and Samuel Hemmings?

Brushing away the steward's offer of a drink, Marshall stared into the darkness outside the plane. If he could only get hold of Teddy Jack, he would explain, tell him it was a case of mistaken identity. After all, hadn't he promised to look after Georgia? *But had he been lying?* Marshall closed his eyes, the noise of the plane's engines echoing against his temples. He would sleep, he would get some sleep. He could do nothing while he was suspended in mid-air over the ocean. There was nothing he could do until he got to New York.

Eventually sleep came over him, along with a sweaty dream, then he woke suddenly and asked for a bottle of water. His thoughts were haphazard, fuzzy. Sleep – he must sleep and the confusion would lift . . . There will be an explanation. Teddy Jack was Owen's confidant, after all. His father would never have let him get so close unless he believed he could trust him. Unless he had fooled Owen Zeigler . . .

Marshall sat up and dialled Teddy Jack's number again, and heard the familiar answer phone message. Closing his eyes, he struggled to breathe, his chest constricting, his skin sheened with sweat as he thought of Georgia.

'Are you all right, sir?' the stewardess asked, bending down to him.

'Fine, fine,' Marshall replied. 'Just tired, that's all.'

She nodded sympathetically. 'D'you want another blanket? It gets colder at night.'

'How long before we get to New York?'

She glanced at her watch. 'Another three hours, sir. Are you sure there's nothing I can get for you?'

'No, nothing,' he said, then hunkered down in his seat and closed his eyes, his right hand resting against his jacket pocket which held the letters.

Sleep came, with memory. With the basement of the

430

Zeigler Gallery and the image of Charlotte Gorday, bleeding. Then Nicolai Kapinski, darting about, panicking, asking for his brother. And Teddy Jack smiling, telling him that they had found Dimitri. Found him at last . . . Waking, Marshall shifted his position and forced himself to sleep again. This time he dreamed of the letters, and of Geertje Dircx. She was very thin, wasted, her hands passing him the paper sheets.

This is the story of me . . .

Waking again, Marshall could feel the beginnings of a sick headache and asked for some tablets. Then he tried Teddy Jack's number once more, and left another message. This time, when he slept, he fell headlong into a dream so vivid he was living the past: He was the boy who had broken the spine of Owen's expensive book; the kid going to the British Museum with Timothy Parker-Ross; the young man reaching out to Georgia and kissing her for the first time.

'I love you,' she had said, her hair falling over her forehead. 'Well, go on, say it back!'

'I love you,' he had replied, pulling a face at her because he was so awkward at his own good fortune.

A sudden jolt of the plane jerked Marshall fully awake. His headache had gone while he slept and he felt rested, his thoughts clearer as he fastened his seat belt for landing and turned off his mobile. Soon he would be able to do something. He glanced round at the passengers. No one had seemed overly interested in him during the flight; perhaps they had missed him at Heathrow. Perhaps he would have some time in New York before they caught up with him ... Impatient, the letters resting against his heart, he willed the journey to end. The early-morning New York skyline seemed to present itself suddenly, visible through the clouds, almost tickling the underbelly of the plane as they came into land.

Tobar Manners had arrived in New York the previous day and was staying at the Four Seasons hotel, where he was complaining about the room service and sending back his water for being stale. His disagreeable mood had been compounded by the ridiculous rituals of communication the seller had insisted upon. He would not talk to Tobar directly, but through an intermediary, a thin American wearing a tight suit. So far, all Tobar had managed to ascertain was that the two Rembrandt portraits were still in storage and would only be delivered to the Museum of Mankind the following day – under escort, two hours before the auction was due to start.

Unable to relax, he had visited the Museum and checked the security, where he managed to irritate the staff and alienate the director. But to Tobar's intense pleasure, they had erected a high stage upon which the two portraits would be shown to their fullest advantage, able to be photographed and televised to the world. Well, Tobar thought, maybe not the world – the recession had knocked the sheen off cultural endeavours – but certainly the art world would be following every moment.

Having pressed Rosella to accompany him, Tobar was

nevertheless surprised that she had accepted. Then, in one of his night-time confessions, he had told her about the Rembrandt letters and the list of fakes.

'Are they genuine?' she had asked, showing no sign that she already knew of their existence.

'Oh yes,' Tobar had replied. 'Marshall Zeigler's got them.'

'But surely,' she said, hesitantly, 'someone will try and stop them coming out?'

'Marshall's put his head on the block, so he can't be surprised if someone cuts it off for him,' Tobar had responded, curling his thin legs against his wife's long limbs. 'I tried to help him.'

'*You* did?'

'I did,' he had insisted, his tone just the wrong side of mawkish. 'But he didn't trust me.'

'Why not? What did you offer to do for him?'

'Withdraw the Rembrandt portraits from the auction – if they were on the list of fakes.'

She had known at once that he was lying, could sense it in the dark. The lie so huge it was like another person in the room.

'What did Marshall say to that?'

'That he wanted to ruin me,' Tobar had replied, his feet against hers. 'He would say anything against me, do anything to discredit me. I wouldn't put it past Marshall Zeigler to claim the portraits were fakes just to ruin me.'

'But no one would believe him, would they?' Rosella asked, her tone all honey. 'Unless Marshall has the list. And if these letters were taken away from him, he would

433

have *no* proof. The person who has the documents has the power.'

Satisfied, Tobar had smiled into the darkness, then risen and left her bed. Relaxing, he realised that his wife had changed sides. The promise of a fortune had tempered her disgust at her husband's treatment of Owen Zeigler, and the promise of riches had made her an ally.

Picking the biggest bank in Manhattan, Marshall walked in and asked for the manager. He got the assistant manager, a man with a large red weal on his neck.

'Are you all right?' he asked the man, who shrugged and explained, 'Wasp sting, hurts like hell.'

Marshall smiled sympathetically. 'My name's Zeigler and I want to open an account at your bank and hire a safety deposit box. I also need to leave something here.'

The assistant manager extended a hand, saying 'I'm Dean Foley, Mr Zeigler. Come this way, sir.'

Marshall followed Foley into a back office and sat down, looking at the man steadily. 'I also need a photocopier.'

'A photocopier?' Foley seemed a little bemused by the request.

Marshall gestured to his bag. 'I'm a translator. I have to take some copies of my work and then I want to leave this bag with you.'

'Well, we'd have to check its contents first.'

'You can check it, by all means. There's just a laptop in it.' Marshall pushed the bag across the table, then stared at the swelling on Foley's neck. 'You should put some ice on that,' he said.

'What?'

'The wasp bite. And check you've got the sting out, that's what hurts.'

Foley smiled lamely, rubbing his neck. 'The insect just flew in and stung me. No one else; just seemed to aim for me.'

Marshall stared at the man, an old memory reviving. His father had been talking to him, telling him a story about the difference between bees and wasps.

. . . Bees warn you before they strike, they give you a chance. But wasps don't. They just pick their victim and go in for the kill. Watch for the wasps, Marshall, the bees will die out long before they do . . .

'Are you staying in New York, Mr Zeigler?'

Marshall nodded. 'For a little while.'

'And you're here because of work?'

'Yes, because of work.'

Foley passed a form across the desk for Marshall's signature. He then studied the signed document and extended a hand, saying, 'If you give me the bag now—'

'I have to do the photocopies first,' Marshall cut in hurriedly. 'Have to send them to my publishers today. They like the work faxed to them.' He shrugged. 'You'd think I could just send it digitally, but they're old fashioned.'

'There isn't a lot to photocopy, is there?'

'No, not much.'

'D'you need any help?' Foley asked, pointing to the photocopier in the corner of the office.

'No, I'm fine,' Marshall replied, flicking the ON switch of the machine. 'It'll take no time at all.'

Marshall watched the man walk off, then looked through the Venetian blinds of the office before taking the letters out of his jacket pocket. Slowly, he weighed them in his hands. He realised that his time had run out. He had no options left. He had to do something, fast . . . If he had hoped to flush out his father's killer, he had been disappointed. Whoever was responsible for the murders was not going to step out of the shadows. There was to be no dénouement, no warning. No one was going to approach him and talk – and why should they? Marshall felt himself suddenly embarrassed by his own naivety. Had he *really* expected a killer to act like a reasonable man? To show his hand?

There was to be no discussion. Four people had already died for the letters, there would be no hesitation in making Marshall the fifth. He was only important as long as he had the documents. When they had been taken from him, his death would follow . . . He paused, now horribly aware of the vulnerability of his situation. He was alone, and in an unfamiliar city. If he even made it back out onto the streets of New York, he wouldn't get far. He had hoped to last until the auction, but he suspected that he had little chance of that. No one could be trusted. Everyone was suspect, and he had nowhere left to go. The Rembrandt fakes would be sold tomorrow for a fortune unless he exposed them – along with the letters, the list and the truth about Rembrandt's monkey.

Marshall knew what he had to do. Not what he had wanted, or hoped for, but what *had* to be done. Carefully, he made two copies of each letter, and two of the list. Every time someone passed the office door, he tensed, waiting for them to come in. Every time he lifted the lid of the copier, he paused. The process seemed to take hours, each warm copy sliding balefully into the plastic tray on the side. Meticulously, Marshall slid the originals into their envelope one by one, handling them carefully because the paper was so worn. The copies seemed different, the reproductions no longer the sepia tones of the originals, but harshly white, crude – worthless on cheap paper.

He was working quickly because he knew he had little time, and that he was probably being watched. Anyone following him would know that he had the letters and would wait for their opportunity to strike. Being in the middle of the largest bank in Manhattan was some protection, but Marshall knew he had been lucky so far. The letters would be safe in the bank, but he would have to leave . . . Walking to the window and looking through the blind once more, his gaze rested on two men who were in the foyer. They looked out of place and, as Marshall watched, they asked one of the tellers something.

The woman turned and pointed to the back of the bank. To the office where Marshall was . . . Gathering up the copies, Marshall took out two envelopes, putting identical copies of the letters in each and addressing them. One to the *New York Times* and the other to *The Times* in London. He had no time to write a note, just sealed the envelopes and tucked them both under his arm. Then, hurriedly, he turned on his laptop. Opening an e-mail, he downloaded the copy of the letters he had made earlier, then typed in the address of the editor of the *New York Times* and wrote.

> *These letters are authentic, and they prove that the Rembrandt paintings coming up for sale at the auction tomorrow are fakes.*

Then he pressed the SEND button, and watched, the process began, then stopped. Baffled, Marshall stared at the screen, just as there was a knock on the door.

'Who is it?'

'Mr Zeigler, it's the manager.'

'Just a minute.'

The door opened but the man who walked in wasn't the one with the wasp sting; this was an older man, un-welcoming and brusque.

'I have to hurry you, sir. Can we take your bag now?'

Marshall glanced at the computer screen. The message had jammed on SEND. 'I just have one more thing to do—'

'We need the room, sir,' the manager said, 'another customer. Besides, there's been a power cut—'

'I just need a few more minutes,' Marshall said imploringly, looking over the man's shoulder into the bank beyond. His instincts were sharpened and he could sense danger. 'Just give me a couple more minutes.'

'Sorry, sir, we need the office,' the manager replied, his tone flat but firm. 'Do you want to leave your bag, or not?'

Defeated, Marshall turned off the laptop, the message unsent. Then he put the laptop into his bag and passed it to the manager.

'Thank you, sir.' He gave Marshall the key to his security box. 'We look forward to seeing you again.'

Suspecting that he had been deliberately interrupted, Marshall walked out of the office and was heading for the foyer when he noticed the two men turn in his direction, both watching him. He looked round, but there was only one exit and to reach it he had to pass them. Trapped, he felt real panic. If only he had managed to send the e-mail, if only . . . He moved forwards, the two men watching him, waiting, Marshall's steps slowing . . . An image of his father's dead body came back to him, and he decided that he wasn't going to make it easy for anyone. Instead he glanced around, then spotted the young assistant manager, Foley, and headed straight for him. The two men, startled, came across the foyer, while Marshall grabbed Foley's arm.

'You have to get the wasp sting out,' he said, propelling the startled man backwards. 'Where's the restroom?'

'In the back,' the man said, shaken, as Marshall half

pushed, half pulled him between the clerks' desks and through the double doors into the corridor beyond. Outside, on the landing, he gripped the man's arm and passed him the two envelopes. His voice was urgent, desperate. 'Send these letters. Mail them for me. *Please.*' And then he ran.

The double doors flung open a moment later, the two men hurrying after him down the exit stairs towards the basement. Confused, the assistant manager watched them pass, then wandered, bewildered, back into the bank. Sitting down, he gazed, baffled, at the letters Marshall had given him.

Then he sighed and dropped them into the waste bin beside his desk.

41

Out of breath, Marshall ran into Central Park, then took out his mobile and punched a number.

'Where the hell have you been!' he snapped down the phone when Teddy Jack finally picked up.

Teddy sounded unperturbed. 'I was about to call you. Where are you?'

'That's not important! What about Georgia? You bastard, why have you hired Dimitri Kapinski?' Marshall yelled, his temper rising. 'If anything happens to my wife—'

'Your *ex*-wife,' Teddy answered, pulling his van over to the side of the street and turning off the engine. 'Georgia's safe.'

'*With Dimitri Kapinski?*'

'Your father would have understood—'

'I don't!' Marshall snapped. 'Enlighten me.'

'Keep your friends close and your enemies closer,' Teddy responded. 'Dimitri *was* working for someone else. What better way to get him onto our side by getting him to work for *us*?'

Looking around, Marshall tried to calm his breathing. He was clammy, his forehead shiny with sweat.

'I don't believe you. In fact, I don't believe anything you say.'

'Remember I told you that I found Dimitri Kapinski years ago? Your father asked me to do it, for Nicolai.'

'So?'

'I told you about Dimitri, but I didn't tell you everything. He's a thug, yes. He can be violent, yes. And he's a thief, true. But above all, he's greedy – and loyal to the person who pays him the most.'

'And how much are you paying him?'

'Enough to keep him on our side.'

'And where did you get the money?'

'I have money.'

'Your flat says otherwise,' Marshall replied. 'Someone else must be giving you money.'

'Lillian Kauffman.'

'*Lillian?*'

'I told you, Marshall, she wanted to help you.' Teddy's tone was brusque. 'She gave me the money. If you want to check, call her, she'll vouch for me.'

Marshall had run from the bank into Central Park, the day sunny and relatively busy as he'd moved through a small underpass and come out into an open space by a lake. Sitting on the bench, which backed onto a stone wall, he could make sure that no one came up behind him, and he could see anyone approach. Around him, women walked with children, a group of schoolboys playing baseball.

'I don't believe you.'

'What don't you believe?'

'Any of it,' Marshall said flatly. 'I know Dimitri Kapinski *was* following me—'

'Yes, I hired him to do that.'

Wrong footed, Marshall paused. '*You* hired him?'

'Yeah, and you managed to lose him in Amsterdam!' Teddy replied, laughing. 'I've told you, Marshall, you can trust me. I wanted him to tell me where you were and what you were doing. When he lost you, I told him to come back to England and I sent him over to Sussex. Listen, I'm not just doing this for you, but for your father. If I'd looked out for Owen more, perhaps he'd still be alive . . . I won't let you down. Or Georgia.'

Wary, Marshall pushed him.

'If that's true, why did you act so surprised when you told me that Dimitri Kapinski was following me?'

'I wanted to make you trust me.' He was all plausibility. 'You were worried about Georgia, Marshall, I had to calm you down.'

'Who was he working for?'

'What?'

'Dimitri Kapinski. Before you hired him, who was he working for?'

'I don't know.'

'I find that hard to believe,' Marshall replied, looking about him. 'If you're jerking me around . . .'

443

'You sound upset, what the hell's going on?'

Rattled, Marshall shook his head. 'Just look after Georgia, that's all I ask. And if you know anything, Teddy, if you know who's behind all this, tell me now. If it's you, tell me.'

'It's not me.'

'If anything happens to Georgia I *will* kill you.'

'Nothing will happen to her. Are you in New York?'

'Don't you know?' Marshall countered wryly, leaning back against the bench.

'What have you done?'

'What I needed to do.'

'Are you in danger?' Teddy asked, his tone anxious.

'Yes, but it doesn't matter that much anymore.'

'Marshall, come back to London.'

'I don't think they'll let me,' he replied simply.

'Who won't?'

'It's *not* you, is it, Teddy?' Marshall asked, ignoring the question. 'I mean, I know you couldn't have planned all of this yourself, I know someone else would have worked it all out. But you *could* have been following orders. And my father would have trusted you. You were his ally, he wouldn't have suspected you.' Suddenly he felt weary. 'You didn't kill my father, did you?'

'No.'

'Who did?'

'I don't know,' Teddy replied. 'Where are the letters?'

'The letters . . . you didn't read them, did you?'

'No.'

'Shame, they would have moved you. '

'Where are they?'

'Was it Charlotte Gorday?' Marshall asked. 'Did *she* betray my father?'

'No.'

'Nicolai Kapinski?'

'No.'

'It has to be someone in the art world. It has to be someone who knows how the business works, and what damage the letters could do. Someone who's cultured, who knows about art. Someone ruthless. Someone ambitious, someone who knows about Rembrandt . . . Is Samuel Hemmings behind it all?'

'I don't know.'

'Guess.'

'I don't know,' Teddy replied, his tone unwavering. 'Where are the letters now?'

'Where they should be. Is it someone I know?' Marshall persisted. 'Lillian Kauffman? It could be her, she's smart enough, and she knows everything that goes on in the business.'

'She's trying to help you—'

Again, Marshall ignored him. 'It has to be someone my father trusted . . .' Marshall leaned forward, watching the pathways. Overhead a plane cut into the sky, the schoolboys argued on the grass, shadows lengthened and twisted under the moving sun. 'I don't think I'm going to get out of this alive.'

'Don't say that—'

'You lied to me.'

'Everybody lies, Marshall.'

'No, not everyone.'

'You'd be surprised. Even the people you think you know, you think you can trust, people you love – even they lie sometimes.'

'What's that supposed to mean?'

'Did you know that Georgia's mother had an affair with Philip Gorday?'

Marshall winced.

'And that your ex-wife is still in contact with Philip Gorday? She spoke to him only the other day,' Teddy went on. 'You *didn't* know, did you? You were married to her and she never mentioned it. Which makes me wonder why. Georgia knew Charlotte Gorday too.'

'I don't believe you.'

'I'm not lying,' Teddy replied. 'Like I said, no one's what they seem. Your father knew that only too well. Then one day he forgot it, and that's what killed him.'

42

'I can't sit here another minute doing nothing,' Georgia said impatiently. 'And why hasn't Marshall phoned?'

Her gaze moved over to Samuel. He was picking listlessly at a sandwich Mrs McKendrick had made for him, pulling out the lettuce and laying it on the side of the plate. His hands moved very slowly, his glasses sliding down his nose. With an effort he pushed them up onto the top of his head, then began picking at the sandwich again.

'If you don't like lettuce, why don't you tell her?' Georgia said, moving over to Samuel and sitting down beside him. 'I could make you something else.'

'This will do,' he said. 'Have you eaten your lunch?'

She nodded and glanced out of the window. The day was folding down as she drew the curtains and turned on the lamps in the study. The room had a sticky feel, an overhang of anxiety which had not been allayed by Teddy Jack's recent phone call. When Georgia questioned him about Dimitri Kapinski he told her what he had told

Marshall, reassuring her that she, and Samuel, were in good hands.

'New York.'

Samuel put down his sandwich. 'What?'

'Marshall will have gone over there for the sale. What time is it there?'

Blinking, he struggled upright in his wheelchair, glad to have something to concentrate his mind upon. 'About four in the afternoon,' he said at last. 'You think that's where he's gone?'

'Yeah, I do.'

'Does Marshall know anyone in New York?'

'No, but I do,' Georgia replied. 'I know someone he could go to for help. I got Marshall's new mobile number off Teddy Jack.'

'But no answer?'

'No.'

'So leave a message.'

'I have, several times,' she admitted, 'but he's not called me back.'

Georgia was hoping that the reason her ex-husband hadn't been back in contact was because he was angry, rather than that he was unable to call her. After all, to advise him to go to Philip Gorday, of all people, would have come as a shock to Marshall. She could imagine only too easily what he would think: Why had she never mentioned Philip before? And had she known about Charlotte Gorday? Chewing the side of her finger nail, Georgia stared at the mobile in her hand. She should have said something a long time ago. Now Marshall would be suspicious, wondering *why* she had kept the relationship a secret. Especially in light of Charlotte's association with Owen, and their inter-related deaths.

Damn it, call me! She willed the mobile to ring, asking herself why she had never told Marshall about knowing the Gordays. It was true she hadn't wanted to think about her past, or her mother, and the subject had never come up – until Marshall found out about Charlotte, that is. Now, seeing the situation through Marshall's eyes, Georgia knew she should have spoken up then, realising that he would wonder now what else she was hiding . . .

Guiltily, she thought about Harry, and remembered what they had told her at the hospital. Georgia had explained the reason for her absence by saying she was having trouble with her pregnancy and had been advised to rest. The lie made a worm in her heart, but at least Harry was improving; he was off the ventilator, breathing for himself, holding his own . . . She thought of her husband and felt, with profound contrition, only partial relief. Surely Harry should have been her first priority? Her first thought? And yet Marshall had usurped him in her present thoughts. Without understanding how it happened, circumstances had revived her feelings for her first husband.

Angrily, Georgia poked at the fire, the flames desultory, then she moved back to the table and sat down again.

'I have to do something . . . *We have to do something.*'

As if he were coming out of a long afternoon sleep, Samuel stirred his sluggish thoughts into activity. If he was honest he had temporarily faltered; unnerved by the gruesome death of Nicolai Kapinski and afraid for himself. The arrival of Georgia had compounded rather than alleviated his fears. Why was Teddy Jack corralling them together? To take care of them? Or make a bigger target? His suspicions had shamed him. After all, hadn't Teddy Jack simply been following Marshall's instructions to protect the people he cared about?

The alternative was too disturbing to contemplate. Being left alone, a man in a wheelchair, in a deserted house . . . He looked at Georgia, remembering that she was pregnant, and shook himself alert.

'What *can* we do?'

'I dunno,' she replied, then asked him, 'How did Owen got hold of the Rembrandt letters?'

'He would never tell me. I asked him many times, but I could never get it out of him.' The lie was smooth, convincing.

Picking at the cuff of his jumper, Samuel avoided Georgia's gaze as his thoughts slid back to a summer day in 1973 and Owen – lit up, blazing like a firework, his usual urbanity giving way to a frenetic, overcharged excitement. Samuel had known the look; that rush of almost erotic triumph, and had felt his heart quiver with envy. *Owen Zeigler had the Rembrandt letters* and Samuel's only consolation was knowing that his protégé would never misuse them. Dry-mouthed, Samuel had studied Owen and seen his own life rear up like a cheap pony in front of him. His learning, his teaching, his theories, would all pale by comparison with the lushness of his pupil's discovery. His own status would be relegated to second, a perpetual Dr Watson of the art world, and his bitterness at the realisation had uncoiled like a snake in his guts.

A bitterness of which he was ashamed. A bitterness he would never admit to anyone.

'I don't believe it,' Georgia said, cutting into Samuel's thoughts. 'Owen must have said *something* about how he got them.'

'He said nothing to me. Perhaps he told Marshall,' Samuel replied, feeling his way tentatively, wondering how much Marshall had confided in his ex-wife. If keeping Georgia in ignorance was meant to protect her.

'Marshall's clammed up entirely about the letters,' she replied, her tone short. 'Why wouldn't Owen tell you how he got hold of them?'

'I don't know!' Samuel replied, emphatically, surprising Georgia. 'I'm sorry, but I still find it difficult to know that Owen didn't trust me.'

Samuel wasn't lying, he *did* find it difficult, but he understood why. He knew he was too covetous, too ambitious to share, and his punishment was not so much in being beaten to the historic find, but in Owen's recognition of his true character. All the years Samuel had believed he had led Owen Zeigler by the nose – grooming him and making him an ally for his old age – his protégé had listened and confided in him, allowed Samuel to believe that he owed him a debt of gratitude and honour – but that was not so. For all the knowledge Owen had been

451

given by his mentor, Samuel had long since been compensated. For the tutelage and insights, he had been rewarded. Owen Zeigler had paid off the debt completely, and added the interest of his charm.

But his complete confidence? Never.

Picking up a sheet of paper and a biro from a container on Samuel's desk, Georgia turned to the old man. 'I tell the kids I teach to write things down, make lists. Put things on paper.'

'Like what?'

'Like what's been happening,' she said firmly, jotting down the names of the victims and the manner of their deaths. 'Can I see the reproductions of the paintings?'

Samuel passed a book over to her, depicting Rembrandt's *The Stoning of St Steven*. 'Stefan van der Helde was forced to swallow stones. He was martyred.'

'What about Owen?'

Samuel turned several pages, stopping at the *Anatomy Lesson of Dr Joan Deyman*. 'This echoes Owen Zeigler's death.'

'Oh, shit.'

'I don't think you should be doing this in your condition.'

Georgia gave Samuel a slow look. 'I have to look at it. I might end up in this condition. I might be killed – *you* might be killed.'

'I'm old.'

'Well, I'm not,' she said flatly. 'I need to try and work this out. Show me the other paintings.'

Reluctantly, Samuel continued. 'This is *The Suicide of Lucretia*—'

'Charlotte Gorday?'

'Yes.' He turned over another dozen or so pages and paused at *The Blinding of Samson*. 'Nicolai Kapinski had his eyes gouged out.'

Horrified, Georgia pulled the book round to face her. In Rembrandt's painting the overpowered Samson was being held down, the triumphant Delilah running away with his shorn hair. But that was not all. Not only was Samson overpowered, but one of his attackers was driving a metal spike into his eye, the socket imploding inwards, blood spurting from the wound.

'People considered the painting melodramatic—' Samuel began.

'Especially Samson,' Georgia finished drily.

'After this work, Rembrandt toned down the content of what he painted. He was never so bloody again.'

Still making notes, Georgia looked at her silent mobile and then turned back to Samuel.

'We know that the killer – or killers – copied the Rembrandt paintings.'

'Yes.'

'Why?'

'To show us they were connected?'

'OK, that would make sense,' Georgia agreed. 'Any other reason? I mean, do they follow a chronological order?'

'No ... but it *is* a way for the killer to show off his knowledge.'

'Why would that matter?'

'It would matter to someone cultured, and to someone who wanted to own the letters. Someone who thought they had a *right* to them.'

'You think the killer just wants to own them?'

'Maybe, or maybe the person wants to feel close to Rembrandt.' Samuel paused, his lethargy was lifting, his brain was regaining its intellectual keenness. 'The killer could be saying that he understood Rembrandt, that he was paying him tribute with the murders. A way of flattering the painter. Or he might actually believe that by getting hold of the letters, he could protect Rembrandt's reputation.'

'*Protect him?*'

'You know what was in the letters,' Samuel said, carrying on immediately. 'If they were exposed, Rembrandt would be seen not as a genial old genius, but as some spiteful, vindictive, greedy bastard. If someone had worshipped the painter, that would be unacceptable.'

'A person wouldn't kill for that!'

'Someone deranged might.'

Thoughtfully, Georgia rested her chin on her hands. 'But if that was true, the killer could simply have stolen the letters from Owen. Or come to some agreement with him.'

'To buy them? No, Owen Zeigler would never have sold them.'

She raised her eyebrows. 'Never?'

A moment passed, Samuel taking a while to reply.

'Normally I would say never, but Owen *was* getting desperate. His business was failing, his friends had turned their backs on him. A desperate man might act out of character.' He paused, then shrugged dismissively. 'But no, even in the mess he was in, I don't think Owen would have sold the letters. Possessing them was everything to him.'

Georgia nodded.

'So it comes down to greed – the killer's greed. He wants to use the letters to control the market. If he – and only he – knows which Rembrandts are fakes, he'd be able to blackmail collectors, even galleries. No one would want to see their priceless Rembrandts demoted.'

Suddenly galvanised, Samuel pushed back his wheelchair and moved over to the furthest bookcase. After looking for a moment, he brought down a narrow volume and wheeled himself back to the table. It was a record of every painting attributed to Rembrandt.

'Did you see the list of fakes, Georgia?'

'No.'

'What if the paintings which coincided with the murders were on that list? What if they were some of those painted by Rembrandt's monkey?'

Her eyebrows rose. 'But no one's seen the list, apart from Marshall. Oh Christ, he's in real trouble, isn't he?'

Her voice dropped as she stood up and moved into the hall. Re-dialling her ex-husband's mobile number, she listened to the recorded message and then began to speak:

Marshall, it's Georgia.

Look, I know it must have been a shock to find out that I knew the Gordays, but I'll explain why I didn't tell you when I see you. In the meantime, Philip Gorday can help you. I've left his details with my last message. He's waiting to hear from you. He's a lawyer with a lot of contacts. Ring him – No! don't ring, go to his home . . . Please go to him for help.

You can't do this alone.

Ringing off, she glanced at the clock, working out that it would be past eleven at night in New York. Marshall was on his own, in the middle of a city he didn't know. And the auction was taking place at ten the following morning. He had eleven hours to get through. Eleven hours to survive . . .

The world was wicked that night.

43

Unable to sleep, Lillian Kauffman got out of bed and padded into the galley kitchen of the flat over her gallery. She then made herself some decaffeinated coffee and took it into the front room, which overlooked Albemarle Street. Without turning on the light, she sat at the window seat and looked out at the unlit Zeigler Gallery. She had lived in the area long enough to remember when it was a café, and the years which followed when no one wanted to take the premises over. Rumours of the ghost kept some away, others balked at the inflated rent, and she had been glad to see the urbane Owen Zeigler arrive. And stay.

They were bosom drinking buddies. Lillian had always been able to hold her drink and Owen was a steady consumer. If they were celebrating a deal, or a big sale, they would open a bottle of Krug; if they were gossiping they would line up several bottles of wine, and drink and talk into the small hours. It was Lillian who was the first to hear of Owen's marriage plans, and they downed a fair amount of Chardonnay when Marshall was born. After

Owen's wife died, Lillian had sat with her old friend and together they had drunk brandy. Lots of it. And stayed very sober.

They had been close in the way only loners can be. Open and affectionate, but always drawing back, keeping themselves intact. It didn't surprise Lillian that Owen had not been a natural father, or that he had been so obsessed with his Rembrandt theory. What *did* surprise her was Marshall's readiness to take over his father's martyrdom. She hadn't expected that, and was sorry for it. She would have liked to see Marshall Zeigler mourn his father and then return to his own life in Holland.

Lillian guessed that no one had expected Marshall to be so relentless. To care so much. Maybe they had thought he would recognise his limitations, come to accept Tobar Manners' betrayal and Owen's murder. Certainly no one – and Lillian had spoken to many people – had anticipated Marshall's fervent, almost Messianic, zeal. From being the truculent, art-loathing kid, he had found a purpose in avenging his father's death and had transformed himself. The attractive, clever, memory-busting translator had metamorphosed into someone else entirely.

Her glance moved back to the empty Zeigler Gallery. Oh, yes, Lillian thought, there were ghosts, all right, and some of them were living. Marshall Zeigler was proof of it.

Slipping into the doorway of an apartment building on Ninth Avenue, Marshall shook the rain off his coat and nodded to the porter. Glancing back, he noticed a man on the street opposite and wondered if it was the same person who had ransacked his hotel room. After leaving Central Park, Marshall had gone back to the hotel to find the door of his room open. There had been no trolley outside, no cleaner's paraphernalia, no reason for anyone to be inside his room – unless they had broken in.

He hadn't stayed around any longer, but had pressed the elevator button for the ground floor, then ducked out of the elevator at the last moment and headed down the fire escape stairs. It had been twenty-two floors to the street, but Marshall carried on down another floor to the basement and found himself in the hotel laundry. A few Oriental women had given him no more than a passing and uninterested glance as he moved quickly through the steam vapour and headed for the smoky outline of the street entrance. Once there, Marshall had looked around him, and then noticed that it had started to rain.

Pulling his coat over his head, he had run out into the street, hailing the first yellow cab he saw and slumping into the back seat. Asking the driver to wait while he checked his messages on the mobile, he found those from Georgia. Tired and suspicious, his first instinct had been to ignore them, but the last message – explaining about Philip Gorday – had decided him. He had a whole New York night to get through and he knew he wasn't going to be able to do it alone. He couldn't return to his hotel, couldn't even get his clothes. All he had he was wearing – with the letters in his pocket.

Resting his head against the back of the car seat, Marshall closed his eyes for an instant, then opened them again, seeing the driver watching him. He directed the man to Gorday's address and, shifting position, he moved out of the man's eyeline and stared out of the steamy window into the rainy night. He tried to console himself with the fact that although he hadn't managed to send the e-mail, copies of the letters would now be on their way to the *New York Times* and *The Times* in London. He thought of Dean Foley, with the insect bite on his neck; of how he had looked so amazed when Marshall had thrust the letters into his hands. Amazed, yes, but compliant. Marshall was sure of that. After all, why *wouldn't* he send the letters? In the morning the *New York Times* would publish them and the Rembrandt auction would be a disaster. No one would buy fakes, not when the letters and the list proved they were copies . . . He tried to smile to himself, to lift his confidence. When the news was out, Marshall told himself, he would be safe. No one would dare to touch him then.

But tonight he was alone. And under threat.

Punching out the number Georgia had given him, Marshall heard the phone connect.

It was answered on the third ring. 'Hello?'

'Philip Gorday? It's . . .' Marshall paused, hurrying on. 'It's your friend from London.'

'Marshall! Get over here. As soon as you can.'

'I'm on my way.'

'Don't stop for anything or anyone,' Philip went on. 'Where are you?'

'Ninth Avenue, coming up for Forty-Ninth Street.'

'OK, you should be here soon. Ring the bell and I'll let you in.' He paused. 'Have you got *them* with you?'

'No.'

'Where are they?'

Marshall caught the eye of the cabbie and changed the subject. 'I'll be with you soon.'

'Are they safe?'

'Yes.'

'In a bank?'

Marshall paused, uneasy. 'I can't hear you, the connection's breaking up—'

'I asked where the letters are,' Philip repeated, raising his voice.

'Safe,' was all Marshall would say, his distrust rising.

'You can trust me.'

'I'm hearing that a lot lately.'

'It's true,' Philip reassured him. 'You have to tell me everything, so I can help you.'

'I'm losing the connection,' Marshall lied. 'If you can hear me, I'll be with you soon.' Then he rang off.

'You want to get a better one.'

Marshall looked at the cabbie through the mirror. 'What?'

'I said, you need a better cellphone. Connection's usually good round here.'

461

Ignoring the comment, Marshall asked, 'How long before we get there?'

'Not long.'

'When we arrive, park a little way from the building, will you?'

'You pay me, I'll do it,' the cabbie replied.

They drove on for another few minutes, the cabbie finally pulling into the kerb and catching Marshall's eye.

'We're here.'

Anxious, Marshall glanced around the street, but he could see no cars following them, or any parked with people inside. Paying the cabbie, he clambered out and then bent down at the driver's window.

'Wait for me.'

Shrugging, the cabbie slipped the car into park, and let the engine idle. The rain had stopped and the streetlamps made oil slick patterns in the puddles as a woman walked her dog. Hurriedly Marshall ran past her into the lobby of the building. There was no doorman behind the desk, so Marshall pressed the buzzer to Gorday's front door and waited. No reply. Apprehensive, Marshall rang again. Then again, jabbing his finger repeatedly on the door bell and wondering why Philip Gorday wouldn't let him in.

Then suddenly he heard a car pull up only yards away from him. Panicked, Marshall rang the bell one last time. No answer. Then he turned and began running towards his waiting cab, but just as he reached it, the car slid into gear and drove off, leaving Marshall on the kerb – standing under the lamplight in full view of the men coming after him.

House of Corrections,
Gouda, 1654

It was the devil's winter. The canals froze in parts, the children skating under the bridges, merchants building fires on the ice. Underfoot there was nothing but milk whiteness until March, when it thawed and a little girl drowned, her body carried off by the callous tide. I remember it. Rembrandt said it would never be so cold again, but he was wrong . . . It is cold here, colder than being held underwater, cold in your lungs, cold in the vessels of your heart.

I am thirty-nine, nearly forty. A good age for a woman, or a whore. They gave me twelve years imprisonment, at his behest, but when my son came and called me his mother, they could have given me twenty lifetimes in hell and I would have borne them.

I told Carel to leave, leave Rembrandt and his greed, take his talent and his family and go away . . . Remote from Amsterdam. And his father. I wanted to say it, but didn't. Couldn't . . .

Carel came back a second time, but he was different. He seemed taller, brooding like the oxen I'd once seen pulled onto the ice for slaughter. As if they knew their fate before seeing the knife. Before feeling the blade cross their throat . . . Carel told me of an argument between them, Rembrandt calling me a prostitute, a drunk. Promiscuous, he said, and Carel struck him.

For me . . . he struck him for me.

For a while there was no contact between them, then Carel was approached again, by Rembrandt's agent. Bringing apologies, promises light as driftwood, bloated like bladder wrack . . . Carel told me this, told me he had agreed to work for Rembrandt again, and had worked throughout the winter, turning out paintings. Signed and passed off as Rembrandts. But not all of them. Not this time.

Sssh . . . There is someone knocking against the outer door, and a dog barking that shrill petulant bark of an animal spoilt, fed well . . . Carel faked the paintings and then sold many of them on himself, cutting out Rembrandt and his agent. Pulling the knife across their throats. They did not know they were even bleeding . . . Carel told me all this and I felt the blade go across my own throat like the ox must have done, shock buckling my legs under me . . .

I made a fortune, he said . . . Whilst the water was still frozen under the canal bridges, and another little girl skated over the thinning ice towards the grey horizon and the echo of the Matins bell.

And he looked so much like his father that my hand went out to touch him and make sure it wasn't van Rijn . . . Greed is a monkey too. Greed clings to its victims and hitches a ride on the backs of whores and crooks . . .

But he saw what I was thinking and whispered in my ear, 'The money is for you.' Then his hand took mine and folded in my palm a bag of coins, so heavy my wrist ached . . . 'Buy yourself out of this place. Buy yourself free . . .'

And then the guard came in . . . I pushed the money bag into my sleeve. The guard told my son to leave. When I watched through the cell window Carel walked off, then turned and put up his hand again. But this time his fingers were together, tight, in rigor like a corpse.

I am putting down the paper now. I cannot write any longer tonight . . .

Today I believe it is my birthday, friends came with sweetbread and a jar of herrings. I could make better, but thanked them. They studied me with that expression which tells you your looks have gone. We have no mirrors here . . . At night I lie on the bag of money and feel it against my hip bone and dream of freedom. I have the means to buy myself a door in the wall; a way out of this place.

For a while knowing that is enough . . .

I begin to plan. I begin to imagine living again. I begin to hope . . . I dream of going to Delft and visiting my son. And know I never will, but will stand on the corner opposite and watch his house. His wife, his children . . . I feel the coins press against my hip bone and think of my brother, my nephew, the neighbours who gave evidence against me, throwing in their lot with Rembrandt and his Stoffels woman . . .

And I keep writing. Because now I know the words will be read. When I buy that door in the wall the world will listen to me . . .

44

New York.

'Christ!' Philip Gorday said, grabbing Marshall's arm and dragging him back into the foyer of the building. 'Lock it! Lock the door!'

Marshall did so, his hand fumbling with the catch, then turned back to his rescuer. Only seconds before Marshall believed he had been set up; the men had been moving towards him just as Philip came out into the street and grabbed hold of his arm. They had raced for the elevator and when, breathing heavily from exertion, they reached Philip's apartment, he had ushered Marshall into the sitting room and poured them both a drink.

'Why didn't you open the door when I rang!' Marshall snapped, downing the brandy.

'I didn't hear it, I was in the basement.'

'You knew I was coming—'

'I'm sorry, I'm sorry,' Philip replied, sitting down and trying to steady his own nerves. 'You got here so quickly.'

'Next time I'll run round the block first,' Marshall said

bitterly, slumping back into the sofa. Then, softening his tone, he said, 'Thanks for taking me in.'

'I told Georgia to send you here.' Marshall said nothing, just waited for Philip to speak again. 'Are you hungry?'

'I don't know . . . yes. Yes, I am.'

Nodding, Philip went into the kitchen and came back a few minutes later with some sandwiches. At once the dog got up from its bed and padded over to the men, sitting between them.

'Don't feed him, he's fat,' Philip said, smiling slightly. 'I should take him out for a walk—'

'I wouldn't.'

'No, maybe not tonight. Who were those men?'

'I have no idea.'

'Have you been followed?'

'All day. To the bank, my hotel. I lost them once, but they caught up with me here.' Marshall paused, staring hard at Philip Gorday. 'My ex-wife never told me that you two knew each other.'

'I was her mother's lover – on and off – for some years.'

'She never mentioned it.'

'Georgia is good at keeping secrets,' Philip replied. 'At least, she was when she was a child. She could bear a grudge too, but she was a strong person to have on your side. Tough little customer. Unfortunately, she was never on my side. In fact, until the other day I hadn't heard from her, or seen her, for years. She contacted me because she thought I might be able to help you.'

'How?'

'I know about the letters.'

'Obviously. You were married to Charlotte.'

'My late wife didn't tell me. Nicolai Kapinski told me.' Philip saw Marshall's surprise, and went on. 'Charlotte and I were close, but she had a private part to her life.'

'My father?'

He nodded. 'It was by mutual agreement. I had my women, and she had Owen Zeigler.'

'Did you ever meet my father?'

'No. I spoke to him over the phone a couple of times, but no, I didn't meet him. When you called me I thought how similar you sounded – and you were kind about Charlotte's death. That was like Owen too.'

Marshall stared at the older man. 'You're all so sophisticated, aren't you? With your lovers and mistresses, all your intrigues hidden under your carefully observed respectability. I have to tell you,' he said flatly, 'if Georgia had taken a lover I'd have wanted to kill him.'

Surprised, Philip stared at Marshall intently. 'You still love your ex-wife, don't you?'

'No.'

'Admit it! I can see it in your face. You're too ardent to be indifferent. Why did you two split up?'

There was a moment's pause before Marshall replied. 'We couldn't live together. I don't know why. It just didn't work. We loved each other, but day-to-day living . . . it just didn't work.'

'Yeah, I know about that,' Philip said, nodding. 'Does Georgia know how you feel about her?'

'She's married to another man, and pregnant. It's too late for us. So, no, she doesn't know how I feel.'

'Five will get you ten she does.' Philip sighed. 'Your father wasn't passionate—'

'Except when it came to his work,' Marshall said, trying to size up the well-groomed man in front of him.

He gauged Philip Gorday to be around fifty-five. Not especially good looking, but confident and charismatic. A man a woman would feel safe with. A man who seemed very grounded and obviously prosperous. Finishing his sandwich, Marshall then emptied his glass and felt his pulse slowing, his heart rate steady as he looked over the mantelpiece at the portrait of Charlotte Gorday.

'It's very like her.'

'Your father organised it, he chose the painter.'

'Who paid for it?'

Philip smiled, ignoring the question. 'Georgia asked me to represent you if you needed a lawyer.'

'I haven't done anything. Yet.'

'Are you thinking of doing something?'

'I'd like to string up the bastard who killed my father,' he said bluntly.

'But you don't know who it is.'

'No, I don't.' Marshall got up and stared at the portrait of Charlotte. 'Did you find her body?'

'Yes.'

'And you found Nicolai Kapinski's too?'

'No,' Philip replied, refilling their glasses. 'I went to his hotel to talk to him, but he was dead when I got there.'

'Did you see his body?'

'Yes. Unfortunately, I did.'

Marshall kept staring at the portrait of the dead woman. 'Nicolai Kapinski was a little man, soft-fleshed, not strong. I don't imagine it would have been difficult for anyone to overpower him. But he wouldn't have just sat there while he was blinded.' He turned to Philip, his expression unreadable. 'There had to be more than one person involved.'

'He could have been drugged?'

'That would have taken planning. The killers would have to have waited for a drug to take effect. No, I don't think Nicolai was drugged. This person kills violently. He takes his time, makes it last; it's brutal and vindictive.' Marshall paused. 'And they knew him.'

'How d'you figure that out?'

'They let him in. Even Nicolai, alone in the middle of New York, scared for his life, trusted the person who came to his door. It had to be someone he knew.' Marshall turned to Philip Gorday, his expression challenging. 'Was it you?'

'Me!' he exclaimed, laughing, and then realised that Marshall was serious. 'You can't think that.'

'My father had known you – albeit from a distance – for years. He wouldn't have thought twice about letting you in. He might have been surprised, curious, but he wouldn't have been afraid.' Marshall paused, watching the sturdy man in front of him. 'And Nicolai had come to you for help. So if you then turned up at his hotel he'd have been delighted to see you. Relieved, in fact.'

'You'd make a bad advocate.'

'Why?'

'No motive.'

'But there *is* a motive, isn't there?' Marshall continued. 'The oldest motive in the world – envy. You might have resented my father for years. You could have killed him for that alone.'

'I'm not the jealous type.'

'You go to great pains to make that clear,' Marshall went on. 'Well, sexual anger would be one motive. Of course, the other motive is simple – you wanted the Rembrandt letters. Perhaps you asked Charlotte to get them for you. Maybe she refused, and you lost your temper. Maybe she got scared after my father was killed—'

'And ran home to me?'

'Maybe she didn't know it *was* you until she got home,' Marshall said, glancing around the room quickly to ascertain his nearest exit. 'Maybe you killed her before she could tell anyone.'

'And Nicolai Kapinski?' Philip asked, helping himself to another drink. 'Why would I kill him?'

'For the same reason you'd have killed Stefan van der Helde. To keep him quiet. Nicolai came to you asking if you had the letters – so then you knew that he didn't have them. But he was running around talking about knowing someone who would want them, would perhaps buy them. And you couldn't have that, could you? *You* wanted the letters.'

'But I don't have the letters,' Philip replied evenly. 'I'm a lawyer, not an art dealer.'

'True, but you're a cultured man, and a greedy one. You could make a fortune with the letters *and* get your own back on your wife's lover at the same time. I know you have a long standing interest in the art world. You know Lillian Kauffman—'

'Ah, Lillian. Has she heard this wild theory of yours?'

'No,' Marshall admitted. 'I didn't even think it was you until a few minutes ago. Then it all fell into place. The fact that you knew Lillian. That Georgia had known you – and your wife. The fact that she had been connected to you in the past. That niggled at me. It was too much of a coincidence.'

'You surely don't think your ex-wife is trying to harm you?'

'No, not Georgia,' Marshall replied, moving a little closer to the door. 'But I think you played her, like you played everyone, for a long time. When I arrived, you didn't open the door immediately, you wanted to make me sweat, think those men would get to me before you did. You did it to make me rely on you. Trust you implicitly. After all, who *wouldn't* trust the person who was protecting them?'

'This is bullshit—'

'When I called you from the cab you asked me where the letters were,' Marshall continued. 'Why would you ask that, if they weren't important to you?'

'Four people have been killed because of those letters. One of them was my wife! It would have seemed fucking odd if I *hadn't* asked about them.' Philip sat down on the window seat, his tone impatient. 'I have nothing to do

472

with any of this. I'm not a murderer, I'm offering to help you, for Christ's sake!' He stared at Marshall, tossing the catalogue of the next day's auction onto the sofa between them. 'I've been invited to the Rembrandt sale, people can attend by private invitation only. I can take you in with me.'

Marshall paused, his tone suspicious. 'Why would I want to go to the auction?'

'I don't know, but you obviously do, otherwise why would you have risked coming to New York?' Philip sighed, folding his arms. 'Your life is in danger – not from me, despite what you think. I'd like to help you, but I need to know a few facts. The people after you want the letters. Do you have them?'

'Next question.'

'All right, if you don't have the letters, you must have got rid of them. Put them somewhere safe. A bank?'

'You tell me.'

'OK, let's say that the letters are in a bank, where no one can reach them. But *you're* out on the street, inviting trouble. Which means that you're confident. That even if something happens to you, you're confident.'

Marshall smiled to himself. Philip Gorday was smart, Georgia had been right about that. He was also beginning to wonder if Gorday was innocent, or simply double bluffing him. If he stayed with Gorday would he last the night? But then again, Marshall thought, if he left where would he go? He thought of the letters, on their way to the newspapers. In the morning the news would be all over the headlines, just in time for the auction. Just in time for Rembrandt's secret to undermine the whole sale. And when the truth was out, Marshall could step forward . . .

All he had to do was to get through the night. But where? And with whom?

'You *are* confident, aren't you?' Philip repeated, almost admiringly. 'Which would imply to me that you think the letters are in the right hands. That they're safe, that whatever happens to you, they're protected.' He glanced away, thoughtful. 'You can't trust anyone, Marshall. Accusing me proves how suspicious you are, how confused. You've got your doubts about everyone, haven't you? So who *would* you consider safe? You must understand that you're making it very difficult for me to help you.'

'I just want somewhere to stay the night.'

'And tomorrow?' Philip queried. 'What about tomorrow? You've got people after you, Marshall, they won't just stop. Even if you gave them the letters, you wouldn't be safe, because you know what's in them. Besides, you could have taken copies . . .' He trailed off and looked closely at the younger man. 'You've gone to the press, haven't you? Your father would never have done that, but you have, haven't you?'

Marshall said nothing, just watched as Philip drew back the curtain and looked down into the street below.

'I'm not risking my neck for some fucking stranger,' he said coldly. 'You want my hospitality, you have to pay for it. And by that, I mean you have to trust me.' He turned back to Marshall. 'You can stay here, I'll give you a room and my protection. These apartments have good security, no one can break in unannounced, and I'll take you to the auction as my guest tomorrow. You won't get in otherwise; as I said, it's invitation only.'

'Why would you do that?'

'Oh, I'm not doing it for you, Marshall, I'm doing it for my own reasons. And one of them is my late wife. You were right – I *am* a jealous man. I was very jealous of your father. I knew he would always come first with Charlotte, but the Rembrandt letters are unimportant to me.'

'I find that hard to believe.'

'I don't give a damn about some dead artist, or if every one of his paintings turned out to be fake. Why should I care? The art world's corrupt anyway, always has been. Perhaps it's time for them to get what's coming to them.'

Surprised by this outburst, Marshall stared at him and asked, 'So why *are* you helping me?'

'Because of Georgia.'

'Because of how you treated her mother?'

'Jesus, you still don't get it, do you?' Philip said, turning away. 'Georgia is my daughter.'

45

At seven in the morning a thin rain covered Manhattan. It came from the river and slid against the high rises, sullen and cool as a shroud. Oyster-coloured clouds scuffed against minuscule slashes of blue sky, the sun making no entrance on the day. It was very cold. As the temperature dropped, the heating came on in Philip Gorday's apartment and the dog scratched at the door to be let out. Rubbing his neck, Philip phoned down to the doorman and asked him to come up for the Labrador. He handed over the dog at the door, relocked it, then flicked over the morning's papers and stared down into the street below.

The previous night he had slept little, rising often and walking to Marshall's door to listen and see if he was also awake. But his visitor slept well, undisturbed, and no noises came from the guest room. Philip did hear the cistern flush once in the early hours, but after that there was silence. Plenty of silence to give him time to think. And – in between dreaming and waking – he thought of his affair with Eve, and of Georgia, his daughter. It had been an arrangement between himself and his lover that she should pass Georgia off as her husband's child. It would be better for both of them, and save both marriages, Eve had said. He had agreed, and their affair continue intermittently.

Never an easy child, Georgia had been difficult to know, and believed that Eve's ex-husband was her father. When he died, Philip had been tempted to step forward, but resisted. Georgia, he surmised, was beyond being able to understand and forgive, and if he was honest he thought it unlikely that she would ever accept him. To Georgia, he was just one of her mother's lovers, no more. Not one of her favourites either, not one she even liked. Keeping the truth to himself, Philip had never confided in Charlotte, and when he heard that Georgia was marrying Owen Zeigler's son he had appreciated the irony.

Opening the fridge for some more fruit juice, Philip remembered Marshall's response when he had confessed last night. He had not reacted violently, just got up from the sofa where he had been sitting and stared at the older man.

'I need somewhere to stay for tonight.'

Subdued, Philip had shown him to the guest room, watched Marshall walk in, and then seen the door closed in his face.

The door which was *still* closed now. Philip went to the guest room door and knocked. No response. He waited, knocked again and then walked in. The bed was made, the curtains drawn – nothing to indicate that Marshall Zeigler had ever been there. He could have left soon after he had retired to bed, or only half an hour ago. But he had gone.

Swearing, Philip moved back into the sitting room and stared at the the mantelpiece: his invitation to the auction had disappeared.

Startled when the phone rang, Georgia reached out for it, her voice groggy.

'Hello?'

'It's me, Marshall.'

She had been sleeping on top of the covers, too nervous to take off her clothes and relax. Samuel had gone to bed early but she had found herself reading, anything and everything she could about Rembrandt and his history. The study was pointless, she knew that, it had just been a way of keeping her mind occupied, her fears at a distance. Several times she had heard footsteps on the gravel outside and tensed, waiting for someone to break in. But no one did. The hours had meandered by, listless and malignant, round the clock. Apparently Greg Horner was also restless, and he seemed to spend a lot of the evening moving back and forwards from the kitchen to one of the guest rooms. Then, for some reason, he had a bath around half past midnight. The action had been oddly comforting to Georgia, and finally she had drifted off to sleep.

But now, at four in the morning, she was alert. 'Marshall, are you all right?'

'I'm fine. Don't worry about Dimitri Kapinski, he's OK. Teddy Jack's looking out for you, you're fine—'

'I know, I got your messages.'

'How's Harry?'

'Off the ventilator, making real progress. He's out of danger now, thank God.'

'I'm glad. I should have never got you involved with all of this,' Marshall said quietly. 'I'm so sorry. Really, Georgia, I'm so sorry. You know I'd never hurt you deliberately.'

Her stomach knotted.

'Marshall, you've got to get some help. I assume you're in New York; did you go to see Philip Gorday?'

He smiled at the name. 'Yes, he gave me all the help he could.'

'So get out of it, while you still can.'

'It's too late for that,' Marshall replied. 'I couldn't get out of it now, even if I wanted to. And I don't want to. I just wanted to make sure you were safe, that's all. You know, just in case something happened to me . . . we had some good times, didn't we?'

She clung to the phone. 'We did. And we will again—'

'No, not like before. You've got a family, a new life. Live it, Georgia, and make it work, OK?'

'Jesus, you sound like you're saying goodbye!'

'I don't regret anything,' Marshall said, his tone sincere. 'I want you to know that, Georgia. Whatever happens to me, I'm glad I got into all of this. I hadn't cared about anything for a long time – not since we split up. It felt good to have something in my life that mattered.

Besides, I wanted to see the art world take a beating, particularly Tobar Manners.'

She felt herself tense up. 'You said *wanted*. What have you done?'

Marshall ignored the question. 'I felt sorry for Geertje Dircx. Just one of the ordinary people that are trampled on. She made me wonder about all the histories which have been blotted out to preserve a reputation or make someone a hero. What Rembrandt did to her was brutal, nothing excuses that. Not even being a genius.'

'Marshall—'

'Look, one way or the other, it'll all be over soon.'

'The auction, you mean?'

'Yes, the auction.'

'Have you got a plan?'

'I *had* a plan,' he said, ruefully. 'Now I have no plan at all.'

'You're scaring me.'

'You never get scared, you're too tough,' he teased. 'I love you.'

Putting down the phone before she could answer, Marshall dropped the mobile into the nearest waste bin and moved on.

He had left Philip Gorday's apartment around eight. From the foyer he could see the men outside, watching him. Getting back into the elevator, Marshall had got out at the next floor, but pushed the button for Philip Gorday's floor, watching the lift rise to the twenty-first floor. Then he took the back stairs to the street and made for the nearest newspaper vendor. Grabbing a copy of the *New York Times*, Marshall had read the front page with surprise, then, panicking, hurried through the rest of the paper. There was no mention of the Rembrandt letters. Not a word about the fakes coming up for sale in two hours time.

He had lost. In that moment Marshall realised that the assistant manager at the bank had *not* sent his letters. They had been thrown away, discarded. The damning news was still hidden; the Rembrandt secret still unknown. Throwing the newspaper onto the street, Marshall began to walk towards the Museum of Mankind. He felt cheated, let down, betrayed. He felt stupid too, and hardly cared if he was being followed.

Angrily he pushed past a pedestrian and stumbled across the road, the traffic blaring its horns, a cab swerving to avoid him. He was aggressively alert, staring at people who passed him like a man looking for a fight. Or someone still drunk from the previous night. Damp from the rain, Marshall arrived at the entrance of the Museum of Mankind and stared up at the posters – REMBRANDT AUCTION. And on the hoardings were images of the portraits. Portraits Rembrandt had never painted, portraits Carel Fabritius had created, many years before in Delft.

Weaving slightly on his feet from tiredness and despair, Marshall stared at the banners and remembered his father.

'*I can't explain it, Marshall, you either have a passion for the work, or not. This is my passion, I would give my life for it.*'

And then he remembered the corpse of Owen Zeigler, the way his father had been butchered, the body suspended from the waste pipe. He remembered touching his father's face and then thought of Tobar Manners. Thought of his lying voice, his threats.

'. . . *start running, Marshall Zeigler, and don't stop.*'

'What do I do? What do I fucking do now?' Marshall said out loud, a man skirting round him as he stood in the rain.

He had no chance and he knew it. At any moment he could be stopped and he wouldn't even see it coming. He had relied on the news being printed, otherwise he would never have left the safety of Philip Gorday's apartment and be standing – out in the open – on a New York street. Angrily, Marshall reached out his arms in the rain.

'Well, come on then!' he said, staring down the portentous street. 'Come and get me!'

But nothing happened, and the rain kept falling.

Laughing to himself, Marshall dropped his arms and walked to the side entrance of the Museum. There he paused in the doorway. His moment of despair had passed; he was suddenly calm and was forming a plan. It was a long shot, unlikely to work, even if he got into the auction – but it was worth trying. Reaching into his pocket, Marshall felt for the invitation he'd purloined from Philip, then realised that no one would let him in looking so dishevelled. He had to get cleaned up, composed.

In a drugstore across the street, he bought a razor and a comb, then returned to the back of the Museum, moving behind a row of waste bins under an awning outside. Wincing at the sharpness of the blade, Marshall shaved himself, stepping out from under the awning and letting the rain cool his face. Then he combed his hair, took off his coat, and – taking a deep breath – walked towards the entrance of the Museum of Mankind. Through inner doors he could see armed security men moving around and members of the Museum staff gathering in the foyer. Knowing that if he was admitted, Marshall would be shown into the auction hall – and anxious that his invitation should not be questioned – he back-tracked. Spotting a side entrance on the left, which led to the main gallery, Marshall took the steps to the next floor. There were four doors facing him, only one open as Marshall entered a deserted office. Walking in, he locked the door behind him and then paused, looking round. The room was obviously used as a store for kitchen supplies; the door which led from the chamber into the main body of the Museum was locked.

Oddly calm, Marshall looked at his watch. There was one hour left until the auction. And he was in the Museum. All that stood between him and the Rembrandts was one door.

On tenterhooks, Tobar Manners kept peering around him. Many of the biggest dealers in London had come to New York, Rufus Ariel and Leon Williams being among the first to arrive for the auction, fanning their invitations like geishas. Both London and New York had been resonating with the news of the letters, but as the day of the auction came around and nothing was exposed, Manners had begun to relax. He would make his bloody fortune and nothing would stop him – especially not Marshall Zeigler. Who had, apparently, disappeared without trace. Him, and the letters – or so people presumed, although there had been another rumour that Marshall had come to New York.

Tobar allowed himself a moment of triumph. If Marshall Zeigler had been able to stop the auction, he would have already done so. For a moment Tobar he did consider the possibility that Marshall might have been killed, like his father, but consoled himself with the fact that someone had to be the winner. If the letters had cost Marshall Zeigler his life, it was hardly Tobar's concern. He knew only too well that Marshall would have seen him ruined without batting an eyelid.

Taking their seats, Leon Williams turned to Rufus Ariel. 'It must have been a hoax, all that fuss about those Rembrandt letters.'

'Four people died for that hoax,' Rufus replied. 'Still, people die everyday, I suppose.'

He glanced towards the dais, staring at the preoccupied man who was going to be holding the auction. Sombrely dressed, he had the air of a churchman, with the right amount of pompous solemnity. As the chairman of one of the world's biggest auction houses, Rufus knew how much the sale meant to him. If the reserve wasn't reached, it would mean a further hit to the art market.

If the reserve was exceeded, the business would see it as an upturn. An indication of recovery.

Having been threatened with a rent rise in the last week, Rufus was hoping for the latter result. Glancing around, he noted the concentration of dealers who were genuinely anxious; in the previous weeks there had been precious few openings on either side of the Atlantic. Rufus nodded to Timothy Parker-Ross, just entering the hall, then turned his attention towards the auctioneer again as the two Rembrandt portraits were brought onto the dais by the security men and placed on a couple of gilded, over-embellished easels. A collective gasp went up around the select gathering. In the chill drizzle of daylight the portraits were coolly compelling, the dark backgrounds flattering the sitters and bringing out the froth of their ruffs, white as azaleas. Both the male sitter and his wife had a sheen of triumph about them. Wealthy Dutch merchants, come into money, hiring the greatest painter of the day to immortalise them. Smug to a fault.

There were perhaps only two hundred people in the room, all clutching their invitation cards, all either seated or scurrying to their places at the last moment. Then, just as ten o'clock struck, Marshall retraced his steps and came in the main entrance, showing his card to one of the security guards. Surprised, Leon Williams nudged Rufus Ariel. The latter glanced over to where Leon was gesturing. 'Bloody hell, it's Zeigler,' he said, surprised.

He wasn't the only one who had spotted the late arrival.

Tobar Manners had seen Marshall enter and, shocked, looked around the gathering. His gaze passed over the security guards one by one, searching for someone out of place, or anyone suspicious, then he glanced back to Marshall again. He had taken his seat at the end of the third row, avoiding Tobar's glance and staring at the paintings instead.

Feeling his mouth empty of saliva, Tobar tried to swallow as someone tapped him on the shoulder.

'Marshall Zeigler's here.'

'I know, I've seen him!' Tobar hissed back to the American dealer.

'Takes some balls just showing up like this, with all the rumours going around,' the man continued. 'Why d'you think he's here? I thought he'd gone into hiding.'

'I don't know, do I?' Tobar countered, watching as the security guards moved to the doors.

In his seat Marshall could hear the doors being closed and locked and felt a hot spasm of fear. Without turning around he couldn't see who was behind him, only the two rows in front. *He was a sitting target.* But who would dare to make a move in the middle of an auction? After the auction, though, how the hell was he going to get out? Staring at his catalogue, Marshall could feel the gossip undulate about the room, and flinched when someone sat down in the seat beside him.

'Hello there.'

He glanced over, then smiled with relief. 'Tim! How are you doing?'

'I'm good,' he said pleasantly. 'What d'you make of the paintings?'

'Impressive. But then again, what do I know about art?'

Tim laughed, crossing his legs, his expression bland. 'I'm sorry.'

Marshall turned to him, puzzled. 'What for?'

'Your father.'

'I know, Tim, you told me before.'

He dropped his voice, his head inclined towards Marshall's. 'You can't get away with this, you know that,' he smiled, benign, almost foolish looking. 'You have to give me the letters. You can't get out of here, and I know where your ex-wife is.'

The room swelled around Marshall, the walls throbbing, the ceiling closing down on him. Slowly, the conversations in the room slid into white noise, the gathering blurred, and only the paintings remained visible, in perfect focus. The shock was so great that Marshall couldn't turn his head for a moment. Could just sit, rigid, in his seat, feeling the warmth of Timothy Parker-Ross's body next to his.

I wonder if I know the person. If it's someone I like, someone I trust.

He could remember his visits to the British Museum with Timothy Parker-Ross, the lanky misfit overshadowed by his charismatic father. The poor lost boy. So out of place he had had to make friends with a kid much younger than he was . . . Marshall could feel the ground slip under his feet, the shock numbing him, making a queasy lilt in

487

his stomach . . . Of all the people he had known, of all the inhabitants of the art world, he had never suspected Timothy Parker-Ross.

Rigid, Marshall watched the auctioneer walk up onto the dais. Timothy rested his hand lightly on Marshall's sleeve. 'Where are the letters?' he asked.

'I burnt them.'

'No, you wouldn't do that,' Timothy replied. 'I know you wouldn't.'

Marshall turned his head to look at his old friend, his voice damning. 'You killed my father?'

'I didn't do it—'

'But you arranged for it to be done?'

'Your father was kind to me, I didn't want it to happen,' Timothy went on, his voice unemotional. 'It became so complicated. I didn't think any of this would happen. Owen could have just given me the letters . . .'

Marshall felt Timothy's grip tighten on his arm. His strength came as a surprise, his fingers clenching the muscle.

'You have to be quiet now. We'll sort it all out after the auction. I'm sorry you got involved, Marshall. I just wanted the letters, that was all. No one was supposed to get hurt.'

Silence fell suddenly. The auction room filled with suspense, everyone watching the action on the raised platform. Then there was an unexpected lull in the proceedings while the auctioneer talked to someone at the side of the dais. Marshall sat rigid as Timothy continued to talk. Aware that the sale was being held up, the audience started murmuring amongst themselves. Timothy's voice was barely audible.

'The letters will make me someone. You watch, Marshall, when they're mine, people will finally take me seriously.' His tone was cajoling, weirdly benevolent. 'Come on, Marshall, you can understand that. You know me. Everyone thought I was a fool. But when I get hold of the letters I'll have the art world in my hands.'

'My father helped you, he cared about you—'

'I know, I know.' Tim's voice was childlike, catching on the vowels. 'I just wanted the letters, that was all.'

Marshall leaned forward in his seat, and Tim gripped his arm even tighter. 'You can't do anything. You're finished,' he said. 'And if you *were* thinking of making some kind of move, remember that I know where Georgia is. And she's pregnant, isn't she?'

His eyes hard, Marshall turned to Timothy, his voice barely controlled. 'I'll make you pay for this.'

'You can't. There's nowhere you can go. Nothing you can do.'

'Jesus, you're even more stupid than I thought,' Marshall said, interrupting him. 'More stupid than *anyone* thought. I felt sorry for you, because you were a misfit—'

Injured, Tim dropped his voice. 'Marshall, don't—'

'*Marshall, don't,*' he parroted. 'You pathetic bastard.' He was baiting Tim, and at the same time keeping an eye on the dais and the preoccupied auctioneer. There was clearly a complication, the delay was continuing. Marshall, glancing to his left, realised that the nearest security guard was several yards away. 'You sick fuck,' he hissed. 'Now I think about it, all those murders made to coincide with Rembrandt's paintings – that's just the kind of puerile schoolboy charade you'd think was sophisticated.'

Timothy flushed. 'Don't say things like that!'

'I can say what I like. You don't impress me. You don't impress anyone. That's your trouble, Tim. Whatever you did people would still laugh at you.'

'When I have the letters—'

'People will still laugh. Because it's *you* that's funny, Tim, and you'd still be the butt of the joke.'

Out of the corner of his eye, Marshall could see that the security guard had turned to talk to the other guard and – in that instant – he took his chance.

Knocking Tim back in his seat, Marshall ran for the dais. Stumbling up the few steps to the platform he reached the nearest painting and took a penknife out of his pocket. Almost as though he was slashing the throat of an animal, he brought the blade across the canvas. The picture sliced into two as the bearded merchant was summarily decapitated from his elegant painted ruff.

Before Marshall had a chance to escape, two security guards overpowered him, almost breaking his arm as they forced him to drop the knife. Hustled out of the auction hall, Marshall was half carried, half dragged, into the foyer. When the police arrived minutes later he was told he was under arrest and would be taken to the police station to be charged. He said nothing. Looking over the shoulder of one of the policemen, Marshall could see the shocked faces surrounding him – many of whom he recognised – and as he was led away he also realised that he was, for the first times in days, safe.

At the police station he made one call – asking for his lawyer, Philip Gorday.

46

'Marshall's safe.'

Relieved, Georgia sighed down the phone. 'Where is he?'

'In jail.'

'Oh,' she said sarcastically, 'well that's OK then, isn't it.'

'I'll get him out soon,' Philip went on. 'Apparently Marshall thought the letters were going to be published before the auction. He'd tried to get them to the papers, but when there was nothing in the news he took some drastic action of his own. You'll read all about it.'

'Spare me the suspense. What did he do?'

'Your ex-husband slashed one of the Rembrandt paintings.'

'*Marshall?*' she said, incredulous.

'It was a fake.'

'Did he know that when he slashed it?'

'Marshall did. The dealers didn't,' Philip said suavely. 'That's why he's in jail. He's an unusual man.'

'Has he given you the Rembrandt letters?'

'Yes,' Philip said, 'and the police have arrested Timothy Parker-Ross for the murders—'

'*Parker-Ross?*' Georgia replied, stunned. 'But he's one of Marshall's oldest friends! Jesus, Parker-Ross! Are they sure it's him?'

'Apparently he confessed. Seemed rather proud of what he'd done.'

Philip could sense Georgia's incredulity. 'What was he like?'

'Someone no one took seriously. Someone who seemed kind, harmless. The last person you'd ever suspect . . .' She glanced towards Samuel Hemmings, sitting by the fire, listening to the conversation. 'What about Dimitri Kapinski?'

'From what I can gather, Kapinski *was* employed by Parker-Ross last year, but moved on. Parker-Ross travelled extensively, seems he picked up Kapinski along the way. He was already a criminal, keen for the money, and when he moved to London, Parker-Ross got him working for him.'

'So why did he leave Parker-Ross? Why change sides?'

'Because his brother was involved,' Philip said. 'Kapinski actually had some scruples and wanted out of it when he found out he was following Nicolai.'

'But Parker-Ross didn't commit the murders himself?'

'No.'

'So he must have had another accomplice.' She looked over to Samuel, holding his gaze as she formed the next words. 'Was it Teddy Jack?'

'No. Teddy Jack was helping Marshall all the time. Teddy Jack hired Kapinski to keep an eye on him.'

'While he was keeping an eye on us?'

'Yeah.'

'Smart.'

'That he was,' Philip agreed. 'He felt bad about what happened to Owen Zeigler and a real need to protect Marshall. To prove himself.'

'So what will happen now?'

'The letters will be published, the list of fakes will be made public, and they'll try to hang a public order notice on Marshall. But it won't stick. He should be home soon.'

'So it's nearly over?'

Drumming his fingers on his desk, Philip stared at the papers in front of him. *So it's nearly over?* The one thing he had never suspected of Georgia was naivety, but here she was, actually hoping that life would return to normal. Philip knew otherwise. He knew that the backlash was just starting. When the list of fakes was published, all hell would break loose. Dealers would claim that the Rembrandt letters were a hoax; they would demand authentications – many of them – to keep the case open and prolonged. Money would change hands for experts who would swear that the letters were fake. But in the end, they would be proved authentic.

And then the market would rock on its already unsteady feet. Collections, museums, private owners would all question their Rembrandts. Those on the list would be uncovered and exposed, virtually priceless works of art relegated to inexpensive forgeries. And with the news of the forgeries would come the revelation of Rembrandt's secret. Rembrandt's monkey. Of Carel Fabritius, Rembrandt's bastard with Geertje Dircx. Very soon, not only Rembrandt's paintings but also his character would be re-evaluated . . . No, Philip thought to himself, it wasn't over and it wouldn't be for years.

'It's not that simple,' he said, finally. 'Marshall will have made a lot of enemies.'

He thought of his conversation with Marshall and of his client's muted triumph at demoting the Rembrandts Tobar Manners had so desperately wanted to sell. Seeing his fortune literally slashed in front of his eyes, Manners had also seen revenge in action. Spooked, he had returned to London and then moved on, no one knew where. Not even Rosella.

'No one can hold anything against Marshall,' Georgia went on. 'The truth was in the letters.'

'Don't shoot the messenger?'

'All right, what else *could* he have done? Died for them? What good would that have been?'

'No good at all, but perhaps Marshall could have thought all this through a little more. He *could* have destroyed the letters when he first got them. Four people died.'

'And he was damn near the fifth!' she said shortly. 'You're such a hypocrite, Philip. I remember you telling my mother how truth was everything in law, and in life. How veracity always triumphed. How it *should* . . . So what changed?'

she challenged him. 'What Rembrandt was, and what he did, is in those letters. And now the world will read them. The woman he tortured will be heard, and his bastard recognised. The truth will come out.'

Philip smiled distantly to himself and said, 'A client once told me that the absolute truth is an instrument that can only be played by an expert.'

'What happened to him?'

'I advised him to start lying.'

Covering his eyes with his arm, Marshall lay back on the bunk in the cell, trying to sleep. He had talked to Philip Gorday at length and was waiting to be released, for the guard to come and tell him he was free to go home. The auction house had wanted to press charges, Philip had told him, but when the truth came out they had hesitated. Marshall's reckless action was excusable, but between the shock of the damage and the exposure of the letters, he was going to be left to sweat a while in jail.

Philip had fielded the media, who were clamouring to line up interviews with Marshall on his release. He told them that Marshall Zeigler *would* be talking – but not for the time being. Exhausted, Marshall kept his eyes closed, remembering the expression on Tobar Manners' face when he had slashed the painting. Marshall had been so quickly overpowered that he hadn't had a chance to look at anyone else, just Manners. And he had held his gaze while the police were handcuffing him and jerking him to his feet.

Tobar's expression had said everything before he skirted the crowd and disappeared out the back of the auction room, a beaten man. Marshall, hoisted to his feet, had been marched out. In passing the crowd, he had caught sight of Rufus Ariel and turned his head to look for Timothy Parker-Ross – but his seat was empty.

Screwing up his eyes, Marshall thought about Parker-Ross. He had never suspected him, not even considered him. He'd suspected every cunning, clever person his father had ever been involved with, but not the kindly fool . . . His mind turned back to his youth, to the two of them jumping onto London buses. Then he remembered the last time he'd seen Timothy Parker-Ross in London, deceptively caring as he called around at the gallery.

'What's up, Marshall?'

'I didn't say anything was wrong.'

'No, but I've known you since we were kids. I can always tell when you're worried . . .'

Marshall flinched as he recalled other conversations.

'You're like me. You've never been really interested in the art business. But then again, you got out, made another career for yourself. I never had the brains to do anything else . . .'

'I'm a fool, everyone knows that.'

A fool. A vicious fool. Overlooked, underestimated. With a character which had brooded on its ill treatment for years. A fool in public, a thug in private. Marshall rubbed his temples with his fingers, trying to understand. How *could* Timothy Parker-Ross be a killer? he thought blankly. Maybe the actual killings had been done by others; perhaps Tim would have focused on the letters, dismissing the murders as an unpleasant necessity. After all, the letters must have seemed his only hope, the one thing that would ensure him status in a world which sneered at him. Perhaps, Marshall thought, his longing for power would have expunged everything else – even the death of a man who had helped him and protected him.

Marshall swallowed. He had to know if Parker-Ross had been at the murders. Had to know if his old friend had watched Owen Zeigler being tortured and gutted. If he had seen Stefan van der Helde sodomised and forced to swallow stones. If he had witnessed the knife go into Charlotte Gorday and split her heart. And if he been in that bleak hotel room and seen Nicolai Kapinski held down, his eyes gouged out, blood choking him as he died . . .

Had Tim seen all this? Jesus, *had* he?

Marshall had been right about one thing – the victims had all let him in. They had all known Timothy Parker-Ross and would never have been frightened of him. Van der Helde, Owen, Charlotte Gorday, Nicolai Kapinski – they would have recognised him as being part of their world. Someone no one feared. Of course Owen would have let Parker-Ross into the gallery, into the basement. Marshall could picture it only too easily, his father talking to the man he had thought of as another son. Perhaps Parker-Ross had asked him for the Rembrandt letters, tried to make some kind of deal. Marshall knew that his father wouldn't have taken him seriously; would have laughed it off.

Letters, Owen would have said. What letters, Tim? He would have looked at him and smiled, thinking that of all people Timothy Parker-Ross wouldn't have the clout to be able to handle something of such importance. No, Owen would have said, there are no letters . . .

With a shudder, Marshall wondered when his father first realised what Parker-Ross really was. When did he first fear him? Did the initial blow come from Parker-Ross, or from his accomplice? Not from Tim, surely. He had always been so afraid of blood, turning his head to one side if anyone cut themselves . . . So when did he turn his head away from Owen Zeigler? At what point did he separate himself from that death and the other violent deaths to come?

Hearing a banging, Marshall opened his eyes and glanced at the door, waiting for it to open. But it stayed closed, locked. Sighing, he stared back up at the ceiling. He would ask to talk to Timothy Parker-Ross, because he wanted to hate him. Wanted to know more. Because Parker-Ross was still partially the playmate of Marshall's childhood, too benign to be feared . . .

And then Marshall realised that everyone would see Parker-Ross in the same way. That a clever lawyer could get him off by pleading insanity. Regurgitate the public-school upbringing, the bullying, the patronising dislike of the art world grandees; the people who admired his father so much, and pitied the son more by comparison. A mirror would be held up to the business, with all its petty spites recalled. Poor Timothy, they would claim, he had money, but nothing else. No affection, no love. Detached, he had rattled around the world as an outsider, and then, obsessively and compulsively, he had fixed his thoughts on the Rembrandt letters. The way, finally, of making his name.

Anyone could understand that, couldn't they? No, Marshall thought, and he had to make sure that no one *ever* understood what Parker-Ross had done.

Sighing, he sat up on his bunk and went to the door, calling out, 'Hey, I need to see my lawyer.'

A guard came down the corridor and paused outside his cell. 'You want something?'

'My lawyer. Philip Gorday. I want to see him. I should have been out of here by now.'

'That so?'

'Yeah, that's so. Please, can you get hold of him for me?'

'Gorday, you say?'

'Philip Gorday.'

'He left a message for you,' the guard went on. 'He said to tell you that he'd be back soon.'

'Where's he gone?'

'London—'

'*London!*' Marshall snapped, incredulous. 'He can't have! He can't leave me here.'

'He can, and he has.'

'Let me out!'

'Mr Zeigler, you must know I can't do that,' the guard replied, shrugging. 'Relax. Your lawyer will be back.'

'Did he say when?'

'No, he just said he'd be back soon.'

'Can I make a phone call?'

'You had your phone call.'

'Can I send a message?'

'Do I look like a fucking pigeon?' the guard replied curtly. 'There's nothing you can do, but wait. So wait.'

House of Corrections,
Gouda, 1654

For many days I did not touch the pen. The nib weighed heavy
as a pail of water.

No one in Delft knew anything. It's being called "'t Sekreet
van Hollandt'. The secret of Holland. So many secrets . . . It was
the 12th October at 10.30 in the morning. It was warm, nothing
unusual, still, without rain, even a small sun . . . They say the
shudder reached the island of Texel in the far north.

No one had known . . . It was a secret, the gunpowder storage
hidden behind trees and under bushes, under greenery which
never shed its leaves in winter, just kept its knowledge to itself.
It was a storage bunker that no one could reach by foot. So no
one knew of it. Not behind the bushes and the trees . . . They say
it was a building on the grounds where the Clarisse convent once
stood, near to where the schutterij – the civic guard – once trained
. . . They say you could hear the explosion in the far north.

When the gunpowder went up the town went with it, a crater
in the earth left like an empty basin, ready to catch the rain.
Trees were mutilated, left as stumps . . . Many hundreds of build-
ings were destroyed, including the Oude Doelen. Many people
were injured.

But only Carel was killed.

Sssh, there is movement outside the window and the guards

look in, watch me. Wonder why I don't move anymore. Not these last days anyway . . . I heard them talking about self murder. Would I do that? they ask themselves. They can't afford to let me die. If I did, there would be no more money coming from van Rijn.

Watch her, they say, watch her. Watch the mad whore.

Friends brought me news of the explosion in Delft. They reported the death of Carel Fabritius because they thought it might interest me, not because they knew my past. Not because he was a blood link, a dead child . . .

Wasn't he apprenticed to Rembrandt? they asked me. Sad he died, and all his works with him . . .

All his works in his studio, his paintings, gone into nothingness. All his drawings, his oils and pigments, his skill and the paintings he created for himself – as Carel Fabritius, not Rembrandt's monkey.

They told me that nothing was left. That the artist was blown into fragments, spun through the air, scattered with his paints and brushes across Holland.

His family lived . . .

Alone, I cried for him. I cried, with the bag of coins pressing against my stomach, where my womb had once held him. And I knew that Rembrandt would have heard the news too, in his house, with his mistress, with the portrait of Saskia watching from the wall . . . He would grieve for his pupil, his accomplice. But for his child? I doubt that. Grieve for his income, his partner, his faker. But for his bastard? . . .

If I bought my freedom, bribed my way out of here, where would I go? What town would want me? What person hire me?

*What future invite me? Where is there on earth that would wel-
come me? So I shall stay here. And keep writing, hiding the letters, adding to the letters, keeping my testament. Stay behind
the locked door, where the damp rises in the late months and
the privy brings flies come May. The winter will eat at my soul,
and the ice will freeze under the canals, and more oxen, showing
the whites of their eyes in terror, will fall to the knife. In the distance, the church bells will glower into the sky and shake the
crows from their nests. And I will be still be here . . .*

*The explosion took away my last hold on Rembrandt van Rijn.
It took my child, my son, my helpmate . . . It blew a hole in my
heart.*

And the door in the wall slammed closed on me.

47

Two weeks after the Rembrandt revelations, Rufus Ariel sold his business for a loss and Leon Williams tried to commit suicide. Faced with the wreck of his business, Williams had found himself confronted by usurers who wanted their loans repaid. And there was no money to satisfy them, nor was there likely to be enough until the market recovered. And no one knew how long that would be.

Worldwide, every Rembrandt was questioned. The most famous Old Master on earth was enjoying his second celebrity as, in every gallery, museum, and private collection, the paintings were checked against the damning list. Despite a hundred legal arguments to delay decisions, the letters and the list were proved, twice more, to be authentic. Despite the conflicting views of handwriting experts and art historians, no one could discredit the Rembrandt letters. Within the first month, thirty-seven paintings previously believed to be by Rembrandt were reattributed to Carel Fabritius. In the second month, another fourteen were found to be fakes.

The market plunged.

Already suspicious, collectors drew back from the cultural blood bath. With the fall of Rembrandt came the scrabble for revaluations. After all, the dealers argued, the list might not be extensive. Geertje Dircx was not always present at Rembrandt's studio and had relied on her son's record – she could be wrong. Perhaps some of the discredited Rembrandts were real, after all. Perhaps others, not listed, were fake? The argument might have been persuasive in another, more buoyant, climate. But in the worst recession since the 1930s, it was seen as just another manoeuvre. Another artistic sleight of hand.

Then the market realised that if one of the biggest names in art could take such a beating, other painters might well suffer from a knock-on effect. Rumours, unsubstantiated and reckless, began to circulate. Were there really secret documents about Titian? Was he going to be the next casualty? The innuendos were absurd, but they put a match to the bonfire of panic. And the dealers looked for a scapegoat.

Oddly enough, it wasn't Timothy Parker-Ross. In the end he had managed to achieve what he always longed for – acceptance. The art market might loathe him for his crimes, but he was one of them as Marshall Zeigler had never been. Immediately after Parker-Ross's arrest, his legal team asked for him to be tried in London, but the plea was rejected and he was kept in New York. His behaviour in prison deteriorated rapidly; he began to hallucinate, became violent and attacked a guard. Put on medication,

Parker-Ross was diagnosed as being a paranoid schizophrenic and transferred to a mental facility, where he was sedated to keep him from harming himself or anyone else. Although he talked endlessly about the letters, when his accomplice was finally caught in Marseilles, he couldn't even recognise the man he had hired – and tutored in murder.

'And you left me here for two weeks while all this happened?' Marshall said bitterly, as Philip faced him across the prison table in the visitors' room.

'You weren't safe. I had to know you were somewhere that no one could get to you.'

'Why didn't you tell me?'

'Would you have agreed to it?'

'No.'

'That's why I didn't tell you,' Philip replied wryly. 'But you can leave today.'

Nodding, Marshall stared at the lawyer. He had thought, when Philip left so suddenly for London, that he had been double crossed. That Gorday would prove to have been involved all along. But Marshall had been wrong there. Instead of betraying him, Philip Gorday had promised his daughter that he would protect Marshall, and he had kept his word. Unsure of what would happen next, and unwilling to let his client leave custody until Parker-Ross's accomplice was found, Philip had left New York for London. Once there he got in touch with Lillian Kauffman and, through her, he discovered the full damage caused by the letters.

Riding the cataclysm, Lillian had done what she had always done: tightened her Hermès belt a couple of notches and decided to brazen it out. Over coffee and half a pack of cigarettes, she listed the victims and told Philip that Tobar Manners had disappeared.

'Disappeared?' Marshall said when Philip passed on the news. 'Where?'

'Just upped and went. No one knows where.'

Disbelieving, Marshall stared at the lawyer. 'He must have left a trace.'

'He left with nothing. The guy's finished. You got what you wanted.'

'You think I wanted *this*?' Marshall challenged. 'You think all this pleases me?'

'You wanted revenge—'

'For my father's death. I didn't want the rest of it.'

'They're blaming you,' Philip said evenly. 'I have to make that clear, Marshall. You're the scapegoat. You have to be, you're not one of them.'

'My father was.'

'You're not your father, and besides, the dealers know that your father wouldn't have released the letters.'

'Maybe he would have done if he'd not been murdered. My father was in real trouble, God knows, he might have been forced into it.'

Philip shrugged. 'But he didn't. You did.'

'And he's dead and I'm alive. Am I supposed to feel sorry for that?' Marshall asked, his tone acid. 'I had no choice but to expose the letters. Parker-Ross told me he was going to go after Georgia. He'd already killed four people, why wouldn't I believe him? And why, in God's name, would I think that any bloody letters were worth another death? Especially not hers.' He stared across the table at Philip Gorday. 'Those letters are the truth – about Rembrandt and about his paintings. I didn't want to bring down the art market—'

'Well, you've made a good fist of it, nonetheless. Thing is, Marshall, you're not going to be able to live like you did before.'

'What?'

'People know you, and what you did is all over the media. That stunt you pulled when you slashed the painting, that was Indiana Jones stuff. I've held the press and TV off for a while, but they want to talk to you. You're a hero to them. Avenging your father's death and taking on the art market single handed.' He paused, almost amused. 'The feminists love you.'

'The *feminists*? Why?'

'For revealing Geertje Dircx's story. It's made you very popular with women. Famous painter puts mistress in asylum makes a good headline in the seventeenth *and* the twenty-first centuries. I don't doubt Oprah will want to interview you.' He paused, looking Marshall full in the face. 'I'm grateful to you. For finding out who killed my wife.'

'So you won't be sending me a bill then?'

Philip smiled and stood up.

'You and Georgia were made for each other.' He put

out his hand, and he and Marshall shook. 'Parker-Ross was insane. Unfortunately, he had the personality and the money to back up his obsession.'

'Meaning?'

'That from now on, you'll always be *persona non grata* in the art world.'

Marshall nodded. 'That's fine. I'm going to sell the gallery anyway.'

'Going back to translating?'

'I don't think so, I don't think that would be enough anymore. I can't see myself getting passionate about any more dead poets. Can't see myself sitting day after day, staring at books.' He glanced at Philip. 'I can get up and walk through that door now. Just walk through it and I'm back into the world. Geertje Dircx couldn't do that. She couldn't escape, could only hear her life being chipped away, piece by piece, and do nothing about it.'

'Everyone's reading her letters, talking about them,' Philip said. 'The originals are now at the Rijksmuseum, as you requested.'

'Good.' Marshall meant it sincerely. 'Geertje was Dutch, the letters should be in her country, read in her language.'

'Will you translate them? Publish them in English?'

Shaking his head, Marshall put up his hands.

'No, not me. That's a job for someone else. For me her words will always be as she wrote them, in Dutch. I memorised every word of those letters and the list that went with them. Every word Geertje wrote, I remember. Every part of her life, her unhappiness, I will *always* remember.'

He tapped his forehead. 'It went in, and stuck. I saw what she saw, felt what she felt. I don't need to write any of it down.'

'She got her revenge in the end, didn't she?' Philip said, walking to the door with Philip. 'Got her own back on Rembrandt. And ruined his reputation in the process.'

'You can't ruin genius.'

'Just taint it.'

'You know who I wonder about?' Marshall said, his tone curious. 'Carel Fabritius, Rembrandt's bastard, his monkey. And if I know the art world at all I think that after a while – when the dust's settled – the dealers will look at Fabritius and decide that he was a very gifted painter, who was underestimated in his lifetime.' Marshall smiled ruefully. 'I doubt we'll live long enough to see it, but with publicity, enough money, and the need to fill a leaky gap in the market, Carel Fabritius might supersede Rembrandt one day. *That* would be the best revenge.'

House of Corrections,
Gouda, 1556

The guard who watched me from the first day I was brought here died last night. They told me that later, when they brought a younger man along, with a beard like froth and a tooth missing at the front. His eyes were quick, and full of malice, and when he passed by later he hissed through the door hatch and jiggled his keys to taunt me.

The flesh fell from me when Carel died. It fell from my arms and legs. And the muscles that had worked so hard, for so long, emptied into folds of dry skin ... Weak, I itched from the bed bugs which bit around my private parts and the fleas which nest in the hair under my arms, smelling frailty. They say insects scent death ...

I ate and threw back my food onto the sawdust and stared from under my eyelids that were often dry. I aged as I watched my hands, the veins rising blue, the liver spots making brown islands of colour against the livid skin ... I tried to stop living, but in spring the cows began lowing as they bore their calves, and a rook, wings open to sunlight, made for the resting trees. Something about that day, that first bird, chimed like the church clock calling for prayer. And hope moved in my ribcage and fluttered under my slowing heart ...

And then I remembered ... I felt for the coins I had carried against me for so long and counted them, and knew there were more than enough. When my friends came I told them to talk to the guard.

'Go to the new man, he's greedy . . .'

I knew greed, could sense it like heat on my skin.

'Go to the guard and bribe him . . .'

I wanted to buy the door in the wall. Wanted to see that bird over my free head and walk towards my home town.

'Go to the guard,' I said again, and pressed half of the coins in their hands.

When the guard came to tell me he would report me for trying to bribe him, I slid my hand through the grill on the door and held out another coin to him. He paused, the church clock rang seven, my friends gone, over the fields, pitying the mad slut grown old in the asylum.

'Take it,' I told the guard, and his eyes fixed on mine and I knew him. That sly greed which counts nothing as precious . . .

He slid the bolt, opened the door, took the coin I offered.

'My last,' I said, and I knew he wouldn't care. Because I was ill and old, and because he had already thought up some cover for my escape . . .

He let me go, and then relocked the door. He let me go and watched me, I am sure of it, as I crossed the darkening court-yard to the wall. To the wall which was opening with a door, a door which said: follow me, follow me . . . and I went to the open door and the memory of sea birds and lowing cows and the soft boom of a ship out to sea.

I walked until I could walk no more, then lay on my back in a field, face up to the flat, white palm of the moon. And she

513

smiled at me when I slyly opened my hand and showed her the last coin. The one I had hidden, the coin which my son had once given me.

A while later, I stood up, put the last coin deep into the front of my dress and then felt for the letters against my heart . . .

Tomorrow I will find the old priest I knew before and give him the letters. He will read them and make of them what he will. I will leave their fate to him, his conscience, and his God . . . And now, no more. No more . . . There is no one listening as I write these last words. There is no one to hide the papers from. No one to say 'Geertje Dircx, the whore of the painter, Rembrandt, gone mad with bitterness'. There is only the moon and the sleeping cows and the day which will come over the flatlands. Only the turn of the windmill and the shaking of new grass. And, on the horizon, the outline of a waterwheel churning over at dawn . . .

This was the story of me.

48

London.
Six months later.

Folding her arms, Georgia watched her pupils in the playground, all of them bundled up against the December bite of frost in primary colours – red hats, green and yellow scarves, blue coats, clashing like cheap, summer flowers after a sudden storm. And yet it was coming up to Christmas, with white cotton wool pinned around the insides of the windows, and a tree in the entrance hall, a manger underneath. Just as it should be, Georgia thought, turning and moving into the empty schoolroom and sitting at her desk.

It had taken a couple of months but Harry had made a full recovery and returned home. But he didn't return to the home he had left, not with his pregnant wife. The house was the same, but Georgia had lost the baby at the end of the fourth month. Stress, the doctors said. And to stop her thinking about what should have been, Georgia nursed Harry back to full health and tried to pretend – as he did – that nothing was different. Both of them put the shift of their emotions down to different reasons. Harry thought it was due to his accident and prolonged recovery, which had turned him from a husband into a dependant. The active, healthy man felt hobbled by his condition, and when Georgia lost their baby there was a moment of relief. He felt shame for it, but felt it none the less.

As for Georgia, she hadn't stopped loving Harry or caring about him – that would have been too easy. What she had lost was their bond, and she put that down to Marshall. Harry never knew that his accident was anything more than a hit and run. The police never found out who did it, and Harry came to terms with the event. It was just one of those random incidents in life, he said: It could have been anyone crossing the road at that moment. That's what he told Georgia, and she didn't dissuade him from that belief because she couldn't. There was no other story to tell – except the truth – and Georgia had long since decided that it was better for her husband never to know he had been targeted. Otherwise, the questions would start – why had she become involved? Why had she not confided in him? Why risk their life, their unborn child's life, for her ex-husband?

So Georgia stayed quiet.

When the news of the events in New York came out, Harry asked her if she had known about the letters. She shrugged, and told him no. Owen had always banged on about some documents, but she had never taken it seriously. And in telling him that, she threw in her lot not with Harry, but with Marshall. She might put it down to the grief over the loss of the baby, but she knew it was more. The Marshall Zeigler she had married had been one man; the Marshall Zeigler who had endangered himself for the Rembrandt letters was quite another. Grief may have done it. Certainly the shock of his father's death and having found Owen's body had brought about a change in Marshall, but he could have walked away at that point. The fact that he didn't, that he risked himself so readily, changed him in her eyes forever.

She *had* asked Marshall about his father's death, wanted him to talk about it, but he never would. And as her feelings for Harry weakened, Marshall returned to Amsterdam. The rift was unexpected and complete. The heady days of being hunted, being bait, were over. Marshall would return to his old life. And she to hers . . .

'*I love you.*'

He had said those words to her on the night before the auction, when he could have been saying goodbye. But instead he had said *I love you*. If he had died that night Georgia would have clung to the words, and used them as their epitaph. But life is seldom so tender. Instead, when she had spoken to Marshall again, he had been reserved, almost embarrassed.

'You did well,' she teased him. 'There was a cartoon in the paper of you slashing the portrait like a regular lunatic . . . Are you coming back to London?'

'Not for a while,' he had replied. 'I'm really sorry for all the trouble I caused you. And the baby—'

'That wasn't down to you,' she interjected quietly, changing the subject. 'I've seen you all over the papers, you photograph well. But I never took you for an action hero, Marshall. What will you do now?'

What will you do now? Everyone had asked him the same question. In interviews, on TV, radio. What was he going to do now? Write a book? Translate the letters? Marshall had never answered. He had hesitated instead, made excuses, said he would have to think about his future. In time he would make a decision. In time . . .

Tracing a pencil line down the spine of her notepad, Georgia stared ahead. In the old days she would have been able to rely on Marshall's constant friendship and advice, but that had changed. It changed when she realised that Marshall still loved her – as much as she loved him . . . But she realised that he was not going to come forward. Not yet, at least. Perhaps, when he realised that her marriage was over, perhaps then. Perhaps in another month, another year.

Perhaps when the loss of his father, the trauma of his actions, the whole heady furore of his disrupted life settled – perhaps then. Yes, Georgia thought, perhaps then.

Lighting up a cigarette, Lillian Kauffman stood in her doorway and looked across Albemarle Street to the Zeigler Gallery. The windows were encrusted with grit, the paint on the door was beginning to peel around the handle, and the 'closed' notice seemed as final and desolate as a gravestone. Her gaze moved upwards to the flat above, then to the top office where Nicolai Kapinski had once worked. Sighing, Lillian stared at the basement steps and remembered them cordoned off with police tape. She also remembered the porters – the ex-Guardsmen, and Owen. Always Owen . . .

'You wanted me?' Teddy Jack said, walking in.

'You took your time,' Lillian replied. She jerked her head towards the Zeigler Gallery. 'Marshall decided what he's going to do with it yet?'

'He can hardly run it, can he?'

'Not unless he wants cat shit through the letter box every morning,' she replied. 'He'd have to get someone in to run it for him.'

'Like you?'

'Jesus, are you joking!' she snorted. 'I can barely keep *this* place afloat at the moment. Anyway, those premises are jinxed. My late husband used to say that, and he was right.'

'So, what did you want to see me about?'

'To have a little chat, Teddy,' she replied, pouring him a coffee and sitting down.

The coffee had been percolating for a long time and was bitter; Teddy winced as he took a sip. Seeing his reaction, Lillian offered him a jug of milk, but it had been warmed and a skin had formed on the surface.

'No, thanks.'

'Suit yourself,' she said indifferently. 'You seen Marshall lately?'

'No, not for a few weeks. He's travelling.'

'Doing what?'

'I dunno. He's been involved with the Rijksmuseum because of the letters, but lately he's not returned my calls.' Teddy took a wary sip of the coffee. 'I'm going see him before I go home.'

'Home?'

'Up North. I reckon if I'm going to be poor, I might as well be poor at home. I know people there, we can be poor together.'

'You'll never stay! You'll miss London. Miss all those sordid adventures of yours.' Lillian paused and looked at Teddy, her expression alert. 'You know, Teddy, something's still troubling me.'

'Oh yes. What?'

'Why did Owen tell everyone about the Rembrandt letters?'

His surprise was genuine. 'How the hell would I know?'

'He wasn't the careless type, not Owen. He was too adept, too cunning to let it slip, so why did he do it? He knew what a hornet's nest it would stir up. Might even have predicted that it would be dangerous. So why would a clever man act like a fool?'

'You're asking another fool. And two fools don't make one wise man.'

'Fuck you, Teddy,' she said dismissively, 'you're no fool. You knew everything about Owen Zeigler. You knew about the letters, about Samuel Hemmings' involvement, about Nicolai Kapinski's brother . . . You *hired* Dimitri Kapinski, for God's sake.'

'To keep an eye on him. It was better he was on our side.'

'Whose side is he on now, hey?' Lillian asked. 'Do you know? Or did you pay Kapinski to disappear?'

'With what? Milk bottle tops?'

'I gave you money, Teddy, money to help Marshall.'

'I used it.'

'I bet you did.' She walked into the back and then returned with some more coffee. 'I won't offer you a refill, I can see you don't like it.'

'Well, it could kill a tree stump.'

She laughed, fiddling with one of her earrings, the pearl ostentatious in her finger tips. 'Why don't you come and work for me,' she said.

'Doing what?'

'The art world's all stirred up, people are panicking. The French think the business will go back to them, but it won't. Some will go the United Emirates, some the Far East, but some will stay here, in London.' She looked directly at Teddy, her manner blunt. 'I've been hearing some interesting things. Without anyone knowing, Tobar Manners came back and tried to empty what was left in his bank account, but Rosella had got there first. He's a broken man, a busted flush. And his gallery's been taken over by the bank.'

'Manners always was a furtive little bastard.'

'Well, you should know, you worked for him before you worked for Owen, didn't you?'

'Not for long. He fired me.'

'Did you do any little jobs for him, like the little jobs you did for Owen?' she asked, raising an eyebrow questioningly. 'I mean, this is a business that prides itself on being furtive. People around here have as many faces as church clocks. They make a virtue of deceit.'

His expression was unreadable. 'Where's all this leading?'

'A clever man – with a lot of patience – could set up a major coup. Like the Rembrandt letters.' Lillian paused, picking the skin off her milk. 'A person could have had those letters for a long time and waited for the perfect moment to release them.'

'Timothy Parker-Ross wasn't that smart.'

'Owen Zeigler was.'

Taken aback, Teddy stared at her. She was composed, her eyes bright with intelligence and perception, her back ramrod straight as she perched on the edge of a gilt chair. The gallery was very quiet, as were most of them. There were no idling customers, no collectors from the USA or Europe looking to buy. Instead the street and most of its galleries were empty, desperate for trade. Which didn't come. Now few trusted the provenance of any of the Old Masters, and the ones which were proven to be genuine were not being traded. Contemporary art had already drawn the coffin lid over itself, but now the previously unassailable artistic Titans were also under doubt.

'I'm a simple man, Mrs Kauffman, I don't understand what you're talking about.'

'Think about it,' Lillian replied, unfazed. 'Just imagine

this scenario: Owen Zeigler had a theory. For years he'd talked about it – it was no secret that Owen believed Rembrandt had a secret – but with the letters he had the means to *prove* it.'

'Much good it did him. He was killed—'

She sighed extravagantly.

'Let me finish. Owen was a complex man, who loved his secrets. He could tell a wonderful tale and give a wonderful ending. Then tell you the same tale a year later, with a different outcome . . . Now, just say that he planned all of this—'

'Are you joking?'

'No. Perhaps Owen had had the letters for a long while and was waiting for the perfect time to make them public.'

'In a recession?'

'Releasing them in a recession would cause the most damage.'

'But he loved the art world.'

'He did,' Lillian agreed, 'until it turned against him. Owen got into debt, he couldn't trade as he used to. His status and his reputation – the things he most valued – were being questioned. People heard he was struggling and turned their backs on him. Then Tobar Manners cheated him with the sale of the Rembrandt, swore blind it was a fake – and that made Owen realise what the business was really like. He knew that painting was genuine, but he was so desperate to pay off his creditors that he let Manners cheat him.'

Teddy Jack shook his head. 'No, that doesn't make sense.

523

Owen could have sold the letters and paid off his debts that way.'

'He would only have done that as a last resort. Those letters were an insurance policy for Owen Zeigler. I think he talked about them to keep them in people's minds, so that when he *did* release them he'd already prepared the ground. He cultivated an interest, whipped it up for years so that his coup would be even greater. He planned it all.' She paused, putting down her coffee cup. 'But then circumstances started to take a sinister turn. When Stefan van der Helde was killed Owen and I talked about it. I didn't know Stefan had authenticated the letters, but Owen was distraught. He insisted it was a gay killing, and he was very firm on the point. Said that Van der Helde had always been sexually promiscuous. Owen was jumpy for a long time after the murder in Holland.'

'Which had nothing to do with me.'

'Who said it did?' Lillian responded, then continued, 'As I say, Owen was uneasy for a long time, but when nothing else happened, he relaxed. Unfortunately, though, he was getting deeper and deeper into trouble in London. His business was failing, the bank was threatening to foreclose, the country house had been remortgaged, he was up to his gills in debt . . . You know this, Teddy, don't deny it.'

'Like you say, Mrs Kauffman, Mr Zeigler never told anyone the whole story. Not even me.'

'I think he told you more than he told anyone,' she answered simply. 'In fact, I'm sure he did. And I think that as he got more deeply into debt, he realised there was only one way out. To sell the Rembrandt letters. I don't think that it was ever Owen's intention to ruin Rembrandt's reputation and bring down the art world. I think that it was only when he saw people turn their backs on him and then realised, when he was on his uppers, that his oldest friend would cheat him, that Owen decided if he was going to go down, he would take the rest of them with him. It was desperation and shock that forced his hand. If one dealer had come to Owen's aid I believe those letters would never have seen the light of day.'

Silent, Teddy shrugged. Lillian leant back in her seat, coolly confident. 'I watched you come and go from that gallery at all hours. You were always reporting to Owen, always busy. Some of the jobs I knew about – like Dimitri Kapinski. Owen was fond of his little accountant and wanted to do him a good turn. I suppose that when you found Dimitri, it was a bonus to discover he was a criminal; someone you could use at a later date . . . You and Owen were very alike, Teddy. You both kept little pockets of your lives secret from the other.'

'This is rubbish—'

'No, not at all,' Lillian replied. 'I've a bloody good brain, and I'm as sneaky as the best. And I knew Owen a lot longer than you did. I imagine that Owen was setting up his coup for a long time, *but you got impatient*. When the recession came, you saw a way to make a killing – fast. Fuck the art world and Rembrandt's reputation – that might interest Owen, but not you. Did you try and convince him, Teddy? Was it before, or after you found a buyer for the letters?'

Teddy blanched, smiling sardonically as he turned his head away from her. 'You've got a vivid imagination,' he said.

'And luckily, I'm an insomniac.' She gestured to the window. 'For years I've watched the comings and goings of Albemarle Street and I saw you bring Timothy Parker-Ross to see Owen. Not once, many times.' She shrugged. 'Of course, Owen was his mentor, so his visits weren't unusual. But what *was* unusual was the argument I overheard the night before I went on holiday—'

'That meant nothing.'

'On its own, no. But together with all the other pointers, it would make anyone think.' She raised her eyebrows. 'You see, I heard Owen *fire* you, Teddy. I heard him tell you to get out and never come back. Now, why would he have done that to his closest ally? Unless he didn't trust you anymore.'

'I was damn nearly killed because of those letters!'

'Of course you were. You'd failed the people who wanted them! What good were you to anyone after that? You were lucky Marshall happened along and found you that night, or you'd be dead too.'

She folded her arms, her varnished nails orange against the black of her tailored jacket, as a man suddenly walked in from the back room. Taken by surprise, Teddy watched Marshall approach, his face set as he glanced over to the little woman on the gilt chair.

'Thanks, Lillian.'

'My pleasure,' she said simply. 'I told you I'd be a good help.'

Nodding, Marshall turned to face Teddy Jack.

'Was that when it all came apart?' he asked, his voice cold. 'Timothy Parker-Ross wasn't the innocent everyone thought and once he caught sight of his particular Valhalla, you were out of the game. He was going to get those letters, no matter what. And *no one* was going to stop him.' He paused. 'You were outclassed, Teddy, and you knew it. To be honest—'

'Marshall, listen to me—'

'No, I don't want to hear it,' Marshall cut in bluntly. 'I've been thinking all of this over for weeks, trying to make sense of it. Then I talked to Lillian and finally, it became clear. You *had* to help me after I'd saved your life, or it would have looked suspicious. Besides, you were really rattled, shaken up. I don't suppose you ever thought you'd be a victim, did you?'

'I didn't want anything to happen to your father.'

'I believe that,' Marshall said. 'I *do* think you felt guilty, up to a point. After all, you didn't know how dangerous things were going to get. You didn't realise people were going to be killed, and I know you were fond of my father. But you were broke, Teddy, skint. No money, a criminal record, no chance of getting a good paying job. Your options were limited and then, suddenly, this opportunity drops in your lap.

'I bet you couldn't understand why my father wouldn't

release the letters. It wouldn't have made sense to you, at all. Sell them and cut your losses, was what you advised him, wasn't it? And when he didn't, you fell out with him. Then you got to thinking – if Owen Zeigler was going to pass up a golden opportunity, you'd get those letters for yourself.'

'I was broke.'

'I understand. Broke and angry,' Marshall said, nodding. 'So what did you do then? My father was dead, you had to stay close to me to find out where the letters were. You had to be my ally to be in with a chance.'

Shifting his position, Teddy stared down at his big hands.

'I didn't hurt anyone.'

'No, you didn't,' Marshall agreed. 'You were used, Teddy. I'm afraid my father used you, and so did Timothy Parker-Ross. When all this started someone said to me 'You can't understand this business because you're not a part of it. It's a closed world, with its own rules and punishments. An outsider can never penetrate it' – and they were right. Owen Zeigler was my father and I *still* couldn't get inside.' He looked at Teddy, his expression resigned. 'You didn't deliberately let my father's killer in—'

Teddy's head shot up.

'Never! I thought Parker-Ross would help him because he had money and besides, your father had always looked out for him. Parker-Ross seemed like he'd be discreet, old school.' Teddy shook his head. 'I just wanted Owen to sell the letters and get himself out of trouble. He was panicking so much, rambling on about the art world and how it had let him down. All those friends who'd been crawling up his arse for years turned their backs on him, no one offered to help. I'd never seen your father like that, so out of control. I thought I was doing him a favour, honestly I did. I even offered to sort out Tobar Manners for him – I could have got that Rembrandt, but your father wouldn't let me. He said Manners would get his come-uppance.' He bowed his head, stricken. 'When it went bad, all I could do was to look out for you. Nothing would have happened to you, or Samuel Hemmings, or Georgia. On my life, I'd never have let anything happen to you . . . You know that, don't you? I owed you that much.'

Silent, Marshall nodded,

Teddy looked at him. 'What d'you want from me?'

'Nothing.'

'Nothing?'

'No, I just wanted to know the truth, that was all,' Marshall said quietly. 'Go home, Teddy, go back up North. You're out of your depth down here and frankly, the game's not worth the candle.'

49

Sussex,
England.

Mrs McKendrick looked around Samuel Hemmings' study, thinking about the old man. He had died two days earlier and she had been drafted in to tidy up the house and make it ready for the auctioneers to take away the furniture and sell off the best pieces. Pleased with her inheritance, Mrs McKendrick took to her task with enthusiasm, clearing out Samuel Hemmings' bedroom first, and feeling genuine sadness when she saw his reading glasses by the bed. Next to them was a book of Giorgione's paintings and an old magazine article written by Bernard Berenson.

In the bathroom she emptied the cupboards, and pushed aside the wheelchair as she passed back into the passage. The days of parties and house guests had long gone, but she remembered when the house had been full most weekends, the garden taking the overspill of people on summer nights. But for the last few years there had been few visitors, just temporary guests who had stayed for a night or two, and Samuel's solicitor, come to make changes in his will. Busily, she returned to the study, sighing at the mounds of books and magazines piled alongside the chimney breast and on either side of the old desk. She then glanced over to the dog bed, remembering the Labrador who had slept there for so many years, and shook her head at the poignancy of it.

There was to be quite a grand funeral. Her employer had been well known and well liked, and if most of his contemporaries were already dead, there were many of younger generations who would want to pay their respects. Obituaries in the papers had been kind, describing Samuel as acerbic but perceptive, and always brave. A man who remained challenging into his ninth decade. They spoke of his disability too, of the debilitating arthritis which had forced him into a wheelchair for the last ten years of his life. Some made reference to the fact that, before his illness, Samuel Hemmings had been a skilled, if amateur, artist. Mrs McKendrick hadn't known that, and wondered why none of her late employer's works had been hung in the house. Perhaps, she thought, it was like so many other abilities, forgotten with the passing of time.

Tossing some yellowed newspapers into a black bin bag, she picked up the worn tartan rug which had always covered the old man's legs. It should be thrown away, she thought, and yet knew that she would take it home. Fold it, put it aside, but keep it none the less . . . Walking over to the desk, she looked at the blotter and saw three letters.

One addressed to herself, one to her solicitor, and one to Marshall Zeigler. Opening her own letter, she read:

> Dear Mrs McKendrick,
>   Thank you for all your many kindnesses over the years and for your loyalty. I do hope you will accept your little inheritance and enjoy it. You looked after me very well indeed and made my life a good deal more comfortable than it might have been, especially in my last, slower years.
>   With very kind regards, and thanks,
>   Samuel Hemmings.
>
> PS. As a last task, would you please make sure that my solicitor and Mr Marshall Zeigler receive their letters?

Glancing at the two remaining missives, Mrs McKendrick tucked them into her basket. When she finally left the house, hours later, she passed by the mail box in the village and posted both letters, pushing them carefully through the slot and making sure she heard them fall to the bottom of the box.

50

Marshall was writing notes, his head bowed, his whole attention focused on the work in hand. The media had tired of him, but the art world hadn't, and when he had called at the Zeigler Gallery earlier in the week, someone had thrown a stone through the front window. It landed at his feet, a smooth grey pebble of disgust. Resigned to his unexpected celebrity, he had gone to the door and looked out, but no one came forward and after another moment he went back inside.

Questioned by the police on both sides of the Atlantic, Marshall had finally been cleared of all charges and had returned to London to oversee the sale of the gallery. His notoriety placed him in demand in some quarters, but his reserve made him back off. The death of his father and the realisation of how little he had known him had changed Marshall, made him a more thoughtful man, and a less trusting one, too. It had also made him dissatisfied with his life. The calm profession of a translator had lost its appeal; the hours of silent work no longer suited him.

He found himself losing concentration, his mind slipping back to Samuel Hemmings, Teddy Jack and Nicolai Kapinski. He found, to his intense surprise, that he missed those days, missed living on the edge, not knowing what was coming next . . .

His thoughts often turned to Georgia, and Marshall would have to force himself to remember that she was married to Harry. Although he had heard about the miscarriage, he kept his distance, comforting her in a phone call but not visiting. Both of them knew that would be dangerous.

And so, in a heightened state of mind, which the passing weeks did nothing to diminish, Marshall Zeigler sifted through the post which had accumulated over the last month. Many letters were still addressed to Owen, many bills too, but there was some mail addressed to himself, care of the Zeigler Gallery. One particular envelope caught his attention and, pushing aside the rest of the pile, he stared at it, recognising Samuel Hemmings' writing. He had known of Samuel's death and was going to attend the funeral, but the letter came as a surprise.

Sitting down, Marshall opened the envelope and took out several folded sheets of paper, all in the same ostentatious handwriting which he knew was Samuel's. For a moment he thought back to the old man and the country house, to the conversations they had had, to the view into the garden beyond. For an instant, he could feel the atmosphere of that study; see the book-lined walls, recall the battered sofa in front of the fire and the way that the sun had faded the fringe of the curtains. And for a second Marshall almost imagined that he heard the sound of the historian's wheelchair rolling over the floorboards.

Moved, Marshall turned to the letter and began to read:

My Dear Marshall,

Of course if you're reading this, I will have passed on. I might be able to see your reaction, or not. I never was much of a believer in life after death, but then again, it wouldn't be the first time I was proved wrong. I appreciated what you did for me at the end, Marshall. I had no family of my own and your concern was touching. It helped me when the days were so full of pain and the nights so full of regret. But I wonder – if you had had any knowledge of what I am about to tell you – would you have been so caring of my safety?

Let me be clear with you – I cared for your father and admired him. From the first time we met, I saw his intelligence and his skill. He had all the potential to be a great dealer, a connoisseur. His intellect was never lacking, it was his character which was threadbare.

Marshall stopped reading, stunned by these words, and took a long pause before reading on:

Owen lacked discipline. And worst of all, he lacked trust. Your father had great charm, but no talent for friendship. I had limited charm, but was a great friend to those I took under my wing. Years ago, Owen Zeigler was introduced to

535

me and he wanted to learn, to know everything he could about the Dutch painters. He worshipped the great artists of Holland: Vermeer, Frans Hals, and Rembrandt. He liked the cool tones, the dour Dutch skies and doughy faces of their sitters. His attraction for this period was heightened when he discovered, and bought, that small Rembrandt he treasured so much. The Rembrandt Tobar Manners lied about. The Rembrandt which was one hundred per cent genuine.

You must understand your father, Marshall, for any of this to make sense. You must also understand me, and the art world. The dealers, the connoisseurs, the traders, the auctioneers and the historians live to uncover some monumental discovery. They dream of it as other men dream of women. Because with knowledge – unknown before, uncovered only by them – they have status. And a hidden, voyeuristic insight into the great. We know we are all dwarves beside Rembrandt, Leonardo and Titian, but we all long for that covert look into the lives of the giants.

I was no different. All my life I strived to uncover something important. Which I did. I wrote perceptively about Goya and the Dutch painters. I argued attributions and mocked Brit Art. I predicted the downturn of contemporary realism, and as far back as 1940 I knew Caravaggio would seduce a new generation of followers. But I'm getting off my story, I must stick to the facts. And they are as follows.

You probably don't remember your grandfather, Neville Zeigler. He was a very secretive character. As a Jewish refugee, he had every right to be suspicious of people and their motives, but he passed this wariness – and weakness – down to his son. Luckily Neville Zeigler was also clever. He knew his ambitions were limited by his foreign status and by the times in which he lived, but Owen was another matter.

Neville's ambition for his son was unbounded. While Neville laboured in markets and later in a dour little bric-a-brac shop in the East End, he coached the boy Owen in art history. He trailed him round galleries and exhibitions, and was rewarded by his son's natural intelligence and instinctive passion for the subject. Who knows what Neville Zeigler's past was? I never knew, but his drive and skill must have had their roots in some wellspring of breeding and culture. By the time Owen was in his teens he was dazzling; Neville was remote as a ghost, driving his star child on.

Of course he was well rewarded. He lived to see Owen go to university and finally slide into the gluey womb of the art world. Father and son were different, but in some ways alike. Both kept secrets. Neville kept his secrets very well, perhaps too well. When I had known your father for a couple of years he introduced me to Neville, and I found him intriguing; we even became friendly. He spoke of what he wanted for his only son, but constantly worried about money. I suspect that Neville had lost a great deal when he came to this country before the war, and his penury rankled. Even when he had made a good sale, he worried about how long the money would last and he used to talk about the art world and rage at the blanket greed of the dealers.

I couldn't argue with that.

537

And Neville had a wish – one of the few he ever confided in me – that he wanted to be able to leave Owen an inheritance so that, whatever might happen in the future, his son would always be secure. He longed to find something valuable, some painting or art work. He wasn't a fantasist, but I know he dreamed of this. Seeing Owen's potential, I had always been keen to mentor him, and Neville was grateful, knowing my name would advance his son further. Owen and I became close, two people dissimilar in age, but identical in interest and ambition. And we talked about that favourite subject of the art world – the theory.

Theories spring up like daisies in this business. Your father and I talked often of such things, and one day, after I had known him for a couple of years, Owen said that he believed Rembrandt had had a bastard son. He said that Geertje Dircx could have borne Rembrandt a child when they were both young. A child who was farmed out to another family – a child called Carel Fabritius. After all, your father went on, Dircx had certainly worked for Rembrandt, and been sent to an asylum. Wasn't that too brutal a punishment for a woman he had simply fallen out of love with? Why would Rembrandt go to the trouble of having an ex-mistress committed?

Unless she knew something so damaging she had to be locked away and silenced.

You know the story, Marshall, you've read the Rembrandt letters, you listened to Geertje Dircx's history. So what you're wondering now is – what am I going to say next? Guess, Marshall, try and guess before you read the next lines. Or

538

perhaps you want to throw this letter away, and never know the answer. You can choose. But be warned, if you read on, you'll be given some information which will change you, and your life. Information which will demand action from you. Or inaction. But certainly a choice.

I think we both know that you've changed. You can't look away now, can you?

It was only supposed to be a joke.

In the 1960s, Neville had been to an auction in Amsterdam. There had been a fire in a synagogue, and the authorities were trying to raise funds for the repairs by selling off anything salvageable. As the items were religious Jewish artefacts, your grandfather was naturally interested. He bought a few items and then spotted a casket, badly scorched. Thinking he could repair it then sell it on as a jewellery box, he was disappointed to find that he couldn't undo the lock. Fire damage and age had warped the casket, so he held onto it, unsold. He kept it in his office, where I spotted it one day and realised just how old it was.

'Fifteenth century,' I told him.

'Worth much?'

'Not if you can't open it.'

It was then the idea occurred to me. Asking if I could have a go at releasing the lock, I took the casket home. After some effort, I _did_ open it and it was empty. But not for long. When I returned the casket to Neville, I lied; telling him that I hadn't been able to open it, but _he_ should keep trying. And then I waited. I knew that the next time Neville tried the lock, it would open and he would find the old

539

papers I had secreted inside. The Rembrandt letters. Yes, Marshall, I hid those letters in Neville Zeigler's box.

You see, I wrote them.

Marshall flinched, read the words again, hardly taking them in. Samuel Hemmings had written the letters? How could that be? No, it couldn't be possible ... His hand shaking, Marshall continued to read.

But days passed and Neville said nothing. Weeks passed, then months, but not one word was uttered. All that changed was Neville's attitude. He became withdrawn, cooler with me. He made excuses to be busy when I called at the shop and would only talk easily of Owen's progress. In fact, he grew even more certain of his son's success, almost jocular, as though he felt secure in a way that people do when they have backing. When they believe themselves rich.

And then it struck me. Neville had *found the letters, but he wasn't going to share his discovery with me. After all, I knew nothing of his coup, did I? Neville didn't know* I *had planted the letters there. I'd told him that I hadn't been able to open the casket, so how would I know of any documents? For a while I wondered if I should confess, but Neville's deliberate choice to keep quiet about his discovery rankled with me. How dare he? I thought. Weren't we friends? Hadn't I mentored his son for years? How deceitful of Neville Zeigler to banish me from his good fortune, from his release from the tyranny of his poverty. He had wanted a find, and I had given him one.*

Yes, I know what you're thinking, Marshall, how did I dare to be angry with Neville? Oh, but I was. Time passed, and he never said one word about the letters. Perhaps he knew I'd planted them and was waiting for me to confess. Or he was turning the joke back on me, but I doubt that. I believe he thought he had found his gilded nest egg and when he hinted, now and again, about having some secret, I wanted to laugh, to tell him the truth. But as the years went on my revenge was watching Neville Zeigler believe he had outsmarted me. Samuel Hemmings, the respected, wealthy art historian, outflanked by an impoverished refugee. I told myself that when Neville died, and the Rembrandt letters had passed to his son – which they would, of course, hadn't he always dreamt of leaving Owen an inheritance? – then would be the time to tell the truth. My protégé and I could laugh about it. Then.

Or so I thought.

In 1973, when Neville died, your father told me he had been left some letters concerning Rembrandt. I smiled over the phone and asked him to bring them to show me. But instead of wanting to share his moment of elation with his mentor, Owen hesitated. His mistrust injured me. For once, he was not his urbane self, and stammered an apology. He said he wasn't being evasive, but that he had wanted to get the letters authenticated before he showed them to me. Me! Of all people. Me! The person who had taught him. Me! The friend and mentor. Me! The man who had trusted him with my knowledge and my affection.

The discovery of the Rembrandt letters changed your father, or maybe his suspicious streak – inherited from Neville – grew until it engulfed his common sense. But, as ever, he took my help quickly enough. On my recommendation, he took the letters to Stefan van der Helde for authentication – yet when your father came back to London he was shifty, unlike himself. Well, Owen said, Van der Helde had authenticated them, but he should get another opinion.

I offered him mine. It was rejected on the grounds that we were too close, I would be biased. That I would obviously want to please him by authenticating the discovery. How could he put me into such a difficult position? Owen asked. We were friends, very close friends, he would be asking me to put my reputation on the line. A reputation I had built up over years . . . The truth was, he didn't trust me. Thought I would expose the letters myself, claim the victory as my own. You thought the same, Marshall. But you were both wrong.

Let me be frank with you. I was a jealous man, with a competitive streak. Yes, sometimes I was envious of other people's triumph, but I never took anything that wasn't my own. I never stole another person's victory, or their work. I didn't have to, my name spoke for itself. All my life I had willingly shared my knowledge with others; opened my home and my heart to people as passionate as myself. As eager to learn and share. But your father could not share. When he inherited the Rembrandt letters he hugged them to himself. I knew from the first he would never let the world enjoy them.

Again, I asked to see them and, finally, he lent them to me. The Rembrandt letters, which were so damning – as you found out. But your father didn't give me all of them to read, he kept back one back, and the list of fakes. I'd written them. I knew the letters made no sense without the last one. But Owen smiled his clubhouse smile and thought he'd fooled me. I was an old man, after all, easy to cheat. And he couldn't risk my having all the information. If I had the list I would know as much as he did – and Owen couldn't bear the thought of that. He had to be the only person on earth who had read all the Rembrandt letters. And owned them.

The day was very hot when he came to see me. We chatted in the garden and I watched this surrogate son of mine – for whom I had cared so deeply and of whom I had been so proud – lie to me. You see, I thought he would relent and share the letters with me. But he didn't. And my affection for him turned into hatred.

Like his father before him, Owen hugged his treasure to himself. I imagine he would have died with the Rembrandt letters still a secret if it hadn't been for the sudden, corrosive downturn in his finances. Your father had been too confident and had gambled in a failing market.

Over the years he had often mentioned his Rembrandt theory, but never suggested that he might have the proof to back it up. When the art world realised Owen Zeigler had the potential to wreak havoc, his fate was determined. Ironically it was the blow Tobar Manners dealt him which was the catalyst. When Manners cheated your father with the Rembrandt sale, Owen realised just how ruthless the business was. He had no real allies, no true friends, all he had were the letters.

But they turned out to be his death sentence, not his salvation.

I must tell you that I didn't believe – not for one moment – that your father's punishment would be so great. I never thought there would be deaths, and my cowardice kept me silent. They say that the man the gods wish to destroy they first make mad. Well, I have been in my own madness of guilt for some time. The joke had festered over the years and turned into a canker which would destroy us all.

Of course you want proof, don't you, Marshall? I mean, I can say I faked the Rembrandt letters, but anyone could say that. So I'll tell you how I did it. I used paper from antique books I had collected, written around the same period as Rembrandt, and made the ink myself. I studied the calligraphy and struggled to emulate the Dutch language, making many copies because sometimes my hands shook. But I told myself that it didn't matter if the writing was uncertain at times. Geertje Dircx had been ill educated, and she was recording her history under extreme circumstances.

The paper I used had come from the flyleaves of books, and was perfectly faded. Indeed, sometimes I looked at what I had written and believed it myself.

For a long time, I had known about Geertje Dircx. It wasn't difficult putting myself into the role of someone who felt betrayed and mistrusted. So I took her story, the court records, the rumours of pupils faking Rembrandt's paint-

ings, and I meshed them into a compelling theory. It was to be a tale Neville would readily have believed. Little did I know when I first wrote them that they would become your father's obsession. One he never doubted. His arrogance did the rest. How could he be wrong?

I _was_ going to tell him the truth, that it was only an elaborate joke I had wanted to play on his father. But this time _I_ was the one who stayed quiet. When I saw my protégé swagger around with those documents, I said nothing. I hinted often, but Owen would never hear a word against the letters. Once I even asked him outright if he believed they were real, and he gave me a slow look before answering. He didn't know I had faked them, but at the back of his mind, the thought had occurred to him that they might not be real, but it didn't matter anymore.

He was such a vain man.

I tell you again I only stayed silent to teach your father a lesson. Show him that his old mentor was wiser and craftier than he was. That I could still teach him a trick or two. But, like his father before him, Owen drew back from me, and his rejection hurt. I heard that he began to gamble more with his sales, take stupid risks.

I suppose having the letters made him feel invincible; that he could always pull this Dutch rabbit out of the hat and save himself.

And so, Marshall, now you know the truth. It is your decision what you do. You can reveal the hoax, and try to undo the devastation the letters have caused. Or keep quiet, and never tell the world your father was duped. Then again, *you can expose me and let my reputation burn to ash. Show me for the petty, jealous coward that I was. You always hated the art world, why would it matter to you that the business got its come-uppance? That the likes of Tobar Manners were ruined? In an enclosed world of secrets, what does one more really matter?*

I wonder which option you will choose. To give Rembrandt van Rijn back his reputation, or allow Owen Zeigler, your father, to keep his?

Yours,

Samuel Hemmings

51

In the months which followed, Georgia's marriage broke down and Harry left the house in Clapham. Marshall phoned and commiserated from a distance, but did not tell her that Samuel Hemmings had confessed to faking the Rembrandt letters. Instead, he travelled, restless, and unable to make a decision. His journeys took him around Europe, but his mind constantly replayed events; the memory of his father intermixed with the memory of him destroying the Rembrandt painting in New York – which, if he believed Samuel Hemmings, wasn't a fake, after all. Marshall could recall effortlessly his many interviews with the media, and his feelings of pride when the Rembrandt letters were finally exhibited in the Rijksmuseum. Notoriously, Marshall had been excommunicated from the artistic Holy See – but that had only served to reassure him that he had taken the right course of action.

Then he would remember Samuel Hemmings' letter and feel the ground shift under his feet. According to the old historian's version of events, Marshall had slashed a masterpiece worth millions.

But that was the historian's version. As time passed, Marshall began to adopt and expand on one of his family's traits – suspicion. He thought back over what he knew about Samuel Hemmings, what he had been told and what he had seen for himself over decades. Despite his kindliness, Samuel had had a bitter edge; malicious enough to create the letters and then risk the ruin of his reputation by having Marshall expose him – albeit after his death. But then again, *would* exposure soil his image? For decades, Samuel Hemmings had been a hookworm in the art world's gut. He had been provocative, argumentative, challenging – perhaps he would have *liked* to be remembered as the man who brought down the art world and toppled Rembrandt's reputation. Perhaps that thought fed his ego, that enormous intellect and conceit which had driven so much of his work. Perhaps, dead and out of reach, Samuel Hemmings had wanted to pull off the biggest scam of his life.

But he had needed Marshall to do it. Needed the younger man's anger, and desire to avenge his dead father.

In the previous months, Marshall Zeigler had learned much that had gone against his nature and assimilated character traits which had been necessary for his survival: how to keep hidden, how to be crafty, how to be suspicious of everyone. Owen Zeigler had never fully trusted his mentor, neither had his son . . .

When he first read the confession, Marshall's impulse

had been to expose Hemmings, thus risking his father's good name in order to reveal a fraud which had, inadvertently, resulted in four deaths. But the more Marshall considered the confession the more he stayed his hand. Could he go to the Rijksmuseum and tell them the letters were fakes? And the list: all those masterpieces now demoted, deemed worthless by comparison to work undeniably by Rembrandt himself; those supposed fakes which had caused such ructions in the business. Could he really come forward and announce that his father, and others, died for the letters, believed in them, but that they – and Marshall himself – were all fooled? Could he really tell the world that not one word of those letters was true; that a bitter, jealous old man faked them to get his revenge?

Conflicted and undecided, Marshall kept travelling. In Italy he considered destroying Samuel Hemmings' confession. In France, he felt a need to own up, to betray his father's memory for the greater good. Weeks passed by; news came that Teddy Jack had been arrested for theft in Manchester. Lillian Kauffman had made an offer for the Zeigler Gallery, which Marshall rejected. In New York, Philip Gorday continued working as a lawyer and kept in intermittent touch with Marshall, passing on the news that Timothy Parker-Ross's mental health had declined and his associate – the man who had actually committed the murders – had been sentenced to life imprisonment.

Soon after Parker-Ross was incarcerated Marshall visited him, but the journey had been a wasted one. He had driven for half a day to reach the mental facility and waited in a confined room for his childhood friend to be brought in. Having planned the meeting and dwelt obsessively on what he would say, Marshall had been shaken when a shuffling, over-sedated creature appeared and sat opposite him, without an iota of recognition. There had been nothing left of the young man he had once counted as a friend. Nothing. Instead there had just been a mental patient in hospital clothing that was too big for him, and with nothing left behind his eyes.

Chastened, Marshall resumed his travels. His contact with Georgia intensified and when she asked him to come back to London he was tempted, but knew he could never return home until the final decision was made. He kept travelling.

In Berlin, Marshall roamed the streets restlessly and then, on a whim, visited the Gemaldegalerie and stood before Rembrandt's painting of *Susannah Surprised by the Elders*. The picture for which Geertje Dircx had been the model. Curious, Marshall looked at the painting, centuries old, depicting a woman long dead. Tormented by Samuel Hemmings' confession, Marshall stood immobile before the picture and stared into the limpid face of Geertje Dircx.

And then, finally, he made his decision.

He would never know – nor would anyone else – if the Rembrandt letters were real or a forgery, but it no longer mattered to him. His choice, he now understood, was not to protect his father's reputation, or take revenge on

Samuel Hemmings. Instead, Marshall realised, the person who most needed consideration was Geertje Dircx. She *had* been Rembrandt's lover, she *had* been rejected and broken. Her freedom *had* been taken from her, her status, her little peck of power. The spite of her ex-lover, the betrayal of her family, her incarceration – all that was true, laid down in the records. When she was taken to the House of Corrections in Gouda she became little more than an animal. Abused and forgotten, she was meant to die in silence.

Relieved, Marshall stared into the unfathomable gaze of Geertje Dircx. He saw in her eyes his father's eyes, Charlotte Gorday's eyes, Nicolai Kapinski's eyes. And he saw in her a history which deserved to be told. Her face was every woman's face; every human's face who had ever had a history to tell. If the chronicle was, in part, wrong, it was also, in part, right.

Marshall turned to go home. He would destroy Samuel Hemmings' confession and let the Rembrandt letters stand – as a final and lasting testimony to Geertje Dircx.

AFTERWORD

Geertje Dircx was Rembrandt's lover and the dry nurse to his son, Titus. Rembrandt loved her enough to give her some of his late wife's jewellery, but she fell out of favour with the painter. It seems very probable that she was ousted by his next mistress, Hendrickje Stoffels. Taking Rembrandt to court, Geertje sued the artist for breach of promise, saying that he had asked her to marry him and given her a ring.

A long battle commenced. Rembrandt denied promising to marry Geertje and offered her a sum of money to remove herself from his house and life. Geertje did not agree and caused a scene in court. Troublesome and difficult, she became irksome to Rembrandt. In a premeditated and vindictive act, he convinced her brother, nephew, and neighbours to give evidence against her, to prove that she was a promiscuous troublemaker.

Their damning testimony resulted in Geertje Dircx being sentenced to twelve years' hard labour and incarcerated at the House of Corrections – a prison/madhouse – in Gouda.

These are true and documented facts on which this novel is based; the rest is open to interpretation.

BIBLIOGRAPHY

Brown, Christopher, *Rembrandt, The Master and his Workshop*, Yale University Press

Sonnenburg, Hubert von, *Rembrandt/Not Rembrandt in the Metropolitan Museum: Aspects of Connoisseurship*, Metropolitan Museum of Art

Constable, W. G., *The Painter's Workshop*, Dover Publications

Esteban, Claude, *Rembrandt*, Ferndale Editions

Bredius, Abraham, *The paintings of Rembrandt*, Phaidon

Lloyd Williams, Julia, *Rembrandt's Women*, Prestel

Boon, K. G., *Rembrandt: the complete etchings*, Abrams

Note: Details on the convent in H. C. Brouwer, 'Stedebouwkundige veranderingen . . .' in exh.cat. De Stad Delft, cultuur en maatschappij van 1752–1667, Vol. I, pp. 37–38. Museum Prinsenhof, Delft, 1981.